THE BLACK DEATH

Taking a deep breath, Killashandra touched the black crystal to the opalescent material, quiveringly ready to drop forceps and all at any sign that the black was going to react.

The black shaft was ingested so swiftly that her reflexes had no time to respond. Forceps, crystal, and her gloved hand were all pulled into the sudden maelstrom of frenzied, turbulent patterns that cascaded down the opalescence and flowed through Killashandra with such devastating force that she felt her death was imminent. Her whole life flashed across her mind, pushing her down into black oblivion.

CRYSTAL LINE

Anne McCaffrey

A Del Rey® Book
BALLANTINE BOOKS • NEW YORK

A Del Rey® Book
Published by The Random House Publishing Group
Copyright © 1992 by Anne McCaffrey

Published in the United States by Del Rey Books, an imprint of The Random House Publishing Group, a division of Random House, Inc., New York, and simultaneously in Canada by Random House of Canada Limited, Toronto.

Del Rey is a registered trademark and the Del Rey colophon is a trademark of Random House, Inc.

www.delreybooks.com

Library of Congress Catalog Card Number: 92-53219

ISBN-13: 978-0-345-38491-1

Manufactured in the United States of America

First Hardcover Edition: November 1992
First Mass Market Edition: May 1993

OPM   21   20   19   18   17   16   15

To my good friend

ELIZABETH MOON

teacher extraordinaire

CHAPTER 1

"'And a star to steer her by,'" Killashandra Ree shouted to herself. Not that Lars Dahl could have heard her over the roar of the sea crashing against the bow of the *Angel* and the humming tension of the wind through the sail stays and across the sloop's mainsail.

She pointed to the first star of the evening in the darkening eastern sky and looked back at him to see if he was watching her. He was and nodded, his grin showing his very white teeth against his very tan skin. She was nearly as dark as he was after their circumnavigation of the main continent of Ballybran. But Lars always *looked* the complete captain, especially as he was standing now—his straddled legs bracing his long lean body on bare feet against the slant of the deck, strong hands firmly on the spokes of the wheel as he kept the *Angel* on the starboard tack under tight sail. The stiff

1

breeze had ruffled his sun-bleached and salt-encrusted hair into a crest, much like the ritual headdress of a primitive religion.

They had plenty of sea room between the *Angel* and the jagged stones of the shore, but soon—all too quickly—they would reach the headland and the harbor that served the Heptite Guild headquarters.

Killashandra sighed. She almost didn't want this voyage to end—and yet this kind of voyage, therapeutic though it was, was not quite enough to ease the surge of crystal in her blood. Lars, not having sung as long as she, was in better shape; but they *had* to strike a good lode of crystal on this next trip into the Ranges and make enough to get off-world for Passover, which was, once again, nearly upon them. She devoutly hoped that their sled was repaired and ready for the Ranges.

Killashandra gritted her teeth, remembering the ignominy of having to be *rescued* when their sled had been buried by a rockslide! Hauling the crushed sled out of the Ranges had sliced a hefty hunk out of their credit balance. The crystal they had cut before the rockslide—which had been preserved in containers sturdy enough to resist collapse—had been sufficient to pay the huge repair bill, but there hadn't been enough credit left for them to take an off-world jaunt while the refit was being done. Once again the *Angel,* and the ever-challenging seas of Ballybran, had rescued them from the ping of crystal in their blood and the boredom of the Heptite Guild quarters.

But, by all the holies, Killashandra swore, this time they would sing good crystals—if they could possibly find that wretched lode again. Communication crystal was always valuable. If they could just cut one set quickly and without foul-ups! She wanted to get off-planet, and *this* time Lars was not going to talk her into going to yet another water world. There *were* other planets that could prove just as interesting. If she didn't get to choose once in a while, she might just seriously consider finding another partner. There was that stocky young redhead with weird eyes and a roguish grin—he reminded her of someone. She grimaced into the wind. The need for "reminders" was becoming more frequent for her. She had been singing crystal a long time now, and she knew very well indeed that her memory was eroding; what or how much she was losing she didn't know. She shrugged. As long as she didn't forget Lars Dahl, nor he her . . .

The *Angel* was nearly round the massive headland, and Killashandra could just see a slice of the eastern face of the great Heptite Guild cube that loomed large from all directions even though it was kilometers inland. The good mood that had sustained her abruptly altered.

"Back to the old grind," she muttered, anticipating Lars's next words.

"Back to the old grind, huh?" Lars bellowed, and she rolled her eyes and gave herself a shake.

Damn! *Knowing* what would come out of his mouth because they had shared so much, so intensely, was also beginning to irritate her. Or maybe all she and Lars needed was new stimulation. He found enough in their sea trips, but suddenly she realized that these were no longer enough for her. She grimaced again. How long was too long?

Lars bellowed for her attention, motioning for her to join him in the cockpit. With cautious but practiced steps she made her way astern, balancing against both wind and the slant of the *Angel,* turning her head against spray and the occasional high wave that broke across the deck.

As she came even with him, Lars reached out an arm

and hooked her to his side, smiling down at her, contented in the elements of the sea/wind/ship, even if the end of their voyage was now in sight. She let herself be held against his long, strong body. She knew him so well! Was that such a bad thing for a crystal singer? Especially when memory began to erode? She glanced up at Lars's profile, elegant despite his peeling nose: Lars Dahl, the constant factor in her life!

"Hey, Killa, Lars! Lanzecki wants to see you soon as you dock," the harbor master yelled as he caught the line Killa deftly threw at him. He bent it neatly about the bollard as she ran aft, leaping lightly onto the marina slip, stern line in hand.

"Ya heard me?" he roared.

"Sure, I heard."

"We both heard," Lars added, grimacing at Killa.

Then, from long-established habit, Killashandra ducked down the companionway to check that everything in the cabin had been stowed properly, her chore as Lars had motored into the harbor. Satisfied, she threw their duffels topside, following more circumspectly with the bag of nondegradable trash.

Lars had shut down the engines and was checking the boom crutch to be sure it was properly secured.

"I'll keep an eye on the boat for ya," the harbor master said anxiously. Singers were not expected to dally when the Guild Master sent for them. This pair made their own rules, but he wasn't about to receive debits for their impudence.

"Sure you will, Pat," Lars said reassuringly as he checked the mast stays, "but old habits die hard. You'll run her in"—he jerked his head toward the spacious boathouse—"if there's a bad blow?"

Pat snorted, jamming his hands indignantly into his jacket pockets. "And when haven't I?"

Lars scooped his duffel bag off the deck and, leaping neatly from the *Angel* to the pier, gave Pat a grateful grin and a clout for the reassurance. Killashandra was a step behind him, adding her nod of appreciation before she matched Lars's stride for stride up the ramp to the wharf. They took the nearest scooter and turned its nose inland, to the Guild Complex.

By the time they had parked the scooter, entered the residential section of the Complex, and taken a lift to the executive floor, nineteen other people had informed them, in tones varying from irritated malice to sheer envy, that Lanzecki wanted to see them.

"Fardles!" Killashandra said, stressing the *f* sound against her teeth and lips. "What's up?"

"Hmmm, we are not in favor with our peer group," Lars said, his expression carefully bland.

"I've got a bad feeling," Killashandra muttered for his ears only.

Lars gave her a long searching look, just as the lift halted at the executive floor. "You think Lanzecki might have one of those choice little extra jobs for us?"

"Uh-huh!"

Then, in step, they swung left to Lanzecki's office. The first thing Killashandra noticed was that Trag was not in sight. A slender man rose from Trag's accustomed place: he bore the fine scars of healing crystal scores on face, neck, and hands, but Killashandra couldn't remember ever seeing him before.

"Killashandra Ree?" the man asked. He looked from her to her companion. "Lars Dahl? Don't you ever turn on your ship comunit?"

"When we're in the cabin," Lars answered pleasantly enough.

"Weren't in it much, not with only two to crew her through some nasty storms," Killa added with mock contrition. "Where's Trag?"

"I'm Bollam." He gave the odd shrug of one shoulder and tilt of his head that told them that Trag was no longer alive. "You know your way?"

"Intimately," Killashandra snapped over her shoulder as she strode angrily around him and toward the door to Lanzecki's sanctum. She didn't like Trag being dead. He had taught her to retune crystal during her apprenticeship, and she vaguely remembered other remote things about him, mainly good. Bollam didn't look like the sort of personality who could manage the duties that Trag had so effortlessly—and unemotionally—executed. If she were Lanzecki, she wouldn't trust that dork-looking weed as a partner in the Ranges. Fardles, she didn't have half that many scars on her arms, and she'd been singing crystal for . . . for a long time!

Slapping the door plate with an angry hand, she pushed through as soon as its identifying mechanism released the lock. She strode across to where Lanzecki was leaning over a worktop.

"You do have a comunit aboard that boat of yours," he began before she could take the initiative.

"Ship," Lars automatically corrected Lanzecki.

"When we turn it on," Killashandra said simultaneously. "What's so earth-shattering?"

Lanzecki tossed the stylus he had been using to the worktop and, straightening, gave the pair a long look. Killa felt something twist inside her. Lanzecki's face looked drawn and—aged. Had Trag's death been that recent?

"In the 478-S-2937 system in the Libran area of space, they've found what they think might be a new version of crystal, opalescent, but purported to be considerably more complex than Terran opals or Vegan firestones, either clear or opaque."

He clicked on the viewing screen, fast-forwarding it so that the exploration ship zoomed in speedy orbit, landed, and early-evaluation processes went at an ever-increasing kaleidoscopic rate.

"Ah! Here!" And Lanzecki pressed for normal speed. "Planet's a shell with an immense cavern system— geologists suggest that the planet cooled too fast."

"No oceans?" Lars asked.

Lanzecki shook his head, and Killa grinned, a trifle sourly, for that was always Lars's first question about a new planet: Were there seas to sail?

"Underground deposits of ice neither drinkable nor," the Guild Master added with a rare display of broad humor, "sailable."

"Damn!"

"Ah!" Killa said, as the vid angled up and a coruscation of what appeared to be liquid was reflected back. The angle altered, and Killa and Lars became aware that the liquidity was actually the reflection of what appeared to be a band of Lanzecki's medium blue opalescent stone.

Abruptly Lanzecki fast-forwarded to another extrusion, this time a deeper blue in a wider band that was almost a complete rib, vaulting across the ceiling from one side of the cavern to the other, nearly to the floor on both sides, seemingly spread from the "pool" in the center of the roof. Curiously, the color seemed to flow as if it were forcing itself downward on both ends, striving to reach the base.

"This is taken with only existing light," Lanzecki

said, his tone laced with amused interest. "The planet has a very slow rotation, taking nearly forty standard hours to complete one diurnal revolution. This was taped in dawn light. Full noon is blazing."

Lars was more vocal in his admiration. "All this one stone, or a vein?" he asked, sounding awed.

"Well, *that* is another matter no one has been able to ascertain," Lanzecki said dryly.

"Oh?" Killa wasn't sure she liked the possibilities becoming apparent in the situation.

"Yes, these tapes are several years old. Every member of the exploration team died within four months of landing on Opal."

"Opal?" Killashandra asked, staving off the gorier details she was sure Lanzecki would give them.

He shrugged, his lips twitching briefly. "The team named it."

"Not knowing it would be their memorial?" Lars commented wryly.

"Happens."

"How did they die?" Lars asked, hitching one leg over the corner of the worktop and settling himself there.

"Not nicely. When the deadman alarm went off, broadcasting a contamination code, the Trundomoux who investigated took every precaution. They recovered the tape cassette in the airlock along with the ship's log and a small chunk of *unflexing* material which turned out to be part of that coruscating stuff. There were notes from the geologist and the doctor of the stricken ship in the log entries. They concurred in the opinion that they had acquired a lethal dose of something on Opal, and it could well have been from contact with the stone. The log said that to get this sample, they had had to laser out the stone around it, as they couldn't detach it in any other way." Lanzecki paused for effect. "The survey guys have identified cesium, gallium, rubidium, and lesser quantities of iron and silicon in the sample. There are also several radioactive isotopes, indicating that at some point the sample included a radioactive element, but we found no trace of one to identify. Odd thing was that the sample did not have the coruscating look of the parent body. Trag thought it had died, being excised from the main body.''

"Trag went?"

Lanzecki looked away from them for a long moment before he answered. Then he made eye contact first with Killashandra, then with Lars.

"The Ballybran symbiont will heal our bodies and reduce degeneration to a very slow crawl, but eventually it, too, loses its resilience. Trag has been on the Guild Roll a long, long time. He knew his symbiont protection was waning. When the Guild was asked to send a representative on the premise that the Ballybran symbiont might protect a Heptite member, Trag volunteered. Presnol put him through exhaustive tests and discovered that the symbiont was still active. Trag insisted that he had protection enough to be safe.''

There were many in the Guild who called Lanzecki "the Stone-face." Even Killashandra had once made the mistake of thinking him emotionless, but later events had corrected that misjudgment. The stony look now was masking at least regret, if not something deeper. Lanzecki had depended on Trag for more than just partnership when he had to cut crystal.

"He spent unshielded time with the stone and suffered no ill effects.''

"Then what killed him?" Killashandra demanded.

Lanzecki gave a snort. "Some damned fool respiratory ailment he caught on the voyage back.'' A twist of his right shoulder indicated his dislike of such an ignoble ending. "Presnol did consider the possibility that contact with the stone had further reduced his symbiont protection, and tissue examination proved that Trag certainly hadn't contracted the same, or a similar, disease to that which affected the geological ship's personnel." Lanzecki paused again. "In his report Trag was confident that the Ballybran symbiont would protect crystal singers, and that further investigations should be carried out by the Heptite Guild. He reported a *resonance* from the stone, unlike anything he ever encountered in the Ranges—unlike but similar."

Killashandra folded her arms across her chest, ignoring the querying expression on Lars's face. "And you want us to explore the possibilities?" she finally asked.

"Yes."

Lars caught her gaze, blinking his left eye in their private code of interest. Killa made Lanzecki wait for their answer.

"How much?"

Lanzecki gave her a shark's grin. "We have quoted them a . . . substantial fee for the services of a Heptite Guild team."

"Ooooh, then the Powers that Be are really interested," she said. When Lanzecki nodded, she went on, "And you have a price in mind—for us, as well as the Guild?"

"I am able to offer you fifty thousand credits. You'd be off-planet during Passover—and you should have more than enough time to complete the investigation before the frenzy overtakes you."

Killashandra dismissed that aspect as she rapidly considered the monetary enticement and decided that the Guild must have asked for twice or three times that amount.

"We wouldn't take less than ninety thousand for that

sort of hazardous work." She flicked a quick glance at Lars. Even the fifty thou would take them anywhere in explored space for as long as they could stand being away from Ballybran.

Lanzecki inclined his head briefly, but the slight upturn of his lips told Killa that he had expected her to haggle. "Sixty. The Guild will have expenses . . ."

"You should have asked for those above and beyond the danger money," Killashandra said with a snort of contempt. "Eighty-five."

"We might have to keep you in isolation on your return from Opal . . ."

"Why else have I been paying dues all these years? And don't you trust Trag's evaluation?"

"As I always trusted him. He was, however, only in the chamber with the stone for a relatively short period."

"How long?" Lars asked.

"Three weeks."

"And you want us to believe that it didn't affect the symbiont?"

"Presnol says not. A simple bronchial infection killed him. Those on the exploration ship—examined by remote probe—died of a rampant lymphatic leukemia which no medication available to any nonaltered humans could combat. There were no indications of lymphatic failure or alteration in Trag."

"Three weeks might not have been long enough for the problem to develop."

Lanzecki shook his head. "Not according to the data in the log of the medic on board the exploration ship. Initial symptoms of fatigue, headache, *et cetera,* appeared in the second week after contact."

Killashandra kept staring at Lanzecki. After the Trundomoux black-crystal installation—a traumatic memory she hadn't been able to eradicate—and some other little special assignments, the memories of which had been reduced over the years to feelings of annoyance rather than specific complaints, Killashandra had an innate distrust of any Lanzecki assignments.

"Eighty buys our time and effort," she told him with terse finality.

"Plus . . ." Lars held up his hand, entering the bidding for the first time. "A half percent of Guild profits arising from viable merchandising of this as a product."

"What!" Lanzecki's blast of surprise startled Lars off his perch.

Killashandra threw her head back in a burst of laughter as he pulled himself back up onto the worktop. "Boy, you're learning!"

"Well, I don't see why not," Lars told her, but he was watching Lanzecki's face. "If we're risking our asses for the Guild, we should see some of the profits!"

"It may be nothing more than a pretty stone!" Lanzecki bit out the words.

"Then there'd be no royalty to be paid."

"It could be sentient," Killashandra put in.

"Whose side are you on?" Lars demanded.

But Lanzecki grinned.

"Done!" And before either crystal singer could protest, he caught Killashandra's hand and slapped it down on the palm pad, effectively registering her agreement. Then he extended the unit to Lars Dahl, who grinned broadly and made a show of wriggling his fingers before placing them down on the pad.

"We could have held out for more," Killashandra said with some disgust.

Lars parted his lips in a broad grin. Bargaining was usually her province, and she was very good at it. He was rather pleased with his initiative in adding the percentage: not too much for Lanzecki to reject out of hand, but if the rock proved useful, they could easily never have to cut crystal unless they needed to renew the symbiont. Still, eighty thousand credits and a royalty was enough to salve pride and greed.

"So, if unaltered humans can't land on this planet, how do we?" Killashandra asked.

"Brain ship's been allocated."

"Our old friends Samel and Chadria?" Lars asked.

The names titillated Killashandra's memory but produced no further recall.

Lanzecki gave Lars a patient stare. "Not them."

Killashandra winced, for his attitude plainly indicated that that pair were no longer alive. She wondered, but only briefly, how long ago their demise had occurred. Brain ships had life expectancies of several hundred years. Could she have been cutting crystal for *that* long?

"They had an awkward accident," Lanzecki amended, and Killashandra relaxed. "I'll inform the Agency that you've taken the contract."

"So there've been no tests or assays or anything completed on this stone? Even by Trag?" Lars asked. "Discounting its effect on humans."

"Trag felt it was sentient."

"Trag did?" Killashandra was astounded. "Then it is."

"And you treat that as a possibility only, Killashandra Ree," Lanzecki said, sternly waggling a blunt finger at her.

"You bet!" She began to feel better about the assignment. If blunt ol' thick-skinned conservative Trag had felt something, she rather supposed that she and Lars would have much better luck. "A silicon sentience has been postulated."

"Will it say it's sorry it killed the team?" Lars asked sarcastically, crossing his arms over his chest.

"Does crystal?" Killashandra responded with a snort.

"At least crystal sings" was Lars's soft rejoinder.

To Lars, Lanzecki passed a flimzie and a thin tape cassette. "That's all we have on the silicon, and the relevant log entries."

"So when do we go?"

"Your transport, the BB-1066—" He held up his hand when Killashandra started to interrupt him. "The Brendan/Boira. Boira's on sick leave, so Brendan's willing to undertake the journey."

"Truly a B-and-B ship," Lars said dryly.

"And I suppose you expect us to depart immediately?" Killashandra asked irascibly.

Lanzecki nodded briefly. "Brendan's been *patiently* waiting your return."

"We just got in," Killashandra protested.

"From a holiday," Lanzecki pointed out.

"Holiday?" Noting Lars Dahl stiffen on his corner of the worktop, she grinned impudently. "Well, from one point of view, but I'd like time to get the salt off my skin and a bit of crystal out of my blood."

"A tub—a double one"—Lanzecki's grin was malicious—"and sufficient radiant fluid are aboard the 1066. With eighty thou to your credit, you can surely see your way clear to a precipitous departure. Everyone you might know—bar Presnol—is out in the Ranges."

Killashandra sniffed her displeasure at what seemed suspiciously close to being part of a maneuver to shanghai them.

"If you'd bothered to keep in contact, you'd've had more time," Lanzecki pointed out.

"C'mon, Killa," Lars said, dismounting from his

perch and draping an affectionate arm about her shoulders.

"I suppose our sled isn't ready?" she said, eyeing Lanzecki sourly.

"It is." Lanzecki never took kindly to any suggestion of Guild inefficiency. "And you'll earn more from this—"

"As well as easy credit for the Guild," Killa put in.

"Not to mention that we're the best ones for this little errand," Lars added.

"That, too," Lanzecki unexpectedly conceded. "Only this time"—his pointed finger stabbed in Lars's direction—"I want on-the-site accounts recorded in Brendan's memory circuits from the moment you land on Opal."

"This time," Killashandra said, smiling in saccharine obedience, "you'll have 'em. We'll just dump our gear and grab a few personal things from our quarters."

"Brendan's stocked your usual brands, and being a B-and-B ship, he's amply supplied with more than the usual trip paraphernalia. Leave for Shanganagh from here. *Now.* There's a shuttle waiting."

Killashandra unslung her duffel and launched it at Lanzecki, who neatly caught it. Lars merely slipped the webbed carry strap from his shoulder.

"Everything needs cleaning," he said.

Lanzecki nodded. "Get out of here!" The phrase combined imperative order as well as gruff farewell.

So they left Lanzecki's office. Being more diplomatic than his partner, Lars nodded briefly to Bollam, who stared back with no response.

"Once in a while Trag'd smile," Lars muttered in Killa's ear as the door slid shut behind them.

"I don't *like* the idea of that dork going out into the Ranges with Lanzecki," she muttered, scowling.

Lars made a comforting noise in his throat. The Guild Master was in the unenviable position of having to keep as much memory current as possible to manage the intricacies of his position. But he also had to renew contact with crystal periodically or lose the vitality of his symbiont, despite being a virtual prisoner on Ballybran.

As they entered the lift and pushed the shuttle-level plate, Killashandra's frown deepened. Lanzecki wasn't stupid. So Bollam must have more substance or intelligence or skill than his appearance suggested. But she couldn't help fretting. Lanzecki was one of those unfortunate singers who became so rapt by the song of the crystal they cut that they could be totally lost to the thrall. A partner was essential to such singers; they dared not sing crystal alone, or they risked never returning from the Ranges. Antona had once told Killashandra that it was an infrequent enough manifestation, more often accompanying the Milekey Transition, the mildest form of adjustment to the Ballybran symbiont.

Lanzecki had always put off cutting crystal as long as he possibly could, even with Trag to accompany him and bring him safely back from the Ranges. Sometimes, as at one time he had done with Killashandra, he could establish an intimate relationship with someone whose body was singing with crystal pulse; that contact supplied surrogate reinforcements, staving off the need for true crystal. Killashandra did remember her interview with Trag, who had all but physically manhandled her off the planet to force Lanzecki out to the Ranges for a thorough revitalization of his symbiont. Would this Bollam have that sort of loyalty to his Guild Master?

The lift door slid back into the brightly banded corri-

dor that led to the shuttle bays. The blinking orange
ready light steered them to the waiting ship.

The pilot waved urgently to them to hurry, but as
they passed him on their way into the vessel, he glowered and pinched his nostrils.

"You reek! Where have you two been?"

"Oh, around and about," Lars said with a grin.

"If I wasn't under orders to—"

"Well, we are all under orders to," said Killashandra,
sliding into the backseat of the otherwise vacant transport, "so the sooner you get us to Shanganagh, the
faster you lose the stink of us."

"Can't be too soon for me," the pilot said sourly,
slamming the door to his cabin after a brief pause to be
sure they had buckled up.

Lars grinned at Killashandra. "Shall we stuff our old
socks somewhere?"

They would have, too, but the pilot had taken their
suggestion and their takeoff was the most perpendicular
Killashandra had ever experienced. They were jammed
so forcefully back into their cushioned seats that she
swore she felt the flexible plastic turn rigid. It was the
shortest trip she remembered making.

As soon as the shuttle had locked on to the Shanganagh Moon facility, the lock opened with such
unusual dispatch that there was no misinterpreting the
urgent invitation to depart.

"The B-and-B is one level above, Bay Eighty-seven,"
the pilot's voice said over the com.

"You are above all a courteous gentleperson, skilled
in the performance of your appointed duties," Lars said
facetiously.

"I'm what?" was the startled comment that followed
them down the lock ramp.

"They must have lowered entrance standards," Killashandra remarked. "I'm first in the bath."

"Lanzecki said it's a double," Lars reminded her.

At the end of the lock tunnel they took turns placing their palms in the ID plate, and the aperture irised open into the corridor.

They encountered no one, which was slightly unusual as Shanganagh was a major stopover point, as well as the Guild's main display and testing center. It also had supply and servicing facilities for vessels of any size.

"You don't suppose that antsy pilot warned everyone off until we've passed and the corridor's been fumigated?" Lars asked.

Killashandra snorted, frowning, and lengthened her stride. "I shall, however, be very grateful for the tub."

"Last one in . . ." Lars began, but then they saw the plate above Bay 87 blinking orange.

"He warned the B-and-B we were here!"

"Last one in . . ."

"*After* we make our duty to Brendan," Killa said quellingly. Of all the myriad manifestations of humans, altered or otherwise, she most respected shell people— to a point of reverence. There was something awesome about knowing that a human being, residing within the main titanium column, ran all the ship's functions and *was* the ship in a way an ordinary pilot could never be. The combination of a shell person with a mobile partner, known as a "brawn," made B&B ships the elite of spacegoing vessels. Traveling with Brendan was truly an honor.

"Of course!" Lars murmured.

As soon as they entered the lock, the panel behind them slid shut.

"Permission to come a—"

"Oh, I never stand on ceremony when I'm solo, kids,"

said a pleasantly resonant baritone voice. "Don't you ever answer your comunit? I've been sitting here on the moon long enough to pick up cobwebs."

"Sorry, Brendan," Lars said, giving as respectful a bow to the titanium column that encased Brendan's shelled body as Killashandra did.

"Ah! A tenor!" Brendan said with delight.

"And he can sing!" Killashandra said. Crystal singers might require perfect pitch, but that did not always accompany a good singing voice or any real musicality.

"So who's going to be last in the tub?" Brendan asked.

"Which way?" the two singers demanded.

"And when can we get under way?" Lars asked, stripping his salt-stiffened garments off. He nearly tripped out of the shorts, trying to keep up with Killa, who had less to shed.

"We are!" Laughter rippled in Brendan's voice. "I don't waste time." Then he laughed again as Killa elbowed Lars to prevent him from getting to the ladder to the tub rim. Lars merely vaulted up and neatly immersed himself in the thick viscous fluid just as Killa slid into the tub. They gave simultaneous sighs of relief as the liquid covered them. Moments later they found the armholds and secured themselves against the pressure of takeoff.

"You're sure you're under power?" Killa asked after a long interval of bracing herself against a shock that never came.

"Most certainly." Abruptly a screen in the corner of the small cabin lit up with a spectacular view of Shanganagh and Ballybran receding at an astonishing speed. "And about to initiate the Singularity Drive. I think you will find that being immersed in radiant fluid will reduce the discomfort the effect often gives you soft shells."

"Never thought of that before," Lars said.

"Here we go," Brendan said, and everything altered before the eyes of the two singers.

Killashandra squeezed her eyes shut against the Singularity Effect. She did not like seeing the decomposition and re-formation of space as the Singularity Drive "surfed" them — Lars liked the nautical analogy — down the long funnel of "interspace" from one relative spatial point to another. And yes, the radiant fluid did reduce that nauseating feeling of falling in on oneself, spinning and yet deprived of any sense of one's own position relative to that spin.

Then they were through.

"Does the fluid help?" Brendan asked solicitously.

"You know," Lars said in surprise, "I do believe it does. Killa?"

"Hmmmm! How many more of these jumps do we have to make to get to Opal?"

"Only two more."

Killashandra groaned.

"Something to eat, perhaps?" Brendan suggested. "I took on all your favorite foods."

Killa rallied hopefully. "Yarran beer?"

Brendan chuckled. "Would I forget *that?*"

"Not if you're as smart a brain as you're supposed to be," Lars said. Disengaging his arms, he pushed himself to the ladder. "You want anything else, Killa?" he asked as he clambered down.

What else she wanted required two trips by Lars, but in the end they were both well supplied. Brendan had even acquired flotation trays for them to use while immersed.

"I think this trip'll be sheer luxury," Killa murmured quietly to Lars.

Brendan heard her anyway. "I'll do my part," he said.

"Ah, Brendan . . ." she began, and was rewarded by a knowing chuckle.

"Just tell me when I'm off-limits and I'll chop the audio system," the ship said.

"Will you really?" Killa asked, trying to keep skepticism out of her tone.

"Actually," Brendan went on conversationally, "if I didn't, Boira would haul off the panel and disconnect *me*. Now there's a gal that liked her privacy . . ."

"How's she doing?" Lars asked.

"Oh, she's regenerating nicely."

The two bathers exchanged glances.

"Do we solicitously ask what happened, or shall we keep our noses short?"

A long silence ensued. "I won't say she was foolish, or stupid—just very unlucky," Brendan said with so little expression that the two would have had to be tone deaf not to appreciate how distressed he was at his partner's injuries. "I was only just able to get her to proper medical assistance in time. It will take a while, but she will completely recover."

"She's been a good partner?" Killa asked gently.

"One of the best I've had." And then his voice altered, not too brightly or lilting falsely. "One tends to nurture the good ones carefully."

"Even if there is only so much one can do?" Killa made it not quite statement, not quite query.

"Exactly. Now, shall I leave you to enjoy your bath in peace?"

Lars and Killa once again exchanged glances. Lars's yawn was not feigned.

"I'm going to have to get some tub-sleep," he said. "Can you monitor this contraption so we don't inadvertently go under?"

"Of course." And by Brendan's tone, the two singers realized they had struck the right attitude with him.

"I could probably sleep a few weeks . . ." Killa said.

"At which point you'd be a wrinkled prune," Lars replied caustically.

"I shall not permit that desecration of your most attractive self, Killashandra Ree," Brendan said in a flirtatious tone.

"Now, wait a mo—" Lars yawned. "—ment, Brendan. This one's mine, you rotten baritone."

Brendan chuckled, a sound that had odd resonances due to the artificial diaphragm he needed to speak or laugh.

"Go to sleep, Lars Dahl. You're no match for me in your present semisomnolent state."

Killa yawned, too, and jammed her arms deeper in the straps, tipping her head back against the padded rim of the tub. She never knew which of them fell asleep first.

CHAPTER 2

"What a cheese hole!" Lars said in a disgusted tone.

Killashandra said nothing. She didn't dare express what she felt about the planet Opal. And especially about Lanzecki for taking advantage of their greed, and need to be off-planet. Only the thought that she and Lars were making eighty thousand credits for this kept her from exploding.

Well, that and wanting to keep Brendan's good opinion. He had turned out to be the most excellent of escorts. Not only did he sing good baritone, but he had the most astonishing repertoire of lewd and salacious, prim and proper cantatas and languishing lieder. He wasn't as fond of opera as Killa was, but he knew all the comic operettas, musicals, lilts, pattern songs, and croons, and a selection of the best of every decade back to the beginning of taped music. He also had the most amazing and catholic files.

"Boira's a mezzo, you see, and while I can only sing the one voice . . ."

"Is the ship who sings . . . whatsername?"

"Helva? Yes, she still is, but no one knows where." Brendan had chuckled. "There's a reward if she's spotted, but I don't know a ship worth its hull who'd tell."

"But couldn't she sing *any* range?"

"So legend has it," Brendan had replied, amused. "It's possible. I could make modifications to my diaphragm and voice production, as she did, but frankly, it'd be damned hard to match the 834. Then, too, Boira *likes* me being baritone."

"Can't fight that," Killashandra had said, grinning at Lars.

But now they were orbiting Opal and musicality was irrelevant.

The pock-holed orb was more moon than planet, one of a dozen similar satellites weaving eccentric patterns about the primary. Opal had no atmosphere and only seven-tenths standard gravity. Its primary still emanated the unusual spectrums, coronal blasts, and violent solar winds that had so adversely affected its dependent bodies. Exploration HQ had decided that circumstances might possibly have resulted in unusual metals. Artifacts from some long-gone alien civilizations had been composed of previously undiscovered metallic components—some not kind to human hands but workable by remote control—that had proved to be invaluable to modern metallurgy, electronics, and engineering. Since those first discoveries, such substances continued to be assiduously sought. Which was why this star system had been surveyed.

"Leaving no turn unstoned," Bren had quipped.

According to the log, the now-deceased team had also discovered some very interesting slag on one of the outer satellites of Libran 2937, samples of which were still being analyzed—and their possible uses extrapolated from the all too small supply.

"Where did the geological survey land, Bren?" Lars asked.

"Their landing of record," Bren began, "is . . . right . . . below us." He magnified the image on his main screen, and the iridescent nauseous green paint that exploration teams used to mark their sites became clearly visible.

Lars and Killashandra turned to examine the close-up of the site, which was being displayed on one of the smaller bridge screens.

"Shall we?" the ship asked in a wry tone.

"Ach! Why not!" Lars said.

"We've time to eat," Killa said, feeling hunger pangs though she was certain they had eaten not too long before.

"Is it that time?" Lars asked with a startled expression. "We've done nothing but eat since we came aboard."

"They used to term it singing for your supper," Brendan added. His chuckle ended abruptly. "Oh, I see. You mean, your home planet's going through one of its Passover periods?"

"It was due to," Killa said. "It must have started. That's the only time we can't stop eating."

"Hmmm. Well, we've plenty aboard," Brendan replied soothingly.

Killashandra grimaced. "But we're going to have to suit up to move around down there, and suit food's not very satisfying."

Lars considered this aspect of the unusual hunger of their symbionts at Passover time: an urge that would overtake their bodies no matter how far they were from

Ballybran, since it was generated by the symbiont, ever in phase with its native planet. "We could work in shifts, one of us eat while the other explores."

"No! Absolutely not," Brendan vetoed firmly. "As a team always. How long do you last between snacks?"

Killa laughed. "Snack? You've never seen a singer eat!"

"Well, tell me how much and I can deliver it to the lock so you don't have to unsuit completely to assuage your need."

Killa brightened. "That's a thought."

"We'll certainly give it a try," Lars said with a grin. "Now, just let's see if we can plan our excursions around our appetites." He accessed the log files of the fateful geology ship.

"How about I land you near the biggest of the vaults? This one!" Bren suggested, calling up the most remarkable of the liquidlike ribs. "That's not the landing of record, but it's certainly the most interesting site they found. Of course, I'm far more flexible than the *Toronto* was. We can pit hop as much as we need—while you're chowing down a good feed."

"Then there's the problem of the Sleep," Killa said, making a sour face.

"Oh?" Brendan prompted.

"Yes. Having stuffed ourselves like hibernators, we then sleep for the duration of the actual Passover."

"Or rather, our symbionts force us to sleep during the combined transit of the three moons," Lars explained.

"How long?"

Lars shrugged. "A week. That's why we stock up so heavily."

"For a week's sleep?"

Lars shrugged, then grinned at Brendan's column. "Not my choice."

"Then you eat again?" Brendan asked solicitously.

"Just before we fall asleep, even the sight of food makes us nauseous. That's generally how we know we'd best get into a comfortable position," Lars explained.

"Most unusual," Brendan said mildly, "though I've heard *and* encountered weirder ones."

"You're most reassuring," Killashandra said dryly.

"I try to be. You'd best belt in," he added. The main screen was showing their precipitous approach to the pock-marked moon. Seeing that, the two singers hastened to obey.

Brendan was an excellent pilot—as he *was* the ship, to all intents and purposes. As he neatly deposited them on the *soi-disant* surface of Opal, Lars and Killa applauded in the traditional manner. Then they concentrated on eating the enormous meal the ship served them—items that Brendan knew they particularly liked and in quantities that should have daunted a normal appetite.

"You really do stow it away, don't you?"

Killa and Lars were too busy stuffing themselves to give any reply other than a distracted "Hmmm . . ."

At last they were replete; and, groaning a bit, they squeezed into their vacuum suits. Killashandra found herself wishing, if only for a moment, that "space suits" had not evolved to be quite so lean and efficient. But these suits were perfect for non-atmospheric explorations. The close-fitting shell provided the wearer with a nearly impervious second skin. Fine controls for digital manipulations were available; sanitary arrangements were as unobtrusive as possible. The helmet afforded complete head mobility and visibility; the tubes for eating and drinking were housed at the neck rim. The oxygen unit fit snugly across the shoulder blades and down to the end of the spine, which it also served to protect. Helmet, digital, and arm lights illuminated a wide area around the wearer. Versatile tools attached to special rigs on the belt and stowed in thigh and leg pouches gave them additional external resources.

"I've stocked your suit packs with a rather tasty high protein, followed by a sweet confection that might just relieve hunger pangs," Brendan began.

"No matter what you feed us, mate, we'll have to come back for more than any suit could supply," Lars said as he and Killashandra entered the airlock. "All right now, Bren, let us out."

They had both studied the log records of the *Toronto,* so they knew to turn left as soon as they exited the outer lock.

"Humpf," Killa said, training her arm light on the fluorescent line the previous expedition had painted on the porous shell. "Nice of them, considering."

"They expected to return," Lars remarked quietly.

"I see the markings," Brendan said in an oblique reminder to narrate their progress more explicitly.

"For posterity then," and Killashandra began the running commentary as they followed the guideline down steps that had been cut by their predecessors. There was even a line sprayed across a low threshold to warn them where to bend and, hunching over, they started down the short passage into the larger chamber.

"Hey, there's light ahead," Lars said, and turned off his beams. "A sort of blue radiance," he went on, gesturing for Killa to extinguish her lamps.

The light source did not actually illuminate the passage, but the glow was sufficient to guide them to its source.

As they entered the big cavern, they were both speechless for a moment. Luminescence cascaded in flinders of brilliance—like sparks, except that they didn't shoot out of their parent substance. The material that arced across the high ceiling seemed to flow, dark blue and dark green and then silver.

"I am not there," Brendan reminded them politely.

Lars turned on his helmet light, and immediately the radiance was quenched. Where the helmet beam touched, the material writhed with bands of black and dark blue and dark green. Almost, Killashandra thought, as if rushing blood to heal a wound. Did light on this lightless world constitute a threat or injury? She wondered if the sun's rays—unfiltered, with no atmosphere to reduce ultraviolet and infrared—penetrated the cavern to the jewel? For jewel it appeared to her, one graceful long sweep of jewel, a living necklace across the vault of the cavern. Or was it a tiara?

"It's the most beautiful thing I've seen in a long time," she murmured. "And I've seen some magnificent crystal." She paused, frowning. "I also don't know why or how, but I agree with Trag, Brendan. This jewel junk is alive. Who knows about sentience—but definitely a living organism!"

"I agree with that," Lars said quietly, then began to examine the chamber while Killashandra concentrated on the gem cascade.

"It's grown, too, Brendan, since the team was here four–five years ago. It's made a complete hoop across the ceiling from floor to floor," Killashandra went on.

"And down into the next cavern, if there is one," Lars added, kneeling to shine the pencil-thin line of his forefinger light where the shimmering opalescent seemed to penetrate the floor of the cavern. The jewel itself darkened and seemed to contract, to retreat from the light source.

"To the basement level for housewares and utensils," Killashandra recited in the tone of a robotic lift device, feeling a need to dispel the unusual sense of reverence that the chamber evoked in her. *"No!"* she cried in sudden fear as she saw Lars reach out to touch the narrow descending—tongue? facet? finger? probe? tentacle?—of the opalescent.

Lars turned his helmeted head toward her, and his white teeth flashed a grin. "Let's not be craven about this. If the symbiont protects me, it protects me. After all, I'm suited . . ."

"Use an extendable," Brendan said in a tone remarkably close to command. "The material of your suit is only guaranteed impervious to *known* hazards."

"Good point, Lars," Killashandra added.

He gave a shrug and snagged a tool from his belt. A light pass of the instrument across the coruscating extrusion gave no results. Then he prodded it gently—and suddenly jerked back his arm.

"Wow!"

"Report?" Killa reminded him.

First he looked at the tool. "Well, I'm glad you stopped me, Bren." He turned the implement toward Killa. She tongue-switched the magnification of her visor and saw that the end had melted, blurring its outline.

"Hot the material is, but it gave on contact," Lars said.

"Pliable?" Brendan asked.

"Hmmm, flexible, maybe, or able to absorb intrusions," Killa suggested. "Or is it semiliquid, like mercury, or that odd stuff they found on Thetis Five?"

"So far, except for your observation that the, ah—" Brendan paused. "—semiliquid has spanned its cave in the four years since discovery, you have trod in the same path the geologists did. They also melted a few instruments trying to probe it."

"I know, I know," Lars said, "but I like to draw my own conclusions." He passed his gloved hand over the material several times, being careful not to touch it. "Any heat readings on record?"

"None, and I'm getting none either from the instrumentation you're carrying," the ship responded, sounding slightly disgusted.

"Any movement?"

"Negatory."

"Can you give us a reading on whether the ground beneath us is solid or not, Brendan?" Killa asked.

"You are currently standing on the intersection of three caves approximately two meters below you. Two of them are large, the other is small, less than half a meter in width and height. My readings corroborate the expedition's report that this satellite is riddled with cavities, probably right down to what used to be its molten core, in irregular layers and with equally irregular cavities."

"Can you keep a scan on possible spots too thin to bear any weight?" Killashandra had a quick vision of herself falling through level after level of cinder.

"Monitoring" was the ship's response.

Killa realized she had been holding her breath and expelled it. That allowed her stomach to mention it was empty, so while she made a confident circuit of the cavern, she sucked up the ration. In several places and with great care, she placed her gloved hand on the walls; her wrist gauge gave not so much as a wiggle. The ambient temperature of the cavern was the same as that on the satellite's surface. But there was something she was missing. Unable to think what that was, she shrugged and sucked on her tube.

"Hey, this glop's not bad, Bren," she said.

"Not eating already?"

"On the hour, every hour," Lars answered. He hunkered down by the visible end of the material and poked, careful not to let his chisel touch the glowing substance as he scraped out a semicircle. He gave a grunt. "It's going down. But where? Any access to the next level, Bren?"

"I think so," the ship answered after a bit. "Sort of a maze, but your suits have tracers on 'em, so I can keep track and direct you. Go out the way you came in . . ."

Following his directions, they traveled one of the more tortuous routes they had ever followed, accustomed as they were to the vagaries of sly crystal in the Milekey Ranges on Ballybran.

"I'm glad we don't have to stay too long in this place," Killa muttered, shining her lights around. The passageways seemed darker than ever after the subtle radiance of the junk-jewel cave. She preferred to have as much light around her as possible in dark burrows. The rock around them seemed to absorb their lights. "You eat it," she growled as she walked.

"What? Me? Oh, you mean the rock?" Lars asked. "Yeah, it does sort of soak it up. Speaking of which . . ."

"Not you, too!" Brendan exclaimed, almost sputtering. "It's scarcely two hours since you consumed an immense meal."

"Hmmm, true!"

"Humpf."

"We can last about another hour, I think," Lars said, and grinned as Killa glanced back at him. Would Brendan catch the teasing note?

"At this rate," Brendan replied trenchantly, "we'll be here for months! Turn obliquely right now, and watch that it *is* oblique—there's a hole!"

"Whoops, so there is," Killa said, teetering on the edge as her hand and head lamps outlined the even deeper blackness. Then, as she swung right, the comforting arch of a passageway was visible. "Nice save there, Bren. And what have we here but another cave!" Her tone was richly facetious. "And," she added, as she shone both lamps in a swing, "our little creepy-crawly has fingers in this pie, too."

Lars stepped around her and walked up to the glittering nubbin just entering the roof of this cavity. He dropped the beam of his light to the floor, and they could both see a small pile of debris. Lars hunkered down and, with the end of his hammer, carefully prodded the mound, examining the end of the tool when he had finished.

"Nope, not a melt. More like simple dust."

"Take a sample," his partner suggested.

"Take a sample of the rock, too," Brendan added.

"Now, look a'that," Killa said, holding her light steady on the opposite wall, where the liquid opal had intruded as well. "How many layers of this cave complex did the geologists explore?"

"At the original landing site, they penetrated several miles below the surface before they could proceed no further, but not here. However, records indicate that, in the cave above, the arch of the junk was incomplete. Nor do they mention that it penetrated below the first level in the landing site."

"Fascinating!" Killa commented. "How many such manifestations were recorded, Bren?" Dammit, she had studied those reports only last night and she couldn't recall the details.

"In nine of the twenty-three sites explored, they observed this opalescence. By then they hadn't found anything else particularly noteworthy, so they decided to proceed to the next system on their route when . . ."

"Hmm, yes, indeed, when!"

"You'd think it would grow up, out of the core," Lars mused, "instead of down from the surface."

"If it *is* indigenous," Brendan suggested.

Lars and Killa were silent a moment, considering that theory. "Well, being alien to this system would answer why it's topside instead of down below," Lars remarked.

"Is there a way to prove alien origin?" Killa asked.

"If you could find a sample that'll submit to examination, possibly," the ship replied wryly.

"Suppose we explain that this won't hurt?" Killa was feeling waggish at this point. Faint from hunger, maybe. She sucked on the tube and got a mouthful of something rather more sweet than she liked. But it did depress the hunger pangs. "An alien substance? Hmm. Wherever could it have originated?"

" 'There are more things in heaven and earth, Horatio . . .' " Brendan intoned in a marvelously sepulchral note.

"Nonsense, Bren, there's usually a scientific explanation for *every*thing," Killa said sharply. The very idea of something like the opal just "dropping" in made her slightly nervous. They hadn't discovered *anything* about it yet. And it had killed a whole exploratory team.

"I wonder," Lars said slowly, "if a quick freeze might not work to get us a sample."

"Work how?" Killa asked, her mind taken off both stomach and apprehension.

"I can't imagine how this stuff generates heat enough to melt an alloy as tough as the chisel, but maybe liquid nitrogen . . ."

"Wouldn't hurt to try," Bren said. "Fight liquid with liquid?"

"Have you got some?" Killa asked, again surprised.

"My dear Killashandra Ree, this ship has everything!" Bren's voice was smug. "My inventory shows that there are two cylinders of liquid nitrogen in storage. I have both spray and stream nozzles that will fit the standard apertures."

"Hmmm."

"I'll have one ready when you return for your next meal," Brendan added at his driest.

"And more luminescent paint, too," Lars added as the last drop dribbled out of his marking tube.

They retraced their steps very carefully, feeling the cindery crunch of the surface under their booted feet. Again something teased at the back of Killa's mind but refused to be identified.

The promised meal awaited them in the airlock, and they could barely wait until the iris had cycled shut and the oxygen level was adequate before they undid their helmets and attacked the food.

"Oh, this is good, Bren," Killa said, gobbling down refried steakbean and reaching for the orange-and-green milsi stalks of which she was particularly fond. Lars, as usual, was munching on grilled protein.

"Is indeed," Lars mumbled.

"You'll notice the nitro tank?" Brendan asked pointedly.

"Hmmm . . ." Killashandra waved a forkful of beans at it. "Appreciate that."

"And the marker tubes?"

It was Lars's turn to reply. "Thanks."

"You're welcome." Brendan sounded a trifle miffed.

"Can't help this," Lars added, glancing up apologetically at the airlock's optic.

Brendan's sigh was audible. "No, I suppose you can't, really. I've just never seen any bodies consume so much food in such a short time. And you're both bone-thin."

"Symbiont," Killashandra managed to say, one hand cramming as many of the bright green vegetable spheres into her mouth as would fit, while she scooped up more milsi stalks in the other. "You'll never see a fat singer," she added after swallowing her mouthful.

Oddly enough, the compulsion to gorge eased off about the time they were mopping up the plates with a yeast bread that was one of Brendan's specialties. Though as a shell person, he was nourished entirely by the fluids pumped into the titanium capsule that contained his stunted body, still he was fascinated by food and did most of the catering, even when Boira was on board.

Replete, Killashandra and Lars exchanged the depleted catering packets in their suits for fresh ones, donned their helmets, picked up the extra equipment, and exited the B&B to resume their explorations.

"Why are we trying to carve a hunk out of the junk?" Killashandra asked as they made their way back to the lower cavern.

"We were sent here to investigate the stuff, *in situ,* make recommendations as to its possible value, and/or usefulness," Lars said. "And see what makes it luminesce. Any report on whether or not the hunk of the junk grew in captivity, Bren?"

"No. I mean, no mention of increase in the sample; however, the report said, once excised, the specimen lost all iridescence."

"The junk doesn't like light," Killa said thoughtfully. "Could be it has to have darkness to sparkle. Or there's something in the composition of this planet that makes it iridescent?"

"And some element that makes it expand, grow, flow, whatever it does," Lars remarked, equally thoughtful. "Down the sides and to the next level. All in four years or so."

"Never heard of anything that *grew* in such a deprived environment as this," Killa said with a snort.

"Well, we ain't seen everything yet, have we?" Lars responded equably.

A ten-second spray of liquid nitrogen turned the entire stalactite colorless, and when Lars gave it a sharp chop with his rock hammer, the end—a piece the length and width of his gloved hand—fell to the ground. Through her boot soles, Killashandra felt a sharp shaking, unexpected and severe enough to unbalance her.

"Did you feel that, Lars?"

"Indeed I did!" Lars had flailed his arms briefly to steady himself.

"Feel what?" Brendan asked sharply.

"A tremor, a shake, a quake. Did you register anything?" Lars asked.

"Hmm. Well, there is a minute blip on the stability gauge. Not enough to set off a stabilizer alarm."

"Look!" Killa shone her light to the opposite wall, and the two singers saw that the other intrusion had disappeared. "A definite reaction to our action. The Junk has enough sense to retract from peril?"

"Sense or reflex?" Lars asked, scooping the colorless stalactite into the duraplas specimen sack he had pulled from his thigh pocket. "Let's see how *far* it's retracting."

Guided by Bren and moving as fast as was safe in the dark maze, they returned to the first chamber. The opalescence was subtly muted, and they had to turn on their suit lights. Then they could see that the Junk had noticeably contracted on both sides of the wall, though the farther "rib" was longer than the one from which they had taken the stalactite. They saw no other change in the central portion of the rib.

"Hey, look, Lars, a channel," Killa said. She pointed to the faint shadow on the wall where the Junk had been. "It makes a channel. Does it absorb rock as it extrudes?"

"Could it be making the caves?" Lars asked. That stunned both listeners into silence.

"Total absorption?" Brendan asked, puzzled. "Most beings excrete some waste material."

"This Junk makes a waste of space," Killashandra replied, grinning at Lars. "I can't see any movement now, but it sure moved incredibly fast in the twenty-odd minutes it took us to get back up here. Getting tape on this, Bren?"

"You bet."

"Well, then, let's try some comparison," Lars said. He motioned for Killashandra to follow him. "The first team found nine such phenomena? Well, let's go see the next one."

"I'm hungry again," Killashandra added apologetically.

Brendan made an exceedingly gross sound, but he had more food ready for them when they reached the airlock. They ate while he changed sites.

And that became the routine of the next ten hours. Search and eat. Eat while searching. At first Brendan had clever, often hilarious comments to make about their "starvation diet," but then he became as fascinated as they by what could only be called the "behavior" of the Junk.

At each of the five sites they investigated, they found

that the opalescence had diminished in size from the
mass that the geologists had recorded.

"Hey, you two, I'm calling a rest period. Your vital
signs are becoming erratic."

"With all the food we're ingesting?" Killa said, half
teasing. "Now that you mention it—whoops!" She
tripped and fell forward into Lars.

"Now that you mention it," Lars continued, steadying her, "I could curl up for a hundred or so hours."

"Hunger would uncurl you in about three," Brendan
replied. "Chow's up!"

They waited long enough before eating to insert their
suits in the cleanser and shower themselves. Bren did
manage to keep them awake long enough after they had
eaten to get to their bunk.

But the next morning, as he served an enormous
breakfast, the two singers were alert and keen to examine the remaining locations. By comparing the exploration notes with the present state of the ribbing, they saw
distinct differences: less alteration the farther the opalescence was from the rib they had sampled.

"Is this a mass defection, migration, withdrawal?"
Lars asked, puzzled.

"Pinch me, you pinch us all?" Killa responded.

"How could one piece of Junk communicate with the
others?" Brendan asked.

"That's the easy one," Killa said with a grin.
"Through the rock mass. We felt that tremble. Maybe
that's communication."

"I'll credit that," Lars said, "but where is the Junk
retreating *to*? Anything show up on the scopes, Bren?"

"Visualize me shrugging," the ship said drolly, "because I *have* checked all my systems for malfunction.
The Junk refuses to have its picture taken. There isn't so
much as a black blob registering on the walls of any of

the caverns you've been in. But the Junk's very much *in situ*."

"Wait a minute, team," Killashandra said, a grin deepening. "I know what I missed . . . crunch underfoot. There's no debris or rubble or pebbles or anything in the caves!"

Lars blinked and lowered his head, frowning as he thought over her remark. "No, you're right, there isn't. Only that small pile of dust."

"Where the rib finger had wormed its way down. It may *eat* its way down."

"I could draw a comparison between your appetites and the—hey!" Brendan protested as Killa lobbed a pencil file at his titanium panel.

"I wonder what it does eat," Lars said. "Shall we whip up some appetizing bits and pieces for it to sample?"

"Didn't the explore team do that, Bren?" Killa asked.

"No, they did not." Bren's voice rippled in amusement. "After they seemed to lose tools to its melt process."

"I don't remember a mention of that," Killa said, frowning. She had only just reviewed the reports during breakfast.

"I gather that by inference, Ki," Brendan said. "And the inventory."

"So, what shall we offer up in sacrifice to the Junk God in the Grotto?" Killa asked.

"A bit of this, a bit of that," Lars said. "Can I have a walk through your spare-parts hold, Bren?"

"And can we return to our first cave?" Killa asked, speaking from an impulse she didn't quite understand. "I'm beginning to feel guilty about carving off that hunk of the Junk. We really ought to make restitution by letting it have first crack at our offerings."

That was granted, and Brendan told them what to take, and graciously offered what little garbage was left from preparing their meals, as well as other samples of protein and carbohydrate. The two resumed their now-clean suits, packed the tube wells for their snack, checked the oxygen tanks, snapped on their helmets, and cycled through the airlock.

"You know, you're right about rubble out here and none in the caves," Lars remarked.

As soon as they saw the blue light, they doused their suit lamps.

"The crunch stops here," Lars added as he strode onto the smooth surface of the cavern. "I don't think it's retracted further, Killa. What d'you think?"

"Hmm. We should have thought to mark it. We can reach this far tip . . ." She took out a sample as she made her way across. "Copper, Bren," she said. Using forceps and stretched at full length upward, she laid the copper on the surface. Then she yanked her arm back. "Muhlah! Talk about hungry. And see, Lars, there's a definite pulse that's copper-toned, running all the way back to the hub. Fascinating . . ."

By the time they exhausted the contents of their sacks, the Junk had accepted every single offering, the metallic ones with noticeable alacrity and reaction.

"Omnivorous."

"Not grateful though," Killa added. "Not so much as a centimeter has it expanded. Humpf."

Lars regarded the central mass. "No, but I think it's brighter. Should we see if any of the others are more receptive?"

She was standing in a pose of thoughtfulness, one arm across her chest, propping the elbow of the gloved hand supporting the tilt of her helmet. "I'm thinking!"

"Are you?"

"And what are you thinking?" Brendan asked.

Killashandra began slowly, formulating her thoughts as she spoke. "I think we ought to return the piece we took. I don't think we ought to carve up the Junk."

Lars regarded her for a long moment. "You know, I think you're right. That should put us in their good . . . gravel? dust?"

"Cinder?" Killa offered coyly.

"Well, we'll just do that wee thing then. Especially as it isn't doing us a blind bit of good as a specimen."

"Which reminds me. When we excised that bit of stalactite, there was that shaking. Was that just a tremor, or an incredibly rapid beat of some kind?"

"A percussive-type signal?" Lars asked.

"Ah, like some primitive groups who wished to make long-distance communications," the ship said. "I'll analyze. Never thought of that." There was a pause during which lights and flicks of messages crossed the main control screen. "Ah, indeed! Spot-on, Killa. The tremor does indeed parse into a variety of infinitesimal pulses of varying length."

"We need some drumsticks, Bren," Killa said, grinning at Lars.

He put his hands on his hips in an attitude of exasperation. "Neither of us could rap *that* fast."

"So we'll be *largo,* but it'll be a beat. We can at least use rhythm to see if we'd get any sort of response. Open some sort of a communications channel to this intelligence."

"Intelligence? The retreat could be no more than a basic survival impulse."

"Impulse is the word," Bren said. "I have no wood in my stores, but would plastic do?"

"Anything strong enough to beat out a pulse . . . Maybe we can get an 'in' to our Junk."

Lars groaned at her whimsy, but he was quite ready to return to the ship and take delivery of two pairs of taper-ended plastic lengths. He gave Killa one pair and, with the other, practiced a roll on the bulkhead of the airlock.

"A little ragged," she said.

"Who's had time to practice for the last seventy years?"

Killashandra frowned in surprise that Lars would even mention a time span. Most singers ignored time references. Seventy years? Since they had been singing duet? Or since they had last done much instrumentalizing? She really didn't want to know which. Unlike herself, Lars often input material to his private file. And after a session in the Ranges, he also accessed his file. She couldn't remember when she had thought to add anything to hers. She shook her head, not wanting to think about *that*. She had far more important things to do than worry about relative time—it was rhythmic time she had to play with right now.

"We are armed and ready," she said flippantly, holding the sticks under her nose as she had seen ceremonial drummers do on some old tape clip. "Front and center, and forward into the fray."

" 'We go, we go,' " Lars sang out.

Long-forgotten neurons rubbed together properly, and Killashandra came out with the beginning of that chorus, altering it slightly to suit their circumstances. " 'Go, we heroes, go to glory/we shall live in song and story . . .' "

" 'Yes, but you *don't* go!' " And Brendan's baritone entered the chorus.

" 'We go! We go!' " Lars toggled the airlock to open, awkwardly hanging on to his drumsticks as he resettled his helmet. Killashandra fastened hers.

" 'Yes, onward to the foe!' " Brendan sang melodiously.

" 'We go! We go!' "

And then the airlock completed its cycle and they could *go* back out into the darkness of Opal. They marched into the nearest of the Junk caves and came to a militarily abrupt halt.

"All right, Ki," Lars said, "where—and what—do we beat?"

"Let's see if we can get its attention. Do we both happen to know a ceremonial roll?"

"I do." Lars proceeded to beat it out.

"Show-off. Now, let's do it together." They did, heads up to see if there was any reaction in the Junk.

"I think you got through," Brendan said. "A hemi-semi-demiquaver of a response, but definitely just after your roll duet."

Lars grinned drolly at Killashandra. "Having said that, what do we say next?"

"Howdy?"

Hunger drove them from the cave, and once they got back into the B&B, sheer fatigue required them to stay. They had beat every tempo they knew, with all the power in their arms, until their muscles had protested. Brendan kept reporting reaction, and once or twice, a repeat—at a much faster speed—of what the two crystal singers had just tapped out. Other patterns of response made no sense to Brendan. But as Killa and Lars reboarded the ship, he told them that he was trying to figure out any code, or pattern, in the Junk's response to their rolls. When he started to tell them, they begged a reprieve.

"Save it, will you, Bren?" Lars said, an edge to his voice.

"Sorry about that. You've seemed indefatigable. I was beginning to think you were crystal analogues. You have, after all, only been on the go today for twenty-seven hours. I'll reprise after you've had some sleep. And I mean, *sleep.*"

"Wicked little man," Killashandra said, struggling out of her suit and tiredly cramming it into the cleanser. Lars had to prop himself up against the wall to balance while he pulled off his suit.

As she stumbled into the main cabin, she yawned, feeling those twenty-seven hours in every sinew in her body—and especially in her weary hands. "I'm almost too tired to eat," she said, but roused herself when the aromas of the feast Brendan had prepared wafted through the main cabin.

"I'm *never* too tired to eat during Passover," Lars announced, and picked up the biggest bowl. He half collapsed into the chair, then settled back with a plate on his chest so he didn't have so far to reach to get food into his mouth. "Can you analyze any particular response from the Junk?"

"In all the caves, it has stopped retreating," Brendan said. "And while I do perceive a definite pattern in the rhythm of its tremors, that's the problem. You could never rap fast enough to 'speak' to them, and they can't seem to slow down enough to 'speak' to you."

"How about us recording something, and you play it back at their tempo, Bren?" Killa asked. "Use one of your extendable tools to hammer the message home?"

Lars tipped respectful fingers in her direction for that notion. "Yeah, but what exactly are we trying to tell them?"

Killa shrugged, her mouth too full to answer just then. She swallowed. "We're singers, not semanticists. I think we've done very well!"

"I concur," Brendan added stoutly. "There are specialists who could handle it from here, now you've established an avenue."

"Yeah, but what about the disease?"

"The specialists do not need to exit their vehicle. I've just monitored the dust your suits left in the cleanser's filters. I can find no contaminants. So the planet must be safe enough. Remember, the geologists had that specimen on board to examine, and I doubt they thought of keeping it shielded."

"You know," Killashandra began, interrupting herself with a great yawn. "We forgot to put the piece back." Her head lolled back.

They fell asleep as they were, half-empty plates balanced on their chests. Brendan decided that he had not been scrupulous enough in monitoring them today—he'd been as fascinated as they had by their attempts to communicate with the Junk. In future, he must remember that singers had phenomenal powers of concentration, as well as appetite.

Then Brendan noticed that weary fingers had left splotches on chairs and carpet. Though he could send the cleaner 'bot to attend to floor spillage, he resigned himself to spots on the chairs until they reached port again. Not that Boira was any neater all the time. He dimmed the lights and raised the ambient temperature, since he couldn't exactly arrange covers for them. Being a ship had a few limitations in dealing with passengers who insisted on falling asleep *off* their bunks.

He was also obscurely delighted by their resolve to restore the specimen to the Junk. It was one thing to take samples of inanimate objects, but to do so to a living, feeling, communicating sentience was quite another matter in his lexicon. Singers were not as insensitive and unfeeling as he had been led to believe. In fact, his opinion of the breed had been raised by several singular leaps.

He must remember to mention it—adroitly, of course, for even to *imply* that he had had his doubts about this mission, and them, was embarrassing. He had a lot to relate to Boira when she was restored to him.

CHAPTER 3

As soon as they returned to the original site with the excised "finger," Killashandra and Lars noticed the increase of the luminescence.

"Well, we fed it, didn't we?" Killa said. "Big Junk looks fatter, too, don't you think?"

Lars shrugged. "Brendan?"

"Ambient light has increased in your present location, but, as you both know, I can read nothing of the Junk itself."

"It should look fatter after all we gave it to eat yesterday," Killashandra repeated, more to herself than to the others.

"I don't see as much expansion on the rib we cut, though," Lars remarked, peering up at it. That extrusion had not moved from the position into which it had retracted.

"Muhlah! I hope we haven't done irremedial harm," she said with genuine remorse.

"The other end had no trouble absorbing what we gave it to eat. Maybe it can . . ." Lars began.

"Can, can, cannibal?"

"Omnivorous, certainly," Lars replied wryly.

"It didn't exactly 'eat,' it sort of absorbed substances," Killa said.

Lars took the "finger" out of the duraplas sack with duraplas calipers and reached up, his extended arm not quite long enough. "Damnation!"

"If you hoist Killa to your shoulders, Lars, that will give you sufficient height," Brendan said.

Lars eyed his partner. She was a lean-bodied woman, and long in the leg.

"C'mon, lover boy, play acrobat. That'll be dead easy in point-seven gravity."

"Just don't wriggle around on my back. Be careful of my oxygen tanks."

"Hmmm. You've got a point. Whoops!"

Lars handed her the tongs and the "finger," then ducked under her legs and, in an athletic heave, raised her from the ground.

"*Don't* obscure my vision!" he exclaimed. Involuntarily, she had grabbed at his helmet before he steadied her with his hands on her belt.

"Two steps forward, and one slightly . . ." Killa caught her balance. "To the left and . . . here we are. Steady!" Even with his almost two-meter height, she had to stretch to reach the end of the rib.

"You're wiggling!"

"Am not! I'm stretching. You're the one who's wiggling. To your right half a step. There!" And she whistled in disbelief as, before her very eyes, the Junk turned even more liquid and flowed over the amputated piece, reabsorbing it. Lars started to waver. "Hey!" She dropped the tongs and clung to him. "Don't move!"

"*I'm* not moving!" And suddenly Lars was down on one knee, Killa falling forward off his shoulders.

"Wooof!" she muttered as she lay sprawled on the ground, automatically checking the panel of lights that ringed the bottom of the helmet join. They were all green, not a flicker into the orange.

"You okay, Ki?" Brendan asked, his tone anxious. "That was a quake, not a tremor!"

"Quite a thank-you!" Killashandra got to her feet.

"Certainly a reaction," Brendan said. "Lars?"

"Oh, I'm all right," Lars replied, checking both knees. "Well, lookee there," he added, pointing to the ceiling. "Come home, all is forgiven!"

Neither could see a demarcation on the rib end.

"Absorption? Not the same reaction though," Killashandra said, "as it gave when we offered it merely metal. Should we recommend that the other piece be returned?"

"After four years or more?"

"It's worth a try—as a peace offering." She grinned at the deliberate pun. Lars groaned.

"It would establish human *bona fides*," Brendan said. "That the people who return it have recognized the attempt as mutilation?"

"Not merely amputation for the sake of investigation," Killa said in a caustic voice.

"So? What do we do for an encore?" Lars asked.

Killa shrugged. "Have we been in all the caves that have Junk?"

"All those recorded," Brendan said.

"And we still haven't found the source, if there is one?"

"That wasn't in our brief, was it?" Lars asked, brushing his gloved hands. "We were to discover if this stuff had some commercial value to the Heptite Guild."

"It doesn't belong under the Guild's aegis. It's sentient," Killa said with more vehemence than she intended.

"We don't know that for a fact," Bren said, "but while it may not be animal, it doesn't appear to be mineral in the strict definition of the word."

"I'll go along with that," Lars said, turning to his partner.

" 'And beings animalculus,' " Killa murmured. "There's something . . ." She struggled with the vague notion she was trying to verbalize and then shrugged. "I dunno, but one sure thing, you can't mine it the way we can crystal, or other gemstones and ores. What's your opinion, Brendan?"

"I'm a minder, not a miner."

"Yes, but you've been a big help."

"As a caterer . . ."

"Yuckh!" The very thought of food suddenly nauseated Killashandra. She and Lars locked eyes. "Oh, blast it."

"I'd say the timing was pretty good," Lars said.

"You're ready for the Sleep phase?" Brendan asked.

"Undeniably," Killa said, moving toward the exit of the cavern. "We've done what we were supposed to, and now it's up to the xenos! This isn't a Heptite matter. So . . ." She looked expectantly toward her partner. "Where are we going to spend all those lovely credits we've just earned, Lars? And if you say 'water world,' I'll excise a few chunks of you."

Following close behind her, Lars rapped her helmet. "No, it's your turn to pick."

"I'll pick *after* I've slept on it," Killashandra said.

"In a week I'll be out of this system," Brendan said. "Which way do I go?"

"Turn left then straight on till morning," Killa said facetiously.

"If that's your wish, it is my command," the ship said.

Once back aboard the ship, the lingering odors of previously delectable meals made them gag.

"You weren't joking, were you?" Brendan said. "Ah, you can restrain the compulsion?" he added urgently.

"Don't worry. We never disgrace ourselves," Lars said grimly, depressing his nausea as he stripped off the suit and stuffed it in the cleanser.

Killashandra had a very set look to her face and swallowed constantly as she peeled off not only her suit but the mesh undergarment.

"Hey!" Lars had not taken off his briefs and stared after her as she strode—regally, he thought—across the lounge.

"Brendan won't mind," Killa said absently.

"Indeed I don't, but I find it difficult to see that all that food—"

"Don't!" Killa held both hands up toward his column. "Don't even *think* that word!" She gagged and hurried to their cabin and into the sanitary unit.

"Anything I can get you?" the ship asked solicitously as Lars hurried after his partner.

"Not a damned thing, Bren," Lars said resignedly.

Killa was already in the shower, sluicing her body down, staggering occasionally as even the mild force of the water unbalanced her. When Lars entered the enclosure, they clung to each other, until they had soaped and soaked themselves clean.

Wrapping the generous towels about their bodies, they reeled to the wide bunk and, with groans of immense relief, crawled on and sprawled across it. As Brendan watched, their limbs relaxed despite what he considered to be uncomfortable postures. They were oblivious to any externals.

"These crystal singers don't do anything by halves. As bad as Boira in some respects." His voice echoed in the silent living quarters.

Delicately, as a mother will carry her sleeping babe to its cot, the Brendan/Boira-1066 lifted off Opal, though his passengers wouldn't have stirred no matter what G force he used in takeoff. A week of sleep? Well, if he "turned left"—now why was that sentence vaguely familiar—made one Singularity Jump and headed straight on, he would reach the Lepus sector, which offered the system Nihal. The primary was G2, and it had an inhabited third planet. Taking that route, Brendan would also have the chance to get a closer look at the very red Mira variable R. Leporis. Boira would be interested in his observations of that anomaly.

Serendipitously, it occurred to him that he was under no obligation to return immediately to Regulus Base. From the last report piped to him, Boira had another six or seven weeks to go in rejuvenation and then time in rehab and retraining. He really didn't have to take another short-term assignment or jump about on a courier route: they'd cleared all 1066's indebtedness with the bonus and danger money from the assignment that had put Boira in hospital.

But was the Nihal system where Killashandra *meant* to go? She'd told Lars that she'd pick *after* she'd had some sleep. Brendan accessed his galactic encyclopedia. Nihal's third planet had some unusual recreational facilities and was regarded as an ideal honeymoon planet. Killa and Lars were well past that stage of a partnership, but they might still appreciate a place like that for the extended vacation they intended to take from Ballybran and singing crystal. If he *had* misinterpreted her remark—and Killa's somewhat incoherent directions had sounded a bit like a quotation—they could change their minds when they woke up.

Then he remembered to do the medscans that he had been programmed to carry out, to insure that the symbiont was indeed protecting the singers. What would the Heptite Guild do if they had been contaminated? Exile them? Where? In those Crystal Ranges, until the next storm took care of the problem? The Guild was known to be ruthless, arrogant, and powerful. This pair had been the best company he'd had the entire time he'd been solo—he'd hate to see them mistreated . . . or worse. But just as the dust of their suits had shown no contaminants, neither did their bodies. Reassured, he added the medical data of this latest investigation to the private file.

"Nihal? Never heard of it," Killashandra said between sips of the fruit beverage she had requested of Brendan. Lars was still slumbering beside her.

"That's where we're going on the heading you gave me."

"What heading?" Killashandra skewed around on the wide bunk until she could see through the open cabin door to his column.

" 'Turn left then straight on till morning.' " Brendan's search through his library files had made him no wiser.

"Shards! That wasn't a direction, Bren."

"So you *were* quoting?"

Killashandra snickered. "And you couldn't find the source? How far back do your files go? No, abort that. I don't want to know. It's from an old children's story, and I didn't even remember that I remembered it. And that spurious direction leads us to Nihal? What's there?"

"A rather nice climate, temperate to cold, recreational, excellent—ah, can I use the *f*-word now?"

"Food? Oh, yeah, but we won't need anything more than liquids for a day or two."

"So was that a direction from your subconscious?"

Killashandra finished the last of her drink and yawned. "I'll know when we get there. How long did I sleep?"

"Five days."

"Wake me in another two, huh?" And she was asleep before Brendan could propose that he stay with them a while longer.

"Have a brain ship as our private yacht?" Lars exclaimed, sipping a clear soup.

"Well, I would have to ask you to pay for fuel, supplies, and landing fees," Bren answered tentatively. "You see, Boira and I have bought ourselves free . . ."

Lars recalled that the brain ships could do so, working off the immense debt with Central Worlds occasioned by their early childhood care and the cost of the ship itself. Some partners never did discharge the debt, but a good pair could earn enough in bonuses to do so. "My sincere congratulations on that feat, Brendan!"

"But I don't want to go into our savings."

"Medical expenses high?" Lars asked solicitiously. Most humans complained about services singers never required.

"Oh, that! Repairs and injuries are part of our contract, and the contractor has to pay the full tab of Boira's rejuv since they neglected to inform us of the hazards inherent in the assignment." Bren sounded both irritated and smug. "So, all her expenses are paid. I just have to—well, sing for my supper."

"How long a contract did you have with Heptite?"

"To the conclusion of your investigations plus travel time to return you to Shankill Moon Base and me to my base."

"And you wouldn't *object* to carting us about?"

"If you defray my costs . . ."

"Sure, we can do that. Any sailing on this Nihal planet?"

"It's more known for its mountain sports."

"Oh!" Lars took the last gulp of his soup, yawned, and settled back down under the thermal beside Killashandra. "Lemme sleep on it, wouldja, Bren? 'S a great ideeeeee . . . ah . . . mmm."

When Killashandra woke from her second sleep, she woke alert, with that sense of having slept deeply and well—and of being mildly hungry. She rolled out of the bunk so as not to rouse Lars and made it to the sanitary facility before she burst. She showered and shrugged into the loose, colorful striped robe she preferred to wear in transit.

She paused by the broad bunk to see how Lars looked—his face was no longer gaunt so she thought he'd awaken soon. As soon as she had closed the door and was out in the short corridor, Brendan gave her a good-morning.

"Is it?"

"Well, it is morning, Nihal time, early morning."

"Oh! Yes, Nihal, of course. That G2—straight on till morning. How far away is it, Bren?" She was in the galley now, making herself a hot caffeine-rich drink.

"Relatively not far at my present speed."

"And it's not a water world?"

"It has water, of course, but mountain sports are featured."

"Hmmm, in that case, I'm not averse to it. Haven't done any hiking or skiing or climbing in—well, I can't remember when."

"There are lakes . . ."

"Lakes don't fascinate Lars as much as seas do," Killa said with some feeling.

"There are seas, but not much traffic on them. The fishing is limited to shoreline nettings, though there are said to be some tasty bivalves."

"Hmmm. You know, I'm hungry but not ravenous, if you appreciate the distinction."

"I appreciate the distinction, Ki." Brendan chuckled. "What might you be hungry for?"

Aware that she couldn't overburden her system, she settled on a light meal of juice and cereal, which she took from the galley into the main room.

"Shards! But we get to be sloppy eaters, don't we," she said with chagrin, noticing the food stains on the arm of her usual chair. "Anything I can use to wash these out, Bren? I don't really want to hand you back to Boira in less than the condition you arrived in. That's not shipshape."

"And Bristol fashion?"

Killa laughed. Then she noticed the view on the main screen. "Muhlah! What's that?"

"Ah, that is the very red Mira variable R. Leporis. It has a four-hundred-and-thirty-two-day cycle. A type N, and with any luck, we'll see it at its hottest. The pulsations should be magnificent as it begins to contract."

Killa squinted. "It's very bright."

"I can darken the screen if it is visually uncomfortable."

"Hmmm, would you? Ah, thanks. That is undoubtedly the very reddest object I've ever seen. What are you seeing?"

"The emission spectra. Stupendous!"

They both, in their separate ways, considered the spectacle blazing light-years away but so vivid.

"Of course, if you find nothing of interest on Nihal Three, I'd be happy to take you elsewhere."

Killashandra snapped her fingers. "Just like that?"

"It's like this, Ki," and Brendan explained what he had offered Lars.

The crystal singer whooped and fell against the back of the chair in a paroxysm of laughter.

"Our own brain ship? Acting the yacht? You've got a deal, man!" She gasped the phrases out between spasms of laughter and ended up wiping her eyes of tears. "You really mean it?" she asked, turning toward Brendan's column.

"I wouldn't suggest it if I didn't."

"Don't huff, Bren, honestly, I didn't mean to offend. But don't you cost a lot?"

"I only need fuel, landing fees, and whatever supplies you and Lars require. To be sure, my larder's a bit bare right now."

"I can well imagine. You were champion to feed us as you did, Bren. I haven't eaten better during any Passover I can remember." Then practicality gripped her. "I think you'd better tell me just how much your fuel and general landing fees run to. We got a great fee for risking skin and symbiont on Opal, but . . ."

Brendan then ran through some figures for her so that she realized the idea was feasible. In fact, downright exciting.

"Of course, we've got to get our report back to Lanzecki. Does Nihal Three have black crystals?"

"It does."

A shiver ran up Killashandra's spine. She didn't like to use black-crystal communications. One of the few crystal singers who could locate and cut black crystal, she was unusually sensitive to its presence in cut or raw form. Especially since she had installed the black-crystal communications system for the Trundomoux: she had never managed to bury the memory of the soul-shattering shock of activating the king crystal. She had asked Lanzecki about that lingering pull, but he hadn't had any answers. Whatever it was, it made her wary of actually *using* black crystal—especially when she wanted to forget crystal for a while.

"There are significant bodies of water down there," Killashandra said as Brendan approached their destination.

"We can go somewhere else," Lars said to pacify her. "I didn't chose Nihal Three, remember. It was your 'straight on till morning' . . ."

His partner glowered at him.

"The chief recreational activity of the planet Sherpa is mountain climbing," Brendan said, raising his voice to distract them. "Downhill and cross-country skiing, skidoo and other snow-based sports, canoeing and kayaking on only designated rivers, trekking on foot or mounted, hunting and fishing. The catering is deemed one of the highlights of the planet and, indeed, wears the Four Comets of Gastronomical Excellence."

Killashandra groaned.

"A little exercise would improve your appetite," Brendan remarked. "Although I never thought I'd have to say that to the pair of you!"

Lars chuckled, and even Killa managed a grin. Then Lars regarded her queryingly, his expression blandly conciliatory.

"Oh, all right. We do mountain sports first," she said in assent, then waggled her finger at him. "I might do some canoeing, but you're on the bow paddle."

"Landing fees are moderate," Brendan said happily. "This won't cost you much," he added cheerfully. "You can send in your report, and I can get an update on Boira's condition. Ah, I'm getting a signal. Oh, really?" he added in surprise. "Penwyn, how good to hear your voice!" To the astonished singers, he added, "The planetary manager was in my class! I'm very glad we decided to come here."

Although Killashandra worked on the official report with Lars, she let him take it to the Communications Center. When they had passed it in the ground vehicle on their way into the settlement, she had experienced the frisson in her guts that told her she had cut the system's king crystal. She had returned as quickly as possible to the B&B. Now, in an atavistic burst, she scrubbed the food stains off the chairs while she waited for Lars to return. When he seemed to have been gone rather longer than the dispatch of a message should have taken, she began to feel ill used, then irritated and finally worried.

"This isn't an overregulated planet, is it? Crystal singers aren't forbidden?" she asked Brendan.

"Not at all. It's a very loosely settled place, though there's a fair competition between recreational facilities to attract visitors. Penwyn handles what administration there is and arbitrates any disputes, as well, but it's an orderly world."

At last Lars came back with promotional holos crammed into every pocket of his shipsuit. He was plainly delighted as he dumped them onto the worktop

by the viewer and gestured dramatically at Killashandra.

"Take your pick! Reports filed—state of the art com-
tower, I'll tell you that, with your friend, Penwyn, handling the transmission, Bren. Guess you won't mind
how long we're away, will you?"

"Hmmm, no, of course I won't," Brendan answered
vaguely. He was busy chatting up Penwyn.

During the day that it took the two crystal singers to
decide where to go first—eventually they settled on
cross-country skiing to get their muscles limbered up for
downhill runs—they didn't hear much from Brendan.

"Must be making up for the last fifty years," Lars
said.

"Must you measure time!" she replied in a burst of
irritation. What did *time* have to do with anything? It
was *today* that mattered, and how well they spent it,
how much they enjoyed it, or, if they were working in
the Ranges, how much they could cut in a day!

Lars regarded her in surprise and then apologized in
such a perfunctory manner that he aggravated her further. The lingering stress put a bit of a damper on their
journey to the resort Killashandra had chosen. But once
at the 'port that serviced the area—a long narrow valley
amidst the most magnificent mountain scenery—her
mood lifted.

The 'port was above the snowline in the mountainous
rim of Sherpa's main continent, Nepal. They were collected at the door by the soberly welcoming rep of the
snotel they had booked into.

"I am Mashid," he told them, making a low, respectful bow. Dark almond-shaped eyes did not so much as
blink as he continued his greeting. "I have been appointed to see that your sojourn with us is all that you
desired."

Killashandra and Lars exchanged quick looks.

"We're remarkably easy to please," Killa said, "so long as you don't show me any large bodies of water." She dug Lars in the ribs.

"All water at this altitude is frozen," Mashid replied stolidly.

"What do we drink then?" Lars asked with a bare twitch of his lips. "Melted snow?"

"Drinking water"—and Mashid's attitude toward drinking *that* was contemptuous—"is of course supplied as needed from protected reservoirs."

"I was joking," Lars said.

"As you wish." Mashid tendered another bow. Sweat had appeared on his forehead, for he was bundled in furs and thick fur-topped boots.

"Lead on," Lars suggested, gesturing to the door. He and Killashandra had bought outerwear suitable to the mountain climate but, though it had been pricey in the spaceport shop, neither jacket was as lush as Mashid's apparel. They learned later that he had caught, tanned, and made his own garments as most of the mountain people here did.

Turning with yet another bow, Mashid led them outside to an animal-drawn sleigh, brightly painted in orange and black stripes with the name of their snotel blazoned in huge letters on its sides. A pair of antlered, rough-coated beasts were harnessed to it, stamping their cloven hooves in the snow. They were nearly as long as the sleigh.

Lars and Killashandra were gestured into the passenger seat, and an immense fur robe was deftly tucked about them. Mashid swung expertly up onto the driver's seat and flicked a whip at the rumps of the beasts. The speed of their departure nearly gave Lars and Killashandra whiplash.

The pace was exhilarating; so was the crisp air, and the unusual method of transportation. Killa laughed aloud in sheer delight. She couldn't remember ever seeing so much snow before. She almost asked Lars if they had and then, as abruptly, didn't want to know: she wanted less to know if she had seen snow than if Lars could remember if they had. Then he turned a happy smile to her and it didn't matter. She was here, with Lars, and they had months before they had to even *think* of crystal and Ballybran. She was then totally distracted by the cold wind nipping at her ears and clamped her gloved hands together to protect them.

In their four months at the snotel, they attempted every single snow sport available, including races on single skis and on sno-bikes down almost vertical slopes. They missed being buried in an avalanche by the length of a ski; they skate-danced, snow-surfed and -planed, and went spelunking through ice and rock caverns of incredible beauty. They absorbed Mashid's instructions and improved on them, until eventually they surprised approval—even compliments—from the sturdy Nepalese, who began to view their near-indestructibility with awe. They doubted he had ever met crystal singers before or knew that their minor bruises, lacerations, and contusions healed overnight, leaving them fully able to cope with the new day's ordeals. They almost regretted leaving him behind in the mountains.

But they had done all they could of the snow sports, and so they moved from the mountains to the vast bowl of the internal plains of Nepal. There they did take to the water and acquired a new guide without the imperturbability of Mashid. With him, they canoed through tortuous canyons on flumes of water, shooting diretoothed rapids.

Once in a while they checked in with Brendan, who informed them that he was quite content and they needn't hurry. So they hunted for two months in the lake districts with a party of mixed planetarials, and rode and camped along the coastline for a month with another, during which time Lars so pointedly said nothing about sailing that Killashandra was sure she would burst with not hearing the words he didn't speak.

"We've done everything else," Killashandra said the night before they were to turn inland, back to the vicinity of the spaceport. "We really can't leave Sherpa without sailing, can we?"

"Can we not?" Lars retorted placidly.

"If you wanted to, we could."

"Wrong," he said, and with his index finger pressed her nose in. "If you wanted to, we could."

Perversely, she ducked away from him and rolled off the bed, unaccountably annoyed with his self-sacrifice.

"It was my turn to pick," she said in a savage tone.

"Hey, honey-love . . ." Lars sprang from the bed to catch her in his arms, his face anxious. "Don't be like this. It *was* your turn to pick the place and activities, and I've enjoyed everything we've done together."

She struggled in his arms, furious with his acquiescence, even with his concern.

"Hey, hey . . ." He tried to gentle her, pulling her against his bare body. "Need a radiant bath?" He stroked her to judge crystal resonance in her body.

"I don't need one. I don't need crystal that badly yet. Ahhhhh!" And her irascibility disappeared as she arched in his arms. "Crystal! We didn't try crystal."

"*Try* crystal? Where? What are you talking about, Killa?"

"We never gave the Junk any crystal."

"It would have absorbed—oh, I see what you mean!"

He blinked in sudden comprehension. "D'you really think Ballybran crystal wouldn't be absorbed by the Junk?" he asked, catching a bit of her excitement despite his skepticism. "What good would that do?"

"Communication. A lot easier than rapping out rhythm. There'd be a useful link with it, if nothing else." Killashandra was as tense with eagerness as she had been with irritation.

"We've done our job," Lars protested. "We've acquitted the assignment . . ."

"But we didn't find out anything."

"We found out the Junk is not a Heptite concern."

"But we didn't try crystal!" she repeated, struggling to release his grip.

"Well, if it means that much to you, let's see what Brendan says about taking us back there—with crystal. There, there, love-heart." Lars soothed her with hand and voice until she relaxed against him again. "Only where will we get some Ballybran crystal here?"

"They've black crystal . . ."

"Huh? You think they'll loan black for this escapade?"

Killa glared at him. "It's not an escapade. It's a point of investigation we neglected to make."

"Well, if they use black crystal, they use others," Lars said, releasing her and marching to the comconsole. "And if they use others, they also abuse them and there'll be sour crystal somewhere on this planet. We can offer to retune, and take the slivers as part of our fee."

"We can't give the Junk sour crystal."

"I don't think anything would give it indigestion," Lars remarked, pausing as he punched in Brendan's on-planet code. "Any scraps large enough can be tuned

to some sort of pitch. You know, it might be fun to tune
crystal when we don't have to."

Brendan was willing enough to return to Opal,
though Killashandra could hear the reservations in his
tone.

"I can't hang about there *too* long," he said, "and get
you back to Ballybran in time to collect Boira. She's
doing splendidly in rehab and retraining." Pride in his
partner's recuperation colored his pleasant voice.

"That's very good news indeed, Bren," Killa said,
meaning it. "We just want to see what effect *our* crystal
might have on the Junk."

"It'll probably gulp it down like it did everything else
and lick its chops at the taste."

"Only sound has any effect on Ballybran crystal,"
Killashandra said with considerable pride. "And there's
no sound on an airless planet."

"Possibly," Brendan said. "And we didn't try diamond either."

"Ballybran crystal's tougher than any diamond ever
compressed from carbon!"

"My, we are loyal!" Lars said facetiously.

Killashandra gave a sniff. "Well, there isn't any substance like Ballybran crystal anywhere else in the uni-
verse."

"Except"—and Lars's eyes glinted with teasing—
"possibly the Junk!"

Crystal resonance *was* beginning to get to Killashandra as Brendan took them back to the Opal system
in one Singularity Jump. It had started when she and
Lars retuned to a minor fifth the sour dominant midblue
crystals that Penwyn had procured for them. As Lars
had thought, there were quite a few soured crystals on

the planet. Though Penwyn didn't ask them to, they tuned them all—the work of three days for such experienced singers—and he canceled Brendan's landing fees. But the sessions had an effect on Killashandra, and she spent a full day in the radiant-fluid tub.

"I'm fine, I'm fine," she insisted to Lars and Brendan when they were too solicitous of her. "Being near black always does it."

Lars desisted then and must have told Brendan to leave off inquiring, for neither of them said another word until the BB-1066 landed near the Big Hungry Junk—as Killa dubbed it—with the sweet-tuned slivers of crystal that they had salvaged.

"Old home week," she said with unforced gaiety as they suited up.

"Do we know what we're doing, Killa?" Lars asked as he settled his helmet over his head.

"No."

"D'you know why you're doing it?"

"No."

"Maybe the Junk *is* sentient."

"You mean, some sort of psionic emanations?" Killashandra was not only skeptical but incredulous.

"Why else would you have such a harebrained notion to feed Ballybran crystal to an opalescent rib?" he demanded.

"I got the notion on Sherpa, not in the cave. I could have understood some sort of a connection if I'd thought of it then."

"You probably did," Lars replied. "You just forgot it. And don't snap at me over your *lapsus memoriae!* Let's get this experiment on the pad."

Even as he spoke he touched the lock release and it cycled open. Oxygen left the airlock with a whoosh.

They stepped out onto Opal's cindery hide and followed the bright paint markings to Hungry Junk's precinct.

"Hey, improvement," Lars said as soon as they had descended to the level of the cavern. The blue radiance, edging toward white, made their suit lights unnecessary. "Wow!"

"Wow what?" Brendan asked when the silence went on for fifty seconds.

"You're sure your instrumentation doesn't read anything?" Lars asked.

"Not a thing. What occasioned your unusual exhortation?" Brendan asked flippantly.

"We fed it too much," Killashandra replied softly.

"Naw," Lars said, "but we fed it good."

"Tell me, do!" was Brendan's slightly sarcastic response.

"Sorry, Bren," Killashandra replied, "but it's a bloody shame you *can't* see. Junk's covered the entire cave, and there are long fingers that we'll probably find have descended to the next level. It's more beautiful than ever, all colors now, reds and oranges and yellows, as well as the blues, dark greens, and purples that it originally had. They seem to flow in and out of patterns . . ."

"Like fractals," Lars added, sounding oddly languid. "I could watch—hey, what'd you do that for?" She had given him such a push that he had nearly lost his balance.

"You were becoming thralled. Junk's hypnotic," Killa said, her voice sharp. "Maybe even addictive."

"*Should* we give it crystal then?" Lars asked, his tone crisp and alert again.

"That's what we came to do. So let's do it!"

"All the crystals to old Hungry Junk?"

"No, just one," Killashandra said. "Let's see what happens."

She pointed to a large swag of the Junk that was flowing toward the floor. Lars took the largest crystal, the B-flat, and, holding it in the calipers, inserted the blue. Junk obligingly flowed over it.

The two crystal singers held their breath as they watched.

"Yup!" Killashandra let out a triumphant crow. "It can't eat crystal."

"It can't?" Brendan asked. "What's it doing?"

"Holding it in its cheek," Lars said flippantly, grinning at Killashandra, "having a good taste." The Junk was rippling back and forth across the crystal insertion, going through all the colors of its visible spectrum without altering the outline of the cube. Then it seemed to push the cube upward, toward the crown in the center of the ceiling. Though apparently drawn deep into the opalescence, the crystal patently retained its integrity.

"Now what?" Brendan asked when the singers had nothing further to report.

"Look!" In astonishment Killashandra pointed to the half-open sack of crystals at her feet. They pulsed from midblue to dark and then paled. "Damn!" She dropped to her knees beside them. "Are they singing? Can't hear a bloody thing."

Tentatively Lars placed the tip of his gloved finger on the faceted surface of the nearest one.

"Vibration all right!" He grinned in triumph. "Communications established?"

"Could be, but pulsations and color alterations are no more intelligible than drum codes—until a code or even a language can be established. And semanticists we are not," Killashandra said, a degree of regret in her voice.

"Then let us by all means leave it to the experts," Brendan said. "Around such an unknown quantity, I find that I get almost as nervous for you as I do for Boira."

"Why, thanks, Bren," Killashandra said, touched by the ship's concern. "But I don't think we're in any danger."

"You are edible," he replied succinctly.

Killashandra laughed and Lars grinned at her.

"I wonder if any of the other Junk has expanded."

"We only fed this one," she replied. "Let's go see."

Lars picked up the remaining crystal, which continued to glow until they had entered the airlock and Brendan had lifted from the immediate vicinity of Big Hungry. They checked the other locations and found that no other formation had increased as significantly as Hungry Junk, although all had begun to flow downward again.

"Got anything on board to feed the starving?" Lars asked.

"In point of fact, I do," Brendan said. "Penwyn had nonrecyclable wastes he did not care to dispose of on-planet . . ."

"Dirty stuff?"

"Obliging I am; stupid I'm not! No, most of it's clean litter from the spacefield. I thought we might use the refuse to better effect."

"Indeed we can," Killa said, pleased. "I think the Junk's starved too long."

Lars was dubious. "We might be making more problems . . ."

"We might," she said with a shrug, "but I can't *not*."

"I've kept a file on the metallic and organic content of what we're feeding it," Brendan said.

"Then we do a comparison, a standard scientific practice," Lars replied, dismissing his reservations. "We feed four metallic and four organic."

It was tiring work, even in .7 gravity, distributing and feeding eight very hungry opalescents. As they trudged back to the 1066, both singers felt a curious satisfaction in the heightened glow and vigorous flow as the Junk ingested their meals.

When they had finished, the two singers returned briefly to the Big Hungry to check on the crystal.

"Not even Junk can eat Ballybran crystal," Killashandra said proudly.

"The cubes you left in the lock, however," Brendan remarked, "have remained dormant."

"Too bad we didn't have any dirty waste to give the Junk," Lars said, "to see if it could digest half-lifes."

Killashandra regarded him warily. "You do want to live dangerously, don't you?"

"Well, I don't think we've done any lasting harm. How long can one good meal last Junk? I think we leave this to the experts. Singers we are; scientists we're not."

"We're a lot smarter than that exploratory team who found Junk," Killa said.

"Are we?"

"Who can say at this juncture?" Brendan said, deftly diverting an argument with his outrageous pun. Lars and Killa groaned in unison as he went on. "You've done more than you were required to. And, while I hate to press you . . ." he added tentatively.

"Yes, yes, of course," Killashandra said, suppressing any comment on the fact that he was indeed pressuring them. "You're anxious to collect Boira."

"I think we've got more than enough to prove to Lanzecki that we earned our fee," Lars added, giving her a meaningful nod.

She exhaled restively, swinging her arms indecisively.

But the men were right: they'd done more than was expected even if *not* what had been anticipated, finding a Heptite use of the Junk. Its fate would now be decided by others.

Lars moved to the exit arch, and with one more backward look at the surging flow of the Big Hungry's questing "finger," she followed. But the feeling that they hadn't done enough remained with her.

CHAPTER 4

The BB-1066 returned them to Shankill Moon Base and deposited them with many expressions of pleasure at their company and hopes to see them again. Wryly Killashandra heard the undertone of polite impatience in his courtesies and nudged Lars to hurry the disembarkation process. Brendan wanted to return, full speed, to Regulus Base, where he would be rejoined by Boira.

They had the pencil files of their report for Lanzecki in their carisaks, which bulged with souvenirs from their months on Sherpa.

Periodically Killashandra cleared out her storage space of items that she could not remember acquiring. Now she couldn't recall if she had corners into which to stuff the new additions. She hated discarding her belongings until they brought back no memories of where they had been used. When she did get rid of things, she preferred to do it when Lars wasn't around. His memory was much better than hers, and he could remember where and when clothes or equipment had been purchased. And why.

They caught the first shuttle down to Ballybran. It was half-full of singers. To the three she recognized she gave a brief nod; Lars smiled at most, though he did not get a response from all.

"Sometimes they act as if they're going to their own executions," he said.

Evidently he said that often enough that her reply was automatic: "Sometimes they are."

That was true enough to be sobering. There was no chatter, no merriment, no laughter at all, and very few grins when singers returned to the planet on which they earned enough to indulge in whatever fancies rocked their jollies. The ambience today was enough to depress anyone—except Lars, who was smiling tenderly at the screen's magnificent view of the broad oceans on the day side. He must be the only singer who enjoyed another aspect of the Guild homeworld, Killa reflected. He was smiling because he could look forward to sailing again.

"You kept your word," she murmured to him. "You choose the next one."

He grinned absently at her. "Hope Pat put her back in the water after Passover."

"We won't have time now for a cruise."

His hand covered hers on the armrest, and his smile was tender and deeply affectionate. "I like the 'we,' Sunny!" His fingers squeezed, and she, too, was suffused with loving warmth for him. They did make a very good team! Then he exhaled. "Lanzecki'll probably have us both out in the Ranges before the morning."

The shuttle was crossing into the night zone as it spiraled down to Ballybran's surface.

"More than likely." Killashandra felt no resistance to the prospect. The *need* to sing crystal had become more insistent during the last leg of their return voyage.

When she had last checked their credit balance, it was sizable enough to reassure her against any eventuality— not finding one of their old lodes of good crystal, a sudden storm flushing them out of the Ranges, even more damage to the sled, though *that* she intended to avoid. The last accident had caused her extreme aggravation. So asinine to have been caught in an avalanche! Lars had maintained that no blame could be attached to them; she railed that they ought to have checked the stability of the projection that had decided to drop on their sled.

She even remembered the piercing, almost pitying, look he had given her. "Look, Killa, you can't be everything in the Ranges. You've got weather sense that has saved our hides more times than I care to count; you're a superb cutter, and you've never cracked a crystal pitching it. Neither of us is geologist enough to have known that projection was unstable. Leave it!"

She remembered his reassurance now. More vivid and embarrassing was her remembered ignominy at having to be hoisted out of the Ranges. She would be grateful when that memory was expunged from her mind by her return to the Ranges. Soon enough only Lars would have access to that embarrassment. Time after time, she had heard him making reports to his private file. He wasn't likely to tease her about the avalanche—she'd give him that—but she almost wished he wouldn't commit *every damn* detail to electronic memory.

The shuttle landed them, and everyone filed out glumly. Only Lars seemed in good spirits. Then the port duty officer signaled to Lars and Killashandra.

"Lanzecki said you're to report to him immediately, forthwith and now!"

"When have I heard that before?" Lars replied with a grin, clipping Killashandra under the elbow as he guided her toward the lift that would take them to the executive level.

As they entered the administration office, Bollam gave them a brief nod of acknowledgment.

"I really don't like that man," Killa murmured to Lars as she placed her hand on the door plate. "He's a dork! A real dork! I wouldn't trust him in the Ranges, and *I* don't have Lanzecki's problem."

Lars jiggled her elbow to move on as the door slid open. It was as if the Guild Master hadn't moved from the position in which they had last seen him. Except, Killa noticed as he raised his head at their approach, he looked more tired and less . . . less substantial. She shook the notion out of her head.

"Good work," he said, nodding at them.

"*Good* work?" Killa was astonished. "But the Junk isn't something the Guild can use."

Lanzecki shrugged. "One less complication. And this Junk of yours couldn't digest Ballybran crystal?" That was more a proud statement than a question, and a slight smile pulled at the corner of Lanzecki's thin mouth.

He was aging, Killa thought, noticing thin vertical lines on his upper lip, the deeper marks from nose to mouth, and the discoloration under his eyes.

"You're working too hard," she said. Lanzecki raised his eyebrows inquiringly. "That dork at the door's no help. You need someone more like Trag. He was efficient—"

She stopped, seeing Lanzecki's expression alter to a courteous mask that rebuked her for her impudence.

"Look, anything we can do to help?" Lars asked. He glanced at Killashandra, not for permission but for her to reinforce his offer of assistance.

Lars never had learned the lesson Moksoon had taught her—that one asked, and expected, no help from anyone in the Ranges. Only . . . the Cube was not the Ranges.

"Neither of us *have* to get out for a while yet," she replied, though it wouldn't be long before an undeniable urgency began to pulse through her veins. Helpfulness and cooperation were not singer characteristics, but even she could remember being obliged to—and alternately infuriated by—Lanzecki's demands on her, and on herself and Lars. However, she was currently grateful for the benefits of the intriguing Junk assignment, and thus in a mood to be generous.

"I appreciate that very much indeed."

"Isn't there *anyone* else more suitable than Bollam?" she demanded.

Lanzecki shrugged. "He has his uses. Now . . ." He turned immediately to red-sheeted Priority notices. "These can no longer be ignored, Lars. And Killa, Enthor's gone and his replacement needs to be overseen. You've a finely tuned sense for crystal's potential. Can you see your way clear to assisting in the Sorting Shed until the woman's less tentative? She's got to be more confident that her judgment's right. I can't be hauled in to mediate her evaluations with disgruntled singers."

Killa made a face. "So I'm Trag's stand-in?"

Lanzecki gave her a level look. "In that aspect of our craft, you were always his superior."

"Well, well," she said, and would have teased him had she not seen the flicker in his eyes that suggested she restrain her flippancy. "Any singers due in?"

"The Tower says that five are on their way back.

Storm gathering over the southeast tip of the Ranges. Met says it's just a squall."

Killa snorted in disgust. Even "just a squall" on Ballybran could be mortally dangerous to any singers caught in it. The high winds that gusted over the canyons stroked mind-blowing resonances out of the crystalline Ranges.

"Who's the new Sorter?"

"Woman name of Clodine," Lanzecki replied. "Don't ride her, Killashandra. Her main fault is being new at the game."

Lars cocked an eyebrow at her and winked conspiratorially. She caught the warning that she would do more good to be patient. She shook her hair back over her shoulder in denial of the reminder and, on her mettle, strode out of the room.

Clodine greeted Killashandra with a nervous blend of gratitude and caution. Sorters, whose particular adjustment to the Ballybran symbiont affected their vision to the point where they did not need any mechanical aid to see intrusions and flaws in crystal, did not suffer the memory deterioration that singers did. Each of the other four Sorters on duty gave Killashandra a pleasant nod or wave as she made her way to Clodine's station— a station that had been Enthor's since before Killa had become a member of the Heptite Guild. She would miss him, too: they'd had some spectacular arguments over his evaluation of the tons of crystal she had presented for his inspection. But she had known him to be exceedingly competent, and fair. The opinion had survived throughout all her trips in the Ranges. Two faces she always remembered, no matter how crystal-mazed she was: Enthor's and Lanzecki's.

Clodine would have to be very good indeed to replace

Enthor in Killashandra's estimation. Ironic to find herself in the position of teaching the woman all the skills she herself had learned from the old Sorter. But Killa *did* know crystal.

The tall, slender girl—Killa judged her to be young in real chronology—kept blinking, her eyes going from one state to the other. Involuntarily she shuddered when the magnification of her enhanced sight made what should have been ordinary images unnerving to behold. She was an attractive girl, too, which might be why Lanzecki had enlisted Killa's aid. There had been a time when Killa would have been intensely jealous of anyone who took Lanzecki's interest, but those days were a long time back in the decades that had not included Lars Dahl. Clodine had lovely blond hair, a lot of it, neatly confined in a thick net. She had the fair complexion of the genuine blonde, and midbrown eyes with light flecks. Yes, very attractive. Some of Killa's unexpected anxiety for Lanzecki's aging dissipated. He still had an eye for a pretty girl and a lissome shape.

"I'm Killashandra Ree," she said, holding out her hand to Clodine. That was a habit most humanoid worlds had adopted, and she had been doing it so much on Sherpa that it had become natural. Singers fresh out of the Ranges never touched anyone if they could help it. Crystal shock sometimes had an adverse affect on others. But Clodine was too new to Ballybran to notice anything out of the ordinary. "Lanzecki sent me down as backup to this grimy lot on their way in. He doesn't want to scare you off the job at too early a date."

The crystal singer noticed that the worn scales and equipment that had served Enthor for so many decades had been replaced. Even the metal worktop, once scraped and scored by hundreds of thousands of cut-crystal forms, was pristine.

Clodine gave a tentative smile, and her eyes flicked into the alter state and then back again. "Oh, Gods, I'll never get the hang of it."

"Make your eyes very round when you want to stay in normal visual mode," Killashandra said in a low voice, aware that the other Sorters were watching them.

Clodine tried to smile *and* widen her eyes, then groaned because her eyes altered despite her efforts.

"It's surprising how soon you will become accustomed to the alteration," Killashandra said in her most sincere "buck up there" tone. "Ah, here they come!"

"They do?" Clodine looked up at the wraparound screens that showed the as-yet empty Hangar where the singers' sled would land. The latest batch of Guild apprentices waited there to help unload the precious crystal. The Met screens showed that the squall, having wreaked brief havoc in the Ranges, was passing harmlessly out to sea, half a continent away. The Hangar crew was lounging about. When storm systems raged close to the Guild's massive cube, their duties became far more urgent and perilous—even to closing the great Hangar doors to incoming singers rather than risk damage to those already safe within. More times than she cared to remember—probably many more times than she *could* remember—Killa had been the last singer to get in over the interlocking jaws of the great portal.

"See?" Killa said, directing Clodine's attention to the long-range screen where the first of the incoming sleds was just now visible as a speeding blip.

"Oh!" Clodine blinked nervously and, shaking her head in distress, looked about to weep.

"Relax," Killa drawled, and pushed herself up to sit on the brand-new worktop. "They're a good half hour out—unless they've had a good scare!" She grinned in amusement and saw Clodine relax a bit. "Where you from?"

"I don't imagine you've ever heard of my home system . . ." the Sorter began apologetically.

"Try me," Killa replied with a laugh.

"A planet named Scarteen—"

"In the Huntsman system," Killashandra said, oddly pleased by the girl's delight in her knowing. "Nice place. Good currents in the Great Oceans."

"You've *sailed* on Scarteen?"

"I've sailed—" Killa paused, censored the ennui in her tone, and smiled kindly at the child. "—on most worlds that are hospitable to our species."

"You sail? I mean, sheet-sail, not motor cruise?"

"Wind-sail, of course." She flicked one shoulder, consigning motor cruising to a suitable nadir. "And you'll find there's good sailing here, too. In fact, if we've time before we go out in the Ranges, my partner and I would be happy to take you out on our ship, show you some of the tricks of sailing Ballybran's currents and coasts."

"Oh, would you?"

Once again, Lars's avocation won her unexpected friendship. Killa sighed and filled in the time until the sleds arrived with sea tales that were honorably unembellished. They didn't need to be! Sorters might not need to leave Ballybran as often as singers, but they took holidays—especially during Passover storms. It didn't hurt to reassure the girl that there was more to life as a Heptite Guild member than remembering to widen her eyes to avoid blinking to crystal-gaze.

Clodine was, as Lanzecki suspected, suffering only from inexperience in dealing with Range-crazed singers. Killashandra's presence quelled the other singer's urge to argue with Clodine's estimate of his crystals—which were a rather good midgreen, currently in scarce supply, so even without arguing he got a better price than Killa knew he had anticipated. He would have had no cause to berate a Sorter, new or experienced, but arguing price with the Sorter got to be an ingrained habit with singers. Some Sorters enjoyed persiflage, and/or getting the better of the singer.

Timing was so often the deciding factor in the value of a cut. If the market was glutted, the price was understandably low. Some colors were always worth the premium price, like black crystals, which were so valuable as communication links. The pale pinks were always low market, but a fine seven-shaft cut of even pink could be valuable in an industrial complex.

When the singer had left, grumbling desultorily, Killashandra touched Clodine's shoulder and grinned at her woeful expression.

"He's all wind and piss. Most of us are. You know your grading, the latest market price is what's on your terminal. Don't let 'em hassle you. Part of it's coming in sudden from the Ranges without as much as you thought you would cut this time out: *I'm* always sure I should have been able to cut longer and more. Most of it's pure singer cussedness. Ignore it, considering the source! Enthor train you up?" she added, for something of the way Clodine had handled the crystal reminded her of the old man.

"Yes." Clodine's eyes widened in astonishment. "How did you know that?"

Killa sniffed. "Enthor loved crystal. He passed that on to you. Remember that the next time a singer gives you a hard time. You"—Killashandra prodded Clodine lightly in the chest—"love crystal. I can see that in how you handle it. Singers"—she turned her thumb into her own sternum—"invariably *hate* crystal."

"You do?"

"For all that it does for us and to us, yes." And, feeling that that sounded like a great exit line, Killashandra left the Sorter Shed.

Lars had not returned to their apartment. She gave herself a long soak in the water tub; then, wearing a loose robe, she began to unpack the carisaks that had been delivered while she was overseeing Clodine. When she got hungry and Lars still hadn't returned, she tapped out a "where is" code on the terminal.

"Here," Lars's voice responded as his features formed on the screen.

"Where?"

"Lanzecki's," he replied, as if she should have known. "C'mon up."

Puzzling over that, Killa changed and returned to the Guild Master's domain.

The pair were sitting at the table where Killa had often dined alone with Lanzecki. There was a third place set, and as Lanzecki gestured her to be seated, Lars rose and met her halfway, giving her a quick embrace and kiss.

Wondering what this was all about, Killa smoothly took her place.

"We waited," Lars said, and he nodded at the array of sumptuous-looking dishes.

"How did Clodine do?" Lanzecki asked, forestalling any query from her.

"She's fine. I told her not to let singers get up her nose. Enthor trained her. She loves crystal. I told her singers hate it. Opened her eyes!" Killa grinned.

"In more ways than one, I trust?" Lanzecki said, quirking his eyebrow. He was being Lanzecki-the-man, as he had been in their old loverly days—a pose he had never before assumed in Lars's presence. For some reason it disturbed her.

"Well, that's the trick, isn't it?" she replied, knowing better than to show her surprise. "Widening the eyes to prevent the alteration? She was only nervous."

"Anything good in?" Lanzecki asked.

Killa regarded him coolly. The Guild Master ought to have been the first to know the answer to that question.

"Lars and I have been discussing the Junk to the exclusion of all else." Lanzecki raised his wineglass in a toast to her, then included Lars. "Interesting . . . Junk. I'm almost sorry I have to turn the matter over to the proper authority."

"Junk's sentient," Killa said flatly, helping herself to food.

"Too bad sentience isn't a marketable commodity," Lanzecki said. "Have some milsi stalks!" he added, passing her the plate and changing the subject.

"What under the suns were you and Lanzecki up to for half a day?" she asked Lars as she swung her legs up onto the sleeping surface of their bedroom.

He yawned mightily, stepping up off the floor and walking to the pillowed end, where he folded down and began to wriggle into a comfortable position.

"The Junk mostly, and speculation as to whether or not it could use the crystal as a comlink. I doubt it. And this and that." Lars punched a pillow into the right contours and stuck it under his head, watching her as she rolled up against him. He lifted one arm, a tacit invitation to nestle against him. She did. "He misses Trag."

"Did you find out what crystal-crazed notion made him pick that dork in Trag's place?"

She settled her cheek against Lars's smooth chest. At

some point he, too, had bathed, for his skin exuded a subtly spicy odor. Lanzecki preferred spicy scents. What could these two be dreaming up together? she wondered. Lars had never used to tolerate Lanzecki at all, he'd been so possessive of her.

His fingers lazily trailed across her back, and she forgot about all other concerns and began to stroke him where it would do the most good. Somehow, despite being reasonably sure that Brendan's shipboard manners were impeccable, they had never quite been able to abandon themselves on the 1066. They proceeded to indulge each other shamelessly.

Uninhibited loving was the best!

The comunit buzzed until they woke, or rather until Lars waved his hand at the panel and accepted the call.

"Lars? Can you spare me the morning?" Lanzecki asked.

Killashandra groaned at the sound of his voice, but she didn't quite take in the message. She flattened her body against the bedding and determinedly resumed her interrupted slumbers. So when she did wake, she wasn't quite certain what had happened to Lars. There was no residual heat left where his body had been.

She roused, washed, and ordered food. As usual, the latter triggered an interruption.

"Killa? I'm up in Lanzecki's office."

"Humph! What's he got you doing now?"

She could hear the amusement in Lars's voice. "Actually, he's got me interested in spite of myself, and you know I'm not an admin type."

"No, you're not."

"Don't be so sour, Sunny. It's a bright day, and we don't have to go cut crystal—yet!"

"Well, I can't say as I mind that . . ." Killa said, as

much because that was the expected answer. Then she began to wonder. "Lars, what are you—" But the call had been disconnected at his end.

More curious than disgruntled, Killa finished her meal, dressed, and went up to Lanzecki's office. There, the mere sight of Bollam, hunched over his terminal, annoyed her. His frantic look and his sudden intense interest in the contents of his screen added to her aggravation.

She couldn't resist twitting him. "Lost something, Bollam?"

"Ah, yes, that is, no! No, I'm merely not sure under what category Trag filed the pencil data files."

"Try the first four letters of whatever file you're hunting, the year if you know it, and hit Search." She meant to be facetious and was irritated that her advice seemed to solve his problem. She caught a glimpse of his relieved smile as she continued on her way into the office.

"Haven't you two moved?" she demanded as she saw them in positions similar to yesterday's.

"I never knew just how much power the Guild wields," Lars said, beckoning to her in an airy fashion.

"You ought to," Killa said, scowling at Lanzecki. "We trade rather heavily on it whenever we leave Ballybran."

"I don't mean as singers, Killa, but the Guild as a force in interstellar politics. And policies."

"Oh?"

"And all without having to leave Ballybran! Whoever needs to speak to the Heptite Guild *must* come here!" Lars chuckled with an almost boyish delight. Lanzecki wore just the slightest smile as he glanced over at her.

To Killashandra that cynical amusement meant that Lanzecki was building to something devious. She cocked her head at him. He shook his head very slightly in denial.

"I've a meeting later today, Killa. I'd appreciate it if you and Lars would sit in on it."

Killa jerked her finger over her shoulder in the direction of Bollam. "He's your assistant."

The fleeting shift of Lanzecki's dark eyes told her that he didn't expect much of Trag's replacement, and his lack of such expectation worried her all the more.

"Yesterday Enthor, today Trag?" she asked, mockingly.

"I'd appreciate your counsel," he said, bending his upper body just slightly toward her in an unexpected bow.

She wondered if he knew that that deference would insure her support. Probably. Lanzecki had usually been able to read her, at times better than Lars did. She realized then that she usually compromised with Lars more than she would have with Lanzecki. But then, she wanted to. She trusted Lars Dahl more than she had ever trusted Lanzecki, even when they had been passionate lovers. Or maybe because of that!

"Bollam? Have you got those trade figures?" Lanzecki called out.

"Still working" was the all too quick reply.

A look of pained patience crossed Lanzecki's face.

"I remember Trag's system," Killa said, turning on her heel and retracing her steps to the worktop where Bollam was plainly unable to find the relevant pencil files. "Move over," she told the flustered man. "Now, who's coming?"

"The Apharian Four Satellite Miners League," he said, both resenting her usurpation and relieved that finding the documentation was now someone else's responsibility.

She typed "Apha4SML.doc" and obediently the recalcitrant entry blossomed across the screen. Bollam groaned.

"I did, I tried that. I really did."

"The library banks know an authoritative punch when they get one," she said, shrugging. She tapped a deliver.

"He wants the Interstellar Miners League, as well."

"What year?"

"Twenty-seven sixty-six."

Killa frowned. Twenty-seven sixty-six? *When* had she left Fuerte, storming out off her native planet with that crystal singer—ah, what *was* his name? Had it been 2699? Or 2599? She shook her head in irritation, then concentrated on tapping out the required sequence. The new files joined the others in the delivery slot. She was a lot better at his job than Bollam was. She gave him not even a look as she gathered up the files and brought them in to Lanzecki and Lars.

Lanzecki gave her a grateful smile as he began feeding them into the reader slot. He folded his arms across his chest as the first one came up on the monitor.

Feeling an obligation to assist the Guild Master, Killa stayed on, as Lars did. She accessed additional data when Lanzecki asked for it, ignoring Bollam when he hovered in an attempt to figure out how she found files so easily. At first it amused her that Lars and Lanzecki worked together so effortlessly. She wondered that, at times, Lanzecki seemed to defer to Lars's opinions. Certainly he tapped them into his own notes.

Then the representatives arrived for the meeting, properly attired against breathing Ballybran air. Lanzecki, hands on the backs of Killashandra and Lars, steered them into the conference room.

* * *

The Apharian Miners League wanted to extend their communications link in the asteroid belt they were currently working. They could not afford black crystal.

"Black crystal isn't needed for belt comunits. Blue will do as well and is half the price," Lanzecki said. "Here are specifications and costs." He inserted a pencil file in the screen reader, and specs and relative costs were displayed on the large monitor for all to see.

"Even that's out of our budget," the head delegate said, shaking his helmeted head.

"I doubt it," Lanzecki said bluntly. A tap of his finger and their trade figures replaced the spec/cost data.

Another delegate, a woman with sharp features and narrow-set eyes, glared first at the screen and then at him. "How did you obtain restricted data?"

"I particularly like to assemble 'restricted' data," Lanzecki replied.

"You could go to a green-crystal connection," Lars suggested. "Of course, there is a longer time lag in communication, especially for any distant units. The blue link is unquestionably faster. Basically you get what you pay for. The option is always yours."

Though Killashandra kept her expression bland, she was amused by Lars's hard-line pose. She had rarely seen that facet of his personality. He was as cool and uncompromising as Lanzecki. An interesting development.

"At present we have the necessary blue-crystal cuts such an installation would require," Killa said smoothly. She gave a little shrug with one shoulder. "Who knows when we'd have sufficient green. It's not an easy color to cut. Nearly as elusive as black. Which we also don't have on hand. You might have a long wait for quality black crystal."

"We can't *afford* that quality crystal," the woman

said, almost spitting the words out over her helmet mike. "But we did expect that, in making the effort to come here and outline our need, you might be amenable to a deal."

Lanzecki cleared his throat dismissively. "Your League has nothing this Guild requires. The Guild has what you require, and at the advertised price." He rose. "You either take it or do without. It's up to you."

Lars and Killa moved to bracket him.

"Wait!" The head of the delegation said, his expression anxious. "You don't understand. We've had accidents, deaths, problems, all due to a lack of adequate communications. We must have a reliable comsystem."

"Blue is available. You can wait for green, if that's all you can afford." Lanzecki spoke with no emotion whatever. He really didn't care one way or another.

Killashandra saw hatred sparkle in the eyes of the woman.

"My husband and my two sons died in an accident . . ."

Lanzecki turned halfway to her and inclined his head. "A singer died and two more were seriously injured acquiring the blue crystal. We have both lost, and we can both gain."

"You heartless—" The woman launched herself at Lanzecki, screaming other epithets in her frustration at his diffidence.

Lars intercepted her neatly even as Killashandra moved to interpose her body to protect Lanzecki's back.

"Lideen, don't!" the leader said, reaching her first. He grabbed her by the arms and passed her to the other members of his party. He took a deep breath before he went on. "Guild Master, I do recognize that sentiment has no place in business."

"In either yours or mine," Lanzecki replied with cool courtesy.

"You singers have crystal for blood! Crystal for hearts!" Lideen yelled as the other two miners' reps hauled her out of the room.

"The Guild does not make deals," Lars added. "The integrity of our price scale has to be maintained. Two options are currently open to you. You can, of course, wait until there is a glut of blue crystal on the market, which would bring the unit price down, but there is no downward market forecast on blue crystal at the moment. Or you can install green when it is available. Your credit balance indicates that your League is able to fund either. It's up to you to decide."

As Killashandra followed Lanzecki and Lars to the door, she sneaked a look over her shoulder and saw the hesitation on the leader's face. He wanted the crystal badly; he knew he could pay for it; he was just trying it on as standard operating procedure. But he had obviously never approached this Guild before. Quite likely, there would be an order from the Apharian League before the Apharians departed Shankill Moon Base. Someone should have warned them not to haggle with Lanzecki and the Heptite Guild. Most people knew that. Still, there were always those who would chance their arms to save a few credits. Only this group had forgotten that mining crystal was not so very much different than mining asteroids: the result of failure bore the same cost.

She shrugged.

"Damn fools," she heard Lanzecki say as she closed the door to the conference room.

He stalked across to the table at which he and Lars had been working, slammed a new file into the reader slot, and stared at the display.

That wasn't like Lanzecki, and Killashandra blinked in surprise. Lars gave an imperceptible shake of his head; she shrugged and dismissed the matter.

By the seventh day, when Lars hadn't mentioned going out into the Ranges, she did.

"Did those Apharians order? Or should we concentrate on finding some green crystal?" she asked when he finally appeared late that evening.

"Huh?"

Lars's mind was clearly on other matters. She felt excluded and that made her irritable. They were partners, close partners, and shared everything.

"I thought we came back to cut crystal, not sit around playing diddly with pencil files."

He gave her one of his quick, apologetic grins. "Well, we can depart in a day or two."

She raised her eyebrows, trying for a light touch.

"Are you aiming to take over from Bollam?"

"From Bollam?" He stared at her in amazement, then laughed, pulling her into his arms. "Not likely, when I've the best partner in the whole Guild. It's just that— well, I can't help being flattered when Lanzecki keeps asking my advice, now can I?"

"I don't mean to denigrate your advice, but that's not like Lanzecki."

"Too true, Sunny, too true," he said with a sad sigh. "I'd hazard that he misses Trag more than he'd admit."

"Then why did he take on such a want-wit as Bollam! There must be someone more qualified!"

Lars grinned at her vehemence and rocked her close in his arms. "Did you *find* anyone to replace him over the last few days?"

She pushed him away, glaring reprovingly at him. She had thought her search discreet enough.

"Oh, there's little going on here that Lanzecki doesn't hear about sooner or later. He said to tell you that he appreciated your efforts. Bollam suits his needs."

Killa swore.

"Hey, I wouldn't mind a late-night snack," Lars said, hauling her with him to the catering unit. "And yes, the Apharians ordered the blue, still registering complaints about the cost and issuing veiled statements about unethical access and invasion of commercial privacy and all that wind and piss."

Two days later Killashandra and Lars lifted their sled out of the Hangar and headed east, toward the Milekey Ranges. Behind them a second sled departed, but immediately struck out on a nor'easterly course.

"That's Lanzecki's," Killashandra said in surprise.

"Yes, that's why he's been working such long hours, to clear all current business. He'll be the better for a spell in the Ranges. That's all he needs, really."

"But with Bollam?"

"I'll grant you that I've qualms, but who knows? Bollam might turn out to be a top-rank cutter. Or why would Lanzecki shepherd him?"

"Shepherd him?" Killa blinked. "Bollam's not been blooded in the Ranges yet?" She recalled the fine crystal scars on Bollam's hands and arms. "He's cuts enough."

Lars grinned. "I heard tell that he was the clumsiest apprentice they ever had on the Hangar floor. He's lucky to find anyone to shepherd him, the number of singers he annoyed dropping crystals when he was unloading sleds."

Killa muttered uncomplimentary epithets about Bollam.

"I suppose that sort of duty does fall with Lanzecki,"

Lars went on with a sigh, "shepherding the ones no one else will take to initiate."

"I don't envy him the job, that's for sure."

"Nor I." Lars turned to grin at her, his eyes deep with affection. "But then, I had the best of all possible partners."

"You!" She faked a cuff to his jaw. She could, and did, envy Bollam the chance to be shepherded by Lanzecki on his first trip into the Ranges: the twit didn't deserve such an honor. Odd, though; she would have thought Lanzecki would have blackmailed someone else to shepherd Bollam, reserving his own talents to take the rough edges off the man once he had been exposed to the Ranges.

"Where'll we head, partner?" Lars asked her as they entered the Milekey.

Killashandra grimaced. The usual ambivalence surged up in mind and body. A singer cut crystal in order to leave the Ranges as frequently as possible. But a singer also had to renew herself with the crystal she cut. The more she cut out of a certain lode, the easier it was to find later. If she went off-planet for any length of time, that attraction diminished. But a singer had to go off-planet to ease the crystal pulse in her blood. Cutting too much was almost, not quite, as much a hazard as cutting too little. With Lars, she had often been able to cut just enough, which was the main advantage of singing duet.

"Can you remember where we cut those greens a couple of trips back?"

Lars gave her a long thoughtful look.

"What's wrong?" she asked. "We have cut greens, and with none available it seems sensible to get top market price on something."

"Why don't we go for black?"

"You know how hard it is to find black, good black,"

she replied in a cranky tone. She didn't *want* to cut
blacks—ever.

"Green it is," he said, and slightly altered the sled's
course. "Our marker may have faded a lot," he went on.
"Lots of storms have passed over since we cut green."

"Not that many!"

He said nothing and accelerated the sled. "It'll be a
while. Settle down."

She watched the jagged pinnacles of the Range. Paint
splotches, old and new, indicated claims. Once she
would have recognized markers by their color and pattern. She didn't try anymore. Theirs was a black and
yellow herringbone design, which Lars had thoughtfully
painted on the console. She often cursed that choice,
because it was hell to paint the pattern on uneven rock
surfaces, but she had to admit that the black and yellow
herringbones had high visibility.

The sled plowed through the skies, the sweep of peak
and pinnacle flowing past her in an almost mesmerizing
blur. Below a relatively fresh paint splotch, she caught
the metallic glitter of a sled half-hidden under a canyon
overhang.

"They ought to watch out," she murmured under her
breath. "Ledges can fall down on top of you."

"What say, Sunny?" Lars asked, and she grinned as
she waved at him to ignore her.

It was late in the morning when he began to circle the
sled. "Think I found one," he said, bringing them down
to hover over the spot.

"Are you sure?" Killa squinted down at rocks bearing
the barest hint of color: the herringbone pattern was all
but indistinguishable.

"Sure as I can be. Shall we put down and see what we
remember of the site?"

"We certainly have to renew the marker," she said,

annoyed that the paint, which was supposed to have a long sun-life, had faded so badly. Markers were what kept other singers from usurping claims. A claim was circular in shape, with a radius of a half kilometer radiating from the painted logo. No one was supposed to enter a space so marked. As further protection, the mark was not required to be at the lode itself—or even anywhere near. The lode could be right at the edge of the enclosed space and still be claimed by the singer.

"Paint first, look later," Lars said, calling the order.

They painted and then took a meal break, all the while looking around the circle, hoping to trigger recollections of this particular site.

"We've got to go down," Killa said after she had swallowed her last mouthful. "Nothing's familiar at this height."

"Eeny, meeny, pitsa teeny," Lars chanted as he circled up from the peak. At "teeny" Lars left the circle in that direction, bringing the sled down into the small canyon. He grinned at Killa: a random choice had often proved lucky. He neatly parked their vehicle in the shadow cast by the higher side, and she nodded approval of his caution. They would be hidden from an aerial view until the morning.

She was first out of the sled, running her fingers along the uneven rock walls of the canyon and hoping to catch a trace of crystal resonance. Or find the scars of a previous working.

Lars struck off in the opposite direction. They met on the far side, having seen nothing to indicate that this canyon was the one they were looking for.

"Shall we go left or right?" Lars asked as they got back into the sled.

"Off the top of my head! Right!" Killashandra said

after a moment's sober thought. "Not that that's any indication."

But she turned out to be correct—for in the narrow ravine to the right of their first landing they came across evidence of cutting.

"I'd know our style anywhere," Lars said.

"You mean yours," she replied, settling in to another of their long debates as they returned to the sled and unpacked their sonic cutters.

"We'd do better if we waited until the sun hits them," Lars said.

"No better or no worse. Hit a C."

Inhaling deeply, he sang a fine powerful true mid-C, his eyes sparkling at her, daring her as he so often did. She sang out a third above his note, as powerfully as he had. Sound bounced back at them, making them both flinch at the undertones.

"Some of it's cracked," Killa said, but, as one, they moved toward the resonating point. "Green, from the power in its echo."

"I told you I remembered where we'd cut green."

Once at the side of the ravine, they sang the pitch notes again and set their cutters to the sound. Killa indicated the cut she would make and set herself for the first wrenching scream of cut crystal. No sooner had she set the cutter than Lars set his a handspan to the right.

The first set cleared away the imperfect crystal to reveal a wide vein of fine green.

"Shards, but those Apharians are going to be furious when they hear about this," she said, slicing away additional marred quartz.

"What'll we try for?"

"Comunit sizes, of course," she said with a snort.

Once the debris cleared, they sang again in case they

had to retune the cutters, but Lars's C and her E rang clearly back at them. Together they placed their cutter edges and, taking a simultaneous breath, turned on the power.

CHAPTER 5

Darkness forced them to stop with twelve fine crystals cut and stored in the padded carrier case carefully strapped in the cargo bay. Quietly, from the ease of long practice, they made a meal and ate it. Then, continuing their rituals, they washed—there would come days when crystal song would override such habits. While Lars made entries in the sled's log, Killashandra pulled down their double bunk and got out the quilts. They were both ready to settle at the same time.

The morning sun, stroking the Ranges awake, provided an alarm no singer could resist: the insidious chiming of crystal as the first rays dispelled the chill of night. The notes were random, pure sound, for only perfect crystal could speak on sunlight. The ringing stirred senses and awoke desires as it grew louder and more insistent. Killashandra and Lars simultaneously turned to each other. She could see his smile in the

shadowy cabin and answered it, lifting her arm to his
shoulders, eager for the touch of his bare skin against
hers. It seemed to Killashandra that as their lips met an
arpeggio rippled through the air, excitingly sensual,
deliciously caressing, ending on a clear high C that shivered over them just as their bodies joined.

This was the real reason men and women sang crystal
together—to hear such music, to experience such sensa-
tions and such ecstasy as only crystal could awaken on
bright, clear mornings. Such unions made up for all the
mundane squabbles and recriminations between partners when crystal cracked or splintered and a whole
day's work might lie in shards at their feet. There was
always the prospect of the incredible combination of
sound and sensation in sunlit crystal to reanimate their
relationship.

"We must get moving, Sunny," Lars murmured,
making an effort to move. Too languorous with remembered passion, Killashandra murmured a throaty denial
and shaded her eyes from the sun splashing into the
cabin.

"C'mon now. Hell, we'll be having a spate of good
clear weather," he said, pushing her toward the edge of
the bunk. "We can afford to do a little work today. I'll
start breakfast. Your turn in the head."

He used the light jocular tone that he knew Killashandra would accept. As she rose and stretched luxuri-
ously, she glanced enticingly over her shoulder at him.

"That won't work on me today, Sunny," he said
wryly and gave her a slap across the buttock. Sometimes
the sight of her at full stretch was enough to tempt him,
despite the fact that they both knew a repeat performance once the sun had risen would be less satisfying
than the first.

She strutted sensually across to the head, flirting with

him, but he only laughed and stuck his right leg into his coverall, pulling the garment up past his unresponsive member. She grabbed up her own clothes and slid open the door. As he took his turn, she finished making the substantial breakfast they would need to fuel them for working crystal all day. On clear days, singers rarely stopped to eat, cutting as long as there was light enough to see where to place their blades.

Killashandra recalled, without remembering when, that there had been a time or two when she had cut throughout a double-moon night: the times when she had struggled to cut enough to afford passage off the fardling planet to get some respite from crystal song.

They had been profitably working that vein for five days when Killashandra's weather sense began to pluck at her consciousness.

"Storm?" Lars knew her so well.

She nodded, and set her cutter for a new level. "Not to worry yet."

"Nardy hell, Killa, we've got eight crates of the stuff. No sense in taking a risk. And the marker's new enough to draw us right back here after the storm."

"We've time. Sing out," she told him in a tone that was half command, half plea. "Greens aren't easy to find, and I'm not about to quit when there's still time to cut. The storm could ruddy well splinter this vein to nothing good enough to spit at."

Lars regarded her levelly. "Just let's not cut it too fine!"

"I wouldn't let you get storm-crazed, lover."

"I'm counting on it. I think this tier's going to be minor key," he added, humming a B-flat and hearing the same tone murmur back at him.

"I'll make mine E, or would A be better?"

He nodded crisp agreement for the A, and they sang,

cutting as soon as they heard the answering notes the crystal flung back at them, its own death knell.

But storm sense caught at Killashandra again, not long after they had crated the nine crystals of that cutting.

"I think we're going," she told him, hefting the cutter in one hand and bending her knees to take one handle of the crate. He did the same, and she set a rapid pace back to the sled. As Lars settled the crate into its strappings, Killa racked up both cutters and took the pilot's seat, closing hatches and starting up the engines.

Lars peered out the window of the right-hand side and muttered a curse. "Angle of the wall's wrong. Can't see anything. Where's it coming from?"

"South." Just then the weather-alert klaxon cut in. It got one hoot out before her hand closed the toggle.

"You're ahead of the best technology the Guild can beg, borrow, or steal, aren't you?" Lars grinned at her, proud of her ability.

"Yup!"

"Don't get cocky."

"It's going to be a bad one, too." She shifted uneasily in the seat, her bones already responding to the distant stroking of the crystal. "I swear, the longer I cut, the more sensitive I get to the intensity of weather systems."

"Saves our skins, and our crystal."

She lifted the sled vertically, and as they rose above the sheltering walls of the ravine, storm clouds could be seen as a smudge of dark, roiling gray on the horizon. She veered the sled about to port and lifted above the higher cliffs, hovering just briefly over their paint mark, satisfied that it would survive this storm and a few more before wind-carried abrasives scoured the rock clean again.

They were nearly out of the Ranges when their com-unit lit up.

"Mayday, Mayday," cried a frantic voice.

"Mayday? What the—" she demanded indignantly, leaning to one side to close the connection.

Lars's hand masked the plate. "That's Bollam's voice."

"Bollam?" Killashandra stared at him in puzzlement: the name meant nothing to her.

"Lanzecki's new partner," Lars muttered, and responded. "Yes, Bollam?"

"It's Lanzecki, I can't get him to stop!"

"Take the crystal out of his hand," Killashandra said angrily. It irritated her that she still couldn't place this Bollam fellow.

"He's not holding crystal. He's cutting and he won't stop. He won't listen. He's—he's thralled!"

"You dork, of course he is, that's why he doesn't cut often. It's your job to stop him. That's why he takes a partner into the Ranges," Lars replied, his tone still reasonable.

"But I've tried, I've tried everything. He's bigger than I am!" Bollam's voice had turned to a distressed whine.

"Knock his feet out from under him," Lars said, concern deepening in his expression.

"I tried that, too."

"Cross-cut with your cutter. Tune it off-pitch, queer his note," Killa roared, becoming more incensed with this dork's stupidity. Where had Lanzecki found such an ineffectual partner?

"I can't. I don't know how to cross-cut. This is my first time in the Ranges. *He* was shepherding *me!*" Now there was grievance and indignation in Bollam's voice. That particular tone triggered the appropriate memory

in Killashandra's mind: it was exactly how Bollam had
sounded when he couldn't find the Apharian files.

"So this is why Bollam suited him," Killashandra
said, bitter with the realization of exactly what Lanzecki
was doing.

Lars stared at her, jerking her arm to pull her around
to face him. "Turn the sled. We've got to try."

"No." She reset her hands on the yoke, gritting her
teeth against the pain that suddenly scored her and the
tears that threatened to blind her. "No, we can't! Rules
and Regs! Mayday means nothing on Ballybran!"

"Nothing?" Lars roared at her. "Lanzecki's been our
friend, your lover! How can you abandon him?"

"I'm *not* abandoning him," Killashandra shrieked
back, glaring her anger, her hurt, the pain of *knowing*
what Lanzecki wanted! "Get out of there, Bollam," she
bellowed at the comunit. "Save your own skin. You
can't save his."

"But I can't just *leave!*" Bollam sounded shocked,
horrified at this heartless advice. "He's the Guild Master. It's my duty . . ."

"There is no such duty in the Rules and Regs, Bollam.
There never was and there never will be. Get out of
there, Bollam, while you still can. *Leave Lanzecki.*"

"I don't believe I'm hearing you say this," Lars cried.

She swiveled around at him, tears streaming down her
face, her throat closing so that she was momentarily
deprived of speech.

"He wants it this way," she managed to choke out.
Then she swallowed hard on her grief and glared
straight into Lars's appalled face. "Consider, Lars,
would there be any other logical reason why Lanzecki
would team up with a dork like Bollam? A novice in the
Ranges? Physically too weak to knock him out of thrall?

We haven't the right to interfere. We owe Lanzecki his choice."

She hooked her elbows through the yoke so that Lars would have to break her arms to get control of the sled. But he didn't try. He sat staring at her as she sent the sled roaring out of the Range, using every ounce of thrust in its powerful new engines.

"Lanzecki *intended* to opt out?"

"Singers have that option, Lars," she said in a voice as low as his. Her throat thickened again, her eyes stinging with tears. It was a hard reality to accept, but she didn't doubt for a moment—now—that that had been Lanzecki's intention. She could even hear his deep voice replying to her puzzled query about Bollam: that the man had his uses. She ought to have *known* what Lanzecki was about and tried to—tried to what? Talk a tired man out of ending a life that had grown too tedious with responsibility, too tiresome with problems, too lonely with his longtime partner dead? "He's been Guild Master for centuries."

Lars was silent until, behind them, they could both hear storm wail creeping inexorably nearer.

"Then is that also why he was so intent on me understanding Guild politics?" Lars asked, softly, shakily.

"What do you mean by that?" she demanded.

"I'm not sure I know," Lars replied, raising his hands in doubt. "It was just that—well, Lanzecki knew you and—whenever we were in from the Ranges, he sought out our company, but I always thought it was you . . ." His voice trailed off.

"Don't get any ideas, Lars Dahl," she said coldly, harshly. "You may be a Milekey Transition . . ."

"So are you."

"But there's no way I'd be Guild Master." She glared at him, willing him to respond in the same vein. "Damn it, Lars, you're my partner. And there's a lot more to being Guild Master than understanding the politics of the job."

"That is true enough," he replied in a muted voice, his eyes looking directly ahead as they passed over the last hills before the Cube.

The flight officer signaled them to park their sled near Sorting with the other half-dozen vehicles that had fled the storm. Killashandra killed the engines and turned to Lars.

"Start with the crates, will you? I'll report," she said bleakly.

"I will, if you want me to," Lars offered, suddenly human again in his unexpressed sympathy.

"No, I was pilot."

The flight officer, a lanky lean man whom Killashandra didn't recognize at all, was trotting in her direction, signaling her to wait for him.

"Were you within range of Bollam? The one Lanzecki was shepherding?"

"Yes," Killashandra said so flatly that the man blinked in surprise. "He couldn't break Lanzecki out of thrall. We told him to get the hell out of the Ranges."

"You mean . . ."

The cargo officer arrived at that point, her face grim.

"I mean Lanzecki *chose!*" Killashandra dared the flight officer to argue her point.

"You're sure, Killa?" the cargo officer asked.

Killashandra rounded on her, away from the accusing eyes of the flight officer.

"Why else would he choose a dork like Bollam? And a novice? Too inexperienced to know how to break thrall and too physically insignificant to be a threat!"

The cargo officer bowed her head, her eyes closed.

"I don't understand . . . Were you near enough, Killashandra Ree, to reach them in time?" the flight officer demanded.

"I accepted Lanzecki's choice. You'd better."

With that Killashandra turned on her heel, returning to her sled at a pace that was nearly a run. Behind her she could hear the flight officer arguing with Cargo, whose low and curt rejoinders told Killashandra that she, at least, accepted Lanzecki's option.

As she helped her silent partner unload their cut, she knew that Lars's feelings about that option were ambivalent. The news seemed to seep through from the Hangar into Sorting, and conversations were muted, arguments over crystal prices conducted in low tones. When the Sorter told them how much they had earned for the green, Killashandra felt none of the elation such a figure should have elicited. Lars only arched his eyebrows, nodded acknowledgment, and turned away. The Sorter shrugged. Dully, Killashandra followed Lars to the lifts. She did listen to the Met report that was being broadcast, even in the lifts, since weather had top priority with most singers. Nothing was said about missing sleds. Nothing ever was.

"That's a relief," Killashandra muttered as the report concluded. The storm had been one of those quick squalls, fierce in its brief life, its only damage that of taking Lanzecki's life in its fury. "We can be back out in the Ranges by tomorrow evening."

"Fardles, Killa!" Lars rounded on her. "Lanzecki's not even found and—"

Her livid expression stopped his words. "The sooner I'm in the Ranges, the sooner I'll forget."

"Forget Lanzecki?" Lars was stunned.

"Forget! Forget!" The lift door opened and she ran

down the hall to their apartment. She heard him following her and wasn't even grateful.

As she slammed into their quarters, she could hear the radiant fluid slopping into the tub. Pulling off her coverall and boots, she stumbled into the room and clambered into the bath. The fluid was no more than calf-deep, so she stood under the spigot and let it roll down her back and shoulders. Dimly she heard Lars's voice, updating his records. She began to curse, so that she couldn't possibly hear a word he said.

All the resident staff of the Cube were quiet and depressed the next noon when Killashandra and Lars reached the dining room. While Killa filled her tray from the alcohol-drinks dispenser, Lars kept looking around, peering at the faces of those sitting in alcoves. Seeing his discreet search for Bollam recharged Killa's vexation.

"Lanzecki opted out, Lars," she said in an intense low voice, jerking him to her side. "What're you drinking?"

"Yarran!" His voice was flat.

"Yarran? This is no time for beer! This is the time to get paralytic drunk!"

He gave her a bitterly amused look. "I thought you wanted to be back in the Ranges tomorrow morning. With a hangover?"

"With the most massive hangover I can acquire between now and then," she told him savagely, and downed the first of the many triple-measure glasses on her tray, pressing for a refill as she tossed the empty glass into the recycler.

"You may just go out alone, then," he said. Taking the Yarran beer from the slot, he left her standing there.

Surprised, she watched him maneuver among the tables, heading for the far alcove where the two Hanger officers were sitting. She hadn't thought Lars had a masochistic streak in him. Or maybe he just had to find out if Bollam had somehow managed to get Lanzecki into the sled and back to the Cube.

The dork couldn't have managed it, or the nonsingers of the Guild wouldn't be so deep in drink. Now that she had looked around, she could see that most of them were as badly gone as she would like to be. She downed another triple and, moving carefully so as not to slosh a drop of liquid anesthesia, made her way toward Lars. The stench of ketones was almost overpowering. These people must have been drinking steadily since the news got out.

"Oh, he'll live," Cargo was saying as Killashandra approached the table. "That's not saying how much good he'll be." She glanced up at Killashandra and, with a brief inclination of her head, indicated that the singer could join them. The flight officer clearly did not agree with that invitation. "Oh, leave it, Murr. You haven't been here long enough to *know.* You did as you should, Killa," she added and patted the cushion beside her. Her eyebrows lifted at the sight of so much liquor on the tray. She raised her mug of coffee. "Happy hangover!"

Suddenly Killashandra lost any taste for the boozing she had planned. Her stomach roiled and growled. She sat down, hands limp in her lap, and stared across at Lars, wanting his reassurance and understanding even more than she had ever wanted to cut black crystal. He pointedly ignored her, and the tears began to stream down her face.

"You did right, Killa. You did," Cargo said softly, and clasped her fingers on the singer's forearm, squeezing briefly with a gentling firmness before releasing. "Didn't she, Lars Dahl?" she added sternly.

Lars looked at Cargo, unable to avoid his partner's tear-streaked face. He closed his eyes, exhaling in defeat. "Yes, if you say so, she did."

"Look here, Dahl." Cargo leaned across the table, her face fierce. "I do say so. If you want, you can ask Medical. They could see." And she waved her hand in the general direction of the infirmary wing where damaged singers were tended until such time as hearts in crippled bodies stopped and empty minds went dark. "*I* could see!" And her tone was fierce. "Murr here didn't know Lanzecki in his prime as I did, and Killa did! And Killa knew him better than most. Face it, Murr, Lars, she did the right thing. Don't know why that ass Bollam even qualified—except he was probably too craven, or too shitless scared to step back after Disclosure, when he heard all the risks he'd be taking on Ballybran. He had a lousy Transition, as if the symbiont working into his bloodstream also discovered it hadn't made a great choice of a home body, and we never thought he'd end up a singer!" The scorn in her voice gave unexpected ease to Killashandra's anguish. "Certainly not as Lanzecki's partner!"

"Lanzecki was shepherding him . . ." Lars said, trying to find some perverse justification.

Cargo snorted bitterly. "When Lanzecki said he'd shepherd the geek, I knew I wouldn't ever see Lanzecki back in the Hangar, Lars. And I told you that, didn't I, Murr?"

"I just don't understand why," Murr said. "Everyone's saying he was the best Guild Master we've ever had . . ."

"There've only been four," Cargo replied.

"Four?" Murr was staggered. "But the Guild's been going close to seven hundred years!"

"Hmmm, so it has, and I've been Cargo for nearly two and a half hundred."

That silenced Murr completely—he stared at the woman as if he expected her active body and attractive face to crumple into dust if he so much as blinked. Despite her grief, Killashandra was amused.

"What did Medical know about Lanzecki?" Lars asked, his expression as bleak as ever. Somehow, though, Killa sensed that his antagonism toward her had eased.

Cargo shrugged. "What happens to all of us eventually? The symbiont is weakened past restoration, and degeneration finally starts. All a fast downhill ride then." That was when she noticed Murr's expression and grinned. "Never fear, Murr, you're stuck with me a while yet. Me and my symbiont are in great shape."

"It doesn't say in Rules and Regs," Lars began after watching Murr try to assume a normal attitude, "how a new Guild Master is elected."

"No, it doesn't," Cargo agreed, frowning slightly. "But, like I say, the problem doesn't come up very often."

Killashandra sent a fierce glare at Lars. The slight grin that tugged at one corner of his mouth did not reassure her.

"It'll take time," Cargo added indifferently. "Politics is involved. What else is new? They have to choose someone acceptable to the majority of the long-term customers."

"Who's 'they'?" Lars asked.

"I dunno." Cargo shrugged again. "Maybe one of the Instructors knows." She looked around the big room. "None of them appears to be sober enough to ask. I gotta get back to work. Do I put your sled into a ready slot? That storm's cleared off."

Killashandra didn't dare look at Lars.

"Yes, we'll be out again tomorrow," he said, and she sagged against the cushions with relief. But her relief was very short-lived as she remembered that Cargo had estimated it would be a long time before the new Guild Master was chosen.

So she didn't get drunk to blunt her acute sense of loss at Lanzecki's death. She endured it as Cargo and Lars did, as Murr couldn't. But she drank glass for glass of Yarran beer with them. A singer could drink Yarran beer for days and barely blunt sensitivities. She heard that Bollam had survived with what wits he originally possessed intact. He had been badly crystal-cut when the rescue ship had found his crashed sled, but he had made it past the storm zone before losing control. What she hated Bollam for was that crystal had wiped all his memories of Lanzecki. She couldn't wait to get out in the Ranges and hope for the same respite. A few days cutting in the Ranges, and one could forget just about anything.

Lars was up before her the next morning, their gear all packed, and silently they made their way to the Hangar. Cargo lifted her hand in acknowledgment; Flight Officer Murr raised his only to give them the go-ahead. Some trainee gave them a formal release.

As if the sled were on some kind of giant spring whose pull could not be resisted, they flew directly back to the black and yellow chevron of the green crystal.

"We shouldn't have gone direct," Killashandra remarked to Lars as he passed over the marker.

"Sky's clear," he said with a diffident shrug. It was. No other singer was aloft to see the direction they took, direct or oblique.

When they landed in the little canyon, they both knew

the vein had been damaged. They spent the rest of the day trying to cut down into clear color.

"Fardles, it's gone, Lars, leave it," Killa said when decades upon decades of experience finally surfaced to remind her how pointless their efforts were. "Green cracks the worst of all when a vein's been exposed."

He kicked at the shards underfoot to relieve his frustration and led the way back to the sled. They stayed there the night, but when crystal song woke desire in them, it was only crystal that spoke, not their hearts.

It took them a week to search the full circle of which that chevron was the center. They found a very light pink, but it wasn't worth the effort of turning on their cutters. They had withdrawn from each other as never before, and Killashandra cursed silently, craving to cut crystal and relieve the tension. Even Lars might forget—at least lose the edge of painful memory—if they could just cut.

Perversely the weather stayed fair, but summer had Ballybran in its thrall and baked the Ranges. As they searched for crystal, they also looked for the deepest, most shadowy canyons in which to spend the night and get some relief from the unmitigated heat.

"I could almost welcome a storm," Lars said. "Unless we can find some water, we're going to have to go back."

"No! Not until we find crystal."

He shrugged, but they did find water, a deep pool under an overhang where water had oozed out of the more porous rock and been collected in the shade. They filled the tank, then stripped and bathed, washing their clothing where a tiny stream trickled out of the pond. The relief was physical, not mental, but they were more in charity with each other than at any time since Bollam's voice had shattered their rapport.

Late the next morning Lars, whose turn it was to pilot the sled, spotted an almost invisible black and yellow chevron.

"What do you think? We cut here?" he asked.

"I don't remember, don't care, I'd even cut pink, so long's we cut *something!*"

"Eeny, meeny, pitsa teeny," and Lars aimed the sled sou'sou'east to a narrow gorge with high walls on the north side. There was a V-shaped notch in the eastern lip. "That looks familiar."

"It's a cut all right." She had both their cutters unracked before Lars landed the sled, and pausing only long enough to grab a water bottle, she half ran to the fracture, slipping on old shards to reach the site. "It's the black, Lars, it's the black!"

Depression lifted from her, and she even remembered to be cautious as she climbed to the top of the shelf. Lars sang out a fine strong C, and she could feel the crystal's response even through the thick soles of her boots. She cut the first shaft, then struggled with Lars when he had to wrest it out of her hands, for it thralled her as black crystal usually did. She was weeping when she saw him nestle the black in the padded crate. He slapped her hard, three times across the face, and she leaned against him, grateful.

"It's all right, Sunny. It's all right," he murmured, caressing her hair briefly. "Now, let's cut. For Lanzecki. He did like to see us bring in the blacks."

"Yeah, but he's not going to make me link 'em! No way will he talk me into linking again!"

She was figuring where to cut next, and how many they could get out of this fine black crystal, so she didn't see the peculiar way Lars looked at her.

* * *

Clodine gave them top market price on their five crates of black. There was enough for two planetary systems—if any could afford the price of black-crystal comunits—and some nice single pieces that might just chord into current installations as auxiliaries. Clodine was full of praise for their work.

"No one cuts the way you two do. I didn't realize singers could be so individual, but you are, you know," she said, slightly shy with embarrassment but sincere in her compliment.

"Where'll we go, Lars?" Killashandra asked. "I think it's your choice."

"I think you're right," he replied, laughing. He was himself again, she knew, but she didn't know why she thought he hadn't been.

Back in their quarters, as usual she plunged directly into the tub while he updated his file.

"That didn't take you long," she said. It seemed only a few moments before he came into the room. Usually an update took him a quarter of an hour.

Still clothed, he was looking in a puzzled fashion at a printout. He held it so she could see the message.

"Report to Conference? What does Lanzecki want you to do *now?*" She hauled at his hand. "You've got to bathe first. We reek!" She laughed because the smell of him could always arouse her no matter how rank he was.

"Lanzecki?" He sighed, his eyes sad, and she wondered what was wrong. "I'd better go find out. This message is several days old."

"He can wait. He has before."

Lars peeled off the perspiration-stained and crystal-sliced overall. "I'll shower. I'll be back as soon as I know what this means." He crumbled the message in a wad and lobbed it at the recycler.

"Oh, Lars! We've got to make plans . . ."

"You start. Just find us a water world that we haven't been to, Sunny," he said, but she sensed his tone was forced.

And so it would be, being required to report so immediately to Lanzecki after a month in the Ranges. Hot summer, at that. It would take several long baths to cleanse her skin of accumulated sweat and dust. Fardles, how she hated Ballybran in the summer. Even her hair had been baked off her head; she fingered the inch-short strands. No, the memory surfaced: they had cut each other's hair scalp-close at one point because they had been so hot and their hair so filthy.

She sank to her chin; the radiant fluid was heavy against her skin, drawing out the vibrations that seemed to throb in every pore. She was tired. She didn't know how Lars was finding the energy to answer Lanzecki's summons. She did remember to pull the shoulder harness from its alcove and get her arms through it. That way, if she did fall asleep, she wouldn't slip beneath the fluid. A singer could drown that way. She had too much awareness of danger to fall into *that* trap the way . . . She paused, unable to remember who it was who had been in danger.

She was just beginning to feel clean when Lars came swinging into the bathroom. He stood for a moment on the threshold, taking her in, and then began the grin she knew too well meant he was about to say something he knew she wouldn't like.

"There's a terminal patient waiting escort at Shankill, Killa," he said, drawling the words out.

She groaned. "And you volunteered? Why does Lanzecki always pick on us?"

He pointed his index finger at her, lifting his eyebrows and grinning rather sheepishly, and she groaned again.

"He picked *me* again?"

An odd expression flashed across Lars's face, and his brows leveled again. "*I* picked you." He strode over to the bath, hooking a towel in one hand as he passed the rack. He held it up to her. "This is a real bad one. She wasn't diagnosed properly and the symbiont is the only chance she has."

Killashandra heaved herself out of the bath, ignoring the entreaty in his eyes and the set of his lips. She stalked to the shower stall, the radiant fluid sleeting off her body with every step. She turned the water shower on full blast. From the curtain of water she glared at him, turning slowly to be sure the fluid rinsed off completely. Slamming the lever in the opposite direction, she deigned to take the towel from his hand. And sighed.

"Does Lanzecki need singers so badly he'll recruit the moribund?" she asked flippantly, drying herself, deliberately making the actions sensual. Catching that same odd expression on her partner's face, she realized that dalliance was the last thing on his mind just then.

"She hails from a planet named Fuerte. *I* thought you'd be the best representative the Guild could send."

She caught the slight emphasis of the personal pronoun. A second flippant remark was on her lips when she sensed that Lars really wanted her to take this assignment.

"Shuttle's waiting, Killa," he said gently. "She doesn't have much time."

"Shards! Why me?" She flipped the towel away, examining her body. "I don't even have a recent scar to show off. I couldn't prove the positive rejuvenation of the symbiont. Much less," she added with a wry smile, "much less that I originated on Fuerte."

"She doesn't have much time." Lars gave her his one-sided grin, though his blue eyes remained sad.

"And you're much better at Disclosure than anyone else I know."

Grumbling to herself, nevertheless Killashandra went to the closet and dragged out the first clean shipsuit she saw, thrusting her feet through the pant legs, shoving her arms down the sleeves, and closing the front as she used her toes to hook boots from the floor. She jammed her feet into them.

"Where've they stashed her?"

Lars's arm came around her shoulders and he nuzzled her ear, kissing fondly but with no hint of sensuality. "In Recruitment."

"Recruitment?"

He nodded. "You'll understand when you get there. Now go!"

In fact, he walked her to the lift and gave her another kiss when she exited at the shuttle level. Killashandra wasn't happy about Lanzecki preempting Lars's assistance, but she didn't really mind about her assignment—she had done it before.

The Ballybran symbiont was the last chance for those whose illnesses could not be cured by modern techniques. In a galactic civilization, minor human mutations could result in major immune reactions to relatively innocuous viruses that refused to respond even with an immense pharmacopoeia and therapeutics cunningly developed from old-world reliables and alien innovations. Exposure to the Ballybran symbiont had proved remarkably effective in almost every single case—at least the ones that reached the planet before the organ damage had gone past the point of retrieval. The obvious deterrent was that the patient then had to take up whatever new life the symbiont provided—and not always that of crystal singer, since that required perfect pitch. But crystal singing was not the only career available on Ballybran. Support skills and professions were always welcomed. Killa wondered what skills this new candidate might have. Maybe replace that dork in Lanzecki's office?

Lanzecki's personal shuttle was parked at the bay, and the pilot ceased lounging the moment she emerged from the lift, gesturing to her urgently to hurry. She gave him a smile, since he appeared to know her.

"What's the gen on this candidate?" she asked as she strapped herself in.

He nodded briefly and completed the formalities with Traffic Control, but he didn't answer until they had cleared Ballybran's atmosphere.

"The daughter of some planetary official . . ."

"Fuerte."

"Yeah, that's the place. Medic says they got her here just about in time. Some bug's doing nasty things to her spinal cord."

Killashandra gave a shudder.

"The irony is that she was trying to find a vaccine for the same infection."

"She's medical?" Medically trained personnel were valuable on Ballybran, despite the symbiont's benefices.

"Research and Development. Not enough R and very little D," he added.

Shankill Base cleared them immediately to the Guild portal.

"I'll wait," the pilot said with a nod as he opened the shuttle's lock.

The recruitment director, a rather portly and impressive-looking man, seemed immensely relieved at her arrival.

"This way, Killashandra Ree," he said. "They oughtn't to have left this so long," he added with a mixture of annoyance and criticism. "She may not make it."

Killa started to give a facetious response, but limited herself to a shrug.

"This way," he said, gesturing her away from the interview rooms toward one of the larger accommodations. "We *have* completed all the necessary formalities . . ."

"Then why—" She broke off, for he had palmed the door open and she was momentarily startled by the number of people crowded into the room. From the expressions on their faces, she began to understand some of the problems. The candidate was on a float, to one side of the room, a medic hovering anxiously and fussing with the dials of the support system that evidently kept the girl alive. Five people whose faces were tanned by Fuertan sun and anxious with fear rushed toward her, each addressing her with such urgency that she could understand nothing.

"Which of you are her parents?" Killashandra asked. "I can plainly see who's the applicant."

Two stepped forward while the other three looked displeased at being excluded.

"I am Governor Fiske-Ulass," the man said, "Donalla's father, and this is her mother, Dian Fiske-Ulass."

"So what's your problem?"

The man gave a twitch to his shoulders that suggested to Killa that he was rarely in the position of petitioner and found it unacceptable.

"We find that we are unable to accompany Donalla to Ballybran . . ."

"You may—if you wish to remain with her," Killa said drolly.

Irritation flickered in his eyes, but he went on, regarding her with growing suspicion. Fuertan officials hated being challenged.

"That there is absolutely no guarantee that this—this unusual symbiosis will cure her . . ."

The medic spoke up from the side of the room. "It *was* her option, Governor. Her option when she was still able to speak. She maintains that position."

Killa made eye contact with the medic. "She can no longer speak?"

"She *can* communicate," the medic replied, sending a glance at the governor, who flicked his fingers in repudiation of that statement.

"How?"

"If you have been in attendance on an invalid, you learn to interpret requirements . . ."

The governor snorted in dismissal, and the mother stifled a sob. Killa nodded her head in acceptance, however, and waited for the medic to continue.

"One blink of the eyelids is no, two is yes." She stepped away from the float, gesturing Killa to see for herself.

"Everyone blinks," the governor said.

Killa ignored him and approached the patient. Looking at the bleached white face, lines of long suffering and pain drawn on the papery-looking dry skin, Killashandra felt a stab of sympathy for this wreck of a human being. Her head was braced, and Killa had to bend slightly over her to see her eyes, light blue, alive and vivid in a sickly yellow that should have been healthy white.

"Is Ballybran symbiosis what you wish?" she asked.

The eyelids closed firmly once, then twice, and then the eyes held Killa's glance with an appeal that was crystal clear.

"What's the prognosis without symbiont?" she asked the medic.

"How she's held on to life this long is beyond me," the medic murmured. "A few more days at the most, and that's close to miraculous."

"And there's been full Disclosure, to which Donalla has agreed," Killa asked, lightly stressing the girl's name as she regarded the recruitment officer.

He nodded. "In strict accordance with regulations. But the parents have to sign in her place, since she is unable to. That's also regs."

"So what *is* your problem?"

"We've heard tales . . ." the mother blurted out while her husband glared suspiciously at Killashandra.

"That the symbiont changes people into monsters?" Killashandra asked, and knew that, indeed, that was their fear.

She snatched an ampoule from the medic's pack, smashed it against the table, and, to the horrified astonishment of those in the room, deliberately gouged her forearm with a shard of the broken glass. The lacerations were satisfactorily long and bled profusely.

"A monster that heals in minutes," Killa said, holding out her arm so that all could see how quickly the symbiont worked to stem blood flow and repair tissue. "Sign!" she said to the parents in her most imperious tone. "You've got thirty seconds before I leave . . . without her and her last chance to live."

It didn't take Dian Fiske-Ulass that long to reach for the document and scrawl her signature. She held the stylus out to her husband. "What *other* chance has Donalla got?" she cried.

"None," the medic said firmly, and closed her lips over whatever else she would have added.

With a shrug of angry resignation, the governor took

the stylus and scribbled his name, illegible, but embellished with rather fancy amendments. "There! You've taken my only daughter from me."

"And you're *governor* of Fuerte?" Killa asked with contempt and then turned to the medic. "Let's get her aboard the shuttle. The Guild Master sent his personal craft." She shot a jaundiced look at Fiske-Ulass.

The others trailed after the float, Dian beginning to sob, the governor trying to recover his public image by appearing sternly resolved.

As soon as the pilot saw them in the corridor, he moved forward to take the front end of the float from Killa, who gently took the other position from the medic.

"Give me your code and I'll let you know the outcome," she told her.

The medic jerked her head back at the retinue. "They're all staying on the station until . . ."

Killashandra snorted. "Our head medic will communicate all details to you. What's your name?"

The medic gave her a very odd smile. "Hendra Ree."

"Ree? You're a relative?" When the medic nodded, her eyes dancing a bit, Killa went on, "So you knew I was here?"

"You're something of a family legend, and I mentioned you, and Ballybran's symbiont, to Donalla when her condition disimproved," the medic told her as they maneuvered the float into the shuttle.

"Legend?" Killashandra asked, surprised, for she hadn't expected *her* family to remember her at all, considering she had left home in the company of an infamous crystal singer. She strapped in the handles of the float.

"Even in today's sophisticated tech societies, legends have their place."

"No, sir, not even in shuttle," they could hear the pilot saying. "Not unless you want to stay. Shards, the air in here was processed on Ballybran. You're getting enough just saying your farewells."

Instantly the governor backed out, restraining his wife from setting foot over the threshold.

The medic gave a little snort, tugged to be sure the straps were secure, and then, in a swift movement, bent to kiss Donalla's cheek. "Good luck, kid!" she whispered.

Hendra turned slightly as she left the shuttle and gave Killa a good-luck sign and a broad grin. Was that what you did when you met a family legend? Killa wondered.

"Let's move it," Killashandra said, belting into her seat as the pilot slipped into the control chair.

As soon as he was released from the satellite dock, he contacted Heptite HQ, telling them to be ready to receive the terminally ill applicant.

The medical team was squeezing through the portal before it was fully dilated. As they angled the float out, Killashandra noticed the tear streaks down the sick girl's pallid face.

"You're okay, Donalla?" she asked.

The eyelids closed twice, each time squeezing out tear drops, oddly emphatic in a bizarre fashion.

"I'll keep in touch, kid!" Killa added as the medical team whisked the girl away to the waiting lift.

Donalla wouldn't be in the Infirmary, but in one of the candidate rooms until she became infected by the symbiont. Killa hoped that it wouldn't take long for a body already so weakened and stressed by illness. There was an aura of courage about Donalla that Killa respected, and she hoped that the girl's stupid, bias-ridden parents hadn't dallied away her last hope of life.

She nodded her thanks to the pilot and then strode to the nearest comunit, asking for Lars Dahl.

"You got her?"

"Let's hope in a timely fashion. She's pretty far gone."

Lars gave a grunt. "All the easier for the symbiont to get to work—according to Medical."

"By the way, being Fuertan was no help!" Killa grinned at his look of query. "Except for the medic."

"That's right, keep me guessing."

"It appears," Killa said with a chuckle, "I'm a family legend."

"And all the time you thought you were a black sheep," Lars replied with a suitably dour expression.

"All this time I thought I had been expunged from the Ree genealogy."

"Well, well! Life has its little surprises, does it not?"

"When one can remember them!"

][CHAPTER 6][

Thinking that a legend ought to be compassion-
ate or kindly or at least welcoming, Killashandra accompanied Donalla to her new
quarters. Green-garbed medical personnel hovered,
checking dials and hooking up remote life-support gear.

Presnol, the Guild's senior medical officer, huddled
over the record printout, tsk-tsking, occasionally swearing, and looking extremely displeased with what he saw.

"Why do they leave it so late?"

"Miracles occur with every passing second," Killa
said.

"Well, it's been left bloody late," Presnol repeated
with a fierce scowl. "Why, her throat muscles aren't
even strong enough to operate an implant. How does
she communicate?"

"One blink is no, two are yes."

Presnol was clearly appalled. "What backwater
planet spawned her?"

Killa grinned. "A mudball named Fuerte. However, there's not a thing wrong with her ears."

Presnol swore again, his skin darkening with embarrassment. Then his expression cleared to a thoughtful look. "Hmmm, I certainly hope the symbiont can do its trick. With her background, she'd be invaluable in the labs."

Lowering her voice, Killa asked, "How long before you see any transitional traces?"

"In her weakened state, it won't take long. It better not take long."

"Here, symbiont. Nice symbiont, come here please," Killa said in a discreet whisper, as if calling a recalcitrant animal, then grinned wickedly at Presnol.

"That's about it." Then Presnol went up to the float, his expression blandly friendly. "I'm Presnol Outerad, head medical officer. I've read your files, and there's every chance that, in your current state, the symbiont has already entered your system. We will know fairly soon, once it has had a chance to filter through your blood, but I hesitate to subject you to unnecessary phlebotomies. There are several degrees the Transition can take. Of that I must apprise you. I think we all hope"—his gesture took in Killashandra—"that you enjoy one of the gentler forms." His grin was more friendly than professional. "I'd like to stay on in attendance, if you don't object?"

Killa was relieved by Presnol's manner and explanations. But then, Antona had trained him out of the false heartiness that some medical personnel affected. He was also dealing with someone medically trained, and the usual medic-patient interface would have been insulting. Her respect for Presnol rose. She saw Donalla blink firmly once.

"Very good. In your condition a monitor wouldn't be

adequate. However, if you become aware of any increase in discomfort, a rapid eyelid motion will attract my instant attention. You could experience . . ." And as he began to enumerate the manifestations, Killa saw Lars at the doorway, watching the scene, his expression somber.

Deciding that Donalla couldn't be in better hands, Killa tiptoed away.

"We could wait a little while, couldn't we, before we go off-planet?" she asked Lars.

He regarded her with no expression whatever for a long moment, and then gave her a quick hug. "We certainly should wait to see how Donalla makes out. Being a fellow Fuertan and all . . ."

He ducked before she could pummel him.

The symbiont took very little time installing itself in Donalla's immune-deficient body. Speech returned first, and she indulged in a near-hysterical spate of weeping, which was certainly understandable and relieved her of a backlog of stress. Weeping could be quite therapeutic, Presnol remarked when he reported to Lars and Killa, as pleased as if he had had more to do with it than the symbiont.

"Back from the jaws of death, and all that," he said proudly.

Killa exchanged glances with Lars, and they both managed not to laugh.

"What's her alteration?" Lars asked.

Presnol regarded him blankly. "How on earth could we know that yet? Why, she's barely—"

"Back from the jaws of death, Lars," Killa said, struggling to keep her expression bland. "How can she possibly know how she's changed?"

"Point." Lars's lips twitched. "We'll look in on her later," he added, and blanked the screen.

Killa let loose the giggle she had been controlling. "The jaws of death, indeed!"

When they came to visit, Donalla was sitting up, propped by pillows, able to move her head and even to raise one limp, wasted hand in greeting.

"I'd hoped to be able to thank you in person, Killashandra Ree," she said.

Although her voice was low, it was a rich, warm contralto. Killa wondered if the woman was actually musically inclined and might have come out of Transition as a singer.

"Why? We Fuertans have to stick together in this alien environment," Killashandra replied genially, appropriating one of the guest chairs while Lars took the other.

Two days had improved Donalla Fiske-Ulass considerably. Her face had lost its gaunt, wasted look; her hazel eyes had gained a sparkle, her skin a healthier color; her lips were pink and less pinched. In fact, from a death's-head she was quickly turning into a rather attractive woman. Perhaps even pretty, and Killa shot a glance at Lars, who, as he had often told her, liked to look—only look—at pretty women. "Easier on the eyes than ugly ones." But there was nothing in his expression other than attentive concern and interest.

Donalla dropped her eyelids, covering either embarrassment or confusion.

"I didn't even know about the Heptite Guild until Hendra mentioned it, and you."

Killa shrugged. "Why should you?"

"It would have saved me a great deal of stress if I *had* known more about Fuertan notables."

Killa snorted just as Lars said, with a mischievous

glint in his eyes, "And here you always gave me the impression you were a renegade, Killa!"

"I suppose in time even renegades become respectable," Killa said diffidently. But she was irritated: she couldn't remember any details of her departure from Fuerte. Except that she had been very glad to go. Perhaps it was just as well that she *had* forgotten the circumstances. Maybe she hadn't *wanted* to remember. Being a crystal singer made that easy enough.

"You told me that you almost didn't make it off the planet with Carrik," Lars said. He turned to Donalla. "Were you given the usual misinformation that crystal singers are wicked, dangerous, eager to entice the unwary into their lairs, corrupting the innocent?"

Donalla gave a little smile, her eyes glinting slightly. "No, but then my informant was a relative, as much of a renegade as I guess you were, Killashandra. She thought you were daring and adventurous. She was thrilled with the chance to meet you, you know."

"Really?" Killashandra was amused. That hadn't come across in Hendra's brief conversation with her, but they had had other priorities at the time. "Certainly I managed to escape Fuerte."

"It's changed since you were there," Donalla said loyally.

"It would have had to," Killa said dryly. She changed the subject. "Presnol tells me you're over the worst of the Transition."

Donalla managed another of her semi-smiles. "I'm unaware of any Transition . . ."

"That's it exactly," Killa said, rather pleased. "The symbiont was kind to you. You won't be bedridden much longer."

"I'm deeply grateful for that, I assure you. I just wish

that I'd been allowed here earlier when the extent of my paralysis was appreciated."

"Just like Fuertans to resist the inevitable," Killa said.

"My parents only wanted the best for me," Donalla said.

Lars rose then. "Let's not tire her, Killa."

Obediently Killa followed his lead, although Donalla protested that she enjoyed company—especially now that she could talk again.

"I've a lot of catching up to do."

"We have, too," Lars said cryptically, guiding Killashandra out of the room.

"What did you mean by that?" she asked him when they were walking down the corridor.

He said nothing, pretending to concentrate on the Met reports as he guided her down the corridor to the lifts to the administrative level. When she realized that their destination was Lanzecki's office, she tried to pull away from him.

"Oh, no! I'm not falling for one of Lanzecki's deals. And you're daft if you let him talk you into anything. We're in good credit, Lars. We can coast for a while. What we need to do is get out in the Ranges again. We've hung about far too long."

"We don't have to worry about Lanzecki," Lars said in a tight voice. "He's not involved, Killa. Come in, please."

She couldn't withstand the entreaty in his voice; she entered the anteroom warily, looking about her.

Trag's desk was empty. Killashandra frowned, realizing vaguely that she wouldn't have seen Trag anyway. Splinters of recall suggested that there had been someone else, someone she didn't like. Lars had his hand on her back now and was propelling her into the office. It was empty. She looked about, wondering where Lanzecki had gone. Lars released her and, striding around the desk, sat down in the Guild Master's big chair.

"Killashandra Ree," Lars began in a tone she had never heard him use before: part entreaty, part frustration, and part anger. "You've simply got to recognize that Lanzecki is dead. You knew that two months ago. You even insisted that no one try to rescue him from Bollam . . ." She recognized that name and put an unattractive face to it. But Lars wasn't finished. "Have you got that lodged in your head? Finally? Lanzecki is dead."

Killashandra stared at Lars, uncomfortably aware that this was something else she had conveniently managed to forget. She shouldn't forget who was Guild Master. He was the most important person to a crystal singer, to all Heptite Guild members.

"There has to be a Guild Master . . ." she began, floundering badly as the discomfort swelled and brushed against concepts and images that she didn't want to remember.

"There is a Guild Master, Killashandra." Lars's tone was kind, soothing, his expression concerned. "I am the Guild Master now."

"No!" She backed away from the desk.

He jumped to his feet and came around the desk, arms outstretched to her, his expression both desperate and supplicatory.

"I know you've been resisting it, Sunny. I know that you've suppressed the fact of Lanzecki's death, but it is a fact. It's also a fact that I've been appointed Guild Master in his place. I would like you to be my executive partner in this, as you have been my partner in the Ranges."

Killashandra shook her head at him, more and more

forcefully as she resisted the sense of his statements. How could Lars become Guild Master? That was absurd. He was *her* partner. They sang crystal together. They were the best duet the Guild had ever had. They *had* to return to the Ranges and sing crystal. With Lanzecki dead it was more important than ever that *they* sing crystal—black crystal, green crystal, blue! A Guild Master didn't have the time to sing crystal. Lars had to sing crystal with her. He couldn't be the Guild Master.

"I know, Sunny," Lars went on more kindly. "His death *is* hard to take. He was such a force for us all. I'd like to be as good a leader, but I want—I need—your help. You're incontestably the best singer the Guild has. You know more about singing crystal than anyone else, and you can explain what you know. Many can't articulate or convey the information they have locked in their brains. You can. Hell, you taught me!" He grinned with wry flattery. "That's only one reason why I need your cooperation and your input." He had come close enough to take her in his arms, trying with his clever hands, to which she had always responded, to soothe her distress and somehow stroke her into acceptance of the hard truths he had given her.

"There, there, Sunny. I see now that I was wrong to let you forget what you didn't want to remember just because I could always remember for you. But now I don't have that luxury. And I *need* you as my partner more than ever."

"But I'm a crystal singer. I'm not a—an office flunky."

Lars gave a brief laugh. "You think Trag was a flunky?"

"Trag was—Trag," Killa finished lamely, casting about for any rebuttal he would accept as her refusal. Lanzecki was Guild Master. He had been and would be.

Trag . . . She wasn't Trag. She wasn't anything like Trag.

"I know it'll take getting used to, Sunny, but accept the reality. Accept me as the Guild Master. I know I'm not Lanzecki, but each Guild Master puts his own stamp on the Guild, and I've got some positive, if bizarre, ideas on how to improve—"

"That's why Lanzecki monopolized you so much," she said in petulant accusation. "That's why you had so many meetings with him!"

"Believe me, Killa, I didn't *know* what Lanzecki was doing. I had no idea that he was briefing me to take over from *him*. But he did think my ideas had merit . . ."

Killa stared at the man who had been her constant companion to the point where she could not envision life without him at her side. She stared at his familiar face and wondered that she knew so little about him.

"You could have said no," she whispered, appalled by what he was saying, and by what he wanted of her. "You didn't *have* to accept the appointment."

"Lanzecki suggested it with terms I couldn't refuse."

"You *want* to be Guild Master!" she accused him.

He shook his head slowly, a sad smile on his lips. "No, Sunny, I didn't *want* to be Guild Master. But I am, and I'm going to improve the Guild, and every kicking, screaming resisting member will benefit."

"Benefit? I don't like the sound of that." She stepped back from him. "What's wrong with the Guild the way it is? Who do you think you are to *change* it?" Her voice rose, shrilling with the growing sense of panic that enveloped her. "You're not Lanzecki! You've never cared about the Guild before. Just sailing. That's all you care about—sailing and seas and ships . . ." And, whirling, she ran from the office.

"Killa, love, let me explain!" he called after her.

She bashed at the lift buttons, begging the door to open and get her out of there. Lars was a seaman, not a Guild Master. Lanzecki was. He always had been. The stable, safe, and secure pivot of her life in the Guild. The door slid open and she jumped inside the car, pounding the panel to make the door close before Lars could reach her. He was going to talk her into this, too, because he could always convince her that his suggestions would work. She wouldn't let him wheedle her into an *office* job. He would keep her out of the Ranges, keep her from cutting crystal, and she would end up like Trag— with less and less symbiont protection. That's what had killed Trag: no protection.

She had to protect herself against Lars now. He would talk her into doing something she did not want to do. The Guild didn't need to be changed! It had run perfectly well for centuries. What could possibly need changing? Well, she wasn't going to help. Best cutter in the Guild, huh? Just the kind of soft talk that had gotten Lars his way with her too often! Make her a stand-in for Trag, would he? She wasn't old sobersides Trag, critical, unswerving, duty-bound. She was Killashandra Ree. She always would be! The door opened again, and she fled. At first she didn't realize where she was; then, when she recognized the Hangar floor, she gasped with relief. She mustn't let Lars catch up with her.

She'd lose herself in the Ranges and then Lars, the Guild Master, wouldn't be able to find her. She'd go as deep as she could, past any claim they had made together. She'd find new ones, ones he didn't dream existed. She'd cut and cut and she'd show the Guild Master that she was too important a cutter to be restricted to an *office!*

She was only peripherally aware that the flight officer was trying to tell her something. She repeated her urgent request for her sled. When he seemed recalcitrant, trying to restate his message, she barged past him, running toward the racks where sleds were stored. Hers was in the first rank, so she climbed to it, palmed the cabin door open, and settled herself in the pilot's seat. She checked the engines, slipped on the headpiece, and heard the babble from Operations.

"I want clearance and I don't want any nonsense. I have got to get out into the Ranges. Is that understood?"

Suddenly the voices that were trying to dissuade her went silent. There was a long pause during which she revved the engines and clenched and unclenched her hands on the yoke, waiting for her release. She'd go without it if she had to. She was reaching for the propulsion toggle when the silence ended.

"Killashandra Ree, clear to go," said a tenor voice, flat with a lack of emotion. "Good luck, singer!"

She was in such a swivet to depart that she didn't realize that it wasn't the flight officer who had released her. She eased the sled out of the rack and headed for the open Hangar door. Once clear, she pointed the nose of the sled north. She allowed the merest margin of distance before she engaged the drive. The relief of her escape diminished the discomfort of gravitational pressure as the sled obediently shot forward, shoving her deep in the cushioning.

The first storm caught her still looking for a possible site. She didn't return to the Guild. She headed farther north, skipping across the sea away from the storm, and settled on the North Continent to wait out the heavy weather. She slept most of the interval, then returned to the Ranges and continued her search.

Lack of supplies, especially water, finally drove her

back. She stayed only long enough to replenish her stores, ignoring all suggestions from both the flight and cargo officers, both of whom were desperately trying to delay her. Lanzecki probably had something in mind for her, and she didn't want any part of it.

"It isn't Lanzecki, Killa," Cargo insisted, her expression troubled. "Donalla—"

"I don't know any Donalla." And Killashandra brushed past the woman and slid into her restocked sled and closed the door firmly.

As she maneuvered the sled out of the Hangar, the flight officer kept wildly pointing to his headphones, wanting her to open up her comline, but she ignored him and sped away, taking a zigzag course at such speed that no one could track her.

She finally found crystal—deep greens in dominants. She was still cutting when the alarms in her sled went off. That made her stop—briefly—and consult her weather sense. For the first time it had not given her advance notice. Or had it? She'd had a few sessions with crystal thrall lately. Perhaps . . . But it was only the first of the warnings. She had time.

She almost didn't, for the last of the greens, a massive plinth, thralled her, and only the lashing of gale-force winds broke the spell by knocking her off balance and out of the trance.

Frantic to load her cartons, for she obviously hadn't bothered to for several days, she worked against the slimmest margin ever. Luck barely hung on to the fins of her sled, for the crash came on the very edge of the storm, near enough for a crew to rescue the crystal and her battered body. The sled was a write-off.

*   *   *

"Whaddid I cut? How much did I earn?" were Killashandra's first coherent questions when she finally roused from accident trauma.

"Enough, I gather, to replace your sled, Killa," a female voice said.

Killashandra managed to open her eyes, though her lids were incredibly heavy to raise. It was hard to focus, but gradually she was able to distinguish a woman's face.

She retrieved a suitable name with effort. "Antona?"

"No, not Antona. Donalla."

"Donalla?" Killa peered earnestly, blinking furiously to clear her sight. She didn't recognize the face. "Do I know *you?*"

"Not very well." There was a slight ripple of amusement in the tone. "But a while ago you saved my life."

"I don't remember cutting crystal with anyone."

"Oh, I'm not a singer. I'm a medic. Do you remember anything at all about helping persuade my parents to let me come to Ballybran?"

"No." When Killa began to shake her head to emphasize the negative, she experienced considerable pain. "I've had little to do with recruitment," she said repressively. "I sing crystal. I don't entice people to it."

"You didn't entice me, Killashandra Ree, but you did give my parents incontrovertible proof that the Ballybran symbiont heals. Fast."

"It has to, doesn't it, to keep singers in the field? I nearly bought it this time, didn't I?"

"As near as makes no never mind," said a man's voice. That one was familiar—and panic welled up in her. Him she didn't want to see. That much she remembered. She turned her head away from the direction of the voice—the Guild Master's voice.

A hand clasped her fingers warmly, the thumb caressing the back of her hand with an intimacy she found both reassuring and insidious. She tried to pull away and hadn't the strength to do so.

"Mangled yourself rather extensively, Sunny. I've always been afraid that would happen. If I'd been there . . ."

Infuriated, she did manage to snatch her hand free. "You weren't. You were in an office. Where the Guild Master has to stay!" She chewed the words out spitefully, and when she saw his face come into her line of vision, she raised her arm, despite the pain, to cover her eyes. "You had your chance to cut crystal with me. Go away." She flung her arm in his direction in an effort to strike him.

"I think you'd better go, Lars. Your presence is definitely not reassuring. She's incoherent."

"On the contrary, Donalla, she's most coherent."

"Please, Lars, don't take her seriously. Not now. She's in considerable pain despite the symbiont."

"She'll survive?"

"Oh, most certainly. The lacerations are healing quickly, and the leg bones are almost completely joined. Strained tendons and pulled muscles take a little longer to mend."

"Let me know when she's . . . herself again, will you, Donalla? And suggest . . ."

"I'll keep you informed, Lars, and I won't suggest anything right now. It would be totally inappropriate."

Killashandra moved restlessly, subconsciously resenting the friendliness of the exchanges, the subtle inference of a relationship between the two speakers: this Donalla and the man she did not want to acknowledge at all.

"I'm giving you something to put you out a while longer, Killashandra," the woman said, and Killa felt the cold of a spray on her neck. "You'll be better when you wake."

"Nothing's ever better when you wake."

It was morning when next she woke, or so the digital on the wall told her. Day, month, and year were never a function of Heptite timekeepers. And, as the Infirmary was deep in the bowels of the Guild, shielded against the ravages of Passover storms, a wall hologram reflected the external weather. Somehow a bright clear morning seemed blasphemous to Killashandra. She groaned. But the bed sensors had already picked up the alteration in her sleep pattern, and the door opened, a bright face peering around it.

"Hungry?"

"Ravenous," Killa said with a groan. Hunger also seemed a travesty to her, and she buried her face in the pillows.

"Be right back."

Food did set immediate needs to rights. Sitting up to eat also emphasized her recuperation. She didn't hurt, though her limbs felt very stiff. She examined her arms and legs and ran wondering fingers down the whitening scars that showed how horrific her wounds had been. Inevitably that reminded her that she had crashed the sled. She couldn't quite face that yet, so she heaved herself out of bed and went into the bathroom to run a deep tub of hot water, full of aromatics to ease the lingering stiffness. Finally, refreshed as well as more flexible, she settled at the room terminal and tapped out her personal code. Ignoring the line that invited her to update her memory data, she accessed her credit balance. For a moment her spirits sank. There wasn't enough to replace the sled.

Wait a minute. There was not enough credit to replace the sled she had crashed, but that one had been a double. She wasn't singing duet anymore. She had enough for a single, maybe not top of the line, but sufficient to get her back into the Ranges and, if she bought just basic rations, enough supplies for a month. She tapped out a query about her cutter. If she had banjaxed the cutter, she would be in heavy debt. Not for long, she assured herself. Not for long. She'd cut—blacks again—and show him! She dialed the cutter's facility, but no one answered. She couldn't remember the current one's name and stewed over that. She called up the Admin roster to see who it was: "Clarend nab Ost" rang no bells and, evidently, answered no calls to his or her quarters. Fortunately the girl arrived with lunch to distract a growing sense of frustration.

By the time she had finished the second hearty meal, she had also managed to contact Clarend nab Ost, who had a few choice words to say about someone who would leave her cutter unracked, crash, and then expect the tool to be ready to go. She hotly insisted that she *always* racked her cutter.

"So how come it was stuck in the cargo hatch door?" he asked snidely.

That silenced her. She was far more appalled by that lapse than she was about crashing the sled or her own injuries. So she apologized profusely, and Clarend finally ended his tirade against careless, derelict, wanton, blasé, feeble-minded, lack-witted singers and their sins, errors, and shame. Then he told her in a less trenchant tone that he hadn't quite finished repairs and he couldn't vouch for its continued efficiency if she abused it her next time in the Ranges and she was bloody lucky she had a cutter at all the way she'd treated it.

Oddly enough, the episode made her feel somewhat better: things were normal when one got properly chewed out by a technician for blatant irresponsibility. She called the Hangar and asked how long she would have to wait for a replacement single.

"I've enough credit—unless you've jacked the cost up again," she told the supply officer.

"The very idea of our benefiting by your misfortune! Single, you want now? I thought—"

"You're not keeping up with the gossip, Ritwili," she said so angrily that there was a long silence. "Haul one out of stock and commission it, provision it. Basic rations for a month. I should be out of here soon."

"Not quite 'soon,'" interrupted the medic who had overheard the last of her conversation.

Killa frowned: the woman looked familiar . . . and yet unfamiliar. Killashandra shrugged, unable to prod recall.

"In case you've forgotten, I'm Donalla Fiske-Ulass, a fellow planetarian from Fuerte," the woman said, advancing to the bed. Her voice ended on an upnote of inquiry.

Killa sighed and shook her head. "I don't remember. Don't expect me to."

"Oh, I do. I expect that the woman who saved my life should remember the fact," Donalla said blandly, shoving her hands in the pockets of her clinical coat. She was a very attractive woman, slender without being thin— although the idea of thinness tweaked Killashandra's memory. Her hair was curly and short, and framed a delicate-featured, clever face. She had lovely eyes and exuded an air of authority and competence. "Especially when I consider myself under obligation to you."

"There're no obligations in the Guild," Killa reminded her.

"Among singers, no, because you lot are, and have to be, competitive, dedicated, and woefully single-minded." Donalla grinned again. "So you'll allow me to discharge my obligation to you."

"I said, I don't recognize that there is one."

"You could if you remembered it," Donalla insisted, and something in the almost wheedling tone made Killashandra wary.

"I avoid people trying to do me good," she said in a flat and, she hoped, discouraging voice.

Donalla perched on the edge of the bed and regarded Killashandra for a moment. "That's because you haven't heard what the good bit is."

"Do I have to?" Killa sighed resignedly.

"Yes, because the Guild Master has asked me to approach every singer on this matter."

"Oh, he has." Killa set up an immediate resistance to the notion.

Donalla laughed lightly, as if she recognized the reaction and had expected it. "Hmmm, yes, well. Quite a few singers have taken me up on my offer."

"Enough of the jollying. Inform me in words of one syllable."

"Don't be churlish, Killashandra Ree." There was a caustic tone to Donalla's voice now that made Killashandra regard her with surprise. "Since I recovered my health here, I've tried to figure a way around the most important drawback that all singers face."

"How kind of you!" Killashandra gave a supercilious snort.

"Kindness has little to do with it. An efficient use of singers' time and energies does. Singers lose memory function every time they go into the Ranges. They lose crucial details of the precise location of valuable sites."

"Detail maybe, but not the resonance that'll lead you right back to a good claim," Killashandra said, shaking her head to dismiss Donalla's faulty logic.

"Only if you go right back into the Ranges. How
much more convenient it would be to *recall* the exact
locations by accurately remembering the relevant landmarks."

"And leave such information around for other singers to access? No way! Try another on me."

"I'm not *trying* anything on you. I've already had
notable success in accessing memory in crystal-mazed
singers' minds."

"You've what?" Killashandra sat up, fury building in
her at such an intrusion. Who did this woman think she
was?

"I had the Guild Master's authority, and it's—"

"Get out of here. I don't want any part of such a
scheme. That Guild Master of yours must be out of his
gourd to permit such harassment. That's the worst example of privacy invasion I've ever heard."

"But so much information can be restored," Donalla
said urgently, bending toward Killashandra in an effort
to win her over. "So much lost memory can be retrieved."

"I haven't lost anything I want retrieved." Killashandra was a decibel away from a shout. "Go peddle
your nonsense to someone else, Donalla. Leave me
alone!"

"But I want to *help* you, Killashandra," Donalla said,
switching tactics.

"I don't need that kind of help. Now go, or do I have
to throw you out? I'm well enough to do so, you know."
And she half rose from her chair.

Donalla pushed off the edge of the bed and took a
step back, flustered. "You'll be helping Lars Dahl as
well, you know. Not to mention your Guild."

"Spare me the sentimental violin passage, Donalla.
Loyalty is another commodity singers lack and don't

need!" Killashandra completed her rise in one fluid movement, delighted that her body would respond so readily. She grabbed Donalla by the arm, turned her toward the door, and forcefully ejected her from the room. "And don't come back."

"If you'd only listen . . ." Donalla began, but Killa shut the door on her entreaty.

"Regression isn't painful!" The woman was incredible, shouting through a closed door at her. With one twist of the volume control, Killa turned on to full whatever program was on the in-room entertainment, drowning out Donalla's voice. Then she threw on the door privacy lock.

For a long moment she seethed, letting the music, some sort of a baroque chorus, roll over her. The song was familiar to her. She picked up the soprano line, surprised and pleased to be able to add words to the notes. She broke off singing when, even to herself, her voice sounded harsh and strident.

Well, wouldn't it? When she was being harassed by a silly bitch who had made a unilateral decision about what Killashandra Ree "needed"? Only Killashandra Ree could make those decisions. She had earned that right, by all the holies! Ridiculous woman! Absurd notion—reviving useless baggage of memories. And the Guild Master agreed?

Killa exhaled in disgust, reviewing what Donalla had said. Her memory might be faulty, but she had been reading voices for years. She snorted again, remembering tonalities and inflections that told her more than Donalla might have intended. The woman had said Lars's name in a tone that indicated more than casual acquaintance with him, intimating a relationship that was more than work-oriented. They were a fine pair, they were! Well suited! If she'd known the woman would take on this way, behaving like a conscience, she'd've let her die in the Recruitment Room!

"There, too, I *can* remember—when I want to!" Killa muttered to herself. Then she laughed as she heard the childish petulance in her voice. She remembered the important things, like how to fly a sled, how to locate claims, how to cut—and, most important of all, she generally remembered *what* to cut in order to get top market value on her crystal. What more did she need to remember? The petty details of everyday life? The trivia that clogged the brain and got in the way: the incidents that humiliated or enraged, the bilge, bosh, claptrap that happened while traveling, things inconsequential when one would only be visiting the world once?

What about remembering the new world?

If it was worthwhile, interesting, or exciting, I'll remember it, she told herself.

Will you?

I can, if I want to! I can!

She slept away the afternoon and awoke to hear a tentative tapping on her door. It was the bright little infirmary aide wanting to serve her dinner. She ate heartily, trying to ignore the fact that someone had gone to the trouble of ordering a selection of her favorite foods. That would pad the charges for her Infirmary usage. Ah, well. She'd always paid for exotics, and the Yarran beer did go down a treat!

She didn't see the irritating Donalla over the next three days but had several sessions with therapists, who worked to help her regain full muscle tone. She retrieved her cutter from Clarend, who warned her again to remember—*remember*—that she couldn't abuse her cutter again or she would have to replace it. She took possession of a sparkling brand-new sled.

"I won't tell you how many you've banged up over the years, Killa," Ritwili told her in a sour tone as he extended the purchase order for her signature. "And stocking it took the rest of your credit. You're in the red right now—so cut well!"

She paused long enough to contact Clodine and find out what crystal she ought to look for.

"Someone's wanting those deep amethysts and, of course, any black you stumble across," Clodine said with a grin. "You've a natural affinity for them anyway, and blacks are always needed."

"Yeah." Killa wasn't all that happy with her affinity. She liked the money from blacks but not cutting them solo. They tended to thrall more easily than any other color. "I'll remember that."

She was not the only singer departing the Guild Hangar that day: fifteen others were making ready and each of them was determined to be the last one out and thus not only see the direction every other singer was taking but conceal his or her own ultimate destination.

Disgusted, Killashandra gave up waiting. At this rate, it would be dark before she made any significant progress into the Range. Noting the marks of age and misuse on most of the other vehicles, she realized that with her new sled, she could easily outfly any of them. She asked, and received, clearance, along with a heartfelt thanks from the flight officer, who was losing patience with the dilatory singers.

"Blinding damn paranoid, the lot of 'em," he muttered, forgetting to close the circuit.

"You better believe it," Killa said with a laugh, and eased her new vehicle through the Hangar's immense outer doors.

The exchange put Killashandra in a good mood, which improved even more when she heard five other singers suddenly demanding clearance. Well, she'd show them!

Capriciously she zipped off at a speed inappropriate for her proximity to the Hangar, laughing at the flight officer's irate reprimand. Running at a recklessly low altitude over the uneven terrain of the foothills, she built the sled up to maximum power as fast as she dared.

"Try to follow me now, you dorks! Shatter yourself on the hills trying!"

She let out a musical hurrah as the ground hurtled past her. Lyrics to the aria deserted her, but she sang on, using vowels and singing at the top of her lungs, reveling in her renewed freedom.

CHAPTER 7

Killashandra came in from the Milekey Mountains with a load of blue-quartz prisms and cylinders in A-sharp or higher. She had always worked well solo in the upper registers, which gave her a distinct advantage over most crystal singers.

She made it into the Hangar on a windy blast from the oncoming storm. Cutting it fine again, but she grinned at having made it without harm to herself or her sled. That was all that mattered: coming back in the same state of mind or body as she had gone out. Still, and in the back of her mind, she allowed herself to be relieved that her recklessness had not exacted a penalty.

Being one of the last in, she had to wait for Clodine to be free to assay her crystal. It was a long wait, especially with every nerve in her body screaming for the radiant fluid that would reduce the resonance to a mild discomfort. The storm outside seemed to stroke her body to an intense pitch. She shuddered from time to time, but managed to survive the waiting.

149

When Clodine told her she had hit the top of the market, she could feel the physical relief course through her despite storm scream.

"I've been due a change of luck," she said, wincing as she remembered the last week in the Range. The sun had been fierce on the scars of her cuttings, half blinding her, and the scream of crystal had sliced through her mind as she had cut. But she had been desperate to hack enough cargo to get off-world for a while—away from crystal song, far away, so her mind would have a chance to heal. "How much?"

Clodine peered up at her from her console, a little smirk bending the left corner of her mouth. "Don't you trust me anymore, Killa?"

"At this point, I wouldn't trust my own mother—if I could remember who she was," Killa replied. She forced a smile for Clodine on her grimy lips and tried to relax. Clodine was her friend. She would know how badly Killa needed to get away from Ballybran and crystal whine. "Is it enough?"

Clodine altered her enhanced eyes and gazed at Killashandra almost maternally. "You've been a singer long enough, Killa, to know when you've cut sufficient crystal."

"Tell me!" With totally irrational fury, Killashandra brought both fists down on the counter, jarring the crystal and startling Clodine to blink into enhancement. Immediately she relented. "I'm sorry, Clodine. I shouldn't shout at my only friend. But . . ."

"You've enough," Clodine said gently. She reached to grasp Killa's arm encouragingly, but drew back her fingers as if she had been burned. The Sorter's expression altered to sadness. Then her gaze switched to someone over her shoulder.

Killashandra jerked her head slightly sideways to see

who had joined them. It was the Guild Master. She looked back at Clodine, ignoring the man as she had done for a long time now.

"Killa," he said, his tenor voice pitched to concern, "that was cutting it too close by half. You shouldn't work solo for a while. Any singer in the Guild would partner you for a couple of runs."

"I'll work as I please," she said, forcing her wretchedly tired body into a straight and obstinate line. "I'm not so ancient that I can't scramble when I have to."

The Guild Master pointed to the weather displayed on the back wall of the Sorting Shed, and despite herself, Killashandra followed his finger. She maintained a show of diffidence, but she felt cold fear in her belly. She hadn't realized the storm was that powerful: twelve-mach-force winds? Had her weather sense betrayed her? Lost its edge? No, but she *had* been deeper in the Ranges than she realized when she started out. She could well have been caught out over crystal. But she hadn't. And she had safely brought in enough crystal to get off-planet again.

"A good blow," she said with a defensive shrug and a wry twist of her lips, "but it's going to knock hell out of my claim."

The Guild Master touched her shoulder lightly; he did not pull away from her as Clodine had. "Just don't go back solo, Killa." She dipped out from under his hand. He continued, "You've sung crystal a long time now. You kited in here just ahead of a mach-twelve storm and one day you'll stay just that moment too long and—poof!" He threw his hands up, fingers wide. "Scrambled brains."

"That's the time, Guild Master," she said, still with her back to him, "that I get some of my own back."

She saw the pity and concern in Clodine's eyes.

"With your ears ruptured and your mind a balloon? Sure, Killa. Sure. Look, there're half a dozen good cutters who'd double you any time you raised your finger. Or don't you *remember*"—and the Guild Master's voice turned soft—"how much you made singing duet . . ."

"With Lars Dahl!" Killashandra made her voice flat and refused to look around.

"We worked well together, Killa." His voice was still soft.

"How kind of you to remember, Guild Master."

She turned away from the counter, but he stepped in front of her.

"I was wrong, Killashandra. It's too late for you to cut duo. Crystal's in your soul." He strode out of the shed, leaving her standing there.

She tried to be amused by the accusation—but, from him, it cut like crystal. As if she would want to sing duet again. Especially with Lars Dahl. She cast her mind back, trying to recall some details of those halcyon days. Nothing came. They must have happened a long, long time ago: many storms, many Passovers, many cuts past.

"Killa?"

At the sound of Clodine's voice, Killashandra jerked herself back to the present: the tote was up on the screen—and the news was good. Even with the Guild tithe, she had enough to keep out of the Ranges for close to a year. Maybe that would be enough to take crystal out of her soul.

The Guild Master had to be wrong about that! He had to be! She thanked Clodine, who seemed relieved that her friend's mood had altered.

She stopped in the Hall long enough to tap in her name and get a locator keyed into her quarters. It had long since stopped irritating her that she couldn't remember where she lived in the great cube of the Heptite Guild. She merely let the locator guide her. The mach winds seemed to follow her, echoing through the lift and the corridor. The key vibrated more imperiously in her hand and she hurried. The sooner she immersed herself in the radiant bath, the sooner she would be rid of the angry pulsing of crystal in her blood.

No, it wasn't in her blood. Not yet.

So there were men willing to cut duo with her, were there? Well, Guild Master, what if it's not just any man who is acceptable to *me?* The door to her quarters sprang open as she neared it, so she began to trot. It was going to take so long to fill the radiant bath. Somehow there ought to be a way to trigger that amenity from afar, especially for singers as crystal-logged as she was. Once, someone—what was his name?—someone had done her that courtesy and she had always returned to her room to find the tub full.

As she turned the corner into the sanitary facility, she was amazed to see the tap running the viscous liquid in a bath that was nearly full. But that someone—she pulled at memory even as she pulled off her grimed jumpsuit—was long dead. She was eternally grateful to whoever had started the bath. The Guild Master? Not likely. What had been that other man's name?

She could abuse her mind no longer with pointless attempts to remember. With an immense sigh of relief, she eased into the liquid, feeling it just slightly heavy against her skin, filling her pores. Her flesh gratefully absorbed the anodyne and she placed her head into the recess, slipping her legs and arms into the restraining straps. She forced muscle after weary muscle to relax, willing the resonances to stop echoing through her bones.

She must have slept: she had been exhausted enough to do so. But she felt slightly better. This would be a four-bath cleansing, she decided, and let the used fluid out.

"Dispenser!" she called, loudly enough to activate the mechanism in the other room, and when it chimed its attention, she ordered food. She waited until the second chime told her the food was ready. "Now if they'd only invent a 'bot to bring it to me . . ."

In her past, she hadn't had to worry about that detail, had she? That much she remembered. She crawled out of the tub, setting it for refill, and, flinging a big towel about her, she made for the dispenser slot, ignoring the puddles made by the fluid that sheeted off her body as she walked. The aroma of the food activated long-unused saliva.

"Don't eat too much, Killa," she warned herself, knowing perfectly well what would happen to her un-derserved stomach if she did. *That* much she always remembered.

She had a few bites and then forced herself to bring the tray back to the tub, where she rested it on the wide rim. Climbing back into the filling tub, she moved her body under the splash from the wide-mouthed tap. With one hand on the rim, she scooped milsi stalks into her mouth, one at a time, chewing conscientiously.

She really must remember to eat when she was in the Ranges. Muhlah knew her sled was well-enough stocked, and since the provisions were paid for, she ought to eat them. If she remembered.

By her fourth bath, she recollected snatches and patches of her last break. They didn't please her. For one thing, she had come in with a light load, forced off the Range a few klicks ahead of a storm. She had reaped the benefits of that blow this trip, of course—that was the way of it with crystal. If a singer could get back to the vicinity of a lode fast enough, the crystal resonated and told her body where it was. But she hadn't had enough credit to get off-planet, a trip she had desperately needed then—though not half as much as she did now.

She'd had to take what relief she could from a handsome and somewhat arrogant young landsman on the upper continent: tone-deaf, sobersided, but he hadn't been man enough to anneal her.

"Crystal in my soul, indeed!" The Guild Master's words stung like crystal scratch.

She made a noise of sheer self-disgust and pulled herself from the tank, knocking the tray off. She turned to the big wall mirror, watching the fluid sheet off her body, as firm and graceful as a youngster's. Killashandra had long since given up keeping track of her chronological age: it was irrelevant anyway, since the symbiont kept her looking and feeling young. Not immortality but close to it—except for the youth of her memory.

"Now where will I go off this fecking planet this time?" she asked her reflection, and then slid open the dresser panel.

She was mildly surprised at the finery there and decided she must have spent what credit she'd had for pretty threads to lure that unwary landsman. He had been a brute of a lover, though a change. Anything had been a change from Lars Dahl. How dare the Guild Master suggest that she'd better duo! He had no right or authority, no lien or hold on her to dictate her choice!

Angrily Killashandra punched for Port Authority and inquired the destinations of imminent departures from Shankill.

"Not much, C. S. Killashandra," she was told politely. "Small freighter is loading for the Armagh system . . ."

"Have I been there?"

Pause. "No, ma'am."

"What does Armagh do for itself?"

"Exports fish oils and glue," was the semidisgusted reply.

"Water world?"

"Not total. Has the usual balance of land and ocean . . ."

"Tropical?" For some reason the idea of a tropical world both appealed to and repelled her.

"It has a very pleasant tropical zone. All water sports, tasty foods if you like a high fruit/fish diet."

"Book me." Crystal singers could be high-handed, at least on Ballybran.

"Blast-off at twenty-two thirty today," Port Authority told her.

"I've just time then." And Killashandra broke the connection.

She drew on the most conservative garments in the press, then randomly selected a half dozen of the brighter things, tossed them into a carisak, and closed it. She hesitated, midroom, glancing about incuriously. It was, of course, the standard member accommodation. Vaguely she remembered a time when there had been paintings and wall hangings, knickknacks that were pretty or odd on the shelves and tables, a different rug on the floor of the main room. Now there was no trace of anything remotely personal, certainly nothing of Killashandra.

"Because," Killashandra said out loud, as if to imprint her voice on the room, "I'm nothing but a crystal singer with only a present to live in."

She slammed the door as she left, but it didn't do

much to satisfy her discontent. She found slightly more pleasure in the realization that, though she might have trouble finding her apartment after a session in the Ranges, she had none finding her way up from the subterranean resident levels to the shuttle bays.

She took the time to get the protective lenses removed from her eyes. It didn't change her outlook much. In fact, Ballybran looked duller that it should have as the shuttle lifted toward Shankill. The storm had cleared away, and she felt a brief twinge as her body ached for the resonances she was leaving, for the dazzle of rainbow light prisms dancing off variegated quartz, for the pure sweet sound of crystal waking in the early morning sun, or sighing in the cold virginal light of one of the larger moons, for the subsonic hum that ate through bone in black cold night.

Then she dealt with the formalities of lifting off-world and was directed to Bay 23, where the Armagh freighter, *Maeve 18,* was docked. She was escorted to her cabin by a youngster who couldn't keep far enough ahead of her—and the crystal resonance that pinged off her—in the narrow corridors.

"Is there a radiant-fluid tub on board?" she asked him with a grim smile at his reaction to her condition.

"In your cabin, Crystal Singer," he said, and then scooted away.

It was a courtesy to call it a tub—it was a two-meter tube, just wide enough to accommodate a body. To reach it one had to perform certain acrobatics over the toilet; and, according to the legend on the dials, the same fluid was flushed and reused. Well, she could count on three to four washes before it became ineffective. That would have to do. She opened the tap and heard the comforting gurgle of the fluid dropping to the bottom of the tub.

From there she flung her carisak to the narrow bunk, shucked off her clothes, and did her acrobatic act, inserting herself just as the flow automatically cut off. There were hand and ankle grips, and she arranged her limbs appropriately, tilted her head back, and let the radiant fluid cleanse her.

She entered the common room for the first time the third day out, having purged sufficient crystal resonance from blood and bone to be socially acceptable. She was hungry, for more than food, a hunger she could keep leashed as far as she was concerned. But the eight male passengers and the two crewmen who circulated in the transit area were obviously affected by her sensuality. There wasn't anyone she wanted, so she retired to her cabin and remained there for the rest of the trip. She had traveled often enough in the shape she was in to practice discretion.

Armagh III's Port Terminal smelled of fish oil and glue. Great casks were being trundled into the hold of the freighter as she bade an impatient farewell to the captain. She flashed her general credentials and was admitted unconditionally to the planet as a leisure guest. She didn't need to use her Guild membership— Armagh III was an open planet.

She rented a flit and checked into the Touristas for a list of resorts. The list turned out to be so lengthy that she merely closed her eyes and bought a ticket to the destination on which her finger settled: Trefoil, on the southeastern coast of the main continent. She paused long enough to obtain a quick change of Armagh clothing, bright patterns in a lightweight porous weave, and was off.

Trefoil reminded her of somewhere. The resemblance nagged at her even as the interoceanic air vehicle circled the small fishing town. Ships tacking across the harbor under sail caused her heart to bump with a curiously painful joy. She knew she must have seen sailships, since the nomenclature—sloop, lateen-rigged, schooner, ketch, yawl—sprang to mind with no hesitation. As did a second pang of regret. She grimaced and decided that such clear recollection might even be an asset on this backward little world.

The landing field wasn't that far from one of the longer wharves, where a huge two-master was moving, with graceful and competent ease, to a berth alongside the port side. That term also came unbidden to her mind. As much because she would not give in to the emotion of the recall as because the ship excited her, she swung the carisak to her shoulder and sauntered down to the wharf. The crew was busy in the yards, reefing the last of the square sails used to make port, and more were bustling about the deck, which glinted with an almost crystalline sheen.

"What makes the decks shine?" she asked another observer.

"Fish oils" was the somewhat terse reply, and then the man, a red-bearded giant, took a second look. Men usually looked twice at Killashandra. "First time on Armagh?"

Killashandra nodded, her eyes intent on the schooner.

"Been here long?"

"Just arrived."

"Got a pad?"

"No."

"Try the Golden Dolphin. Best food in town and best brewman."

Killashandra turned to look at him then. "You pad there?"

"How else could I judge?" the man replied with charming candor.

Killashandra smiled back at him, neither coldly nor invitingly. Neutral. He reminded her of someone. They both turned back to watch the docking ship.

Killashandra found the process fascinating and reminiscent, but she forced memory out and concentrated on the landing, silently applauding the well-drilled crew. Each man seemed to perform his set task without apparent instruction from the captain in the bridge house. The big hull drifted slowly sideways toward the wharf. The last of the sails had now been fastened along the spars. Two crewmen flung lines ashore, fore and aft, then leaped after them when the distance closed, flipping the heavy lines deftly around the bollards and snubbing the ship securely.

Armagh men ran to height, tanned skins, and strong backs, Killashandra noticed approvingly. Redbeard was watching her out of the corner of his eye. He was interested in her all right. Just then, the nearest sailor turned landside and waved in her direction. His teeth were startlingly white against the mahogany of his skin. He tossed back a streaked blond curly mane of hair and waved again. He wore the long oil-shiny pants of his profession and an oddly fashioned vest, which left chest and arms bare and seemed stiff with double hide along the ribs. He looked incredibly muscular.

Why was he waving at her? No, the greeting was for Redbeard beside her, who now walked forward to meet his friend. A third man, black-bearded and tangle-maned, joined them and was embraced by Redbeard.

The trio stood facing the ship and talking among themselves until a fearsome machine glided along the rails to their side of the dock. It extruded a ramp out and down and into the deck of the boat, where it hovered expectantly. The two sailors had jumped back aboard, the blond man moving with the instinctive grace of the natural athlete. In comparison, the black-haired man looked clumsy. As a team, they heaved open the hatch. The hesitant ramp extruded clamps that fastened to the deck and the lip of the opened hold. More ramp disappeared into the maw of the ship. Moments later the ramp belt moved upward and Killashandra saw her first lunk, the great oil fish of Armagh, borne away on its last journey.

She became absorbed in the unloading process, which, for all the automated assistance of the machine, still required a human element. The oil scales of the huge fish did not always stay on the rough surface of the ramp belt and had to be forced back on manually. The blonde used an enormous barbed hook, planting it deep in what was actually the very tough hide of the elusive fish and deftly flipping the body into place again. Redbeard seemed to have some official position, for he made notes of the machine's dials, used the throat mike often, and seemed to have forgotten her existence entirely. Killashandra approved. A man should get on with his work.

Yes, especially when he worked with such laudable economy of motion and effort. Like the young blonde.

In fact, Killashandra was rather surprised when the ramp suddenly retracted and the machine slid sideways to the next hold. A small barefoot rascal of a lad slipped up to the crewmen, a tray of hot pies balanced on his head. The aroma was tantalizing, and Killashandra realized that she had not eaten since leaving the freighter that morning. Before she could signal the rascal to her, his merchandise had been bought up by the seamen. Irritated, Killashandra looked landward. The docks couldn't be dependent on the services of small boys. There must be other eating facilities nearby. With a backward glance at her blond sailor, contentedly munching on a pie in each hand, she left the wharf.

As it happened, the eating house she chose displayed a placard advertising the Golden Dolphin. The hostelry was up the beach, set back amid a grove of frond-leaved trees, which also reminded her of something and excited an irritation in her. She wouldn't give in to it. The inn was set far enough around a headland from the town and the wharf so that commercial noise was muted. She took a room with a veranda looking out over the water. She changed into native clothing and retraced her steps along the quiet corridor to the public room.

"What's the native brew?" she asked the barman, settling herself on the quaint high wooden stool.

"Depends on your capacity, m'dear," the little black man told her, grinning a welcome.

"I've never disgraced myself."

"Tart or sweet?"

"Hmmmm . . . tart, cool, and long."

"There's a concoction of fermented fruits, native to this globe, called 'harmat.' Powerful."

"Keep an eye on me then, man. You call the limit."

He nodded respectfully. He couldn't know that a crystal singer had a metabolism that compensated for drug, narcotic, or excess alcohol. A blessing-curse. Particularly if she were injured off-world, with no crystal around to draw the noise of accidental pain from her bones and muscles. Quietly cursing to herself, she knew she had enough crystal resonance still in her to reduce even an amputation to minimal discomfort.

Harmat *was* tart, cool, and long, with a pleasant aftertaste that kept the mouth sweet and soothed the throat.

"A good drink for a sun world," she commented. "And sailors."

"Aye, it is," the barman said, his eyes twinkling. "And if it weren't for them, we could export more."

"I thought Armagh's trade was fish oils and glue."

The barman wrinkled his nose disdainfully. "It is. Harmat off-world commands a price, only trade rules say home consumption comes first."

"Invent another drink."

The barman frowned. "I try. Oh, I try. But they drink me dry of anything I brew."

"You're brewman, as well?"

He drew himself up, straight and proud. "I gather the fruit from my own land, prepare it, press it, keg it, age it."

She questioned him further, interested in another's exacting trade, and thought if she weren't a crystal singer, brewmaking would have been fun.

Biyanco, for that was the brewman's name, chatted with her amiably until the laughter and talk of a large crowd penetrated the quiet gloom of the public room.

"The fishermen," he told her, busying himself by filling glass after glass of harmat and lining them up along the bar.

He was none too soon, for the wide doors of the public room swung open and a horde of oil-trousered, vested men and women surged up to the bar, tanned hands closing on the nearest glass, coins spinning and clicking to the wooden surface. Killashandra remained on her stool, but she was pressed hard on both sides by thirty or so people who spared her no glance until they had finished the first glass and were bawling for a refill.

Then she was, rather casually, she felt, dismissed as the fisherfolk laughed among themselves and talked trade.

"You'd best watch that stuff," said a voice in her ear, and she saw Redbeard.

"I've been warned," she answered, grinning.

"Biyanco makes the best harmat this side of the canal. It's not a drink for the novice."

"I've been warned," she repeated, mildly amused at the half insult. Of course, the man couldn't know that she was a crystal singer. So his warning had been kindly meant.

A huge bronzed fist brushed past her left breast. Startled, she looked up into the brilliant blue eyes of the blond sailor, who gazed at her in an incurious appraisal that warmed briefly in the way a man will look at a woman, and then grew cautious.

Killashandra looked away first, oddly disturbed by the blue eyes, somehow familiar but not the same, and disappointed. This one was much too young for her. She turned back to Redbeard, who grinned as if he had watched the swift exchange of glances and was somehow amused by it.

"I'm Thursday, Orric Thursday, ma'am," the redbeard said.

"Killashandra Ree is my name," she replied, and extended her hand.

He couldn't have guessed her profession by her grip, but she could see that the strength of it surprised him. Killashandra was not a tall or heavily boned woman: cutting crystal did not need mass, only controlled energy, and that could be developed in any arm.

Thursday gestured to the blond. "This is my good friend, Shad Tucker."

Thankful that the press of bodies made it impossible

for her to do the courteous handshake, Killashandra
nodded to Shad Tucker.

"And my old comrade of the wars, Tir Od Nell."
Orric Thursday motioned to the blackbeard, who also
contented himself with a nod and a grin at her. "You'd
be here for a rest, Killashandra?" Thursday asked. And
when she nodded, he went on. "Now, why would you
pick such a dull fisherman's world as Armagh if you'd
the galaxy to choose from?"

Killashandra had heard that sort of question before,
how many times she couldn't remember. She had also
heard the same charming invitation for confidences.

"Perhaps I like water sports," she replied, smiling
back at him and not bothering to hide her appraisal.

To her surprise, he threw back his head and laughed.
She could see where he had trimmed the hairs from his
throat, leaving a narrow band of white flesh that never
saw sun. His two friends said nothing, but their eyes
were on her.

"Perhaps you do, ma'am. And this is the place. Did
you want the long wave ride? There's a boat out every
dawn." Orric looked at her questioningly. "Then water
skating? Submarining? Dolphin swimming? What is
your pleasure, Killashandra Ree?"

"Rest! I'm tired!"

"Oh, I'd never think you'd ever known fatigue." The
expression in his eyes invited her to edify him.

"For someone unfamiliar with the condition, how
would you know it?"

Tir Od Nell roared.

"She's got you there, Orr," he said, clapping his
friend on the shoulder. Shad Tucker smiled, a sort of
shy, amused smile, as if he hadn't suspected her capable
of caustic reply and wasn't sure he should enjoy it at his
friend's expense.

Orric grinned, shrugged, and eyed Killashandra with respect. Then he bawled to Biyanco that his glass had a hole in it.

When the edge of their thirst had been satisfied, most of the fishermen left. "In search of other diversions," Orric said, but he, Tir Od Nell, and Shad Tucker merely settled stools around Killashandra and continued to drink.

She matched them, paid her rounds, and enjoyed Orric's attempts to pry personal information from her.

He was not, she discovered, easily put off, nor shy of giving facts about himself and his friends. They had all worked the same fishing boat five seasons back, leaving the sea as bad fishing turned them off temporarily. Orric had an interest in computers and often did wharfman's chores if the regular men were away when the ships came in. Tir Od Nell was working the lunk season to earn some ready credit, and would return to his regular job inland. Shad Tucker, the only off-worlder, had sailed the seas of four planets before he was landed on Armagh.

"Shad keeps saying he'll move on, but he's been here five years and more," Orric told Killashandra, "and no sign of applying for a ticket-off."

Tucker only smiled, the slight tolerant smile playing at the corner of his mouth, as if he was chary of admitting even that much about himself.

"Don't let Shad's reticence mislead you, Killashandra Ree," Orric went on, laying a hand on his friend's shoulder. "He's accredited for more than a lunk fisher. Indeed he is." Killashandra felt yet another tweak of pain that she masked with a smile for Orric. "Shad's got first mate's tickets on four water worlds that make sailing Armagh look like tank bathing. Came here with a submarine rig one of the Anchorite companies was touting." He shrugged, eloquently indicating that the company's praise had fallen on deaf Armaghan ears.

"They're conservative here on Armagh," Tucker said, his voice a nice change, soft after Orric's near-bellow. She almost had to sharpen her hearing to catch what he said.

"How so?" she asked Shad.

"They feel there is one good way to catch lunk when it's in oil. By long line. That way you don't bruise the flesh so much and the lunk doesn't struggle the way it does in a net and sour the oil. The captains, they've a sense of location that doesn't need sonic gear. I've sailed with five, six of the best and they always know when and where lunk are running. And how many they can bring from that deep."

And, Killashandra thought, bemused by Shad's soft accent, you'd give your arm to develop that sense.

"You've fished on other worlds," she said out loud.

"Aye."

"Where, for instance?"

He was as unforthcoming as a fish—or herself.

"Oh, all over. Spiderfish, crackerjaw, bluefin, skaters, and Welladay whales."

The young man spoke casually, as if encounters with aquatic monsters were of no account. And how, Killashandra wondered to herself, did she know that's what he'd named? Nervously, she glanced to one side and saw Orric's eyes light up, as if he had hoped that the catalog would impress her.

"A crackerjaw opened his back for him on Spindrift," Orric said proudly. "And he flew five miles with a skater and brought it down, the largest one ever recorded on Mandalay."

Killashandra wasn't sure why Orric Thursday wished to extol his friend. But it made *him* more acceptable in her eyes. Shad was too young, anyhow. Killashandra made no further attempt to draw Shad out but turned to Tir and Orric.

Despite a continued concern for her consumption of harmat, Orric kept ordering until full dark closed down abruptly on the planet and the artificial lights came on in the room.

"Mealtime," Biyanco announced in a loud, penetrating voice, and activated a barrier that dropped over the bar. He appeared through a side door and briskly gestured them to a table for four on the other side of the room. Killashandra made no resistance to Orric's suggestion that they all dine together, and she spent the rest of the evening—listening to fish stories—in their company. She spent her night alone—by choice. She had not made up her mind yet.

When the sun came up over the edge of the sea, she was down in the hotel's private lagoon, floating on the buoyant waters, just as the lunk ships, sails fat with dawn winds, slid out to open sea with incredible speed.

To her surprise, Orric appeared at midday and offered to show her Trefoil's few diversions. Nothing loath, she went and found him most agreeable company, conversant on every phase of Trefoil's domestic industry. He steered her from the usual tourist path, for which she was grateful. She abhorred that label, though tourist she was, on any world but Ballybran. Nor did she give Orric Thursday any hint of her profession, despite all his attempts to wheedle the information from her.

It wasn't that she liked being secretive, but few worlds understood the function of crystal singers, and some very odd habits and practices had been attributed to them. Killashandra's discretion and caution was instinctive by now.

Late that afternoon, a bleeper on Orric's belt alerted him to return to the dock: the fishing boats had been sighted.

"Sorry, m'dear," he said as he executed a dipping turn of his fast airflipper. "Duty calls."

She elected to join him on the wharf, allowing him to think it was his company she preferred. Actually, she wanted to watch the silent teamwork of docking, and see the mahogany figure of Shad Tucker again. He was much too young for her, she told herself again, but a right graceful person to observe.

They had made a quick plenteous catch that day, Killashandra was told as the fishermen drowned their thirsts in harmat at the Golden Dolphin. Tucker seemed unusually pleased, and Killashandra couldn't resist asking why.

"He's made enough now to go off-world," Orric said when Shad replied with an indolent shrug. "He won't go." Orric shook his head, a wry grin on his face. "He never does. He's been here longer than on any other planet."

"Why?" Killashandra asked Shad, then had to hush Orric. "Let Tucker reply. He knows his own mind, doesn't he?"

Shad regarded her with mild surprise, and the indolent look left his blue eyes, replaced by an intensity she found hard to ignore.

"This is a real sea world," Shad said, picking his words in his soft-accented way, "not some half-evolved plankton planet."

He doesn't open his lips wide enough to enunciate properly, she thought, and wondered why he guarded himself so.

"You've lunk for profit, territ and flatfish for fine eating, the crustaceans and bivalves for high livers, then the sea fruits for a constant harvest. Variety. I might buy myself a strip of land and stay."

"You do ship on more than the lunk boats?"

Shad was surprised by her question. "All the boats fish lunk when it runs. Then you go after the others."

"If you've a mind for drudgery," Tir Od Nell said gloomily.

Shad gave Tir a forbearing glance. "Lunk requires only muscle," he said with a sly grin.

This appeared to be an old challenge, for Tir launched into a debate that Shad parried with the habit of long practice.

For the sake of being perverse, Killashandra took Tir to bed that night. She didn't regret the experience, although there was no harmony between them. If it gave her no peace, his vehemence did take the edge off her hunger. She did not encourage him to ask for more. Somewhere, long ago, she had learned the way to do that without aggravating a lover.

He was gone by dawn. Orric dropped by a few hours later and took her to see a sea-fruit farm on the peninsula, ten klicks from Trefoil to the south. When she assured Max Ennert, the farmer, of her experience, they were all fitted out with breather tanks and went submarine.

Enclosed by water, isolated by her trail of bubbles, though attached by guideline to Max and Orric, she realized—probably not for the first time—why crystal singers sought water worlds. Below sea level, there was insulation against aural sound, relief from the play of noise against weary eardrums.

They drifted inches above the carefully tended sea gardens, Max and Orric occasionally pruning off a ripe frond of grape or plum and shoving them in the net bags they towed. They bypassed reapers in a vast sea valley where weed was being harvested. Occasionally, loose strands would drift past them, the fuller, longer ones deftly caught and netted by the men.

Killashandra was content to follow, slightly behind Max, slightly ahead of Orric, craning her neck, angling her body to enjoy as much of the clear-sea view as possible. One or the other man checked her gauges from time to time. Euphoria could be a curse undersea, and they didn't know of the professional immunity she enjoyed.

Perhaps that was why Orric argued with Max at one point, when they had been below some two hours. But they stayed down almost three more before they completed the circuit. As they walked out of the sea at Max's landing, night was approaching with the usual tropical dispatch.

"Stay on, Orric, Killashandra, if you've no other plans," Max said, but the words sounded rehearsed, strained.

She entered the room where she had changed to sea dress and heard Orric's footsteps right behind her. She didn't bother closing the door. He did, and had her in his arms the next instant. She made no resistance to his advance nor did she respond. He held her from him, surprised, a question in his eyes.

"I'm not susceptible to euphorics, Orric," she told him.

"What are you talking about?" he asked, gray eyes wide with innocence.

"And I've submarined on more worlds than Shad has sailed."

"Is it Tucker you're after?" He didn't seem jealous, merely curious.

"Shad's . . ." She shrugged, unwilling to place the young man in any category.

"But you don't fancy me?" He did not seem aggrieved—again, merely curious.

She looked at him a long moment. "I think . . ." She paused then voiced an opinion that had been subconscious till that moment. "You remind me too much of someone I've been trying to forget."

"Oh, just remind you?" Orric's voice was soft and coaxing, almost like Tucker's. She put that young man firmly out of her mind.

"No offense intended, Orric. The resemblance is purely superficial."

His eyes twinkled merrily, and Killashandra realized that the resemblance was not purely superficial, for the other man would have responded in just the same way, amused with her and taking no offense. Perversely that annoyed her more.

"So, dark and mysterious lady, when you get to know me better . . ."

"Let me get to know you better first."

They flitted back to Trefoil, circling over quays empty of any fishing craft.

"Lunk is moving offshore," Orric said. "Season's about over, I'd say."

"Does Tucker really have enough for a ticket-off?"

"Probably." Orric was busy setting the little craft down in dim light. "But Tir needs one more good haul. And so, I suspect, does Skipper Garnish. They'll track school as far as there's trace before they head in."

Which was the substance of the message left for Orric at the Golden Dolphin. So Killashandra, Orric, and Biyanco talked most of the evening with a few other drinkers at the bar.

That was why Killashandra got an invitation to go

with Biyanco fruit-harvesting. "Land fruit for harmat," Biyanco said with an odd shudder.

Orric laughed and called him an incorrigible lubber. "Biyanco swears he's never touched sea fruit in his life."

"Never been that poor," Biyanco said with some dignity.

The brewman roused her before dawn, his tractor-float purring outside her veranda. She dressed in the overall he had advised and the combi-boots, and braided her hair tightly to her skull. On the outward leg of their trip, Trefoil nestled on the curved sands of a giant horseshoe bay, foothills at its back. Rain forests that were all but impenetrable swept up the hills, sending rank streamers across the acid road in vain attempts to cover that man-made tunnel to the drier interior.

Biyanco was amiable company, quiet at times, garrulous but interesting at others. He stopped off on the far side of the first range of foothills for lorries and climbers. None of the small boys and girls waiting there looked old enough to be absent from schooling, Killashandra thought. All carried knives half again as long as their legs from sheaths thong-tied to their backs. All wore the coveralls and combi-boots with spurred clamp-ons for tree-climbing.

They chattered and sang, dangling their legs from the lorries as the tractor hovered above the acid road. Occasionally one of them would wield a knife, chopping an impertinent streamer that had clasped itself to a lorry.

Biyanco climbed farther above sea level by the winding acid road until he finally slowed down, peering at the roadside. Five kilometers later he let out an exclamation and veered the tract-float to the left, his hands busy with dials and switches. A warning hoot brought every climber's legs back into the lorries. Flanges, tilting downward, appeared along the lorry load beds, and

acid began to drop from them. It sprayed out, arcing
well past the tract-float's leading edge, dissolving vege-
tation. Suddenly the float halted, as if trying to push
against an impenetrable barrier. Biyanco pushed a few
toggles, closed a switch, and suddenly the tract-float
moved smoothly in a new direction.

"Own this side of the mountain, you know," Biyanco
said, glancing at Killashandra to see the effect of his
announcement. "Ah, you thought I was only a bar
brewman, didn't you? Surprised you, didn't I? Ha!" The
little man was pleased.

"You did."

"I'll surprise you more before the day is out."

At last they reached their destination, a permaformed
clearing with acid-proofed buildings that housed his
processing unit and temporary living quarters. The
climbers he had escorted went farther on, sending the
lorries off on automated tracks, six climbers to each
lorry. They had evidently climbed for him before and in
the same teams, for he gave a minimum of instruction
before dismissing them to pick.

Then he showed Killashandra into the processing
plant and explained the works succinctly.

Each of the teams worked a different fruit, he told
her. The secret of good harmat lay in the careful propor-
tions and the blending of dead ripe fruit. There were as
many blends of harmat as there were fish in the sea. His
had made the Golden Dolphin famous; that's why so
many Armaghans patronized the hostelry. No vapid,
innocuous stuff came from his stills. Harmat took
months to bring to perfection: the fruit he'd process
today would be fermented for nine months and would
not be offered for sale for six years. Then he took her
below ground, to the cool dark storage area, deep in the
permaform. He showed her the automatic alarms that

would go off if the vicious digger roots of the jungle ever penetrated the permaform. He wore a bleeper on his belt at all times (he never did remove the belt, but it was made of soft, tough fiber). He let her sample the brews, and it amused her that he would sip abstemiously while filling her cup full. Because she liked him and she learned about harmat from him, she gradually imitated drunk.

And Biyanco did indeed surprise her, sprier than she had ever thought him and elated with his success. She was glad for his sake and somewhat puzzled on her own account. He was adept enough that she ought to have enjoyed it, too. He had tried his damnedest to bring her to pitch but the frequency was wrong, as it had been with Tir, would have been with Orric, and this badly puzzled Killashandra. She ought not to have such trouble off-world. Was there crystal in her soul, after all? Was she too old to love?

While Biyanco slept, before the full lorries glided back to the clearing, she probed her patchy memory again and again, stopped each time by the Guild Master's cynical laugh. Damn the man! He was haunting her even on Armagh. He had no right to taint everything she touched, every association she tried to enjoy. She could remember, too, enough snatches to know that her previous break had been as disastrous. Probably other journeys, too. In the quiet cool dark of the sleeping room, Biyanco motionless with exhaustion beside her, Killashandra bleakly cursed Lars Dahl. Why was it she found so little fulfillment with other lovers? How could he have spoiled her for everyone else when she could barely remember him or his lovemaking? She had refused to stay with him, sure then of herself where she was completely unsure now. Crystal in her soul?

Experimentally, she ran her hand down her bare

body, to the hard flesh of her thighs, the softness of her belly, her firm breasts. A woman never conceived once she had sung crystal. Small loss, she thought, and then, suddenly, wasn't sure.

Damn! Damn! Damn Lars Dahl. How could he have left her? What was rank to singing black crystal? They had been the most productive duo ever paired in the annals of the Heptite Guild. And he had given *that* up for power. What good did power do him now? It did her none whatsoever. Without him, black eluded her.

The sound of the returning lorries and the singing of the climbers roused Biyanco. He blinked at her, having forgotten in his sleeping that he had taken a woman again. With solemn courtesy, he thanked her for their intercourse and, having dressed, excused himself with grave ceremony. At least a man had found pleasure in her body, she thought.

She bathed, dressed, and joined him as the full fruit bins began spilling their colorful contents into the washing pool. Biyanco was seated at the controls, his nimble fingers darting here and there as he weighed each bin, computed the price, and awarded each chief his crew's chit. It was evidently a good pick, judging by the grins on every face, including Biyanco's.

As each lorry emptied, it swiveled around and joined the line on the tract-float that was also headed homeward. All were shortly in place, and the second part of the processing began. The climbers took themselves off under the shade of the encroaching jungle and ate their lunches.

Abruptly, noise pierced Killashandra's ears. She let out a scream, stifling a repetition against her hand but not soon enough to escape Biyanco's notice. The noise ceased. Trembling with relief, Killashandra looked around, astonished that no one else seemed affected by that appalling shriek.

"You are a crystal singer, then, aren't you?" Biyanco asked, steadying her as she rocked on her feet. "I'm sorry. I wasn't sure you were, and I've not such good pitch myself that I'd hear if the drive crystals were off. Honest, or I'd have warned you." He was embarrassed and earnest.

"You should have them balanced," Killashandra replied angrily, and immediately apologized. "What made you think I might be a crystal singer?"

Biyanco looked away from her now. "Things I've heard."

"What have you heard?"

He looked at her then, his black eyes steady. "That a crystal singer can sound notes that'll drive a man mad. That they lure men to them, seduce them, and then kidnap 'em away to Ballybran, and they never come back."

Killashandra smiled, a little weakly because her ears still ached. "What made you think I wasn't?"

"Me!" He jabbed at his chest with a juice-stained finger. "You slept with *me!*"

She reached out and touched his cheek gently. "You are a good man, Biyanco, besides being the best brewman on Armagh. And I like you. But you should get those crystals balanced before they splinter on you."

Biyanco glanced over at the offending machinery and grimaced. "The tuner's got a waiting list as long as Murtagh River," he said. "You look pale. How about a drink? Harmat'll help—oh, you are a witch," he added, chuckling as he realized that she could not have been as drunk as she had acted. Then a smile tugged at his lips. "Oh-ho, you are a something, Killashandra of Ballybran. I should've spotted your phony drunk, and me a barman all these decades." He chuckled again. "Well, harmat'll help your nerves." He clicked his fingers at one of the climber chiefs, and the boy scampered into the living quarters, returning with glasses and a flask of chilled harmat.

She drank eagerly, both hands on the glass because she was still shaky. The cool tartness was soothing, though, and she wordlessly held the glass out for a refill. Biyanco's eyes were kind and somewhat anxious. Somehow he could appreciate what unbalanced crystalline shrieks could do to sensitive nerves.

"You've not been harmed by it, have you?"

"No. No, Biyanco. We're tougher than that. It was the surprise. I wasn't expecting you to have crystal-driven equipment . . ."

He grinned slyly. "We're not backward on Armagh, for all we're quiet and peaceful." He leaned back from her, regarding her with fresh interest. "Is it true that crystal singers don't grow old?"

"There're disadvantages to that, my friend."

He raised his eyebrows in polite contradiction. But she only smiled as she steadily sipped the harmat until all trace of pain had eased.

"You told me you've only a certain time to process ripe fruit. If you'll let me take the tractor down the rails past the first turn—No . . ." She vetoed her own suggestion, arriving at an impulsive alternative. "How long do you have left before the pick sours?"

"Three hours." And in Biyanco's widening eyes she saw incredulous gratitude as he understood her intention. "You wouldn't?" he asked in a voiceless whisper.

"I could and I would. That is, if you've the tools I need."

"I've tools." As if afraid she would renege, he propelled her toward the machine shed.

He had what she needed, but the bare minimum. Fortunately, the all-important crystal saw was still very sharp and true. With two pairs of knowledgeable hands—Biyanco, he told her, had put the driver together himself when he had updated the plant's machinery thirty years before—it was no trick at all to get down to the crystals.

"They're in thirds," he told her needlessly.

"Pitch?"

"B-flat minor."

"Minor? For heavy work like this?"

"Minor because it isn't that continuous a load and minors don't cost what majors do," Biyanco replied crisply.

Killashandra nodded. Majors would be far too expensive for a brewman, however successful, on a tertiary fishing world. She hit the B-flat, and that piece of crystal hummed sweetly in tune. So did the D. It was the E that was sour—off by a halftone. She cut off the resonance before the sound did more than ruffle her nerves. With Biyanco carefully assisting her, she freed the crystal of its brackets, cradling it tenderly in her hands. It was a blue, from the Ghanghe Range, more than likely, and old, because the blues were worked out there now.

"The break's in the top of the prism, here," she said, tracing the flaw. "The bracket may have shifted with vibration."

"G'delpme, I weighed those brackets and felted them proper . . ."

"No blame to you, Biyanco. Probably the expansion coefficient differs in this rain forest enough to make even properly set felt slip. Thirty years they've been in? You worked well. Wish more people would take such good care of their crystal."

"That'd mean less call for crystal, bring the price down, wouldn't it?"

Killa laughed, shaking her head. "The Guild keeps finding new ways to use crystal. Singers'll never be out of work."

They decided to shift the pitch down, which meant she had to recut all three crystals, but that way he would have a major triad. Because she trusted him, she let him watch as she cut and tuned. She had to sustain pitch with her voice after she had warmed them enough to sing, but she could hold a true pitch long enough to place the initial, and all-important, cuts.

It was wringing-wet work, even with the best of equipment and in a moderate climate. She was exhausted by the time they reset the felted brackets. In fact, Biyanco elbowed her out of the way when he saw how her hands were trembling.

"Just check me," he said, but she didn't need to. He was spry in more than one way. She was glad she had tuned the crystals for him. But he was too old for her.

She felt better when he started the processor again and there was no crystal torment.

"You get some rest, Killashandra. This'll take a couple more hours. Why don't you stretch out on the tractor van seat? It's wide enough. That way you can rest all the way back to Trefoil."

"And yourself, Biyanco?"

He grinned like the old black imp he was. "I'm maybe a shade younger than you, Crystal Singer Killashandra. But we'll never know, will we?"

She slept, enervated by the pitching and cutting, but she woke when Biyanco opened the float door. The hinge squeaked in C-sharp.

"Good press," he said when he saw she was awake. Behind, in the lorries, the weary climbers chanted to

themselves. One was a monotone. Fortunately they
reached the village before the sound could get on her
nerves. The lorries were detached, and the climbers
melted into the darkness. Biyanco and Killashandra
continued on the acid road back to Trefoil.

It was close to dawn before they pulled up at the
Golden Dolphin.

"Killashandra?"

"Yes, Biyanco?"

"I'm in your debt."

"No, for we exchanged favors."

He made a rude noise. And she smiled at him. "We
did. But, if you need a price, Biyanco, then it's your
silence on the subject of crystal singers."

"Why?"

"Because I'm human, no matter what you've heard of
us. And I must have that humanity on equal terms or I'll
shatter one day among the crystal. It's why we have to
go off-world."

"You don't lure men back to Ballybran?"

"Would you come with me to Ballybran?"

He snorted. "You can't make harmat on Ballybran."

She laughed, for he had given the right answer to ease
his own mind. As the tract-float moved off slowly, she
wondered if he had ever heard of Yarran beer. A chilled
one would go down a treat right now.

She slept the sun around and woke the second dawn
refreshed. She lazed in the water, having been told by
the pug-nosed host that the lunk ships were still out.
Biyanco greeted her that noonday with pleasantries and
no references to favors past, present, or future. He was
old enough, that brewman, she thought, to know what
not to say.

She wondered if she should leave Trefoil and flit
around the planet. There would be other ports to visit,

other fishermen to snare in the net of her attraction. One of them might be strong enough—*must* be strong enough—to melt the crystal in her. But she tarried and drank harmat all afternoon until Biyanco made her go eat something.

She knew the lunk boats were in even before the parched seamen came thronging up the beach road, chanting their need. She helped Biyanco draw glasses against their demand, laughing at their surprise to see her working behind the bar. Only Shad Tucker seemed unamazed.

Orric was there, too, with Tir Od Nell, teasing her as men have teased barmaids for centuries. Tucker sat on a stool in the corner of the bar and watched her, though he drank a good deal of harmat to "unstick his tongue from the roof of his mouth."

Biyanco made them all stop drinking for a meal, to lay a foundation for more harmat, he said. And when they came back, they brought a squeeze box, a fiddle, two guitars, and a flute. The tables were stacked against the wall, and the music and dancing began.

It was good music, too, true-pitched so Killashandra could enjoy it, tapping her foot in time. And it went on until the musicians pleaded for a respite and, leaving their instruments on the bar, swept out to the cool evening beach to get a second wind.

Killashandra had been dancing as hot and heavy as any woman, partnered with anyone who felt like dancing, including Biyanco. Everyone except Tucker, who stayed in his corner and watched . . . her.

When the others left to cool off, she wandered over to him. His eyes were a brighter blue in the new red-tan of his face. He was picking his hands now and again because the lunks had an acid in their scales that ate flesh, and he'd had to grab some barehanded at the last.

"Will they heal?" she asked.

"Oh, sure. Be dry tomorrow. New skin in a week. Doesn't hurt." Shad looked at his hands impersonally and then continued absently sloughing off the dying skin.

"You weren't dancing."

The shy grin twisted up one corner of his mouth, and he ducked his head a little, looking at her from the side of his eyes.

"I've done my dancing. With the fish the past days. I prefer to watch, anyhow."

He unwound himself from the stool to reach out and secure the nearest guitar. He picked a chord and winced; he didn't see her shudder at the discord. Lightly he plucked the strings, twisting the tuning knob on the soured G, adjusting the E string slightly, striking the chord again and nodding with approval.

Killashandra blinked. The man had perfect pitch.

He began to play softly, in a style totally different from the raucous tempi of the previous musicians. His picking was intricate and his rhythm sophisticated, yet the result was a delicate shifting of pattern and tone that enchanted Killashandra. It was improvisation at its best, with the player as intent upon the melody he produced as his only audience.

The beauty of his playing, the beauty of his face as he played, struck an aching in her bones. When his playing ceased, she felt empty.

She had been leaning toward him, perched on a stool, elbows on her knees, supporting her chin with cradled hands. So he leaned forward, across the guitar, and kissed her gently on the mouth. They rose, as one, Shad putting the guitar aside to fold her in his arms and kiss her deeply. She felt the silk of his bare flesh beneath her hands, the warmth of his strong body against hers and then . . . the others came pouring back with disruptive noise.

As well, Killashandra thought as Orric boisterously swung her up to the beat of a rough dance. When next she looked over her shoulder, Shad was in his corner, watching, the slight smile on his lips, his eyes still on her.

He is very much too young for me, she told herself, and I am brittle with too much living.

The next day she nursed what must have been her first hangover in a century. She had worked hard enough to acquire one. She lay on the beach in the shade and tried not to move unnecessarily. No one bothered her until midday—presumably everyone else was nursing a hangover as well. Then Shad's big feet stopped on the sand beside her pallet. His knees cracked as he bent over her and his compelling hand tipped back the wide hat she wore against sun glare.

"You'll feel better if you eat this," he said, speaking very softly. He held out a small tray with a frosted glass and a plate of fruit chips on it.

She wondered if he was enunciating with extra care, for she understood every soft word, even if she resented the gist of them. She groaned, and he repeated his advice. Then he put gentle hands on her, raising her torso so she could drink without spilling. He fed her, piece by piece as a man feeds a sick and fretful child.

She felt sick and she was fretful, but when all the food and drink were in her belly, she had to admit that his advice was sound.

"I never get drunk."

"Probably not. But you also don't dance yourself bloody-footed either."

Her feet were tender, come to think of it, and when

she examined the soles, she discovered blisters and myriad thin scratches.

Tucker sat with her all afternoon, saying little. When
he suggested a swim, she complied. The lagoon water
was cooler than she had remembered, or maybe she was
hotter for all she had been lying in the shade.

When they emerged from the water, she felt human,
even for a crystal singer. And she admired his straight
tall body, the easy grace of his carriage, and the fineness
of his handsome face. But he was much too young for
her. She would have to try Orric, for she needed a man's
favors again.

Evidently it was not Shad's intention that she find
Orric: he persuaded her that she didn't want to eat in the
hostelry; that it would be more fun to dig bivalves where
the tide was going out, in a cove he knew of, a short
walk away. It was difficult to argue with a soft-spoken
man, who was taller than she by several centimeters,
and could carry her easily under one arm . . . even if he
was a century or so younger.

And it was impossible not to touch his silky flesh
when he brushed past her to tend the baking shellfish, or
when he passed her wine-steeped fruit chips and
steamed roots.

When he looked at her, sideways, his blue eyes darker
now, reflecting the fire and the night, it was beyond her
to resist his subtle importunities.

She woke on the dark beach, before the dying fire,
with his sleeping weight against her side. Her arms were
wrapped around his right arm, her head cradled in the
cup of his shoulder. Without moving her head, she
could see his profile. And she knew there wasn't any
crystal in her soul. She could still give, and receive. For

all she sang crystal, she still possessed that priceless human quality, annealed in the fire of his youth.

She had been wrong to dismiss him for what was a mere chronological accident, irrelevant to the peace and solace he brought her. Her body was exultant, renewed.

Her stretching roused him to smile with unexpected sweetness into her eyes. He gathered her against him, the vibrant strength of his arms tempered to tenderness for her slighter frame.

"You crazy woman," he said, in a wondering voice, as he lightly scrubbed her scalp with his long fingers and played with her fine hair. "I've never met anyone like you before."

"Not likely to again." Please!

He grinned down at her, delighted by her arrogance. "Do you travel much?" he asked.

"When the mood strikes me."

"Don't travel for a while."

"I'll have to one day. I've got to go back to work, you know."

"What work?"

"I'm a guild member."

His grin broadened and he hugged her. "All right, I won't pry." His finger delicately traced the line of her jaw. "You can't be as old as you make out," he said. She had been honest enough earlier to tell him they were not contemporary.

She answered him with a laugh, but his comment brought a chill to her. It couldn't have been an accident that he could relieve her, she thought, caressing his curving thigh. She panicked suddenly at the idea that, once she had tasted, she could not drink again and strained herself to him.

His arms tightened and his low laugh was loving to her ears. And their bodies fit together again as fully and sweetly in harmony as before. Yes, with Shad Tucker, she could dismiss all fear as baseless.

Their pairing-off was accepted by Orric and Tir, who had his ready credit now and was off to apply it to whatever end he'd had in mind. Only Biyanco searched her face, and she had shrugged and given the brewman a little reassuring smile. Then he had peered closely at Shad and smiled back.

That was why he said nothing. As she had known he wouldn't. For Shad Tucker wasn't ready to settle on one woman. Killashandra was an adventure to him, a willing companion for a man just finished with a hard season's work.

They spent the days together as well, exploring the coastline in both directions from Trefoil, for Shad had a mind to put his earnings in land or seafront. She had never felt so . . . so vital and alive. He had a guitar of his own that he would bring, playing for hours little tunes he made up when they were becalmed in his small sloop and had to take shelter from Armagh's biting noonday sun in the shade of the sail. She loved to look at him while he played: his absorption had the quality of an innocent boy discovering major Truths of Beauty, Music, and Love. Indeed, his face, when he caressed her to a fever pitch of love, retained that same youthful innocence and intent concentration. Because he was so strong, because his youth was so powerful, his delicate, restrained lovemaking was all the more surprising to her.

The days multiplied and became weeks, but so deep was her contentment that the first twinge of uneasiness caught her unawares. She knew what it was, though: her body's cry for crystal song.

"Did I hurt you?" Shad asked, for she was in his arms.

She couldn't answer, so she shook her head. He began to kiss her slowly, leisurely, sure of himself. She felt the second brutal knock along her spine and twisted herself closer in his arms so he wouldn't feel it and she could forget it had happened.

"What's wrong, Killa?"

"Nothing. Nothing you can't cure."

So he did. But afterward, she couldn't sleep and stared up at the spinning moons. She couldn't leave Shad now. Time and again he had worked his magic with her, until she would have sworn all crystal thought was purged . . . until she had even toyed with the notion of resigning from the Guild. No one ever had, according to the Rules and Regs she had reviewed over and over. No one ever had, but likely no one had wanted to. When she *had* to have crystal, she could tune sour crystal. There was always a need for that service, anywhere, on any world. But she had to stay with Shad. He held back fear; he brought her peace. She had waited for a love like Shad Tucker for so long, she had the right to enjoy the relationship.

The next moment another spasm struck her, hard, sharp, fierce. She fought it through a body arched with pain. And she knew that she was being inexorably drawn back. And she did not want to leave Shad Tucker.

To him, she was a novelty, a woman to make love to—now—when the lunk season had been good and a man needed to relax. But Killashandra was not the sort of woman he would build a home for on his acres of seafront. On her part, she loved him: for his youth, for his absurd gentleness and courtesy; because, in his arms, she was briefly ageless.

The profound cruelty of her situation was driven home to her mind as bitterly as the next hunger pain for crystal sound.

It isn't fair, she cried piteously. It isn't fair. I can't love him. It isn't fair. He's too young. He'll forget me in other loves. And I—I'll not be able to remember him. That was the cruelest part.

She began to cry, Killashandra who had forsworn tears for any man half a century before, when the harmony between herself and Lars Dahl had turned chaotic. Her weeping, soft as it was, woke Shad. He comforted her lovingly and complicated her feelings for him by asking no questions at all. Maybe, she thought with the desperation of fearful hope, he isn't that young. He might want to remember me.

And, when her tears had dried on her face, he kissed her again, with an urgency that demanded to be answered. And was, as fully and sweetly as ever.

The summons came two days later. Biyanco tracked them in the cove and told her only that she had an urgent message. She was grateful for that courtesy, but she hated the brewman for bringing the message at all.

It was a Guild summons, all right: a large order for black crystal had been received. All who had sung black crystal were needed in the Ranges. Implicit in the message was a Guild warning: she had been away too long from crystal. What crystal gave, it took away. She stared at her reflection in the glass panel of the message booth. Yes, crystal could take away her appearance of youthfulness. How long would Shad remember the old woman she would shortly become?

So she started out to say good-bye to him. Best have it done quickly and now! Then back to Ballybran and forgetfulness in the crystal song. She felt cold all over.

He was sitting by the lagoon, strumming his guitar, absorbed in a melody he had composed for her. It was a pretty tune, one that stayed in the mind and woke you humming it the next day.

Killashandra caught back her breath. Shad had perfect pitch—he could come with her to Ballybran. She would train him herself to be a crystal singer.

"Don't," Biyanco said, stepping to her side.

"Don't what?" she asked coldly.

"If you really love the boy, Killashandra, don't. He'll remember you this way. That's what you want, isn't it?"

It was, of course, because she wouldn't remember him. So she stood there, beside Biyanco, and listened to Shad sing, watched the boyish intensity on his beloved face, and let cruelty wash hope out of her.

"It never works, does it, Killashandra?" Biyanco asked gently.

"No." She had a fleeting recollection of Lars Dahl. They had met somewhere, off-world. Hadn't they? His had been a water world, too. Hadn't it? Had she chosen another such world, hoping to find Lars Dahl again? Or merely anyone? Like Shad Tucker. Had she herself been lured to Ballybran by some ageless lover? Perhaps. Who could remember details like that? The difference was that now she was old enough not to play the siren for crystal. Old enough to leave love while he was young and still in love enough to remember her only as a woman.

"No one forgets you, Killashandra," Biyanco said, his eyes dark and sad, as she turned to leave.

"Maybe I can remember that much."

[[CHAPTER 8]]

"The Guild has received the biggest order ever requested, to facilitate the colonization and exploitation of seven new systems," the Guild Master told the twenty singers he had called back from their travels. "We must be able to fill these orders for black crystal. All of you"—and his blue eyes settled on one after the other—"have cut black crystal from time to time."

"When I could find it," someone said facetiously.

"The chosen few," another added.

He wasn't really all that much like Shad, Killashandra thought, her mind jumping as much from crystal deprivation as deliberate inattention because it was Lars Dahl who was talking in his Guild Master role. Just because they both have blue eyes and love the sea, that doesn't make them comparable. Or it shouldn't. And if any of us could find black crystal, we would, without him having to order us!

"To facilitate that search," Lars Dahl continued as the screen behind him lit up with a variety of paint emblems, "the Guild is canceling the markers of singers who, for one reason or another, are not actively working in the Ranges." That caused a stir and some consternation. "I should amend that—singers who have been known to bring in black crystal," he went on, raising his voice slightly over the murmuring. "We must follow up every potential source of black crystal."

"Leaving no stone unturned?" the wit asked, rousing some laughter and groans.

Lars Dahl grinned in response. "That's it. Now"—he gestured behind to the screen—"these are the canceled markers. If, however, one of you finds black on the claim of a still-existing singer . . ."

"Can't regress 'em back far enough to tell you where they cut black yet, eh, Lars?" someone asked, ending with a malicious laugh.

Regress? The word reverberated, jogging an uneasy memory, and Killa sat upright, trying to locate the speaker. "Regress"? Why should that word alarm her?

"I'll be forced to use that option, Fanerine, if you sane and active ones can't cut the blacks the Guild is obligated to supply. As I was saying, if an existing singer's claim is worked, there'll be a levy of twenty-five percent on your cut which is to go to the original claimant." He held up his hand to interrupt the sharp protests. "That will include the Guild tithe, so you aren't losing much to gain a viable site. Of course, you have to find it, first." Killashandra rather liked that droll touch. Lanzecki had reserved his humor for private moments. "Now, here're copies of these released markers for you to take with you. Secure it somewhere highly visible and *try* to remember why the sheet's there. First comer to any of these reopened claims has possession: mark it with your own colors.

"Most of you realize that we've just had Passover, so that's one hazard that won't interrupt the search. Met says there's a period of stable weather due us—isn't it always after Passover?" His remark generated a few polite chuckles, but Killashandra regarded him stony-faced.

He shouldn't think he could jolly them into doing the impossible even with that ploy of reopening worked claims that might possibly be black crystal. Why was the Guild "obligated" to supply anything? Worlds should be grateful for whatever the singers cut. She flicked her gaze around the room from one face to the next. Of the twenty, she recognized two or three. She ought to be able to recognize more. The buzz in her body made it hard for her to think. On the other hand, did any of the twenty recognize her? But then, she was seated at the back and hoping to get this meeting over with. She hugged herself, wishing she could squeeze out the itch. Maybe she could sneak out, but there was someone standing right in front of the door. To prevent premature exits?

Resignedly she listened to Lars go through his act, stirring the singers up to do the impossible—find enough black crystal to fill those contracts. Muhlah! She gave a humorless snort. He was doing a good job of communicating the urgency of this search. She couldn't recall another such all-out effort! Or that Lanzecki had ever thrown open unused claims before the paint marker was completely obliterated.

She rose when the others did, but was not unduly surprised when her name was called out. The Guild Master pushed his way through to her.

"Killa, can we let bygones be and cooperate duo on

this?" he asked in a quiet voice so that only she could hear him.

She was unnerved to have the regard of those intense and brilliant blue eyes focused on her alone. That was one difference between Shad and Lars Dahl—Shad's eyes were kinder, milder, undemanding. She turned her face away.

Damn that Biyanco! She shouldn't have let herself be persuaded out of a good partner by sentiment. True, even if she had brought Shad back with her, he wouldn't have been ready for a massive search this soon, even had he been lucky enough to have a Milekey Transition. But she would have had such fun shepherding him, deftly guiding him to learn the intricacies of a new trade, watching his sensitive face perceiving new and marvelous things . . . and especially hearing the dawn song of crystal with someone as gentle and loving as Shad Tucker. And how he would have enjoyed the seas of Ballybran! What sort of a ship would he have bought with his first big cut?

"Killa!"

Someone had her by the shoulders, firm hands giving her a shake to focus her attention.

"Killa?"

"What?"

The Guild Master frowned at her with concern. "One thing sure, Killashandra Ree, you've got to get back to the Ranges whether you sing black, green, or pink! You left your return mighty late. How do you stand the itch?" The sudden tender concern in his voice startled her, but she gave no hint of that surprise.

"I'll be all right as soon as I make the Ranges," she said wearily, her spine twisting with crystal hunger.

"If you can in this condition. So I'm not asking permission now. I am coming with you. It'd be outright murder to send you out solo in your present state. I'll meet you at the Hangar. Donalla . . ."

Killa peered at the woman who stepped forward. Her face was vaguely familiar, and although her smile was warm and friendly, Killa felt a flash of anxiety.

"Glad to see you safely back, Killashandra." When Killa recoiled slightly, the woman smiled reassuringly. "We're only going straight to the Hangar. You really can trust me that far, you know."

"I'll need . . ." Killa pulled at the clothes she was wearing—they wouldn't last an hour in the Ranges. "I've no boots . . ."

"Let Donalla take care of the details, Sunny, will you?" The loving tone of the Guild Master was gently supportive.

Some part of Killa was unconvinced, but the other, more dominant need for a respite from the crystal itch made that hesitation short. The hands that replaced Lars's were gentle, warm, and subtly persuasive. It was easier to submit and be guided.

Killa rubbed at her forehead. How could she have let herself get into such a state? She ought not to be led about like a child. Surely, she wasn't that bad, that decrepit? She had walked off the transport ship on her own, hadn't she? Found the shuttle bay with no trouble! Why was she suddenly incapable of managing something as simple as getting to the Hangar? Her feet ought to know the way even if her head didn't.

But she let herself be taken. She really couldn't think straight with all that noise in her head and that buzz along her veins, spiking into her heart and lungs—a crystal shiver that no amount of radiant fluid would reduce, only cutting crystal.

She hated to admit it, even to herself, but the Guild Master had been correct. She had cut it fine. She ought

to have started back to Ballybran the day she had felt
the first shock of crystal deprivation. And that was what
was shorting out her decision-making faculty, too.

Now that she put a reason to her mazedness, she also
knew how to cure it: cut crystal! Let it sing through her
body, bones, and blood. Let it clear the confusion in her
mind and strengthen her flagging energies. Crystal! The
worst addiction in the galaxy: difficult to live with and
impossible to live without.

She stumbled, and Donalla's helping hand steadied
her.

Then the noise and ordered confusion of the Hangar
swirled about her. Faces peered at her; large blurred
objects moved slowly past. She was gently propelled
into a space that shut out much of the noise. Hands
turned her body this way and that as she was inserted
into a shipsuit; her feet were pushed into the familiar
restriction of boots.

"My cutter . . ."

Her right hand was pressed against a hard cold surface, and her fingers, of their own accord, fitted themselves around the grip, slipping into grooves exactly
carved to fit her grasp. The tension within her eased
further.

She was settled into the appropriate contour chair,
and the harness was buckled about her. Passive now,
because she didn't have to make any movement or decision, she waited. The air around her smelled familiar—
and new, of paint and oil, with enough of the pungent
fuel odor to be acrid—and somehow comforting.

A sudden burst of noise, and a wave of fuel- and
grease-laden air whooshed across the sensitive skin of
her face. Someone had entered the sled, not so much
noisily as confidently. She felt the throb of engines rev-
ving up, increasing the stink of fuel in the air, which also

oddly reassured her. The sled moved forward, and she sighed with relief. Slowly she was pushed back against the seat cushions as the sled gathered speed. Sunlight pierced the windows, too brilliant for her tired eyes, and she made a protest as she closed them against the glare. Had she remembered to put in the refractive lenses? She blinked. She had, but it always took a few seconds for them to alter to the necessary refractory index. The blaze diminished, the backward pressure of takeoff eased, and she opened her eyes, suddenly more aware of her surroundings. Lars's lithe figure occupied the pilot's chair.

"Get some rest, Sunny," he said as he had so often said as they departed the Guild for the Ranges.

Because it was easier to obey than resist, she wriggled into the cushions, dropped her head back against the rest, and let herself slip into sleep.

"Eeny, meeny, pitsa teeny . . ." The old choosing phrase roused her.

"Muhlah! Any time I need to blackmail the Guild Master . . ." she murmured.

Lars laughed, the infectious laugh that had been one of his most endearing traits, and despite herself, she felt her mouth curving up in a grin.

"Works every time," he replied, and when she gargled a denial at him, he amended it. "Well, sooner or later, it works."

She struggled upright in the seat, biting her lip as the movement stirred up the crystal sting that pinched at blood and bone. She was in the Ranges, and it would ease soon . . . ease when she finally cut again. She released the harness and peered out at the steeples and ridges of deep Range. "Where are we?"

"Scouring the parameters of an old claim."

She frowned and stared at him until recent memory returned. "Oh? Whose?"

Lars grinned. "Such details are irrelevant. The marker's on the list: that's enough."

"Where did you find a statute of limitation in Rules and Regs?"

"In the Guild Master's prerogatives." Lars grinned at her. When she snorted derisively, he added, "Why have the rule and not put it into effect? The Guild has to supply legitimate demands. Like Lanzecki, I use every trick I'm allowed—"

"You're not Lanzecki!"

"Thank you for that vote of confidence," he replied, and the buoyancy had gone out of his voice. After a long silence while she rubbed surreptitiously to ease the crystal sting, he asked, "Is it bad?" His tone held genuine concern.

"I've been worse," she said diffidently—though, candidly, she doubted that. She would have remembered it—and tried to avoid a repetition.

"Ha! Try that on someone who doesn't know you as well as I do, Sunny. Take heart. We're nearly there."

"Where?" Her voice had an edge on it. "Oh, quick! Mark *there!*" And she pointed imperiously to starboard. The evening sunlight had just briefly glinted off crystal shard.

Lars gave an appreciative chuckle. "You may be writhing with crystal itch, but your eye's as keen as ever." He veered to the right, slowing the sled and neatly landing it on the bottom of the ravine. "You're one of the best in the Guild," he murmured as they saw the unmistakable evidence of a cutter's discards.

Killa could not control the trembling that racked her body. She fumbled with the door release, managed it the second time, and half fell from the sled.

"Careful now, Sunny," Lars called, rapidly flicking through essential landing procedures at the console.

She stumbled forward to the shards, crouching to gather handfuls, closing her fingers about them, oblivious to the sharp edges, even grateful for the caressing cut of crystal, grateful to spill blood and ease the sting that made artery, vein, and capillary itch.

"Easy, Sunny, easy," Lars cried, and gripped her firmly by the shoulders, pulling her to standing position.

"Muhlah!" she sighed with relief. "I needed that!"

"I don't think you need go to extremes, however," Lars said dryly. He leaned down and picked up a hunk that had crazed in faulty cutting. He tilted her bloody hands to tip the fragments out and replaced them with the larger, blunter piece. Putting his arm about her, he guided her back into the sled and washed each hand, while she held the shaft against her in the other like the talisman it was. The tiny crystal slices were already healing as he finished.

"You'd better eat, Sunny," Lars went on, still using that gently matter-of-fact tone. And he prepared a meal while she sat rocking the crystal against her, feeling it draw the sting from her, damaged as it was, as contact warmed it to her body temperature.

As she mechanically ate the meal he placed in front of her, she kept up her rocking motion, shifting the crystal to her thighs, bending her knees so the crystal touched her belly. She didn't resist when he put her to bed, letting her wrap herself around the crystal in a semifetal position. And that was how she spent the long night, comforted by crazed crystal.

When crystal song woke her the next morning, the damaged shaft sent out painful emanations. With a cry, she unwound, pushing the crystal from her as if it were polluted. Lars picked it up and flung it from the sled, relieving her of the sudden agony.

Then he spread himself across her body—she was arching in the agony of crystal song, too long away from it to be stimulated in the usual way.

"It'll ease, Sunny, it'll ease . . ." he murmured, struggling to keep her from straining herself in the paroxysms that were shaking her. If she had been alone in such a state, she would have launched herself to the nearby lode. In such disorientation, compelled by the irresistible need to reestablish contact with the ecstasy of sunwarmed singing crystal, she could have done herself a fatal injury.

Writhing against his restraint, she screamed at him, desperate to get to the crystal face and ease the intolerable sting and achings.

"Let me go! I'm begging you, Lars, let me go! I've got to get to—"

"You do and you're dead," he yelled back at her, resetting his hands on her wrists, managing, each time she nearly squirmed free, to cover her body with his and deny her freedom. "Hang on, Sunny. It won't be long now. Just let the sun get up!"

She twisted and bit at him, tried to knee his crotch, but he was quicker, stronger, and fitter than she and evaded her savage attempts to inflict enough pain to get free.

Abruptly the dawn chorus ended as the sun's rays flicked up and over the surrounding ridges and lit the ravine. She sagged against the hands that held her, limp, weeping because the itch was back, intensified. The compulsion to seek crystal, however, had eased. Wearily, she rubbed sweat and tears from her face on the quilt beneath her.

"Let me up, Lars," she said dully.

He kept his grip a moment longer, and then his fingers slowly released her wrists and he slid off her.

"Sorry about that, Killa, but you know I was right."

"Yes, I know," she replied, absently rubbing her wrists before she elbowed herself to a sitting position. "You're sneakier than an Altairian tangler," she said nastily. But the purely physical aches distracted her nerves from the interior throb of crystal sting.

A mug of some warm liquid was thrust at her.

"Drink this. Stuffed full of stimulants," Lars said, and she obeyed.

The beverage coursed down her gullet and seemed to find an immediate path to her armpits and stomach, radiating out from those points to her extremities.

"Thanks, Lars," she said.

He ruffled her hair. "That's my Sunny!"

"I am *not* your Sunny," she said, shooting him a brief dark scowl of denial.

"No, you're not much like *my* Sunny, are you?" his voice had gone expressionless again.

She tried not to care, but perhaps it was as well. "We're here to cut, aren't we? Let's do it."

Stiffly she got to her feet and walked as firmly as she could to the cutter rack. The weight of the tool was almost more than her flaccid arm could support, but just as Lars's hand came to her assistance, she managed to heave the cutter strap onto her shoulder.

"Let's go."

As she descended from the sled onto the rock- and shard-strewn ground, she was vaguely aware that he had slung more than his cutter over his shoulder. By the time she had scrambled to the rock face only fifteen meters from the sled, she was panting with exertion. She paused long enough to catch her breath to sing. She chose an A; heard Lars sing out in C and the face echo it back. Not a strong rebound but enough to encourage her. With her hand flat on the rock, she tried to find the source of the echo.

"It's stronger over here," Lars said, and she closed the distance between them with a leap. "Don't break a leg!" he shouted.

She sang A again, and the reverberation rippled through her hand.

"Easy, girl," he said, but she was too busy tuning her cutter.

Old habit guided them both, and Killa managed to hold her cutter against the buck of the subsonic blade through the crystal that had lain hidden since the tectonic pressures had formed it.

"Hold it steady!" Lars's voice penetrated her cutting fever and steadied her just enough so that their initial cut was true. Lars did the underslice as Killa held out eager hands to receive the excision. Her fingers clawed it free, ignoring the lacerations, and she held it up—a form in green, clear and solid.

Sunlight caught it, making it sing in her hands. The shaft sang on and on, its sound coruscating through her skin to bone and blood, flowing down her arms to her body, through her body to her legs, flowing and blotting out the sting with its resonance, leeching the agony of her long absence from the crystal that rejuvenated her.

When someone wrenched the shaft from her, she screamed and received a hard slap across her face; she dropped to the ground, bruising her knees on the scattered crystal debris.

"*Killa!* You've been thralled!" Lars's voice caught her just as she was about to launch herself at him, a formless silhouette in the haze beyond her crystal rapture.

Slowly she got to her feet, crawling her hands arduously up her legs to straighten a body shaking with fatigue and the residue of thrall. Lars reached out to support her, one hand gently brushing dirt and sweat from her face. Instinctively she leaned into his body, accepting support, unconsciously entreating sympathy, and his arms closed about her, his chin on her head, in the way they had so often stood after a good cutting.

"There, there, Sunny," he said, patting her shoulder and cuddling her. "You needed that. Feel somewhat better?" he asked, tipping her head back and looking down into her haggard face.

"How long did you let thrall last?" she asked, aware of her incredible weariness.

"Considering your condition," he said with a laugh, "most of the day."

She pushed away from him. "You mean, you let me thrall all day long when I could have been cutting? An hour or so at most would have been enough!"

He stepped back from her ire, grinning more broadly now, holding up his hands in mock appeal. "That's more like my Sunny."

"I'm not your Sunny," she said, needing to rant and rave herself back to a more normal humor, disgusted by the limp and nauseating lug she knew she had been.

"Well, then, it's a good deep green, and I cut around you, in case you didn't hear, locked in that thrall."

She both hated and admired Lars in this sort of a mood: far too amenable, far too effective, far too . . . *right!* Shard his soul!

Glaring at him, she sang out a high C, lost it for lack of support in her weakened condition, set her diaphragm muscles, and sang it again. She could hear his A an octave below. The green resonated, and their blades touched its bright surface as one.

When they had excised five shafts, Lars refused to let her pitch for more. He even refused to let her help him carry the carton back to the sled. When they got back and had racked their cutters, he insisted that she needed to wash, however briefly, and when she was obviously unable to stand up under the dribble coming from the shower head, he undressed, too, and supported her.

He made her lie down under the quilt while, buff naked, he made a quick meal for them both. She managed to spoon it into her, but the effort was all she had left and he caught the sagging plate before it tipped over onto the quilt.

"Can't mess it up. It's the only one we've got."

She tried to think of a smart reply to that. Honor demanded that she not let Lars get away with the last word today, but she fell asleep before she could think of something appropriately scathing.

Crystal song woke her and, aware of the warmth of the body beside her, she turned, eager for the benison of relief. She matched the eagerness of her partner, accepting and returning the passion she found. The gentleness and tenderness he displayed reminded her of Shad, and yet, as she opened her eyes, it wasn't Shad's engagingly innocent face that she saw. It was Lars Dahl's.

He gazed down at her for a long moment, his blue eyes dark with unspoken words as he searched her face. When she gave a little impatient twitch, he moved away.

"A better day today, isn't it, Sunny?" he said noncommittally.

"Yes, it is," she said with an equal lack of emphasis as she snagged her clothes from the floor.

It was easy to fall into the old habits. She might rail silently at finding herself accepting their former routine, but it helped. They didn't have much to discuss. Except the cutting.

"We shouldn't stay here," she said after they had

finished eating. "Green's not black, and that's what we're after."

"Feeling up to it?" he asked offhandedly.

She shrugged. "I'd rather waste time on looking than on cutting."

"Green's easier to cut to get back into the swing of it."

"Ha! I'm back already."

He cocked an eyebrow at her. "When thrall can hold you for hours?"

"That," she said, snapping her words out, "was *your* fault. I wouldn't have needed more than an hour."

"Ha!" he mimicked her.

But they were already, out of long habit, setting the cabin of the sled to rights to take off.

They bickered with some heat and contempt for the first hour in the air. Some equity was reached when they came across another worn paint mark that bore enough resemblance to one of the released ones for them to land. But as they were surveying the canyons, they caught sight of a sled in one of the gorges and quickly left the area, Killa swearing under her breath.

"What about one of the claims we cut? Aren't there any in the vicinity?"

Lars frowned thoughtfully. "Should be." Then he banged his fist on the console. "If only we could establish some method by which singers could register the location of sites . . ."

"Ha! And have renegades spend weeks trying to break into the program?"

"There are security measures available now that no singer could break."

"Ha! I don't believe you! I won't believe you."

"I know," he said, shrugging away her anger, and

grinned over his shoulder at her. "But I'll win 'em over to my way of thinking!"

"That'll be the day!"

"It'll come, Sunny. The Guild has to reorganize. It can't continue to operate on guidelines that're centuries old, incredibly obsolete, and damned naive."

"Naive?"

"It's a rough galaxy we live in. The business ethics that motivated the earliest Guild Masters simply don't exist, and modernization is long overdue."

"Modernization?" Killa swept her hand around the cabin, where sophisticated equipment was installed in small, discreet, and effective packages.

"I don't mean the hardware. I mean"—he jammed a finger to his temple—"the software. The thinking, the ethos, the management."

Killa made a disparaging noise in her throat. "This Guild Mastership has addled *your* software, that's for sure."

"Has it?" He cast her a sideways glance. "I think you'll come to agree that updates are essential."

"Hmmm. Hey, isn't that a marker of ours to starboard . . ."

It was, though nearly rubbed completely off the flat summit. They touched down, as much to refurbish the marker as to see if anything was familiar.

"Vaguely" was Killashandra's verdict. Something nagged at her, something quite insistent. "I think," she began hesitantly, "I think it's black."

"You don't sound sure . . ."

"I think you were also right to ask me if I was up to it." She fought the frisson that racked her.

"We can go back and cut more green."

"No, we're here to cut black and black we'll cut, if it kills me."

"I draw the line at suicide, no matter how badly the Guild needs black right now."

She gave him a wry grin.

What they found was a deep blue crystal, one of the loveliest colors either had ever cut. They got three cartons of it and were back at the sled, filling up their water bottles, when the first twinge of storm warning caught Killashandra. She sucked in her breath at the intensity of it. The crystal deprivation must have made her doubly vulnerable. She caught at the side of the cistern, and Lars reached out to support her.

"What's the matter? And don't you dare say 'nothing,' Killa," he said, eyes piercing hers with his growing recognition of the probable cause. "Storm?" When she nodded, he cursed under his breath. Then he closed the water tap and covered his half-filled canteen, stowing it in place. He took hers from her limp hand and put it away, as well. "All right, let's get ready."

"But it's only the—"

"Fardles, Killa, I can tell just from your reaction that it's going to be a bad blow."

"It's only because—"

"I don't care what it's because," he cried, irritably chopping his hand downward to interrupt her. He took her arm and turned her toward the galley. "We're returning, and that's that. I'm not risking you to even the mildest blow. Your head's not on straight yet from deprivation."

Though she protested vehemently, she had to recognize the fact that he was absolutely correct in assessing her state. She wouldn't admit it to him—she argued out of habit. He refused to entertain her contention that they would have enough time to cut at least five; he agreed but discounted the fact that this was the best blue lode they had seen in decades.

"It isn't black," he said, his mouth and eyes angry. "Try not to forget that, Sunny. It's black we need!"

"Then why did we waste time cutting this blue?"

"You thought there was black here!" He was moving around his side of the sled, securing cabinets and stowing oddments away.

"We cut good blue . . ." she began, going meek on him, a tactic that had often worked. "I don't remember how many times you've told me that . . ."

The anger went out of him all at once, and reaching across the narrow space that separated them, he caressed her cheek briefly, his smile penitent. "Sorry, Sunny, no matter how you try to slice it, we're not cutting any more . . . here . . . today."

"It should be a partners' decision, not one way," she said, wondering if he was weakening. "You've never been this arbitrary before."

He gave a weary sigh. "I'm arbitrary now! As Guild Master, I have more than a partner's stake in keeping your brain unscrambled."

"I didn't want you to be Guild Master."

"You've made that clear," he said, and his eyes flashed at her before once again he relented. "We were the best duet the Guild ever had. I've seen the printout of our aggregate cuttings. Impressive!" The smile he gave her was suddenly boyish, and she felt her heart unseize as the Lars she knew so intimately surfaced briefly. "Now let's scramble. I'm not risking you, or me."

In far better charity with each other, they returned to the Guild. By then the storm warnings were far-flung, and sleds from all sectors began pouring into the Hangar. Lars was calling for assistance to unload their crystal just as the flight officer handed him a comunit with the message that the call had top priority.

"I'll take ours through Sorting," Killa told him when he looked expectantly at her.

For a moment she watched his tall figure stride to the nearest exit, his head bent as he listened to the priority call. Someone else needing black crystal?

Guild Master's cut also took priority in the Sorting Shed and Killa waved her cartons toward Clodine's stall. She ignored the Sorter's initial nervousness and did her best to be pleasant. It was the cut that helped restore Clodine to their previous easy relationship. The market price of the blues would have been enough to appease the most desperate singer.

Once assured of the hefty credit balance, Killashandra became aware of externals—like the crystal pong emanating from her person and her clothes. Jauntily she strode to her quarters. As she palmed open the door, she heard the radiant liquid splashing into the tub and smiled. That was nice of Lars. A good long soak, something to eat, and she would be back to normal. Well, as normal as any crystal singer ever was. At least she had worked free of all that crystal cramp. Good cutting was what she had really needed to cure it.

The moment she toggled the food dispenser, the screen lit up to display Lars's face.

"Killa? That's a handy total on the blues," he said.

"Shards, I wanted to tell you myself," she said, feeling a surge of disgruntlement.

"I've ordered up a meal here, if you'd care to join me . . ." The hesitant tone of his invitation struck her as atypical, but it pleased her that this Guild Master was not as autocratic as Lanzecki had been.

"I think I might at that," Killa said graciously, and canceled the order she had just placed. Dinner with Lars, or for that matter, dinner with the Guild Master, tagged elusive wisps of memory, most of them pleasant.

Looking at the garments in her closet, she picked the one that suited a slightly smug mood and dressed carefully, spending time to comb out her snagged hair and arrange it attractively. She ought to get it cut short again, she reflected. It had been a nuisance in the Range, sweating up and falling into her eyes when she wanted a clear view of her cuts. She peered at her face: she had a tan again, making her eyes brighter, canceling the yellow that had begun to tint the white. She pulled her hands down her cheeks: they were still gaunt, and were those age grooves from her nose to her mouth? She grimaced to smooth them away. Then she frowned. She did look older. She would have to be very careful not to tax her symbiont again as badly as she must have done to look *this* way.

As she entered the Guild Master's offices, the first thing she saw was the empty desk, its surface clear of pencil files or any work at all. She frowned. Trag? No, Trag was gone. Lars had not found a suitable assistant. He would have to. No wonder he had been snapping at her in the Ranges. She knew from the amount of work she had seen Lanzecki get through—and that with Trag's help—that the Guild Mastership was no sinecure. She snorted to herself: Lars had been a damned fool to get roped into the job. She bet he hadn't been sailing once since he had become Guild Master!

"When" was not a word she often used, but it suddenly flicked across her consciousness. *When* had he taken over from Lanzecki? She grunted, canceling that irritating consideration as she continued across the floor to the inner office.

Lars was deep in contemplation of whatever was on his desk screen. He had had time to shower and change; his hair was still damp. To one side, in front of the wide window that overlooked the immense doors of the Hangar, a table had been set, and the enticing odors of some of her favorite foods wafted to her. Becoming aware of someone else in the room, he looked up with a scowl that shifted into a smile as he jumped to his feet.

"Sunny!" He gestured for her to join him at the table, then seated her.

"What are you after now?" she asked, a teasing note in her voice to draw the sting of her cynicism.

"Ah, lovey," he said, dropping a kiss on her cheek before he took his own seat, "give me credit for some altruism."

"Why should I?"

Grinning at her, he searched her face and was evidently satisfied by what he saw. She cocked her head at him.

"So?"

"Eat first, talk later. I'd like to see a little more flesh on your bones before we go out again."

She groaned. "So we're not going back out as soon as the storm clears?"

In place of an answer, he served generous portions of her favorite foods onto her plate. When he started to help himself, she saw that he had ordered the nicco spikes she hated even to smell. He grinned when she twitched her nose in disgust.

"You see, I'm not catering entirely to you, Killa Ree, and no, we're not able to go out immediately. Black crystal's not the only one of our products in demand." He ended the sentence abruptly. "I'd be able to go quicker if you could see your way clear to giving me a little help."

"I thought helping you was finding black. I'll go alone."

"No!" The single word was so forceful that she stared

at him in surprise. Lars hadn't used to take such a tone with her. She bristled, but he reached for her arm, shaking some of the milsi stalks from her half-raised spoon, before his touch softened in apology. "No, Killa. Too dangerous. You're not completely over the deprivation and you'd thrall. Especially if you were cutting black alone."

While she still resisted his prohibition, she had to admit that she would be extremely vulnerable to black thrall. She also had to admit that she had been in a terrible state when they had gone out: as near as made no never mind to being a crystallized cripple. They might have been searching for black crystal, but she was bloody lucky they hadn't found any. Green thrall had been deep enough. She owed him a lot for risking his own neck taking her out at all in that state.

"So, what do you need done, Guild Master?" she asked flippantly.

He smiled with genuine relief. "Thanks, Sunny, I really appreciate it."

"So?"

"Eat first," he said. "I can't think when my stomach's clinging to my backbone."

She was hungrier than she had thought and quite willing to concentrate on eating. Odd how a full belly could reduce resistance to unpalatable business.

When they had cleared the last morsel from the platters, Lars leaned back, patting his stomach and smiling.

"That's better. Now, if you could finish rounding up the figures and prices on the accounts I have on the screen, then I can go salve wounded feelings."

"Whose?"

"Clarend and Ritwili have legitimate grievances which must be addressed, and I've a delegation to meet at Shankill that I can no longer postpone."

"I might be better with the delegation than with the files," she suggested warily.

"It's the sort of thing you've done for Lanzecki before. D'you remember the Apharian contingent? Well, I've got the Blackwell Triad looking for favors now. Similar circumstances, similar solution, but I need the account figures on hand."

"Bor-ring," she said, rolling her eyes.

"A lot of what I have to do is boring, and yet . . ." Lars regarded her, his wide mouth curling in a grin. "I rather like finding out how this Guild hangs together against all comers."

Killashandra snorted. "We've a unique product that no one else can produce, no matter how hard they try. We're in control."

"I like that 'we,' Sunny." He reached across the table to fondle her hand. "I'll go heal fractured feelings; you find me figures."

"Just this once, because I owe you," she warned him, pulling her hand away and shaking her finger at him. "Don't think you can rope me into this full time. I'm a singer, not a key tapper! Find yourself a recruit with business training."

"I'm trying to," he said with a sly grin.

Once she became absorbed in the analysis, Killashandra found it more interesting than she had expected. Certainly the scope of the Guild's authority— and its unassailable position as the only source of communication-crystal systems—was wider than she had imagined. Her job—the cutting—was but the beginning of a multitude of complex processes with end uses in constant demand throughout the inhabited galaxy. Deprive a world of Ballybran crystal, and its economy would collapse, so vital were the shafts, and even the splinters, to technology on all levels. The pure research buffos in the labs here kept finding new applications of crystal—even ground shards had uses as abrasives. The more brilliant of the smaller splinters could be made into resonating jewelry, much in vogue again. She wondered how the galaxy had let one Guild gain so much power. What had Lars been on about? Reorganizing? Modernizing? What? The Guild bought state-of-the-art technology in other fields.

Unable to resist the temptation of having unrestricted access to the Guild's master files, Killashandra ran some that she might never again have a chance to discover. Lars had said something about aggregate cutting figures. She wanted to know just how much she, Killashandra Ree, had contributed to the success of the Guild. Once in the ultraconfidential files, those entries were easy enough to find. But the dating of their first duet journey was a shock. They couldn't have been cutting *that* long. They couldn't . . .

She canceled the file and sat looking at the screen, patiently blinking a readiness to oblige her. She couldn't . . .

"Sunny?" Lars's voice on the comunit broke through the fugue such knowledge caused. "Sunny, got those figures for me? Sunny? Sunny, what's wrong?"

His voice, concerned and increasingly anxious, roused her.

"I got 'em . . ." She managed to get the words out.

"Sunny, what's the matter?"

"Am I old, Lars?"

There wasn't much of a pause and, later on, she was never sure if there had been any before he laughed. "Old? A singer never gets old, Sunny." His voice rippled with a laughter that sounded genuine to her critical ear. She couldn't even imagine that his amusement was forced. "That's why we became singers. To never get old. Give me those figures, will you, and then I can get back from Shankill and show you just how ageless we both are! Don't get sidetracked by trivia like that, Killa. Now, what are those figures? I'm nearly at Shankill Base. Patch them through, will you?"

Like an AI, she performed the necessary function and then leaned back in the Guild Master's comfortable but too big chair and tried to remember how she could possibly have cut so many tons of crystal over so many decades.

Lars found her there when he returned long after night had fallen over Ballybran. Nor could he, using all his skill as lover or persuader, bring her out of her fugue. He did the only thing possible: took her out into the Ranges again.

She broke out herself when she realized that they were deep in the Milekey Range. On that trip they found the elusive black crystal, a full octave in E that was likely to sing messages around the biggest of the systems vying for comcrystals. But cutting the blacks enervated Killa to the point that she did not argue with Lars when he reluctantly but firmly turned the sled back to the Guild complex. For the first time it wasn't a storm that drove them in.

Dimly Killa realized that he carried her in his arms all the way down to the Infirmary, refusing any assistance or the grav-gurney. He undressed her himself while Donalla attached the monitors and Presnol fussed over which medication would produce the best results in the optimum time.

"Shard the optimum!" Lars raved. "Juice up her symbiont! Heal her!"

He saw her harnessed into the radiant-fluid bath before he stormed off. She let herself drift then and didn't even wonder how much credit that octave of blacks had earned them.

CHAPTER 9

"**D**id you get enough blacks in?" Killa asked Lars the first time she saw him after she began to pull out of the traumatic exhaustion.

"Enough to reduce the clamor a few decibels, Sunny." He bent to kiss her cheek and then pinched it, a gleam of mischief in his eyes. "The ones we cut together were the best."

"Naturally," she said with a flash of her usual arrogance.

"Seen the figures on that octave?" he asked.

"One of my first conscious acts." She leaned into the fingers that stroked her cheek. "I've a bird to pluck with you. You gave me part of those you brought in when you went back out by yourself, and that's not in Rules and Regs. You cut by yourself," she said, scowling at him but well pleased at his generosity.

"Ah, but it's your site. All things being equal,

you'd've continued cutting with me until the weather turned."

"So," she said, moving her head slightly back from his caresses and eyeing him speculatively, "what is such charity going to cost me?"

Lars gave a hearty laugh, throwing his head back and tipping the chair away from the bed, balancing it deftly on the back legs. "I wasn't so much charitable as conscious of my administrative edict that those whose claims were cut without their participation would be awarded a settlement."

"I'm an existing and active singer," she said, outraged. "I'm not—not yet, at any rate . . ." And she waved her hand in agitated denial toward the section of the Infirmary that cared for the brain-damaged singers.

"No, of course you're not. The fact remains that I was compelled by press of orders to obtain black crystal from any viable site," he said, solemn for a moment. "And you did cut there earlier with me, so it was only just, meet, and fair that you got your share—especially at the current market price of blacks." He rolled his eyes. "Best ever."

"Yes, it was, wasn't it!" Killa grinned back at him. Blacks always generated top earnings. Their octave had earned her more than she had made in—her mind stumbled over the time factor. Quickly she turned away from such speculations. "Has that octave been processed yet?" She was still annoyed with Donalla and Presnol for not allowing her to access that information. They had kept her restricted to a simple voice-only comunit.

"Oooh, as fast as it could be shaped and bracketed. The Blackwell Triad drooled when I made it available to them. Eight was what they needed, and eight matched was a plus. Which they paid for."

"Too right!"

"Terasolli installed them." Lars's grin turned sour. "Then lost himself so well in Maxim's Planet I haven't been able to locate a trace of him. Even with what the pricey establishments on Maxim's charge, he's got enough to lose himself for months."

"I remember going to Maxim's once with you," Killa said, though she could recall no details of the legendary exotic pleasances that the leisure planet offered. Though some singers risked mind and body to cut enough for repeated visits to Maxim's, she couldn't recall any desire to do so.

"Once. No seas, not even lakes, so no sailing." He cocked her a malicious grin. "Which reminds me. Care to get out of here for a few days' R and R? You can crew for me."

"To get out of here I'd even crew!"

Counterfeiting irritation at her gibe, he ruffled her hair into snarls and left, whistling a chanty.

Three days later, when she made her way down to the pier, she was surprised to find Donalla, Presnol, and Clodine already there, carisaks at their feet. She very much resented Lars's extending his invitation to anyone else, much less these three. She had wanted—expected—only his company on board the *Angel*. The ship was more than enough rival for his attention. Then she experienced a second, more disjointing shock when she got a good look at the ship moored to the long pier: it was not the *Angel* she *thought* she remembered clearly, but a craft some ten or fifteen meters longer. A sloop, but a much bigger one. That somewhat explained the extra hands but did not disperse her disgruntlement.

Lars arrived before she got past a stiff greeting to the others. He jogged down the pier, grinning broadly at the success of his surprise.

"She's great, isn't she?" he said, his face boyish and more like the Lars she had known than the Guild Master he had become. "This'll be her maiden voyage. You're the shakedown crew."

Not even Killashandra had the effrontery to blight his pleasure as he shepherded them on board, pointing out the technological improvements and amenities, the spaciousness, the luxury of the several cabins and wardroom, still smelling of varnish, paint, and that indefinable odor of "unused." There was even space for a body-sleeve-sized radiant bath. Killa lost the edge of her vexation when Lars guided her to the captain's cabin, genially waving the other three to pick out their own bunks. There would be much more privacy on *Angel II*—unless, of course, Lars insisted on standing a different watch. Maybe they would have to, for she had no idea how much seamanship the two medics and the Sorter had.

"Like it, Sunny?" Lars said, tossing his duffel to the wide bunk and gesturing around the beautifully appointed cabin. "The rewards of cutting black!"

"Must have cost you every bit you made," she murmured, looking about her appreciatively. "State-of-the-art?"

"She was when she left the boatyard on Optheria." Lars slipped his arms about her waist, enfolding her to him and burying his face in her short crisp curls. "Probably still is, though I waited to sail her until I could have my Sunny aboard. No fun for me to sail without you, you know." He kissed her, then let her go to swing his arms about expansively. "She's a beaut, isn't she? Saw her sister ships on Flag Three and I've lusted after one like her ever since."

"Do the others know how to sail?" she asked, curious and still somewhat resentful.

"They sailed on the old ship a couple of times," he admitted casually. "They don't get seasick, if that's your worry, and, while this baby should run herself, they know their way about a deck."

"Who cooks?" Killa asked, half teasing.

"Whoever's off-duty," he replied gaily, and then hugged her to him. "It's good to have you back on board, lovey. Real good. Now"—and his manner turned brisk—"let's get this cruise under way."

It turned out to be a very good cruise, especially when Killashandra realized that she was a much more capable sailor than any of the others. And, as usual, she responded automatically, and correctly, to any of Lars's orders.

The important things to remember she remembered, she told herself. The rest was chaff, which time would have winnowed out of active memory anyway.

And, as they anchored every evening in a cove and the ship could be rigged to rouse the crew if its monitors received any critical readings, Lars and she spent their nights together in the captain's double bunk.

They fished and ate the panfried catch, sweet and delicate in flavor and flesh. They sailed, or rather Lars did—he would let no one take the helm for very long, even Killa. By the afternoon of the third day out, they encountered some stormy weather. She reveled in it, for it brought back to mind flashes of other storms she had experienced on ships with Lars. It was four days before the pressures of the Guild had to be considered. Lars tried to settle one set of problems that were patched through to him, but since he had no assistant to handle matters during an absence, they regretfully had to turn back.

"I thought you were going to find yourself an aide,"

Killa said, unhappy at having the halcyon trip truncated.

"I've been trying to find the right personality for the past seven years, Sunny. Isn't easy to find anyone suitable. Oh, there've been a couple of recruits who had some potential, passable as temporaries, but none who had the breadth of experience to be effective executives. I need someone who knows and understands Guild tenets, has or could cut crystal, has managerial skills without being a power freak. Most especially someone I can trust . . ."

"Not to usurp your prerogatives?" Killa asked facetiously.

"That, too," he agreed, grinning at her. "It's not an easy position to fill. I've learned to do as much as I can myself without delegating it to others because, bluntly, singers forget too much."

Killa heard that on several levels and winced. His arm came about her, lovingly tucking her against him, and she felt his kiss on the nape of her neck.

"Worse, they sublimate—Donalla's word—crystal singing into the most important aspect of their lives, which, in many senses, it *has* to be. The disadvantage to that is the balance: they end up with such narrow parameters in which they can function that they're bloody useless for any broader view. They're either singing or they flee *from* singing until they can no longer ignore the need for crystal. That sort of myopia compromises a lot of otherwise good people. Life holds more—hey, Sunny, what's the matter with you?" Killa had stiffened in his arms, and tried to push him away. "Hey, no need to take offense!" He laughed at her and pulled her back into his arms, caressing her until she began to relax. "Silly chunk!"

She made herself soften in his arms because they were

nearly back at the Guild harbor, but whether or not he denied it, she felt that his comments had not been as casual as he pretended. And yet . . . nothing in the past few days had suggested to her that there had been any other, subtle alteration to their long relationship. Donalla was patently interested in Presnol, and Clodine apparently had a like-for-like preference.

Then Lars issued the necessary orders to ready the ship for docking, and there was no time for any further conversation. On the one hand, Killa resented that Lars had left her so unsettled with his remarks unclarified, but, on the other, she wanted time to mull over what he *had* said. If the suit fits, wear it, she thought.

With utter honesty, she recognized that she was guilty of compressing her personal parameters into just such a narrow track. Had Lars seen that? Was he hoping that his remarks would jolt her out of that myopia? Only how? Something teased at the edge of her mind. Something important. She couldn't catch so much as a hint.

She sighed and finished cleaning up the galley and removing the last of the perishable foods. Well, maybe she wasn't as myopic as some. She sailed, didn't she? And she could remember seeing more water worlds than any galaxy had the right to offer.

Sailing had given Lars Dahl some respite from the pressures of his responsibility, but the main one had doubled on him—more black crystal was ordered.

"I left instructions that no further orders were to be taken," Lars said, angrily furrowing his brows as he glared at the comscreen. It had been buzzing for his attention the moment he opened the hatch on his private ground vehicle.

"Guild Master, we *never* refuse orders for black," he was told.

"We can't fill the orders we've got." Lars leaned out of the open door. "Donalla, you're going to have to lean on Borella and Rimbol."

The names were vaguely familiar to Killashandra.

"I'll do what I can, Lars," Donalla called back to him, but she shrugged as if she was none too sanguine about success.

"Rimbol? I knew him—I think," Killashandra said as a hazy image of an ingenuous smile on a boyish face flickered in recall. "And Borella . . ." The woman's face was not clear; memory centered on a tall strong body and a badly lacerated leg. "I haven't seen them in a long time," she added.

"You're not likely to, Sunny," Lars said kindly. "They both turned off storm warnings once too often."

"Oh!" She paused, considering that information. "Then how can Donalla lean on them?"

Lars had stowed their two duffels; he strapped into his seat, motioning for Killa to do the same, as he prepared to drive back to the Cube.

"Regression," he replied succinctly.

That was the word.

"What's that?"

"It's an old technique of accessing segments of memories lost on purpose or from brain injury. We don't use but two-fifths of the brains we've got. As Donalla explained, some functions can be switched to unused portions of the mind, and often memories get shunted out of active recall. Off and on, there have been fads of regression, usually to former lives." He chuckled before continuing, an indication of his opinion of such an exercise. "We're using it to tap memory strings. Donalla's research on memory loss suggests that we don't actually lose anything we've seen, heard, and felt. The unpleasant we tend to bury as deep as possible, depending on its effect on our psyches. Oddly enough, good memories get dropped just as thoroughly. Through a careful use of hypnosis, Donalla has been able to reclaim lost knowledge."

"That's illegal!" She saw Lars shake his head at her outburst. "Isn't it?"

"No, it isn't. I had that point clarified. We are the custodians of those husks of former singers, and they get the best physical care we can supply. Some of them, under Donalla's care, have actually been restored as functioning humans."

Killa stared at him, aghast. "You can't possibly put them back in the Ranges!"

Lars laughed harshly. "I'm not sadistic, Killa, it's a plus to me if they are able to care for themselves. Some have improved enough to undertake simple duties in the infirmary."

"That's macabre, Lars," Killa said with a shudder.

"It's also expedient. The infirmary is damned near full, and I won't short anyone on the care they need if they've totaled their minds. The other problem is that the Guild is not attracting enough new recruits to make up for those losses . . ."

She felt both anger at him and a stirring of terror. She had come all too close to being one of the "totals" herself. "If I'd totaled, would you . . ."

His eyes on the ground speeding past them, Lars reached out to grab her hand. "If you were totaled, Killa, you wouldn't be aware of anything that was happening to you."

"But would you subject me to . . ." She couldn't continue, horrified at the very idea of someone crawling about her mind without permission, at that ultimate loss of privacy. The painful grip of his fingers increased, jolting her out of such considerations.

"I told you I didn't want to be Guild Master. Lanzecki left me with quite a mess to cope with, only when I agreed, I didn't know the half of it. Full disclosure wasn't required of him." Lars's smile was droll. "But I did have some ideas on how to revitalize the Guild, to reorganize it for efficiency and predictability. I can't leave so much to the vagaries of the singers and the weather."

"Vagaries?" she repeated indignantly. *"Vagaries?"* His choice of word infuriated her.

"Yes, singers are permitted far too much leeway—"

"Too much? When we risk our sanity every time we go into the Ranges?"

"That's the most haphazard part of the whole operation," Lars said scornfully. "Most singers—and you are not in that category, Sunny, so relax and listen up—cut just enough to get off-planet. They leave viable sites long before they need to quit because of an approaching storm. They don't remember from one time to the next where they've profitably cut and waste a lot of time trying to locate old sites or find new ones. This paranoia that keeps a singer from noting coordinates of claims is absurd. It's easy enough to use codes."

"If you can remember it later," Killa put in.

"Numbers aren't that hard to remember," he said, "and something has to be done to make such invaluable information available to the individual. It'd cut out the guesswork and make every trip into the Ranges far more profitable. Our friend Terasolli's another example of wasted time. He gets top price to set that octave, and he won't come back to Ballybran until crystal itch drives him back. That'll be a year or so—a year or so of unproductivity. That's got to stop."

"Stop?" She sputtered the word in her amazement at his uncompromising attitude.

"Two, maybe three months, should be respite enough for a singer."

"How the fardles would *you* know?" Killa demanded. "You've never set black crystal. You don't know . . ." She had to stop, she was trembling so badly. "Set this thing down. I'm not going any further with you. I'd rather walk back to the Guild than stay another minute . . ."

Lars did set the vehicle down, but he also shoved in the doorlock and swung his back against it so she couldn't reach it. His face was set and his eyes flashing with anger. He took her by the shoulders.

"You'll stay and you'll listen! If I can persuade a mind as closed as yours against any change in wasteful habits and stupid archaic perks, maybe I have a chance of pulling the Guild out of the hole it's in." He gave her a little shake, his fingers digging into the flesh of her upper arms. He ignored her squirming. "I'm trying my damnedest to save this Guild. Its position in communications is no longer as secure as it used to be because people have got tired of waiting for Ballybran crystals and have developed alternatives. Not as good as our crystal but performing much the same functions and . . . always . . . available . . . for replacement . . ." He spaced the last words for emphasis. "I've got nine orders for black crystal I can*not* fill because my singers can*not* relocate the sites where they've found black. So they go wandering about in the Ranges, looking, trying to remember. I want them to remember. I've been patient long enough—just as Lanzecki was patient—but there's an end to patience and I've reached it. I'll do anything I can to supply black crystal, to build up a backlog of the stuff, to reinstate the Guild to its former prominence. And if it means I have to plumb the depths of crazed minds to find out where black crystal is, I will.

But it'd be much easier to have a live singer willing, and able, to cooperate with me."

His bitter gaze held hers, and she could see his deep anxiety, his frustration, his fears in the dark agony of his clouded eyes. His voice was harsh with desperation.

"How could I cooperate any more than I have?" she asked in a low voice, shivering internally with fear of what this compliance might do to her.

"Oh, Sunny . . ." He embraced her tightly, holding her head under his chin with one hand, stroking her body as if contact would express his gratitude and relief. Then he held her slightly away, her face in his hands, stroking her cheeks with gentle thumbs, looking deep into her eyes. "You *know* where you cut blacks. It's there in your memory." One hand cupped her head tenderly. "We just have to access those memories . . . it'll all come back. Donalla says that with the proper clues, you could remember everything . . ."

Killashandra stiffened, regretting her impulse, pulling herself free. "I don't *need* to remember everything, Lars. I don't *want* to remember everything. Get that straight now."

"Honey, all I'm asking is landmarks for the black-crystal sites you've cut. I've remembered only two, and I know there were more. I have *got* to have black crystal!" And he pounded his fist into the plas above the control panel with such force that it left a dent.

She reached for his hand, to prevent him from repeating the blow. Immediately he covered her hand with both of his.

"If we could only"—and his voice was low now, his frustration vented—"get singers to note down landmarks so they can get themselves back to the best sites . . ."

Killa gave a snort, not as derisive as she might have

been because she was not going to exacerbate Lars's despair. "Now that's asking a lot, love," she said wryly. "You know how paranoid singers are. Put something down that another singer could find and locate?" She shook her head. "Not to mention roping singers back to Ballybran before they absolutely have to return."

Lars looked deeply into her eyes. "That's why your cooperation is so vital, Sunny. You're senior among the working singers. If *you* can be seen to accede to executive orders," he said with a bitter smile, "the others will accept them. Especially if you start bringing in more crystal, better crystal, because you know *exactly* how to get back to workable sites."

"I've already cut more crystal than any other singer . . ."

"You have that enviable reputation, Sunny," he said with a hint of his customary ebullience.

"So how does this regression process work?"

He straightened up, his eyes losing their grimness. "Under hypnosis. Donalla's become expert. She found the coordinates I needed to access one of our old claims the last time I went out."

"You—by yourself?" The notion that he had risked himself like that made her choke with fear.

"As Guild Master, I had to set the example, despite my partner's illness. I can't ask singers to do what I won't do myself, you know."

"And you talk about capricious singers!"

"Don't shout, Killa. I cut, I got back, and at least filled another order."

"Order? *Order!*" She was indignant.

"An order that's been unfilled for twenty years, Killa! It's no wonder the Guild's reputation has been suffering. I've finally got permission to inaugurate a more active recruitment campaign, but it's experienced singers I need and right now—and out in the Ranges, not carousing on Maxim's or Baliol and spread out across the galaxy."

The bleak expression of a man who was not given to desperation, the flat, despairing edge to a voice that had always been rich with humor and optimism, moved her more deeply than she had been moved at any other moment in a basically egocentric and selfish life. She owed Lars Dahl, and now was the time to repay him in the only coin that mattered.

"So, let's get back to the Cube and let Donalla beguile me, or whatever it is she needs to do."

"Regress your memory."

"I can't, and that's that," Donalla said, swinging her stool around and projecting herself off it. She paced angrily about the room. "You don't trust me, Killa. It's as simple as that. Until you *can* trust me, hypnosis can't happen."

"But I *do* trust you, Donalla," Killa insisted, as she had over the past few days and the increasingly frustrating sessions she had had with the medic.

"Look, ladies," Presnol said, coming out of the corner of the room where he had been as unobtrusive as possible, "there are some folk who are psychologically unable to release control of their minds to anyone, no matter how they trust the operator. Killa's been a singer a very long time now . . ."

"Don't keep reminding me of that." Killa heard the edge on her voice, but she was too keyed up by failure to control the reaction.

"Habits are ingrained . . ."

"I've never been a creature of habit," Killa protested, trying to inject a little humor into the tensions that crackled about them all.

"But," he said, turning to her, "protecting your site locations has played a dominant role in your subconscious. I mean, I've sat in on Donalla's sessions with some of the inactive singers"—Killa approved of his euphemism—"and often it's sounded to me as if they were keeping the information from themselves: the subconscious refusing to permit access of knowledge to the conscious."

"Ha!" Killa folded her arms across her chest. "I go to sleep telling myself to remember. To dredge up the necessary referents. I *dream* of fardling spires and ranges and canyons and ravines. I *dream* of the act of cutting; I *dream* of crystal until I wake myself up thinking I'm asleep on a bed of the nardling shards!"

"Like a mystic?" Donalla tried to cover up the giggle that had slipped out.

Presnol looked shocked, but Killa grinned. "I know the sort you mean—total disregard of the purely physical. Mind over matter! Oh, Muhlah, if I only could . . ." And she groaned, covering her face with her hands.

"Wait a minute," Donalla said, drawing herself erect at a sudden inspiration. "You get thralled, don't you? By crystal?"

"It can happen to any singer," Killa said guardedly.

"Yes, but thrall's a form of hypnosis, isn't it? I mean, the crystal triggers the mesmerism, doesn't it?"

"Indeed it does."

Presnol caught the significance of their exchange. "But that would mean you'd have to go into the Ranges."

"What's wrong with that, Presnol?" Killashandra asked, slapping her hands to her knees. "I'd be doing something constructive at the same time, instead of sitting on my buns here accomplishing *nothing*. Sorry,

Donalla. You've tried. I just can't comply! Maybe, in the Ranges, and in thrall, you can get through."

"But—but—" Presnol floundered.

"But you've never been out, have you?"

"Only to rescue singers." A convulsive spasm shook the medic's frame.

"Well, it's about time you saw the Ranges at their best," Killa said, amused.

Presnol gulped.

"No, I'll go," Donalla said, giving her lover a reassuring smile. "I'm—supposedly—the hypnotist. And I'm not afraid of the Ranges."

"I'm not, either," Presnol protested, but the women exchanged knowing glances. "I'm not, truly."

"Donalla's presence is sufficient, I'd say," Killa said.

"One of us should remain here, Pres," Donalla said, "and you could continue the hypnotics with—" She hesitated, glancing at Killashandra. "—another patient."

"Yes, I could," Presnol said, beginning to relax. He was not as adept at the process as Donalla, but he had been successful with two of the inactive singers. "That would be a much more useful disposition of my time right now. Ah, when will you be going?" he asked, turning back at the door.

Killa and Donalla looked at each other. Killa shrugged. "We'll check with Lars . . ."

But when they explained their plan to Lars Dahl, Killa could see plainly his resistance to the idea of her going out into the Ranges without him. She herself had had to override her own reluctance to go out in the company of a nonsinger, however dispassionately involved with the singing of crystal.

"There's been no tradition of nonsingers—" Lars began.

"Ha! Since you've been demolishing tradition all over the place, why cavil at this one? The results could be exactly what's needed. At least with me," Killa said. "As you point out, I'm one of the oldest still active singers . . ."

"Killa!" His tone held a warning not to try his patience just then.

"Look, we can rig lots of safeguards. Weather's behaving itself right now, so we can cancel that worry. Donalla can wear a combutton direct to your console, so if you have to do a rescue flit, you'll be the first to hear," Killa went on, perversely determined to undermine any argument he might voice. "Donalla's stronger than she looks, if it comes to her having to break thrall." She grinned. "Know any good throws?" she asked Donalla, who dismissed the question. "So, teach her your special techniques, up to and including setting my cutter sour. Muhlah knows that the reward could be worth the price of a cutter."

"Don't let Clarend hear you say that," Lars remarked with a good attempt at genuine humor.

"Hmmm, too right." Killa grinned back at him. Over the decades they had both taken plenty of abuse from the cutter.

"You'll lend us the double sled then?" Killa asked. She looked out the broad window, beyond the Hangar. "Hell, it's only midday. We could be deep in the Ranges and cutting in a couple of hours." She leaned across the desk toward him, daring him, silently urging him to agree. "Of course, if you happened to have some black-crystal coordinates handy, I could be productive on several levels."

"Killa, you do *know* what you're doing, don't you?"

"No, but Donalla thinks that thrall will help her get past the barriers I can't seem to lower."

He sighed deeply and threw his hands out in capitulation. "If you could come back with some black . . ." He set his lips firmly, hearing the desperation in his own voice.

He propelled himself out of his chair, and while Killashandra contacted the Hangar and arranged for his sled to be readied and stocked, he demonstrated to Donalla the various ways in which thrall could be broken.

"I didn't realize thrall was that dangerous," Donalla said, her eyes wide with the newly acquired information. "And you *let* Killashandra stay thralled to green . . ."

"That was a most unusual situation. Killa needed the overdose of crystal to counteract deprivation. I would never have permitted her to thrall to black—it's far harder to break out of. And that's why I *don't* like just the pair of you going."

"Well, if you want another singer along to see where we've cut black . . ." Killa teased.

"There isn't another singer *in* or you can believe I'd send someone."

"Who's that dork at Trag's desk then?"

"Certainly not yet a singer," Lars said sarcastically, "but she does have business management experience and she's capable of organizing pencil files and auditing accounts."

Killa smiled, relieved by his disparagement of the very pretty girl's abilities.

"Now, if you can't break thrall by any of the methods I've demonstrated, you club her behind the ear and haul her bodily out of the Ranges. You are checked out on sleds, aren't you?"

"You know we all are, Lars," Donalla said, giving him an almost condescending smile. "I've even driven some of the worksleds when there was extensive storm damage to patch up." Lars nodded acceptance of her competence. "But I'm not charmed by the idea of bludgeoning Killashandra Ree into submission. I'll bring along something soothing."

"You have to be careful, though." Lars held up a warning hand. "A singer in thrall can become violent. Strap her down in the sled if it comes to that."

"Now that you've given her the worst-case scenario, how else can you scare her out of this attempt?" Killa asked in some disgust. She turned to Donalla. "Anyone would think he didn't want this to succeed. I've never slugged him yet. Though I might start . . ." And she lifted her fist in mock anger.

He raised both arms and pretended to cringe from her blow. "Just in case," he added, his manner lighter and a sparkle in his blue eyes, "have you any idea where you're going?"

She grinned at him. "You need black. So, since you have already bared the location of your latest black location to Donalla, I thought you wouldn't mind entrusting it to me, your partner."

His smile deepened. "Here." He thrust a slip of paper at her. "When you're on course, eat it!"

"You are all heart, Lars Dahl," Killa said, and marched Donalla out of the office and to the lift.

In the descending car, Killa was amused by the way Donalla eyed her.

"Sorry?"

"Not a bit," Donalla said, scowling sternly; then her expression altered to anxiety. "It's just I hadn't realized the possible complications."

Killa laughed. "You don't, unless you've had to work with 'em. Lars shouldn't have scared you like that."

"He doesn't want to lose you again, Killa," Donalla said, her fine eyes intent. "He idolizes you."

"He has an odd way of showing it at times," Killa

replied, trying for a casual acceptance to conceal her surprise at Donalla's appraisal.

"Sometimes that's because it's too important to admit, even to himself."

The intensity of those quiet words rang in Killa's mind. Lars had so often told her he loved her, but usually in a sort of offhand manner, as if he didn't really mean it, or was astonished by blurting out the declaration. Always his hands and eyes had conveyed more than he actually said aloud. Even when she was denying him, she couldn't genuinely deny her love for him, just her dependence on the affection of any other human being.

The lift door opened and, taking a deep breath, she led the way out to the Hangar and the double sled waiting and ready.

As there was no other sled in sight, Killa set the course directly toward the coordinates Lars had given her and, making a little display of it, dutifully chewed and swallowed the note. Donalla gave her a nervous smile. Killa found the fidgeting of the usually self-confident medic amusing. Well, her self-confidence was only to be expected—in an infirmary. But now she was in the singer's bailiwick, and the Ranges were awesome. No question of that.

When Donalla relaxed enough to watch the spectacular scenery streaming by, Killa made something hot to drink and broke out some munchables. They hadn't had any noon meal, and she wanted something in her belly if she was to let herself get thralled.

There was one problem, Killa mused, now that she focused her mind on the actual process. She never remembered a thing from any period in which she had been thralled. It was all a blank from the moment she

lifted the crystal free to the moment thrall lifted. Of
course, Donalla had carefully explained that one didn't
remember the span of a hypnotic incident, either. Well,
Killa thought with a shrug, finishing the last of her
ration bar, it was worth a try! Lars needed the boost a
success would give him.

Between sessions with Donalla, Killa had done some
surreptitious poking in general files, from Recruitment
to Deliveries, all readily accessible information. There
certainly had been a drop in the numbers of applicants
to the Guild. There had only been six in the last bunch
to be processed, and a mere ninety signing up for Guild
membership over the last decade. She checked back
over four decades, when the totals had been up to the
two hundred mark. More singers were rated "inactive"
than active on the roster. No deaths listed in the past
twenty years. Killa's thoughts were grim. The cost of
caring for singers was higher than the budgets for Research and Development, yet profits were dwindling.
Lars had been all too correct in saying that the Guild
was in serious trouble. She really should have brought
in . . . she frowned, for the name escaped her. She had
found someone, hadn't she? With the perfect pitch required. Could that sort of ability be on the wane in the
modern world? It was a trick of the ear and the mind.

Gradually as the state of affairs of the Guild became
obvious, her initial repugnance over invading singers'
damaged minds to find the location of their sites began
to subside. At Donalla's suggestion, she sat in on a
hypnotic session with a man whose symbiont was visi-
bly failing him. He was gnarled and wrinkled with age,
joints thick with calcium deposits, veins engorged on
fleshless limbs and digits. He seemed content, though,
wrapped in a warm, soft blanket and smelling of a recent bath. There hadn't been much intelligence in the

dull, deeply receding eyes, despite the fact that they were following the movement of the random fractals ever-shifting on the large screen in the corner of his room. He was an improvement over some of the living corpses Killa had seen on her way to his small single room.

"I chose Rimbol, because at least he's tracking what's on the screen," Donalla said. "I've had some luck in restimulating one or two of the least damaged singers. I've just turned off the music in here, but we've found he does respond to aural as well as visual stimuli. I think whatever we do to try to reach their brains is better than just letting these poor hulks have nothing to see and hear. Rimbol's more receptive to hypnotism than some of the others."

She held up the prism and turned Rimbol's head slightly so that the crystal was on a level with his eyes. She twisted the chain so that the prism caught the light, and immediately Rimbol's eyes were captured.

"Watch the prism, Rimbol, watch the lovely colors, shifting and changing. Your eyes are getting heavy, you can't hold them open because your lids are so very heavy and you're falling asleep, gently falling asleep . . ." Donalla pitched her pleasant contralto into a slow rhythmic pattern, and Rimbol's eyes did flicker and close, and a sigh escaped his lips.

"You will sleep and you will not resist. You will answer my questions as best you can. You will remember where you were when you have cut black crystal. You will remember what the landscape was like, if there were any prominent landmarks. You will also tell me the coordinates, because you *do* remember them. And you *do* remember this particular site because you cut black crystal there, four fine crystals in the key of E major. You made enough credits to leave Ballybran for over a year. Records show that you went to your homeworld on that occasion. Do you remember that time, Rimbol? Do remember the landmarks about that site, Rimbol?"

"Ah, the E majors? Best I ever cut. I 'member." The words were slurred, but both medic and singer listened hard. "I 'member. Two peaks, like cones, and then the flat part . . ." The words became more distinct; the voice even sounded younger, more vibrant. "Narrow ravine, winds like an S, had to tip the sled and damned near lost her but I knew there was black around. Fardling steep slope up to the peaks, sharp to climb, slipped often but crystal's there . . . feel it in my knees and hands . . ."

"The coordinates, Rimbol. What are the coordinates? You saw them when you finally set the sled down. You know you did. So put yourself back then, when you're looking down at your console. Now, you can see the figures on the scope, can't you?"

"See 'em . . ."

"What do you see, Rimbol? Look closely. The numbers are very clear, aren't they?"

"Clear . . ."

"What numbers do you see?"

"Ah . . ." And another sigh escaped the old man. "Longitude, one fifty-two degrees twenty-two, latitude sixteen degrees fifteen. Didn't think I'd 'member that. I did!" He smiled contentedly and his closed eyelids trembled.

Killashandra had jotted down the coordinates and then looked at the figures, still uneasy about obtaining such information.

"He'll never make it there again, Killa," Donalla said softly. "He doesn't need them. The Guild which cares for him does."

"Someone else could probably find the claim without scouring it out of his mind," Killashandra said, resisting the intrusion for Rimbol's sake. His name sounded familiar, but he had altered far too much for her to recall what he had looked like as a young and vigorous man.

"There isn't time for random chance." Then Donalla turned back to her patient. "Thanks, Rimbol. You have been marvelously helpful."

"Have?"

Killashandra was astounded to see a smile return to tremble on the wasted lips, a smile that remained even after Donalla ended the hypnotic session. She said nothing when she noted that Killashandra had seen that smile. She turned up the music, a lilting, merry tune, and, as the two women left, Killashandra turned back and saw a distorted finger lift in time to the rhythm.

When they had finished their snack, Killashandra checked their flight path and estimated that they were nearly there. They overflew the black-and-yellow chevrons ten minutes later, and she circled, mentally chanting Lars's choosing rhyme—eeny, meeny—as she looked for the landmarks he had told her marked the exact location of the black crystal.

She had turned 160 degrees before she recognized the configuration of ravines: three, one rising behind the other, in frozen waves of stone. At the base of the third, she should find signs of workings. She did: recent workings because sunlit sparkles caught her eye.

"Here we are," she caroled out to Donalla. "Behold!" She gestured expansively out the front window. "An actual crystal site!"

Donalla's lips parted and then a slight frown marred her high forehead.

"No, it's not much to look at," Killa said, lightly teasing. "A place known only to few and treasured by many." She locked down the controls, noting as she did so, as she always did whether she had realized it before or not, the coordinates on the screen before she shut the engines off. She had to admit that such an automatic scan was as much a part of a landing routine as turning off the engine—so automatic that she wouldn't remember she had done it three seconds after she had. There would be hundreds of such flashes for Donalla to probe . . .

She reached for her cutter and gave the lined carrier for cut crystal to Donalla to tote and opened the sled door. Through the soles of her heavy work boots, she could feel the ripple of the nearby black. She swallowed hard. The call of black was strong. Maybe Lars had been right: she wasn't ready for black yet. But they hadn't much choice, had they?

She led the way to the face, visible because of the regular steps where crystal had been recently cut. Nothing looked familiar. She knew from checking files that he had cut alone for nearly a decade—a decade she hadn't even known had passed while they were estranged. But, and she shook her head in surprise, the claim bore *their* chevron markings. Lars was a bundle of contradictions, wasn't he? He was too sentimental to be a good Guild Master, she thought; then, thinking of recent examples of his ruthlessness, she reversed her opinion.

As she narrowed the distance, she explained once more to Donalla exactly how a singer proceeded on site: finding a clear side of crystal, sounding a tuning note, setting the cutter, and then excising the crystal.

"The dangerous part is when I hold the crystal up. If sun hits it, I'll go into thrall." Wryly she glanced up to check the position of the sun, trying to ignore the hard cold knot developing in her stomach. "Well," she said, exhaling a deep breath, "here goes!" She motioned for

Donalla to step back a bit, farther away from the business edge of the cutter.

Killashandra eyed the crystal face. Yes, these were Lars's cuttings. She would know them anywhere. Recent storms had not damaged his distinctive style. She brushed some loose splinters away and felt the crystal resonance just a note away. She pressed her hand flat against the surface and, setting her diaphragm, sang a clear mid-C. The crystal vibrated almost excitedly to the sound. She set the cutter. Putting the blade perpendicular to the face, she rammed it in, disengaged the blade, sliced from the top to her lower cut, then quickly shifted position to make the second downward cut, freeing the shaft. She turned off the cutter, letting it slip down the harness that held it to her shoulder.

"Now, Donalla," she said. She lifted the black crystal high, high enough to catch the sun, and felt the beginnings of thrall paralyze her. She could no more have evaded that than Rimbol had been able to evade Donalla.

Hard grit dug into her face, irregular hard objects poked her the length of her body, and her ears rang with an unpleasant dissonance that would soon split her skull. Abruptly the unendurable noise quit.

"Killa! Killa! Are you all right?"

A hand on her shoulder shook her, tentatively at first, then more urgently. But the voice was female. She had never cut with a woman! She propped herself up, one hand automatically feeling for the cutter. Her cutter? Where was it? She couldn't have lost her cutter! Dazed, she looked about, patting the ground. Her eyes were dry in their sockets and ached.

"Killa?"

Boots scrabbled on the litter and someone's face

peered anxiously at her. But the someone held her precious cutter in one hand and a black-crystal shaft in the other.

"I didn't drop it . . ." Killa was weak with relief.

"I was about to shatter it if the cutter noise hadn't worked," the woman said.

Killa peered at the anxious face. It was familiar. She forced a tired mind to put name to face. Ah! "Donalla!"

"Who did you expect?" Relief made Donalla's voice sharp.

Killa eased herself to a sitting position. She couldn't trust her legs yet. Her right shoulder ached, and her arm was riddled with sharp needles of renewed circulation. She massaged her shoulder, gradually becoming aware that darkness was rapidly shadowing the narrow ravine.

"So?" she asked Donalla curtly as memory flooded back. She had cut black to go into thrall, which she had obviously done, and the thrall had lasted much longer than planned.

The look on the medic's face answered her question. "You were more impenetrable than when I tried back at the Infirmary," she said, with a weary sigh. "You just stood there, holding this wretched thing." She gave the black shaft a careless waggle. Killa lunged to save it. Donalla drew it sharply back into her chest.

"I'm all right now, Donalla. It can't thrall me again. Just don't damage the thing."

"After what it did to you? I thought I'd never get it out of your hand." Donalla regarded her burden warily.

"Then put it in the carrier." Killa wrenched her upper body about, looking for the carrier, and jabbed her finger at it. "Just don't drop it," she added as Donalla obeyed. Her voice was strident with anxiety. She cleared her throat and went on, controlling her voice, "For some reason, fresh crystal cracks faster than at any other time. Ah!" She sighed in relief as the medic stowed and covered the shaft.

Killa got to her feet then, brushing off clinging bits and pieces of dirt and crystal. She was tired, but glancing at the sun, she saw there was enough light left to make a couple more cuts to add to this bigger C.

"What are you doing?" Donalla asked, her voice sharp with concern.

"I'm going to cut." She had to use force to get Donalla to release the cutter.

"But I couldn't break through the thrall."

"Shouldn't keep me from cutting. Especially as it's black."

Killa went down a fifth, sang loud and clear, heard the answering note, and set her cutter. Donalla stepped in front of her.

"Out of my way," Killa said, appalled that she had been about to swing the cutter into position—a movement that would have brought the blade slicing right through Donalla's thighs.

"I can't let you."

"Ah, leave off, Donalla!" Killa tried to push her away. "There's no sun. It's the sun that starts thrall. For the love of anything you hold sacred, let me use the light that's left."

"You're sure? It took me hours . . ."

"Well, it won't happen at this time of day." Killa blew out with exasperation. Donalla was worse than any novice she had ever shepherded. "Sun's nearly down. Now, move out of my way!"

Hesitantly and watching Killa very warily indeed, Donalla stepped aside. Killa sang again and tuned the cutter, neatly slicing beyond her first cut. She excised that one, managed two more quick ones in the same level—smallish and stocky but black! She had the cutter poised for a third when the face turned sour. There was an intrusion or a flaw. Cursing under her breath, she stepped back and signaled Donalla to bring the carrier over. She finished packing crystal just as the last of the sunlight faded from the ridges above them.

The two women stumbled back to the sled, the carrier between them. Only when she had seen the carrier secured behind straps and the cutter properly racked did Killashandra allow fatigue to creep up on her.

"How long did you say I was thralled?" she asked, slumping into the pilot's chair.

"I forgot to check the time right away," Donalla admitted, "but from the time I did till I threw you down, it took three and a half hours!"

Killa chuckled weakly. "Don't doubt it." She rubbed at shoulder muscles still twinging from a long inactivity. "And I wouldn't answer?"

"You kept staring at the crystal. I tried every single maneuver Lars showed me and you might as well have been crystal yourself for all the blind good it did me."

She had been scared, Killashandra decided; that's what was making her angry now.

"Don't reproach yourself, Donalla. I got out, and the crystal's okay. I'd've been out of thrall once the sun went down. Or did Lars remember to mention that?" He hadn't, to judge by the expression on Donalla's face. "Fix me something to drink, will you? I'm too tired to move, and my throat's so dry . . ."

Donalla banged the cup on the counter as she hauled the water out of the cooler, her movements revealing more plainly than any words the state of her feelings.

With food in her stomach, Killashandra took a hand beam and went out to examine the face. If she could cut past the damaged crystal to clear stuff, she ought to. She was damned lucky to find black—then she laughed, recalling that luck hadn't entered into the discovery. *Knowing* that she would have black to cut in this site took some of the elation out of the work. It was the mystery, the challenge of having to *find* the elusive material. But the work was still rewarding—and Donalla had had the chance to acquire firsthand Range experience to augment her clinical knowledge of crystal singers.

Killa hummed softly, listened for an answering resonance, and heard none. Cursing under her breath, she went back to the sled. She would have to wait till morning to see how deep the flaw was. Worse than not finding black was finding it uncuttable.

She woke in the night, aware of the warm body beside her and instantly recognizing it as Donalla's, not Lars's. That was another matter they had neglected to explain to Donalla. As the woman was apparently unremittingly heterosexual, Killa decided she would have to manage on her own—morning song could be rather more of a shock than Donalla was ready to handle.

Moving carefully, Killa rose. She found an extra thermal blanket in the cupboard and let herself out of the sled. This wouldn't be the first time she had slept on the ground. Rolling herself up under the prow of the sled where she would be protected from any heavy dew, she wriggled around until she got comfortable and dropped off to sleep again.

Dawn and crystal woke, singing her awake. She took deep breaths to reduce the effect on her until she heard Donalla crying out. Grinning, but as uncomfortable as Donalla probably was, Killa endured. She waited until the effects had faded before returning to the cabin.

"What was that? Where did you go?" Donalla demanded, her tone almost accusatory.

"That's crystal waking up to sunlight. Fabulous experience, isn't it?" Killa grinned unrepentantly, folding her thermal to stow it away again. "I felt discretion was the better part of retaining our growing friendship."

"Oh!" Donalla flushed beet red and turned away, looking anywhere but at Killashandra. "No one told me about this."

"I know," Killashandra said sympathetically. "It's another case of us knowing it so well we think everyone else knows it."

Donalla took another deep breath and managed a weak smile. "I gather—I mean—well, is that why certain partnerships . . . Oh, I'm not sure what I mean."

Killa laughed, flicking the switch on the hot-water heater as she began preparations for cooking breakfast. "It has a tendency to make minor quarrels disappear in the morning."

By the time she had eaten, Donalla had turned clinical in her examination of the sensual effect of sun-warmed crystal on human libido. Killa answered honestly and fully, amused at Donalla's professional curiosity.

"What's astonishing is that more singers don't sing duet," the medic finally announced, turning inquiringly to Killa, who shrugged.

"I suppose it's like anything else," she said. "Palls after a few score years."

"You and Lars were partners for—" Donalla bit off the rest of her sentence.

Killa regarded her for a long moment. Those of the Guild who did not lose "time" in the Ranges were taught not to make comparisons that could upset singers.

"A long time," Killa said. "A very long time." She

paused. "It doesn't seem like a long time. How old am I, Donalla?"

"You certainly don't look your age, Killashandra," Donalla said, temporizing, "and I won't put a figure to it."

Killa grunted and heaved a big sigh. "You're right, you know, and I don't really want a figure."

"You don't look older than four, maybe five decades," Donalla offered as compensation.

"Thanks." Then Killa rose, having finished her meal. "I've got black I might be able to cut out of that face. I've got to try." She waggled a finger at Donalla. "Only today, you make bloody sure you take any cut right out of my hand the moment I've pulled it free. You wrench it from me, if necessary; and carefully, mind you, stow it in the carton."

Donalla stood ready all day to follow those orders, but they were never needed. The black had fractured right down into the base of the site. Killa swore, because she had cut so carefully the day before. She hadn't heard the fracture note as she finished cutting the third shaft. Usually a crack like that was not only audible but sensed even through the thick soles of her boots.

"Damn, damn, and double damn," she said, admitting defeat in midafternoon. She had even tried to find an outcropping somewhere else in the rock but hadn't heard so much as a murmur from crystal.

"What?" Donalla asked, rousing from a state of somnolence. She had been patiently watching Killa's explorations from a perch on the height.

"It's gone. No point in staying here."

"We're going back?" Donalla's expression brightened.

"We shouldn't. We should look around."

"Lars only gave you these coordinates."

"Yes, but somewhere around here," Killa said, waving her hand in a comprehensive sweep that took in the entire ravine, "there'll be more black crystal."

"How long will it take you to find it?"

"Ah . . ." Killa waggled her forefinger. "That's the rub. I don't know where."

"Well, then, let's go back to the Cube and get coordinates to another known black-crystal site," Donalla said, pushing herself off her perch and brushing dust from her trousers.

"It'll take us three hours to get back," Killa heard herself protesting. "Why, I could be—"

"Circling the area unprofitably for hours, days, more likely," Donalla said. "Let's do it the easy way, with another set of coordinates. Huh?"

Killa considered this, sweeping aside all the arguments she was ranging against the common sense Donalla was speaking. She owed it to Lars. He had been right. She had some black to return with. She shouldn't waste time. She should cut where they knew there was more.

"You're right. Absolutely right. We go back. We do it Lars's way."

][CHAPTER 10][

Lars was pleased with the four she brought back, disappointed by Donalla's failure, and relieved that they had returned. He had other coordinates for Killa to use.

"I don't really *like* this," she told him. "It still feels like claim jumping."

Lars grinned at her. "You won't say that when you have to share the proceeds, Sunny."

"There's that, too, of course," she said, making a face at him.

She went out by herself within the hour, after getting a severe lecture from Lars about remembering to stow black the instant she cut it.

"If I find it!"

"You will."

She did, but whatever crystal might have been there once was now buried under a mass of rubble and boulders too big to be shifted. She sang at the top of her excellent lungs and didn't hear so much as a squeak from the buried crystal.

So she returned to the Guild, arriving just before dark and, while Lars was willing to give her another set of coordinates, he wasn't willing to let her start until the next morning.

"Take a long bath, have a good meal, sleep in a good bed," he said with a wink and a leer. "Missed you, Sunny," he added in a soft voice, and pulled her to him, to kiss her neck. He pulled a face as he licked his lips. "Yugh! You need the bath."

"Thanks!"

"Look," he said, becoming serious, "I badly need your help, Sunny. Really, more your presence and a nod or two when necessary. If you seem to be going along with my scheme, the others're more apt to."

"Go along with what scheme?" she demanded warily. Lars was wearing his Guild Master's face.

"I've got three other singers who I believe—I hope—are still flexible enough to go along with me in this."

"In what?"

"Easy, Killa!" He grinned down at her, a twinkle returning to his eyes. "Using coordinates from the inactives."

"Oh." She began to see both his problem and his scheme.

"I also want to see how they respond to that alternative Donalla's suggested."

"Which is?" She had slightly eased herself back from his embrace.

He scrubbed his head with his knuckles, a sure sign that he was uncertain and nervous. "If singers didn't spend so much time trying to *find* claims they haven't worked in a while, if they could just go right back to them, they'd save a lot of time."

"So you want them to permit Donalla to hypnotize them and force memory of their coordinates?" Killa asked, cutting to the gist.

He nodded.

"I don't think they'll go for it," she said, shaking her head.

"You took mine and found the black. You took Rimbol's and got to his site."

"I know it can be done, and you might get some singers to use inactives' coordinates, but I don't think you'll get them to submit to hypnotic recall of their own sites. You know how paranoid we all are about claim locations."

"Paranoia doesn't have to enter the picture."

"Ha!"

"Look, Donalla's not a cutter and she's demonstrated her integrity as a medic. She's certainly not going to violate their trust."

"First she has to get it."

"All right, but she's not about to go mouthing off coordinates. Muhlah, but she could implant—in herself—a posthypnotic command to forget what she's just heard."

"She could?" Killashandra was surprised.

"Even better, she wants to give each singer who'll go for this a keyword. She may have to keep track of keywords, knowing the fragile memory of singers"— and Lars gave Killa a wry grin—"but that keyword would allow them to recall their own coordinates without any other further assist.

"I mean," Lars continued, beginning to pace the room in his enthusiasm, "this is the way it'd work, according to Donalla. She gives them a posthypnotic command to remember coordinates whenever they set down the sled. That's locked in their memories. Guild records show what they cut, if not where they cut. When they want to return to a site, they say the password, and that makes the information accessible again. To them, and to them only, so their privacy hasn't been violated."

"It sounds feasible—for those who accept hypnosis."

"You seem to be one of the few who don't," he said, resignation in his voice.

"I've always marched to my own drumbeat," she said in a light tone that masked her own sense of failure. She really did want to help him. "Count on me for support—for however much good it does you."

"Your support'll mean more than you imagine, Sunny," he said, and gave an emphatic nod of his head. "Go on and get cleaned up. I've got a few more things to clear off my screens." And he gestured to a desk littered with pencil files. "I'll meet you in the main dining hall in an hour, all right?"

When she had bathed and dressed with some care, she made her way to the dining hall she had not patronized at all in recent years. There weren't that many diners in the big room, and most of the alcoves were dark. It made her shiver a little. Was it just that all working singers happened to be out in the Ranges right now? That there wasn't a group of novices waiting around to be infected by the symbiont? That the large number of support staff had all decided to eat in their quarters this evening?

She looked around for Lars and then heard his distinctive whistle. He was just loading a tray with beakers of what looked like Yarran beer. Beside him were Donalla and Presnol and three singers, the same three she had recognized at the meeting at which Lars had officially opened inactive claims.

Now he nodded toward a banquet table off to one

side of the huge low-ceilinged room, and she turned to meet them there. She managed to drag one singer's name to mind: Borton. Pushing harder, she remembered that he had been in the group she had "graduated" with. He didn't look much older than he had looked back then. But why should he, if his symbiont was doing its job?

"Borton, how nice to see you," she said, smugly pleased that she had placed him. She smiled at the other two, a man and a woman, as if she remembered them, as well. She gave Lars a quick glance.

"Tiagana, Jaygrin," he put in quickly, "do you recall Killashandra?"

"I think we've met either on ships leaving Shankill," Killashandra said, addressing Jaygrin, "or wandering around the moon waiting for a shuttle." She glanced at Tiagana. "Ah, Yarran beer. What would we do without it?"

That seemed to bridge the gap. Everyone reached for a glass from Lars's tray and then helped transfer platters and covered dishes to the round table. Lars acted the genial and diligent host and sent Presnol back for more Yarran beer when the first beakers were empty. Killa saw flashes of amusement in the other singers' faces, as if they were well aware of how Lars was trying to lull them. It had been a long time since she had been in a peer group, or in a dinner party of any kind. If it hadn't been for Presnol and Donalla deftly stimulating conversation, this party might never have come to life. But it did.

"All right, Lars, you've dined us and beered us, so what's this really about?" Borton asked, settling back in his chair as he pushed his empty dinner plate away from him.

"All four of you have been profiting from cutting on

inactive singers' claims," Lars began, "and that's exactly what I hoped would happen. But I'd like you four to take this a step further." He went on, using almost the same explanation he had given Killa an hour before. Had he been rehearsing it on her? she wondered. But since she had heard it already, she could pay more attention to the way the other three were responding to his scheme.

Tiagana didn't bother to disguise her reluctance. She leaned away from Lars, toward Borton, who was sitting beside her. He was not as unreceptive. And as for Jaygrin, Killa could almost see the credits dancing in his eyes, and his smile was positively greedy.

"How do we know that Donalla can't unhypnotize herself and consciously *know* our claim locations?"

"She can't," Presnol said flatly, his tone brooking no argument.

"I wouldn't want to," Donalla said. "It would be pointless, since I don't sing crystal, and the cutter is always paid on what he or she brings in. I couldn't count on you to remember to give me a bribe, now could I?"

Jaygrin laughed, showing narrow, almost feral teeth. "So the deal is, Lars, that we'll get inactive singer sites plus this hypnotic business to remember where we cut?"

Lars nodded.

"And no share out of the cut?" Borton asked.

"On the first cut of an inactive, you pay the twenty-five percent, but only the Guild tithe on any subsequent cuttings."

Even Tiagana looked interested now.

"It works," Killa said, deciding to enter the discussion. "I've flown out and cut as long as the claim was good. Came back in, got another set, and flew directly to it, ready to cut again. Of course, one claim was buried too far to be reached, but the coordinates were accurate. Saves a lot of time and wasted effort."

"You've been doing what Lars described?" Tiagana asked.

"I have," Killa replied, nodding and managing a slightly smug curl to her smile. "A snap." She snapped her fingers to match her words. "I think it's a lot easier on a body, too," she added, indolently easing her buttocks down in her chair. "Muhlah, when I think of the days I've spent trying to find a site, trying to remember if it was still workable. Sure saves a lot of stress." She debated putting a word or two about loyalty to the Guild but knew that wouldn't cut much with singers. Only credit did. And Lars's new scheme was indeed the key to larger credit balances and fewer dry runs in the Ranges. "No more dry runs," she reminded the three singers as they mulled what had been said.

Presnol slipped away from the table and returned with more Yarran beer. Wisely Lars switched to a discussion of the dinner they had just eaten, criticizing the preparation of one or two dishes and asking if anyone else had found them wanting.

Singers could talk food till the galaxy grew cold, and Presnol and Donalla kept the beer circulating until only Lars and Killa, who had been more abstemious than was her custom, were able to walk straight.

"Do you think it'll work?" she asked him as they made their way to their quarters.

"We'll know tomorrow. But that Jaygrin's going to try it." Lars chuckled. "Avaricious bastard! But then, he's never come in with any of the darker colors on his own."

Which, in crystal-singer parlance, was the most insulting thing one could say about another cutter.

CHAPTER 11

As Killa was setting off for the next set of coordinates Donalla had obtained for her, she saw the other three singers readying their sleds in the Hangar. When she came back two days later, she had a full carton of deep amethyst crystals in fifths and thirds. They were not, of course, the black she had been after. But she had remembered that Clodine had said the darker shades were in short supply, so she had stayed to cut rather than return empty-handed.

Before she had lifted from the site, she had jotted down the coordinates and slipped the notation under the sheet of liberated markers taped to her console. In plain sight and yet hidden. Now if she could only remember *that!* She ought to think of some sort of code, something she would twig to the moment she saw it. She began to regret that she wasn't a good subject for hypnosis. She wondered how Tiagana, Borton, and Jaygrin were getting on. She was pleased that she could recall their names so easily. If she wanted to remember something, she really could!

She was in rare good spirits when she brought the cartons in to Clodine.

"Haven't I seen you here a lot lately?" the Sorter asked, grinning because Killa was.

"Sure! I'm enjoying an excellent streak of luck. It was bound to happen," Killashandra said blithely, "given the probabilities. Even if these aren't blacks."

Clodine held up the heaviest of the fifths, adjusting her eyesight to scrutinize the crystal. She put it on the scales and made minute adjustments, nodding all the while.

"Well, you remembered amethyst, and there's a good market for them right now. Two space stations are being constructed, and the big Altairian way station is expanding, so darks are needed for their life-support systems. Lars'll be real pleased to know these have come in."

"I'll tell him myself, hear?" Killa winked at Clodine.

"It's nice to see you like this, Killa," Clodine said, and gave Killa's arm a tentative pat. "And you're not even buzzing."

"No, I'm not. I feel as if I could cut forever these days."

"I'd heard you already had!" Clodine said with rare flippancy.

In great good humor, Killashandra laughed, then chuckled more heartily from her gut when she saw the final figure on two days' work. Many were the times in her past when she would have killed for such totals. Yes, Lars's idea of getting coordinates out of inactives was brilliant.

Before she went down to her quarters, she stopped in

the Hangar office to ask for her sled to be ready for the morning.

"Why don't you just stay out, like you usually do, Killa?" Murr asked. "You're like an overnight homer, in one day and out the next."

"I find what the Guild needs, I cut, I bring it in. Much more efficient that way, isn't it?"

"You're using a lot of fuel," he cautioned.

"I've the credit to pay for it, Murr. Humor me."

She left him there, but his morose attitude had brought her down a bit. The moment she entered her quarters, the comunit buzzed.

"Muhlah! Can't I even have a bath first?"

"Killa?" Lars's image came up on the screen. "Glad you're in, C.S. Ree. Would you join me as soon as possible in my office?"

She started to say something snide about his formality, but before she could speak he stepped to one side and she saw that he had visitors in his office: visitors who were wearing the clear plastic suits and breathing masks that meant their errand was urgent enough for them to risk possible contamination by the Ballybran symbiont.

"Permit me time to become presentable, Guild Master Lars Dahl," she said in a similar manner, and waved the comunit off.

Curiosity moved her to shower and change quickly. Very few people would take the chance these were. Urgent was almost always interesting. As she strode into the office, there was a new person at Trag's desk who looked up, seemed about to challenge her presence, hesitated, and then looked quickly back to the screen. She palmed the door and entered Lars's office.

"Ah, Crystal Singer Ree, I appreciate your alacrity. These are Klera and Rudney Saplinson-Trill. Klera,

Rudney, this is the other member of the original Guild survey team." He gestured for Killashandra to be seated.

She noticed that there were snacks on the table beside her and blessed him for such thoughtfulness. He had even managed drinkers for the suited Saplinson-Trills. But he hadn't managed to indicate why they were braving the dangers of Ballybran.

"I'm not sure if you can recall the planet we visited some years back . . ." Lars began.

"Twenty-four years, five months, and two weeks, to be precise," Rudney Saplinson-Trill said with the quick, humorless smile of someone to whom accuracy is more important than courtesy. The tinny and nasal quality the helmet speakers gave his voice increased the impudence of that unnecessary correction.

"Yes, the one with the opalescence which we investigated for the late Guild Master," Lars continued. "It was posited at the time that Heptite Guild members, protected by their symbiont, would be safe from the infection which had killed the original exploratory team exposed to the opalescence—"

"Fluid metal, Guild Master," Rudney said, "is a more accurate term for the material—FM for short."

"We called it Jewel Junk," Killashandra said, mimicking him. He didn't notice, but Klera did.

"Yes, we did, didn't we?" Lars said, clearing his throat. "For lack of a more accurate designation," he added, nodding toward Rudney. "You will remember that we actually made two trips there, the second one after our visit to Nihal Three. On the second one we fed some trash to several of the Jewel Junk aka FM."

Killashandra wanted to giggle at Lars, but mastered the urge.

"Actually, *nine* of the now twenty FM manifestations," Rudney said.

"Yes. As I was saying . . ." Lars's nostrils flared, a sign of rare impatience in him, and he gave Rudney a quelling glance. "We also tried to establish communications with the, ah, FM opalescence." When the scientist seemed about to correct him yet again he said more firmly, "Or has the opalescence abated?" Lars fixed the scientist with a cold glare, then looked back to Killashandra, rattling his strong fingers on the table in a complex roll.

What appeared to be a nervous habit of his, plus the use of the words "opalescence," "Nihal Three," and "the infection" began to stir memories for Killa.

"We established a form of communication with it," she said. "Have you managed to enlarge on that beginning?" Why else would they be risking their lives visiting Ballybran?

"We are pure research scientists," Rudney said stiffly. "We are attempting to establish the parameters of an extremely complex life-form."

"Then you agree that the Junk is sentient?"

Rudney made a gesture, discounting her assumption. "We are only beginning to analyze its substance."

"Wasn't it impervious to diagnostic instrumentation?" Killa asked Lars.

"Ours is considerably more sensitive," Rudney continued inexorably, "and therefore we have made progress where the usual sort of instrumentation was inadequate to the purpose."

"So," Killa said, crossing her arms over her chest and focusing her entire attention on him. She had found this to disconcert the unwary. "What is it?"

"We have not yet finished our initial survey," Rudney admitted.

"After twenty-four years, five months, and two weeks?"

"With such an unusual material, one does not rush to conclusions," Rudney informed her.

"Did it ever digest the Ballybran crystal we gave it?" Killa was very pleased with herself for that recollection.

"Ah, no," Rudney replied, and cleared his throat, causing an awful rasping sound to be broadcast. The nonabsorption seemed to worry him.

"In fact," Klera said, plunging in, "all nine FM units prominently display the crystal shards in the center of the reservoir. That's what we call the central node. Though 'node' is not exactly accurate either."

"Would blob do?" Killa found scholarly precision tedious.

"Fluid metal is the proper description of its composition and, even, of its function," Klera said, her round face solemn.

"But have you established any level of communication with my Jewel Junk?"

"Yyyeesss, and nn-no," Klera said, momentarily flustered. "Our xenolinguist had hundreds of hours of recording but . . ." She sagged with a weary sigh.

"No mutual lexicon," Killa said, adding her own sigh.

"The individual FMs, however," Klera said, brightening, "*seem* to be communicating on some level. Though whether or not it's through use of the crystal shards, we haven't been able to ascertain." She shot a worried look at Rudney.

"Just the nine, or the other Junks you've discovered?" Killa asked, wondering if that was the problem.

"We can't be positive that they don't have another means of interacting. But we have established that the crystals send bursts of piezoelectric current," Klera said.

"Though we have been unable to determine the exact reason for the activity," Rudney said, smoothly taking over the explanations. "All the twenty FM deposits show irrefutable evidence of a thermoelectric effect, generating a voltage flow which, we have posited, is due to the extremes of temperature through which the planet goes. There is a recognizable tide, as it were, in the fluctuations of the thermoelectric effect that can be timed to the onset of deviations in the planet's rotation around its primary.

"Naturally, we established a control group of three," he went on, settling himself in his chair for a long lecture. "Caves Three, Nine, and Fifteen remain as we found them on our arrival, complete with their central nub of crystal. We've divided the others into three groups according to size, giving each group a special diet: organic wastes, which seem to have little effect on growth; inorganic wastes, which demonstrably increase the size exponentially to the amount offered; and a mixture, half and half, to the third group, which seems to thrive the best."

"We've done hours of recordings," Klera managed to slip in while Rudney took a deep breath, "which I do maintain are not merely thermoelectric statics. Fizal, our linguist, is certain that the various rhythms are conversations of some sort."

"That's not as immediate or as interesting as the history we have postulated about the primary 478-S-2937 and the planet's relationship to it," Rudney went on. "Star 478-S has been through many stages, and our investigations point to the probability that the planet, Opal, was formed from ejecta of the various stages of the star's development."

"Now, Rudney," Klera said firmly, "you know that Sarianus's theory is equally viable." She turned to Lars. "Our astrophysicist is of the opinion that the star was a huge *new* star, formed near the remnants of others."

"That has yet to be proved, Klera. That theory does not explain—"

"The flares, Rudney," Klera said, and the pair ignored the others in the room to continue what was obviously a long-standing argument. "The solar flares affect the planet. We've noted the exceptional activity of the 'static' messages shortly before and after solar flares."

"Klera, you cannot seriously believe that FM is controlling the flares?"

"I do, Rudney, and there is much evidence to support this." She looked at Killa as if requesting her support. "I believe that the FM has developed intelligence—a bizarre form, to be sure." She pointedly ignored Rudney's crackling snort. "Its vision and sensory systems would be electric and magnetic fields, ions and electrons. Its pain would be changes in the strengths of those fields and their threat to its existence when the solar flares are especially violent. Until recently—well, recently in solar terms—it has been the sun which has manipulated the planet's environment, and therefore it tries to control the sun by emanations of its own thermoelectric fields, making sunspots come and go as needed. Our geologist has noted that the planet has had more than its share of magnetic pole charges, many earthquakes, and some major readjustments in consequence of the polarities. You might say that it's attempting to avoid 'pain.' But it follows that the FM is intelligent, because it is attempting to adjust its environment. Only intelligence seeks to do this. I also think," she added, shooting a repressive glance at Rudney, who kept opening his mouth to interrupt, "it is capable of reproducing itself by asexual fission in order to increase its ability to control the sun. We have monitored a steady growth in all FM units . . ."

"How many levels do they go now?" Killashandra asked, suddenly remembering that part of their investigation.

"FMs with crystal nubs receiving the mixed diet have descended nineteen levels," Klera said, as pleased with such growth as a doting mother. "Those without crystal do not make significant progress and . . ." She faltered, glancing nervously at Rudney.

"Food plus crystal means growth?" Killashandra asked.

"*And* intelligence," Klera said emphatically. "The FMs with crystal nubs exhibit more thermoelectric activity than those deprived of crystal. Who knows what progress could be made in measuring FM intelligence if they were all equal in opportunity? Or if they had undamaged crystal!"

That sentence came out in a rush—and the purpose of their visit became clear to Killashandra.

"We've tried," Rudney said, his tone nearly apologetic, "to obtain a modest budget from the Solar Investigative Society to cover the cost of small pieces of undamaged Ballybran crystal . . ." He trailed off lamely and raised his hands in appeal.

She glanced at Lars's bland expression, not sure if she was amused or annoyed with him. When he was trying to put the Guild on a more solid commercial basis, how could he entertain what was clearly an appeal for a *donation* of crystal for these scientific types on a project that had nothing to do with the Guild? It seemed to her that Lars was seriously contemplating this request. Why else had he invited her to the conference?

As the silence lengthened, Rudney turned redder inside his protective suit; Klera just kept running her finger up and down the seam of her sleeve.

"I gather that no more deaths have resulted from contact with the opalescence?" Killa asked.

"Of course not," Saplinson-Trill said, flicking away that consideration with his fingers as he resumed his professional manner. "We follow a strict regimen of decontam and weekly med checks. We are extremely careful not to touch the FM with anything but the instruments kept in the cave for that purpose which have been made of a special alloy that FM does not melt."

"The lapses certainly haven't proved fatal," Klera added candidly.

Rudney smothered an oath as he glared at her.

"What lapses?" Killa asked, covering her delight with a bland, inquiring expression.

"Nothing fatal, or even producing physical discomfort," Klera said quickly.

"What sort of lapse? Memory loss?" Killa remembered that both she and Lars had spent long moments admiring the brilliant, shifting coruscation in the caves. Like a very sophisticated fractal, it had been beautiful to watch, almost mesmeric.

"What Klera refers to," Rudney told them, the rasping edge to his voice communicating clearly his wish that she had not spoken, "are periods when the FM displays the most thermoelectric activity. Several of our team members experienced what, ah, I suppose, *could* be termed time lapses . . ."

"The Jewel Junk's shifting patterns had a certain hypnotic rhythm to them when we were there, didn't they, Guild Master?" Favoring Lars with a quick glance, Killashandra began to perceive another reason why he had wanted her in on this meeting.

"Yes, they did," he agreed amiably. "While the Guild does not make a practice of assisting outside research in crystal applications, it just happens that there are some useful shapes and colors available from apprentice cuttings that could be released to you. They are now unflawed crystal, having been returned, but not of the size, color, or warrantable stability of pitch to be offered for commercial sale."

Utter relief flooded Rudney's face. Klera, after giving a squeak of delighted surprise, covered her mouth as if afraid she might say something wrong and compromise the offer.

"However, the Guild requires that a singer install the crystal," Lars said, "and right now, the Guild needs all experienced singers in the Range. We can't spare one for the time it would take to make the trip."

"But, Guild Master, we've the services of a B-and-B ship," Rudney surprised both singers by saying. "That's the only way we, as leaders of the FM Project, could justify our absence."

"A brain-and-brawn ship with a Singularity Drive?" Lars asked, expecting a negative response.

"Yes, indeed, Guild Master," Rudney said. "Archeological and Exploratory are exceedingly interested in the FM project and put a ship at our disposal for this important mission. The BB-1066."

"How very convenient," Killa said, twitching an eyebrow at Lars. "I'd be tempted to take the assignment, if only to see Brendan again."

"You are, C.S. Ree, one of my most experienced singers," Lars began repressively, and Killa wondered why he was glaring at her. Surely he was merely priming the pump to haggle a good fee for her services. As he had the right to do. The Guild had a reputation to maintain—especially right now.

"I am due some relief time away from Ballybran," she said.

To her surprise, Lars frowned. "This really isn't the time for you to be away from the Ranges, C.S. Ree."

He spoke so firmly that she was uncertain of how to proceed. She was also peeved at him, for she really could use some time off-planet. And who else had previous experience with the Jewel Junk? As Guild Master, he really couldn't leave Ballybran, but she could. Muhlah!

"In that case, I shall plan to return to my duties tomorrow," she said stiffly and, bowing courteously to the scientists, marched out of the office.

"Well?" she asked Lars as he entered their quarters much later that evening.

"Well, what?" he said, scrubbing at his hair with irritation and fatigue.

"Did you give them crystal?"

"You heard me. FM, indeed," he muttered. She had ordered Yarran beer and some light snacks, which she served him. "Thanks!" He sighed with gratitude as he tipped the recliner back.

"So, how much did you get?"

"Hummm?" he mumbled over a long pull of the beer.

"How much for a singer to go install the crystals, and whom have you chosen? Because I insist on going."

"Sunny, I need you here . . ." he began.

"You can do without me for the eight–ten days it'll take by way of the B-and-B. And frankly, I could use the break."

"Not when you're cutting crystal every time you go out."

"Aren't Tiagana, Borton, and Jaygrin?"

"Of course, but—"

"And anyone else you can talk into this direct-line approach to cutting, I'm sure," she said. "I thought that was why you had me sit in."

"I had you sit in to see how much you could remember," he said. He gave her a quick grin. "You did better than I expected."

"I did, did I? Well, *thank* you, Guild Master."

"Donalla says a lot of memory is association. The more—"

"And *thank* you not for discussing *me* with Donalla!" Killa wasn't certain why that made her so mad, but it did. "I'm not inactive yet, by a long twig, Lars Dahl. *And* I don't need hypnosis to *remember!*"

"You proved that conclusively today," he said in the mild tone he used whenever he wished to defuse her anger.

"Now *stop* manipulating me, will you?"

"I'm not, Sunny." There was a genuine note of surprise in his voice. In one lithe movement, he slipped from the recliner to her chair and embraced her. She kept herself rigid, refusing to relax and let him think he had cajoled her into a better humor.

"I also had to get someone else in the office or I'd've kicked Rudney out," he went on. "Wasn't he the pompous ass!"

Killa did relax a bit then, glowering and still suspicious. "Asshole, you mean. Though she wasn't as bad. Why would she put up with him?"

"Why do you put up with me?" And Lars flashed a smile at her.

"Then *why* did you give them the crystal?"

"Ah, yes." Nudging his hip against her to make her give him some room, he slid his arm about her. "Well, I received an urgent burst requesting assistance from

Archeological and Exploratory. Seems our Jewel Junk is exceedingly important."

"Then why do they entrust it to a dork like Saplinson-Trill?"

"Because, despite his manner, he's tops in his field."

"Which is?"

"Planetary mechanics. His is not the first group to try to solve the mystery of our opalescent junk, but he's had far more demonstrable success than any other. And Ballybran crystal is very important to the success of the next phase of their investigations. Or so A and E seems to think."

"Why didn't A and E pay for the crystal?"

"Too many slices out of their budget already."

"Then who's paying for a singer to install 'em?"

Lars cleared his throat. "The Guild was asked to absorb the cost."

She hauled herself about to face him, scowling. He pinched her lips shut.

"Oh don't worry," he said. "The Guild got concessions I've been trying to wangle for the last three years."

"Such as?"

"Permission to publicize the employment opportunities of the Guild . . ."

"What?" That was an exceptional concession.

Lars grinned smugly. "*And* the Guild is being allowed to actively recruit specialists on nineteen human planets."

"That must be a first!"

"In living memory."

"So, they've finally realized how important Ballybran crystal is."

"I'd say that's a fair comment." He stretched languorously beside her, arching his back, before he cocked his free arm to cushion his head. "A good day, all totaled."

"Who's the new dork at the desk?" she asked after a moment.

"Oh." The frown returned. "Him. Well, he's a spare pair of hands, and he'll be more useful when he becomes accustomed to the filing codes."

"I'd hazard the guess," she said after a long pause, "that you also can't afford to annoy the Council and A and E by sending an incompetent singer to set those crystals."

"I'm *not* letting you go, Sunny," he said sternly.

"Who else can you send?" she asked reasonably. "I'm the only one qualified, and you can't afford to have the installation messed up, can you?"

Lars gave her a long searching look and then sighed. "You're right there. Much is at stake."

Just as he gathered her closer, she caught a fleeting expression on his face that might have been satisfaction. She didn't have time, then, to sift the matter through, because he distracted her thoroughly.

Being aboard the Brendan/Boira 1066 was a mixed pleasure, since Killashandra had to share the ship's good company with Rudney and Klera. Fortunately the two scientists had brought reports with them to study, and they spent most of their time in their cabin, or using Brendan's powerful and complex computer banks.

"They did the same thing on the way out," Boira told Killa.

"The tedium was palpable," Brendan added, in the exact affected tone Rudney used.

Killa and Boira smothered laughs. Killa had taken to Boira the moment she had seen the 1066 brawn. Not that Boira could be described as brawny: she was of

medium height, and her figure was compact. She was
very attractive, smooth-skinned and with the symmetry
provided by reconstruction; her eyes were dark, and her
dark hair was kept at shoulder length. She moved with
an odd grace that Killa suspected was also due to the
accident that had left Brendan unpartnered during the
singers' first expedition to Opal. Best of all, Boira had
the same quick wit and ready humor that had made
Brendan such a good travel companion.

"Do be careful, Bren," Boira murmured. "You'll set
me off again. Bren had me in kinks," she told Killashandra. "It got to be embarrassing, because every time
they ventured out of their cabin, they'd say something
that Bren had lampooned and I'd dissolve—in a cough-
ing fit, of course. Wouldn't do to laugh in their faces!"

"Then it isn't just me," Killa said, grinning broadly.

"Oh, no," Boira assured her. "It's them! The only
time they acted human at all was during decomposition."

"Then they were *very* human," Bren said caustically.
"Had to circulate and clean the air nine times."

"D'you still have the radiant-fluid tub on board?"

"Indeed we do," Boira said, "and back in your
cabin."

"What'll you do about them, then?" Killa asked,
jerking her finger in the direction of the Saplinson-
Trills.

"Oh, them! This time we may let them stew in their
own juices, as it were," Brendan said. "I can close off the
vents to their cabin so we're spared the stench. At least
they cleaned themselves up afterward."

"And what about you?" Killashandra asked Boira.
But apart from a mild headache, Boira was not adversely affected by decomposition.

"Repetition dulls the effect," she told Killashandra,

"though it'll never be my favorite way to spend five of the longest minutes ever invented by the mind of man."

"So, did you see much of the FMs?" Killa asked, drawling the term sarcastically.

Boira gave a snort. "After a very lengthy briefing and all sorts of dire warnings about keeping my mitts to myself and going through a rather ridiculously involved decontam. It was worth the effort," she said. "The brilliance, the design . . . I really think they ought to pay attention to the complex patterns—what did you call them? Jewel Junk? I suggested," she added, grimacing at her recollection, "that the patterns the Junk displays could be another attempt at communication."

"And?"

"I got told in long chapters how such a theory was ludicrous and had no possible scientific basis." She shrugged. "I am entitled to an opinion."

Killa mulled that over. "Pattern is as good a method of communication as any other. Aren't *words* patterns?"

"Hmmm. Hadn't thought of it in quite that way, but they are, you know," Bren said. "Full marks to you, Killa."

"I gather they didn't test your theory, Boira?"

"Fardles, no! What does a ship's brawn know about esoteric life-forms?"

"Fifteen minutes until the first Singularity Jump," Brendan announced, and Killa immediately adjourned to her radiant fluid tank.

Awash in the fluid, Killa had only the mildest of decomposition willies. When she returned to the main cabin, where Boira and Brendan were running a systems check, she jerked her head in the scientists' direction.

"Oh, them?" Boira grinned. "This time they took the precautions we always recommend. Never have understood why the cerebral types think I don't know as much about my profession as they know about theirs. Hungry?" She smiled slyly.

"Brendan, did you have to tell Boira about that?" Killa asked, halfway between irritation and amusement.

"She insisted that I explain why I spent so much credit on food stores."

"Why? Did she think you'd wined and dined pretty girls all in a row while she was incapacitated? And thank you, Boira, I am hungry, but not starved and certainly nowhere near another Passover gorge."

Boira liked food as much as Killa did, and they compared notes until the next Jump. Both women were spared the company of the Saplinson-Trills, though Boira periodically inquired solicitously after their health and well-being. The two did emerge when the last Jump brought them into the Opal system. Rudney asked Brendan to open a channel for them, so that he and Klera could get caught up on any new developments. There were enough to send Killa and Boira into the galley to get away from the scientific jargon.

"You'd think, from all that gibberish, that they were activating a sorcerous spell or something," Boira said.

"Equations are a form of spell, aren't they?" Killashandra asked.

"Hmmmm, perhaps, if you get the right answer."

They batted the notion about until Brendan quietly informed them that they would be landing in fifteen minutes.

Rudney and Klera were excited about something, the upshot of which was that they wanted Killa to install the crystals as soon as possible. Rudney sputtered, close to being inarticulate in his instructions. Fortunately he had a diagram of where he wanted crystal installed, though to judge by the strikeouts, the list of priorities had altered several times. He wanted the biggest, or strongest, of the crystal pieces to go in Cave Fifteen, which Killa shortly learned was the one that she and Lars had named Big Hungry Junk.

"It already has crystal," she began.

"It must have the best of the crystals," Rudney insisted, spittle spattering Killa in the face.

"I really don't believe that FM Fifteen will surrender the one it has when the larger unit is installed," Klera said, her face screwed up with concern. "I really do feel that we have no way of adequately explaining that we need the old shard for one of the smaller FMs."

"Is that what you want to do? Exchange?" Killa asked, surprised.

"Of course, of course. You only supplied us with twelve crystals. We now have thirty FMs to be brought into the comnet we posit."

"Have you ever tried to remove anything from a Junk?"

"A Junk?" For a moment, Rudney was confused. "Oh, please employ the proper nomenclature."

Killa gave him the sort of look that had once been extremely effective in reducing affectations.

"No, we actually haven't," Klera admitted.

"It's always been on the receiving end, though, hasn't it?" Killa said. "Well, I'll try, but I'm not risking a finger or a hand."

"We're most certainly not asking you to take a physical risk," Rudney said.

To prove that, he and Klera were among those in the A&E installation who suited up to watch Killashandra install the crystal. When Rudney pompously introduced her, she got the usual guarded reaction from the staff assembled in the decontamination room, but there were several broad smiles of welcome as well as help when she began suiting up.

There was one black crystal, not a large shaft but tuned to a dominant, and this was the one she felt Big Hungry Junk deserved.

"Surely this one," Rudney said, pointing officiously to the largest, a pale blue, "would be more suitable."

"It's blue, a minor, and considerably less stable than the black," she said in a tone that she hoped would end the matter.

"But—but—"

"Rudney," she said loudly and firmly, "I am the crystal singer, not you!"

Rudney seemed surprised at her vehemence and stood there, blinking in astonishment. She became aware that everyone else was regarding her with similar surprise. Well, Rudney might be a boor to *her,* but he was clearly held in considerable respect by his staff.

"Black," she began in a milder tone, "is the most powerful of the Ballybran crystal range. Even a small one, like this, is three times as useful as the large pale blue. The paler colors are notoriously fragile." She held up the black, though she could feel the tingle of the damned thing right through her heavy vacuum gloves. "The black is also in a dominant key, which increases its potential threefold. Minors are good for small repetitive jobs, but you want some character for Big Hungry Junk to work with. Now, let's go."

She gestured for the two who had been assigned to carry the crystal-packing carton to put on their helmets as she adjusted her own. A few more moments sufficed for the usual pre-exit tests, and then everyone was checked out as ready to go. She activated her private com to Brendan and Boira.

The airlock cycled open to the black bleakness of Opal's surface. Changes had been made: light flooded the cindery surface, illuminating paths from the facility to the various caves, each path neatly signposted for its destinations. Big Hungry, posing as Cave Fifteen, seemed to be the most popular direction—that path was the smoothest in appearance. Killa struck out, leading the way, Rudney having missed the chance to get in front of her.

As she neared the cave, she could see splotches of brilliance penetrating to the surface. "Big Hungry must be really big," she murmured to herself.

"I can pick you up at that level, Killa," said Brendan softly.

"What did you say, Crystal Singer?" Rudney asked, reaching forward to tap her arm.

"I mutter a lot," she said loudly enough for her voice to carry to his comsystem. Then she smiled. Nice to be one up on Rudney! "You really have improved the place," she added. The approach had been cleared of all rubble, and the steps down to the entrance of the cave widened. Lights weren't needed: blue radiance leaked up the first five steps. And suddenly dimmed as Killa's helmet filter adjusted to the increased exterior illumination.

Even with that aid, she was nearly blinded by light as she turned the corner into Big Hungry's cave. Her gasp elicited a concerned request for explanation from Brendan and a smug chuckle from Rudney, which turned into a gargle of surprise.

"Great Muhlah on the mountains of Za!" She was transfixed in the entrance until Rudney brushed past her.

"Can I have a reading on why the pattern has so dramatically altered?" he asked in a sharp tone.

No one could miss the shower of complex interlacing designs that expanded from the center core. They were different from the idle banding she had first seen as she paused on the threshold. Majestic, they radiated down the sides of the cave, to disappear below the floor.

"It's most unusual, Doctor. First time this one has been screened," one of the technicians told Rudney.

"Maybe it's a welcome for me," Killashandra said facetiously.

Rudney shot her a fierce look of disgust and denial as he brushed past her and into the cave.

"There is a considerably higher level of static," the technician added. "Now it's dropping to normal output."

Hastily, Killa stepped to one side, watching the last of the fractal-like design slide out of sight. She shivered. To divert herself, she looked about the magnificently festooned cave. No one had told her that the fluid metal completely covered the walls of its site. She had thought it had merely sent tendrils to the lower levels. How many had Klera said Big Hungry went down? Nineteen? Incredible and yet . . . All it may have needed in order to grow was some decent food.

As the plasglas of her helmet darkened sufficiently in the gloriously lighted cave, she finally made out the central hub of the Junk, a now-infinitesimal sliver of crystal standing upright at the pulsing core. Rudney probably used a more accurate scientific name for the heart of the Junk. Odd, though, Killa thought, searching her memory for details of that earlier visit. She could resurrect little beyond knowing that Big Hungry had grown.

"Bren," she asked softly, "did we ever measure the original center of Junk?"

"We did, and . . ." He paused briefly. "Circumference is the same, but I'd say it was denser, thicker. Ask Rudney. The sort of thing he'd know."

She heard Bren, but her attention was somewhat dis-

tracted by the shift and play of color and pattern that
radiated from the core down the sheet of opalescence. It
was more colorful, too, than it had been: speeding up
and down the spectrum of visible color even as arcs of
shifting hues and shades rippled across. Try as she
would to follow one pattern, it melded or was overrun
by others. She remembered Junk doing that before but
surely not as rapidly.

"Our instrumentation is picking up considerable exci-
tation but not on a band usually occupied," someone
said over the comunit.

"Crystal Singer," Rudney said, bouncing over to her
and tapping her shoulder, "let's proceed. There's
unusual activity recorded . . ."

"I heard," she said repressively. Abruptly the thought
of setting black crystal in that throbbing heart of
opalescence disturbed her to a degree she had never
experienced before. "Having seen this one, I believe it
would be wiser to install crystals in the lesser units first."

"I disagree," Rudney said, appalled at the sudden
change of plans. "Cave Fifteen is responding to some
sort of—"

"Exactly! I'm not risking my wits on black until the
last possible moment," she said, and, gesturing imperiously to the two carrying the carton, she started from
the cave. "I'll start with Three."

Rudney objected; he even jumped in front of her
when they had left Cave Fifteen in his effort to stop her.
She bounced away from him, urging the carton carriers
to follow her. He tried to get them to follow his orders.

"You want crystal installed. I do it. I do it my way,"
she roared at him, and saw people recoil. "Now, do I
proceed to Three, or back to the 1066? Because if you
don't let me handle the installation *my* way, I'll leave.

With the crystals, too, by the way, since they're the *gift* of the Guild!''

That threat, combined with pleas from Klera and one of the other senior members of the team, silenced Rudney's objections, and she was allowed to proceed.

Three had been a small, pretty cap of Jewel Junk when she and Lars had first seen it. Sothi, one of the carton carriers, told her that it had insinuated itself down three levels now. Smack dab in the center of its core was the original splinter of pink. Muhlah, if the Junk could do this well with only bloody pink, it would flood with the good green destined for its second crystalline intrusion.

The rest of the observers had filed into the cave by then, and the portable ladder was erected right under the core. Killa hefted the green shaft and peered at it in the radiance to be sure it had not somehow become flawed in transit. She clamped the forceps about the green and, carefully examining the position of the pink splinter, started to insert the new crystal. The moment it touched the opalescence, it was sucked up so rapidly that only her trained reflexes kept her hand from following it into the core. The forceps were gone. In the next instant, the pink splinter fell, and there was a flailing of gloved hands as three people tried to catch it.

"Got it!" Sothi exclaimed, holding up the splinter for all to see.

"More than a mouthful is impolite," Killa said drolly. She hadn't anticipated any success in trying to yank out the old splinter.

"Ooooh!" Klera's exclamation, anxious and fearful, brought everyone's attention back to the core.

"Bloody hell, it swallowed it!" Killa announced, unable to perceive any trace of the green. "Of all the ungrateful . . ."

"Oh, there it is," Klera went on, pointing as the green slowly came into view again, positioned in the exact center of the core, with two-thirds of its length visible.

"We are monitoring increased activity in Three" was the report from the base.

"No quarrel with that," Killa said, delighted with the effect. And yes, she thought, Boira's theory about pattern talk was an avenue that ought to be explored. She found herself tracking a brilliant display of green, blue, and yellow herringbones that flashed from the core to the floor and disappeared.

"Crystal Singer . . ." Sothi had her by both hands, gripping tightly. "You were swaying . . ."

Killa accepted his help down from the ladder. He pressed his helmet against hers. "Don't watch the patterns, C.S. You lose time that way," he murmured.

Her lapse had gone unnoticed, save by Sothi, for the other observers were helmet to helmet in deep consultations. Killa wondered how much time she had lost.

"Does it happen often, Sothi?" she asked.

"Often enough to need to be cautious."

"Which cave is next?" she asked him. In that moment of distraction, she had forgotten.

"Two, which is only a step away," he answered, and suddenly she remembered the entire sequence and where each crystal was supposed to go. Time was not the only thing you lost following Junk patterns, she thought.

Then, when Sothi would have signaled to Rudney that they were leaving Three, she caught his hand and waggled her finger at him. "C'mon," she said, touching her helmet to his. "We can get this all done in half the time if we leave these science types to talk."

Sothi seemed hesitant, but his companion whose suit bore the name "Asramantal," pulled him toward the entrance.

Killashandra had done four, with Sothi or Asra neatly catching the discarded slivers, before Rudney and the observers caught up. She ignored Rudney's harangue and continued on her scheduled round. If she kept herself busy, watching her feet on the cindery paths, even doing a bit of pattern watching, with Sothi or Asramantal to pull her out if she dallied too long, she didn't have to think about installing the black in Big Hungry. As they had trudged from one cave to the next, she had confided some of her anxiety to Brendan and Boira.

"Can I count on you two for a bit of help?" she asked.

"What kind?" Boira asked.

"I might have trouble with Big Hungry . . ."

"What sort of trouble?"

"I'm not sure, really. Ah, well, it's mainly that I hate installing blacks anywhere for any reason," she said, trying not to infuse her voice with the anxiety that she could feel building into full-blown stress. Muhlah! This black wasn't being used—not in the normal sense—as a comcrystal. Maybe she was borrowing trouble.

"Feedback?" Brendan asked.

"Like you never felt before," she said.

"What can we do?"

"Stay tuned—and talk me out of the backlash."

"What form does that take?"

"It sings back through me."

"Gives you quite a jolt, huh?"

"That's putting it mildly."

"How do we help?" Boira asked.

"Could you suit up, Boira, and come down to Fifteen for the finale?"

"Sure. Be with you in two strokes of a hand pump. Only what do I do if you do freak out?"

"Get me back to Bren as fast as possible! I think I'll pull out on my own as long as there's distance between me and the black. And, by the way, Boira, your theory about patterns is not so far-fetched. The Junk radiates them in ever-changing displays."

"Hmm. Int—" Boira's voice was cut off.

"Boira?"

"She's in her suit and has not turned on the com," Brendan said in the patient tone of someone who was accustomed to such bungles.

With her confidence shored up by Boira's promise to be present, Killa completed the other installations. On her way to Big Hungry, she took a swallow of the suit's emergency ration—and immediately wished she hadn't. Somehow she had been expecting something considerably more palatable.

"Yecht!" she muttered.

"What's the matter?" Brendan asked.

"The suit's food!"

"Oh? So you do appreciate the lengths to which I went for you the last time?"

"If that's what I thought I was getting, yes." And the memory of more delectable flavors was indeed vivid in her mind.

She had no time for a pleasant review, for she had reached the cave entrance. Boira stood out from the others lining the big cavern: her suit was not only a vivid citron yellow but of a different design. She lifted her gloved hand in a salute to Killashandra. That alerted the other suited figures. Killa guessed that every member of Rudney's team who could be spared from the laboratory was present. There was a jumble of comments that told her there had been a draw to see who got to attend. Killa also heard excited reports from the few technicians still manning the instrumentation. Activity in the Junks had speeded up, pushing the monitors to designer limits to process the incoming data.

"Watch out, you guys and gals," Killashandra said as Sothi and Asra positioned the ladder under the core. "You ain't seen nothin' yet."

"What precisely do you mean by that remark, Crystal Singer?" Rudney demanded, his apprehension reflected in his voice as well as the sudden stiffening of his suited figure.

Killa had been talking to bolster her own confidence and wished Rudney didn't require so many explanations of casual comments. She sighed as she clamped the forceps firmly about the black. If she could avoid touching it at all, its effect on her would be reduced. She had gotten the hang of jamming crystal into cores now, and she didn't plan to bungle this final, and most crucial, insertion.

"Watch and observe, Dr. Saplinson-Trill." She extended her arm, noting that Sothi and Asra stood ready to catch the old splinter. Oh, Muhlah! she swore silently as a new thought struck her. This wasn't the last she had to install. There were all the old slivers to be put into the new Junks.

"Observe what?"

"Wait and see," she said. Taking a deep breath, she touched the black to the Junk, quiveringly ready to drop forceps and all at any sign that the black was going to react.

The black shaft was ingested so swiftly that her reflexes had no time to respond. Forceps, crystal, and her gloved hand were all pulled into the sudden maelstrom of frenzied, turbulent patterns that cascaded down the Junk—and flowed through Killashandra with such devastating force that she felt her death was imminent! Her whole life flashed across her mind, pushing her down into black oblivion.

[CHAPTER 12]

K illashandra Ree was vastly surprised to
waken once more to the living world.

"She's back," a low voice murmured, and
a cool hand rested lightly on her forehead. "Hey, you
made it!" The cheery tone rich with relief was Boira's.

"I'm not so sure of that," Killa replied, spacing her
words carefully. Her head felt several sizes too large,
and while it didn't ache, it might just as well have. A
brightness pressed unmercifully against her eyelids, and
she squeezed them tighter. "Got any analgesics?"

"What? A crystal singer needing medication?"

"There's always a first time. I certainly wouldn't
blame my symbiont for decamping after that. Whatever
it was."

"There's considerable debate on that score back at
the base," Brendan said, his whisper rippling with
mirth. Or maybe her hearing was impaired.

"Are you whispering for my benefit?" she asked.

"Yes," Boira said in a more normal tone. "You kept complaining about noise, and bright lights. Not that I blame you for that. Big Hungry Junk nearly turned nova when you fed it the black. D'you remember anything?"

"I remember dying."

"You didn't," Boira said. "First thing I did was check your suit readings and, mind you, you were rigid . . ."

"I died," Killashandra insisted.

"Not according to your suit readings, friend, and when I got you back here—"

"Against heavy opposition," Brendan added. "You'd have been real proud of Boira. She mowed 'em down."

"Sothi and Asra helped," Boira went on graciously. "What on earth can I give you that might help?" Killa heard a rattling that rumbled like an avalanche inside her head.

"Try one of the homeopathics, Boira," Brendan suggested. "I think that wouldn't interfere with the symbiont."

"Why isn't it working when I need it?" Killa moaned. "How much light do you have on out there?" The brilliance was instantly dimmed. "Thanks, Bren."

"Ah, this says it's a specific for trauma, injury, and systemic malfunction. See, Bren? What d'you think?"

"Try it," Killashandra said urgently.

The spray was cool against her skin, and she could actually feel the preparation diffusing—diffusing and easing the intolerable and unidentifiable malaise that gripped her.

"Oh, Muhlah! It's working . . ." Killa sighed with infinite relief, feeling taut muscles and stressed nerves beginning to relax. The noise level began to drop, and the light beating against her eyelids diminished to a comfortable level.

"I'm thirsty," she said then, suddenly aware of her parched throat and mouth. She didn't quite have the courage to open her eyes.

Very gently, Boira laid an arm under her and raised her head enough to make it easy to drink from the beaker pressed against her lips.

"It's full of electrolytes and the other stuff a convalescent needs," Boira said.

She couldn't taste a definite flavor, but the moisture was very welcome. It, too, was traceable all the way down her gullet and into her stomach. She could feel her body absorbing the wetness. Was her bloody symbiont fast asleep, zapped out of existence, or working overtime? She had been injured often enough to know that the symbiont's work was generally too subtle to be noticeable. What had Big Hungry done to her?

"Our diagnostic unit says you're in perfect physical condition," Boira said, "in case you're worried."

"I wish I could agree." Killa forced her lids open to a slit and, finding that this was not painful, opened them further. She was in her cabin on the 1066, and the digital dateline over the door informed her that she had lost two full days. "So, tell me what happened?" she bravely asked Boira, who was sitting beside her bunk, an open medical chest on a stand next to her.

"First you went rigid . . ."

"I remember that very clearly." And Killa did, with a clarity that astounded her. In the moment she had anticipated her death, every bone had seemed to harden; every artery, vein, and capillary had solidified. Color had coruscated through her eyes into every cell of her body, rippling in an inexorable tide, lapping back and plunging forward again, as if she were being swirled in some liquid element . . . and all the while her life had been fast-forwarding through her mind.

"I got to you before Rudney did, and your two cronies helped me get you off the ladder. Even the suit material felt petrified but, as I said, your life signs registered normal."

"Normal was not what happened to me."

"Agreed, but that's what the monitors told *me*. And I was relieved. Meanwhile, all hell had broken loose. I mean, the Junk was indescribable. Brendan'll show you his recordings . . ."

"Later," Killa suggested weakly. The thought of seeing all that color again was more than she could handle.

"Of course, whenever you wish," Brendan said gently. "Talk about scientific detachment and impartial observation . . ." He chortled maliciously. "Rudney and his crew were hysterical. Everyone tried to get through the exit at the same time. 'S a wonder suits weren't ripped in the press."

"I don't blame them for being scared," Killa said charitably.

"They weren't scared," Brendan replied in a scathing tone. "They just wanted to get back to the base to see what the instruments were logging. Rudney kept trying to shut 'em up so he could hear the broadcasts."

"Sothi and Asra were marvelous, by the way," Boira went on. "They helped me get you out of the cave, and then you sort of folded, like an empty sheet. Thought we'd nearly lost you, but Bren was monitoring and kept telling us to hurry you to him. Sothi worried that perhaps we were wrong to remove you from Big Junk . . ."

"Big Junk had just done all it could to me and for me," Killa murmured, though she still had no idea of the extent of the alteration. She merely knew there had *been* one.

"D'you know what it's done?" Boira asked tentatively. "Nothing new registers?"

"Sensory overload doesn't always produce measurable output," Brendan said.

"Is that your diagnosis, Bren?" Killa asked.

"Empiric only, Killa, since it's obvious by your comments and the need for supplemental medication that what you're experiencing is not corroborated by the med monitors."

"Well, maybe it's nothing more than a good night's sleep won't set right in next to no time, huh?" Killa kept her tone facetious because she could not discuss, even with such staunch friends as Boira and Brendan, what seemed to have happened to her during that sensory overload. "I do feel as if I'd been turned inside out, back to front, and then wrung dry . . ."

The emotional and psychical discharge of her first black-crystal installation had now paled to the insignificance of an insect sting. Lars was going to be furious with her, but there was no way she would ever again cut black crystal. Of that, if nothing else at this particular moment in time, she was certain. On the plus side, she would be able to tell him every single location where she had cut black. Indeed, she now remembered every site she had ever cut, and the type, size, number, and tuning note of every cutting she had ever made over the past one hundred and ninety-seven years. She remembered everything, and completely, to the last petty detail, and the weight of such total recall was worse than having it restored to her.

"Hungry?" Boira asked gently.

Killashandra considered this. "Yes, I think I am."

"Then you must be on the road to complete recovery," Boira said, smiling as she rose. "Any special requests?"

"Chicken soup?"

"The very thing," Brendan replied so heartily that Killa winced. "I've an old family recipe that's supposed to cure anything from ingrown toenails to the worst degree of space fug."

Killa closed her eyes. Chicken soup, no matter how efficacious, was not going to cure what really ailed her. Who needed to remember *everything?* Everything except how Big Hungry Junk had done what it had done to her.

Being aboard the BB-1066 had other advantages besides excellent nursing care and incredible food. Rudney could not get to her, though he demanded interviews on an hourly basis, insisting that she finish installing the crystal according to the contract he had made with the Guild Master. He threatened to sue her and the Guild for breach of contract.

"Tell him I installed the crystals as per the contract. Nothing in it said I had to do the old splinters, too. And I won't."

When Rudney exhorted the 1066 to turn the crystal singer over to him, Brendan informed him that he had no such authority over his passengers.

They remained on Opal's surface only long enough to be sure Killa had sufficiently recovered from the physical depletion to withstand the disorientation of a Singularity Jump. Then Brendan lifted his tail from the planet.

After the second of the three Jumps, curiosity got the better of Killashandra. She wanted to know what had happened to Big Hungry after it had gobbled the black crystal. Maybe that would distract her mind from a constant survey of memories she really didn't want to have on replay.

"Rudney's group haven't come to any conclusions,"

Brendan said, having discreetly continued to monitor all their transmissions and internal conversation. "They're still examining their data. Thermoelectric emissions have gone off the scale of their instrumentation. Significant growth of all the FM units—"

"Jewels, please, Bren, or Junk," Boira interposed.

"They seem to be oozing into every available cave, crack, crevice, cranny. The planet's rotation has shifted erratically, and sunspot activity has also increased. All the crystals glow, and the static they emit is constant."

"Junk is using the crystals for communication, then?" Killa asked.

"It would appear so," Brendan said, "though to what end, Rudney's group doesn't know. Their semanticist is analyzing the frequency and consistency of patterns, and the rhythm at which they flow, which varies."

"Klera was correct?" Killa asked, quite delighted at the thought.

"They won't commit themselves," Brendan said in a mildly snide tone of voice.

"Naturally. They don't deny the sentience of Junk, do they?"

"They can't when it is obviously altering its environment," Boira said, grinning broadly. "Oh, by the way, Rudney sent off a request for another singer to install the splinters."

"For all the good it'll do him," Killa said caustically.

"Fifteen minutes to the last Jump," Brendan said, and Killa scurried to the radiant-fluid tank.

Lars was waiting for her at Shankill, his worried expression clearing when he saw her striding down the corridor toward him. He embraced her hungrily, burying his face in her hair, his fingers biting into her shoulder blades and then her waist. She leaned into him, grasping him as tightly as he did her. He was warm, strong, and just as lean as he had been when they had first met so many years before on Optheria. The essential Lars Dahl hadn't changed . . . she cut off the other memories that threatened to swamp her. She was getting the hang of censoring recall when she had all she needed. Otherwise all that memory could be overwhelming.

"Honest, Sunny, I had no idea what I was asking of you!" he murmured.

"You didn't ask anything," she said, surprised. "I volunteered. Remember?"

He held her off, his expression wretched. "Sunny, I maneuvered you into volunteering."

She reviewed the occasion quickly, laughed, and pulled him back to her. "So you did, but I didn't resist much, did I?"

"How could you, crystal-mazed as you were?" He was so miserably repentant that she chuckled.

"At least you have the grace to apologize," she said. "Lanzecki never did."

She felt the change in him, and this time when he held her away, he apprehensively searched her face.

"What happened, Sunny?" His anxiety was palpable; even the grip of his hands on her arms altered as if she had become noticeably fragile.

"It would appear—" She gave a breathless laugh. "—that Big Hungry Junk reconnected all my memory circuits when it zapped me. The brain's electric, you know, and it got recharged, right back to my first conscious memory."

"Muhlah!" Lars stared at her, appalled.

"And I thought placing that Trundomoux king crystal was bad. The merest piffle in comparison. It's all right, love," she reassured him as she saw his eyes blink frantically. "Now let's get back to Ballybran, which, incidentally, I have never been more glad to see. By the way, did you get Rudney off your back?"

"I did, finally! I had to threaten to sue him for placing my best singer in jeopardy. And you got all your memories back?" She knew that he had briefly assumed his Guild Master's role. "Maybe I should send another singer in . . ."

"Lars Dahl!" She stopped dead in her tracks, pulling him off balance. "Don't you dare, Lars Dahl, don't you dare consider for one moment sending any member of the Guild to Opal for any reason!"

"Was it that bad, Sunny?" Lars was instantly solicitous.

"Was, is, and shall be, I suspect, my love, but I can handle it." She anticipated his next question. "And yes, as a bonus, I can give you the coordinates of every single claim I ever cut. I can't wait to get that off my mind." She began to hurry him along to the airlock where his shuttle awaited them.

"*All* your coordinates?"

"That's right."

She would explain the other side of that coin to him later, and as gently as possible. Maybe out sailing in the *Angel II*. Then she had to cope with a flood of memories, all associated with the word "angel": sailing to Island Angel's back, the storm, sheltering in the command post, meeting Nahia and Hauness, meeting his father, Olav, marrying Lars formally by island rites . . . Ruthlessly she cut off the stream; resolutely she closed down those reminiscences.

Lars handed her into the cabin of the shuttle and would have fastened her harness; but, laughing, she slapped at his hands, saying she could do it herself.

"Oddest thing, Lars," she said in a low tone so that

Flicken, the pilot, wouldn't hear. She was going to freak a lot of folk out by suddenly remembering their names, she thought, amused. She forced her errant mind back to what she had to tell Lars. "Big Junk recognized me. I remembered that little bit during the last Singularity Jump. I don't mean it said 'hello,' but I think I was aware of its recognition when I got to its cavern the first time. That's why I panicked and did Three first."

"Hmmm. Interesting."

"Yeah." She smiled in a somewhat maudlin fashion. "I'm glad we put its piece back."

"Is that what it remembered?"

She shrugged. "Who knows what passes for memory with Junk? Rudney certainly doesn't and we decided—"

"We who?"

"Brendan, Boira, and me . . . decided that Klera had the right idea about the *patterns* being part of the communication effort."

"Pattern and rhythm?"

"Pattern, rhythm, and color."

"Hmmm. Complex."

"Too much for this back-planet girl."

"You remember everything?" he asked, dismayed for her sake.

She nodded. "But I'm learning to chop 'em off before they overwhelm me. Too much is not a good thing."

"Hmmm."

He laced his fingers in hers, and she let her head roll to rest on his shoulder. She had been exceedingly lucky to have been kidnapped by Lars Dahl. She hadn't really had any guide by which to measure that serendipity or realize how truly Donalla had spoken when she had said that Lars was devoted to her. She could see it now, in the tapestry of their years together—all hundred and twenty-three of them, incredible as that total was—that he had been more than friend, lover, partner, and alter ego. She remembered how devastated, how lost, she had been when he had been falsely disciplined for the Optherian affair . . . She remembered, with great relish, their first sexual encounter on the beach at Angel—and, more importantly, how the mutual attraction had only strengthened and deepened throughout the years. "Everlasting love" took on a new dimension when applied to what she and Lars shared.

And now she could share even more with him: his duties as Guild Master. She would be Trag to his Lanzecki. Muhlah! Had Lanzecki and Trag . . . She stifled a giggle. Lanzecki had been quite willing, but she had never known if Trag had had any liaisons with Guild members. Lack of memory, a fear of displaying the gaps and embarrassing herself, and Lars, had been behind her resistance to his offers. She couldn't be less than the best for Lars, and now she could take on those responsibilities with a clear conscience—and an infallible memory.

Odd how so many things worked out—if one waited long enough. That initial humiliation back on Fuerte when she had been refused solo status by the bombastic little Maestro Valdi had resulted in her meeting Carrik and discovering the covert Heptite Guild. "Silicate spider," "crystal cuckoo"—Valdi's accusations rang in her head. Foolish little man. Singing crystal had been so much more rewarding than being a mere concert singer, who could expect only three or four decades of a "good" voice! She was still "singing" after a hundred and ninety-seven years.

She turned her head and caught her reflection in the porthole. Well, a quadruple thickness of plasglas might blur lines, but she really didn't have many, thanks to the

Ballybran symbiont. She certainly didn't look any two hundred and fifteen years. She smiled at her image. She wasn't much changed from the girl who had left Fuerte with a mind-damaged crystal singer. She gripped Lars's fingers tightly.

Now, if she could manage to cushion his shock that she could never again cut black crystal, she was good for another couple of hundred years.

"You won't mind letting Presnol and Donalla give you a good checkup, will you, Sunny?" he asked, his eyes dark and anxious.

"Not at all," she replied blithely. "Though I'm sure Bren and Boira sent a report on ahead, didn't they?"

"That was hardly reassuring," he remarked dryly. "Especially the part where you were sure you were dead. I don't exaggerate when I say that the heart went out of me."

She stroked his hand. "But as it was me saying it, you had no cause to worry."

He gave her a long and trenchant look. "By any chance, among your newly revived memories, do you have the one of our first night together?"

She ducked her head: the recall was instant, and almost embarrassing in its intensity.

"Did I not tell you then," he said, his voice intimately low and rich with emotion, "that you gave me the most incredible love experience of my life?"

"Lars! You don't remember that?"

He smiled at her, his eyes so filled with passion that she could feel the blood rising to suffuse her face.

"It's one of my fondest recollections, Sunny, and it is so wonderful that you remember it now, too."

He kept gazing into her eyes, stroking her hand, so that she felt like a giddy youngling. Which, she remembered, she had never been, for even at that age she had

already been dedicated to the notion of herself as a
singer.

"Ah, ahem . . ." Flicken, standing by the open shuttle
door, was clearing his throat.

"Thanks, Flick," Lars said, suavely recovering. He
reached across Killashandra to release her harness and
then handed her out as regally as if she were indeed a
queen.

"The courier's scheduled for an oh-eight-thirty docking at Bay Forty-three, Guild Master. Shall I be ready
at oh-seven-hundred?"

"That'll be fine," Lars said, and hurried Killa out,
obviously wishing that Flicken had not spoken.

"Who's going where tomorrow in a courier, Lars?"
Killa demanded as he guided her toward the lift. As they
entered, he ran his hand through his crisp blond hair.

"I've put it off as long as I could, Killa," he said
apologetically. "Presnol said he'd sit in for me. I
shouldn't be gone long."

"Where?" She felt a definite sinking feeling.

He scratched the back of his neck. "I've been putting
it off because you were away, and I wasn't leaving until
you got back after what Big Hungry did to you . . ."

"Out with it!"

"I'm not sure if you'd remember . . ."

She quirked an eyebrow at him, grinning. "Try me."

He jabbed an impatient finger on the control pad, and
she didn't take her eyes off his face.

"All right." He grinned, his eyes sparkling with the
challenge. "Recruitment . . ."

"You've got permission for overt recruitment," she
replied without hesitating, precisely remembering the
scene and where they had stood in his office in relation
to each other, "and the courier's taking you where
there're some live ones."

"My, my, we are vastly improved," he said, slightly mocking, but his fingers wrapped tenderly about her forearm.

The lift stopped, and he tugged her out. She stopped in the foyer.

"This is not the medical level."

"No, it is not. It is our level, and you can spend tomorrow with Presnol and Donalla, but you are spending the next hours with me, your Guild Master, and your ardent lover who is overjoyed to have his Sunny *compos mentis,* hale, whole, and hearty, back again." With a deft twist of his wrist, he pulled her into his arms and demonstrated his overjoy!

Sometime during the loverly reenactment of their first night together, he spoke of his trip to three over-populated city-planets where he hoped to find recruits. He also had permission to enlist specific technicians to fill the empty positions or to train up in the specialist support skills.

"We desperately need more medical staff," he told her, stroking her hair as they lay entwined on the sleeping platform. "Too many singers are so long in their craft that they get arrogant about their abilities and lose all common sense and any caution they might have once possessed."

"And a one-way trip to the Infirmary." She thought of Rimbol, poignantly remembering the bright gay chap he had been when they had both first come to Ballybran. That was not a comfortable memory when contrasted with his current condition. She shuddered.

"Which will have to be enlarged unless we can some-how stop the stupid mistake singers are making . . ."

"You know, Lars, it can be stopped," she said, de-scribing idle circles on his chest as she chose her words.

"By knowing where exactly to go to cut, cutting, and coming right back out."

"You tell 'em, Sunny," he said wearily. "They're not listening to me. And if you can get them to listen, I'll love you forever."

"You already have, Lars, you already have."

Such a statement demanded ratification. Later he returned to the subject. "A few of them are, because Tiagana, Borton, and Jaygrin have been loudly declaring how much credit they've made in easy straight-out-in runs. But so many singers are running on instinct now, there's no way to get through to them."

"Maybe I was hasty a bit ago, Lars," she said, "saying you mustn't send other singers to Big Hungry. If he could bring my memory back . . ."

"I think we'll leave that as the solution of last resort. I may be prejudiced," he said, kissing her cheek, "but you were always more than *just* a singer, Sunny."

"Being *just* a singer would have been rather limiting," she remarked, but she meant something different than he. "Which reminds me, why on earth saddle Presnol with pro-tem duties? I'm much better qualified than he is."

"Are you volunteering, Killa?"

"I believe so . . ." She grinned up at him in the dim light of their sleeping room. "But only while you're away. You don't want to risk me getting to enjoy the power, you know."

He gave a snort and wiggled his shoulders into the pillows. "Not bloody likely. You *are* the best singer I've got."

She didn't like the way he said that, but by the time she had thought of a suitable response, his breathing had slowed into a sleep rhythm. An infectious one, because she slipped into it, too.

* * *

Donalla and Presnol ran Killashandra through a gamut of tests, sampling her bodily juices and wiring her up to all kinds of monitors that provided reams of print-out.

"All of which only tells us that you're in great physical shape . . ."

"For a gal my age," Killa added, preening in front of the mirror. She had been allowed to dress again and was hoping they would think of feeding her sometime soon.

"Ah, yes," Donalla responded, needing to clear her throat.

Killashandra laughed. "Whatever zapped me seems to have burned off the outlived dross and stupidities any human collects along the way. I don't mind being two hundred and fifteen years old. In fact, it's fun, in a bizarre fashion. How's my symbiont, by the way? I'm keenly interested in its continued functioning."

"Oh, that." Presnol flicked his fingers dismissively. "It's as vigorous as mine or Donalla's, and we're both much much younger than you."

"I," Killashandra said quellingly, "may make comments, and even jokes, about my antiquity, Presnol, but"—she waggled her finger at them—"no one else can. Read me?"

Presnol looked properly subdued, but Donalla had to cover her mouth to suppress her laughter. Killashandra focused all her attention on the medic.

"And you, you ingrate," she added sternly, "had better watch your step, too! Imagine! Not showing proper respect to a legend of your planet! Who is exceedingly hungry right now. And I don't care if you need to make more tests. I'm eating first."

"We'll join you."

* * *

There were as few diners in the big room as there had
been on her last appearance there, Killa noted. "How
many singers are actually active?" she asked Donalla,
vividly remembering the room packed so many years
before.

"Four hundred and forty-two," Donalla said sadly.

"Ouch! That's ridiculous." Killashandra was stunned,
all too aware that there had been 4,425 singers when she
had joined the Guild. "How many are off-planet right
now?"

"Three hundred and five."

"How many inactives?"

Presnol made a face. "Three hundred and seventy-
five."

Killa could not recall the appropriate total of that
category, but then, she hadn't been interested in the
figures. In any event the number was depressing.

"Seventy-four," Donalla said with a sigh. "Rimbol
passed on this morning. I hadn't had a chance to mention it."

"Rimbol!" Killa's throat closed after she spoke his
name. She swallowed and felt tears forming in her eyes.
She hadn't cried in—no, that she couldn't bring to
mind. She ducked her head and struggled to get control
of herself. A beaker of Yarran beer was pushed into her
line of sight. She picked it up, nodding her appreciation
to Presnol, and held it aloft. "To Rimbol, a gay lad with
a kind heart and a fine tenor voice." Then she downed
the beer in one draft.

She looked around her then, to see if she could put
names to the handful of singers dining. She recognized
two: they had been in the batch of twenty that Lars had
recalled to cut black crystal. The tall thin fellow with the
long jaw was Marichandim. But search as she did, she
could not dredge up a name for the blond woman.

"D'you know her name, Donalla?"

Donalla craned her head over her shoulder. "The one with Marichandim? That's Siglinda. They've done quite well cutting from coordinates."

"How many *have* joined in that program?"

"Of the active singers, only twelve." Donalla shook her head, and Presnol looked solemn. "The others won't even listen. They run if you try to approach them. They're too far gone in their sublimations."

"Well," Killashandra said, rising, "I think I want to go over the Orientation program. If it's the same as I had under Tukolom, I think we'd better overhaul the whole thing. That's where the trouble started. Whatever singers Lars brings back are going to learn more than Rules and Regs!"

It was strange to be in this office, Killashandra thought as she entered the Guild Master's quarters. Trag's desk was clear, empty, waiting. Waiting for her, she decided with a wry grin, even if she had done her damnedest to delay the inevitable.

Lars's desk was neat, with pencil files set in four platoons across the broad surface. One group had the notation "Orient. Revis." And she smiled. She should have known he would consider that vitally important. She peered at the other notations: "Coords," and there were nine files in that group; "Recruit" had seven; "R&D" was the sparsest with only three.

There were several scrawled notes that she couldn't decipher stuck to one side, near his comunit, and a hologram base. She flicked it on and was gratified to see herself—a shot taken while they were on Nihal III— and then she noticed that the unit, which could hold a hundred 'grams, was full. She flicked the change switch and there she was again, in the orange wet suit he had bought her for Flag, where he had seen the prototype of *Angel II.* She joggled the switch again and again, pausing only long enough to identify where the 'gram had been taken. She turned the holo off and, hauling the chair firmly under her, resolutely turned to the big monitor and called up the Guild Roster. She had a lot of work to do before Lars got back.

As she had discovered once before on her single foray into administrative work for Lanzecki—she must remember to find out what happened to that dorkish Bollam, she reminded herself—she enjoyed rooting among the files and collating information.

The Guild's operating costs, of which the Infirmary was now requiring an increasingly larger share, came from tithing every singer's cut, a bone of contention between singer and Sorter. Other costs, which the singer bore for sled, fuel, equipment, living accommodations, and food, were presented at market rate. That sank her notion that the Guild took a cut from the supplies, jacking the prices up periodically. The files proved that there was no markup whatever, merely a gradual increase in wholesale costs throughout the inhabited galaxy. There had been an increase of farming on Ballybran and, to give the Guild fair credit, they paid above the average market price for foods produced on Guild lands.

There were, however, far fewer active singers to produce any tithes for the Guild and more inactive ones—some of those in a vegetable state—who had to be supported by an ever-dwindling income. Fewer cutters in the field meant less crystal to offer, and Killashandra came across orders three and four years old that were waiting to be filled. Black crystal figured largely in these back orders, but all the dark crystals were needed.

Before she could be totally depressed by the outlook,

she saw a remarkable upswing over the past few
months—since Lars had thrown open unused claims.
Her cuts were significant in that revival, though both
Tiagana and Jaygrin had brought in more. To comfort
herself, she reviewed the total of one hundred and
ninety-five years of cutting and compared it with the
records of any other singer. She was tons ahead of the
two younger singers.

She then reviewed Lars's comments on Orientation.
They showed the continued emphasis on note-taking
after every Range trip and on the return from off-planet
jaunts: he planned to have an automatic reminder on
each singer's console. He had also been listing the ways
in which coordinates might be inviolably kept on file.
There were notes on compulsory hypnotic sessions that
would access such memories.

Lars also had notes on how to modernize the various
departments of the Guild, what new technology there
was to replace worn machines and at what cost; and
many notes on how to capitalize on the talents of the
support staff with appropriate bonuses. Most of these
possibilities would have to wait on a continued upward
turn of filled orders.

He had taken the trouble to investigate the alternatives used by people weary of waiting for the Guild to
supply crystal. Advantage one to the Guild: Ballybran
crystal had a longer work life and, if damaged, did not
need to be jettisoned but could be retuned and used in
other installations. Its competitors could not be recy-
cled. Some of the original shafts of Ballybran crystal,
cut by Barry Milekey, for whom the Milekey Range was
named, were still in use after eight hundred years.

"What we need is an advertising campaign, too," she
murmured, and tried to think—without much success—of interesting slogans. Ballybran crystal hadn't

needed hype: it sold itself. So long as supply met demand.

"Well, there is an improvement," she told herself, leaning back in the conformchair and stretching. "We'll build on it."

The lights had come up when the sensors registered a diminution in available illumination. She swiveled the chair and noted that night had fallen—Shanganagh and Shilmore were chasing each other across the sky, but they were soon to be occluded by the clouds billowing in from the west. She turned the chair enough to see the weatherline blinking on its strip across the top of the room. Barometer was dropping, and the isobars were tight with gale-force winds. Storm warnings had been broadcast. She altered the monitor to pick up the Hangar scan and saw the blips of forty or so sleds homing in.

Good! She would have a chance to speak to some of the less productive singers. She accessed the program that would identify returning craft and asked for details of each singer as they came in. She would approach them with facts and figures: the productive time charts on those working from coordinates, and the credit they raked in. Something that appealed to any singer was how to make enough credit quickly enough to get offplanet for as long as possible. Only "as long as possible" was going to be curtailed to "as long as necessary" until the Guild had returned to its once-prestigious position.

Somewhat to Killashandra's surprise, she was received with a good deal of awe by the first group of singers she approached. She had quickly scanned the details of the forty-seven who had left the storm-bound Ranges, so she knew what and how much they had cut and how long it had taken them, and she was prepared to talk them out of resisting the proposal.

She marked her victims as she sat drinking with them:
the ones who didn't have enough credit to go anywhere
interesting. She had been to a staggering number of
R&R and vacation planets in nearly two centuries, so
she was able to spin tales to make them yearn to visit
such fabulous places. It didn't take her long to interest
this group, eighteen in all, in using a surefire way to
achieve their ends.

The insistent buzz of the comunit roused her from a
deep, dreamless sleep. Once she heard it, she also recognized the emergency code and floundered with her blan-
kets to roll to the control panel at the edge of the sleep
panel.

"Killashandra!" The caller was Flicken, his face stark
with grief. "Oh, how can I tell you?"

"Tell me what?"

"The B-and-B courier—it's sent out a Mayday."

"A B-and-B courier . . ." She stopped, gasping. Lars
had been on a courier ship. "Lars?"

Flicken nodded slowly, his chin quivering and his
mouth working. "Just came in."

"How? What? Couriers are . . ."

"Singularity trouble!" Flicken gasped out again.
"That's all I know. All I can find out. Mayday and a
Jump disaster tag."

"Where?"

He shook his head more vigorously, but there were
tears falling down his cheeks and he couldn't control the
trembling of his mouth.

"Keep me informed," she said, amazed that she could
sound so calm, that she wasn't raging at how abruptly
her life had been shattered once again. She palmed the
lights up and sat there a long, long time, her mind going
in tight circles. B&B ships were very sophisticated ves-

sels. Courier ships were the best of the B&Bs. Both brains and brawn could be expected to function under the most adverse conditions and survive against incredible odds. Singularity Jump disasters were few, but they could happen. Brendan had mentioned, in passing, that, while he was equipped to handle thousands of minute calculations during a Jump, he had several back-up, worst-scenario corrective capabilities. Furthermore, and she began to revive from the shocking news, every B&B ship, every naval vessel, every liner, every tanker, freighter, private yacht anywhere in the sector where the courier ship had been lost would be looking for it. If a Singularity disaster had to happen to a ship, then a courier B&B was the most likely one to survive.

She forced her mind to hang on to that thought and found something to wear. She went to the Guild Master's office and palmed up all the lights. She sat down in the conformchair, brought up the comsystem, and accessed Shanganagh Port Authority.

"Deputy Guild Master Ree, here," she said in an even tone. "Keep me informed on any developments of the—"

"Yes, of course, Deputy Ree. We've initiated emergency proceedings and requested all naval, mercantile, and private spaceships to forward all messages."

"By crystal coms, I trust," she said, mildly surprised that she could be droll at a time like this. A time like this was when a bit of drollery kept you sane, she amended.

"Yes, yes, of course, Deputy. The blacks we have here will pick up whispers in the farthest sectors of inhabited space."

"I think we'll have to find crystal that operates in Singularity space."

"Nothing works in decomposition space, Deputy."

She wondered if Jewel Junk would.

"We'll keep you informed, Deputy."

Deputy! Had she the right to use that title? Well, why not? Lars had appointed her, hadn't he? She was a better deputy than Presnol would be. She was a singer, a sometime diplomat, spy . . . she grinned sadly to herself. Then she pulled the multiholo base to her and called up the earliest 'gram it had stored. What appeared was the holo of herself, sun-bleached hair, the garlands Olav had given her the morning they left Angel about her neck, accenting the color of the lovely gown of Teradia's making. When had Lars taken that? But he had—for here it was.

She sat there, looking at the holo, remembering all that had happened before and after it had been taken. She jumped when someone rapped at the door.

"I've only just been informed, Killa," Donalla said. "Is there *anything* I can do?"

"Yes, there is," Killashandra said, adopting a brisk tone. She had idled away enough time in private meditations. "Would you dial me some breakfast? I haven't had time with so much to put in motion."

"Put in motion?" Donalla stared at her.

"Yes, I must implement the plans Lars made." She gestured at the neat piles of pencil files. "It'll take my mind off the waiting."

"Oh! Then you think there's hope that—"

"There's always hope, Donalla, but I think Lars would prefer it if I didn't sit about moping like a fool, don't you?"

She had her breakfast and then arranged appointments with the Hangar-bound singers she had talked to the previous evening. Since everyone was dazed by the news that had swept through the Cube, she obtained more agreement than argument and sent seventeen of the eighteen off with three sets of coordinates each and a mission to cut where possible—for some claims were likely to be unworkable—and return as soon as they had collected at least a carton of back-ordered colors. She didn't want to see a single shaft of pink or any of the pale blues and greens. Darks, and blacks, whenever possible.

She managed to bury herself so deeply in revitalizing the Orientation program that she was astonished to hear multiple sleds leaving the Hangar: she had worked through the night! She allowed herself four hours' sleep and then was back at the desk, going back over Guild affairs of the past decade.

By the fifth day, she had digested every current file and reviewed older ones on merchandising and research and development so that she was fully up-to-date on Guild business. She had talked four more singers into foraging by coordinates and seen eight of the original seventeen back in with viable crystal cuts, all dark. She encouraged the happy singers to stay overnight, have a good meal, relax with their peers, and talk about how easy it was to work known coordinates.

Each day she allowed herself a glimpse of a new holo-gram from Lars's incredible collection. With each new 'gram, she accessed the memories of that excursion, as fresh in her mind now as when she and Lars had lived those lovely moments. She could never be grateful enough to Big Hungry Junk for restoring the memories that allowed her to continue living. When she was dead, too, there would be no one to remember Lars Dahl as vividly as she could now. And that would be a real pity.

The restoration of memory brought with it a desire not to lose it again. She would eventually have to go out into the Ranges and cut crystal, but she did not want to jeopardize the reinstatement of so much valuable information. She had a long chat one day with the meteorologists and then asked Presnol and Donalla to have dinner with her.

"It's like this," she began when they were on their cheese and beer. "The Met guys tell me that Ballybran storms are apt to produce more electricity in the air than storms on other planets. Is it possible that an overload of such electrical discharges could affect singers' minds? I mean, most of us *wait* until the last possible moment before leaving the Ranges. Is that why we tend to forget between trips? The electricity has somehow affected our circuits?"

"It *is* a possibility, isn't it?" Donalla said, looking to Presnol.

He mulled it over. "I think we could profitably check memory retention on, say, those singers who are working coordinates regularly, and those who prospect right up until a storm drives them out of the Ranges. See if we can get any relevant data. We could also check just how much electricity is discharged into the atmosphere—sort of a continuous measurement. I'm sure we could find instrumentation to register that sort of emission. Hmm, rather interesting. But what good would it do?"

"If we can prove any correlation between the intensity of a particular storm and memory loss, all the more reason for us to teach the next candidates to come in at the first warning," Killa said. "Or, if we can manage it, keep them all on coordinate mining."

"That would be quite a departure from tradition," Presnol said, clearing his throat. He had been on Ballybran a lot longer than Donalla.

"That's exactly the attitude that needs changing, Presnol," Killa said. "The Guild needs to alter a lot of its thinking and its 'traditions' "—and she imbued that word with disgust—"if it wants to improve. And keep singers active and productive."

"Let's see what we can discover, Pres," Donalla said, smiling winningly at her lover. She gave Killa a wink that suggested the matter could be left safely in the medics' hands now.

The fourth week brought the first of the recruits from Lars's ill-fated journey. Forty-four young, eager persons trained in a variety of skills, and fifteen others with the perfect pitch required for crystal singers. That was more than had applied to the Guild in several years. There were two more groups scheduled to arrive over the next weeks, but once the first group had been processed, Killashandra ordered them right down to Ballybran. She would take the first Orientation sessions herself. She would show them the way to go, to be successful singers. They, and others like them, would revitalize the Guild—in Lars's memory.

The Council, composed of the heads of departments of the Heptite Guild on Ballybran, were becoming more insistent that she formally accept the position of Guild Master, but she resisted. Acceptance meant, in her lexicon, that she had accepted Lars's death, and she couldn't. She still didn't *want* to be Guild Master, no matter how many people told her she had taken command as if she had trained all her life to assume the rank. What she *could* do was implement Lars's plans and have the Guild operating efficiently again.

When Donalla insisted she take a break from the console before her eyes turned square, she would go down to the *Angel II* in its big shed. She felt close to Lars there and could dwell on the memories of their many sea voyages together. Oh, how she longed to sail with him just one more time! She grieved over her acrimonious griping about his love for the sea, her perverse opposition to his choice of water planets for their holidays. She had been unkind, and ungrateful, to insist on her turn at choosing a vacation place, when she knew how much the sea and sailing meant to him.

She had just returned from another maudlin review of her shortcomings, foibles, and limitations and listlessly entered the office that now felt more hers than Lars's. She was wondering which chore she could use to occupy her mind until fatigue pushed her into sleep when the comunit beeped.

"Now what?" she demanded, irritated to have duties press in on her so quickly.

"Patching through" was the excited comment, and then there was an intolerable rasping, squeaking, high-pitched blast.

"Sunny?"

"Lars!" His name came out of her mouth in a scream. There was no one else in the Galaxy who called her "Sunny" and no voice with quite the same timbre as his. "You're alive?"

"Kicking, too."

"Turn on the vision, Lars. I've got to *see* you!" Tears streamed down her face, and she had to grip the edge of the desk to keep on her feet. But the voice, the words: it had to be Lars.

His chuckle reassured her again. "Not on your life, Sunny, or mine. Overimmersion in radiant fluid produces curious effects on skin and muscle, but it saved the lives of me and the ship's brawn. They say that we'll look human again soon, but I've my doubts. Brendan and Boira found us. That pair refused to give up. Praise be to Muhlah! We're all safe, though the courier ship'll need a new shell—no, that's wrong way round—the shell person will need a new ship; hers got Singularly twisted."

She didn't care *what* he looked like: he sounded like

himself and that was what counted. "But you're a

"I repeat, I am alive! I even survived the Singularity Jump we just made." His voice quavered briefly. "Had to, according to Boira. And I suppose I'll have to again, but not soon! Not soon!" He sighed gustily.

"Where *are* you?"

He chuckled again, teasing her. "Estimated time of arrival at Shankill Base is four hours!"

"Four *hours!*" She was shrieking again. How could she wait that long to set eyes on him! To hold him to her, to feel his arms about her. "Oh, Lars love . . ."

"What did you call me, Sunny?" His voice was tender with surprise.

She swallowed. "I called you 'Lars love,' " she said almost defiantly.

"D'you know," he said, and his laugh was tentative, "you've never called me 'love' before."

"I'll remember to call you that every other breath— Lars love. I've had a lot of time to remember things, while you've been—away." Her voice broke slightly, and she hastily cleared her throat. "I remember all the love you've given me," she went on, determined to say what had become so imperative he know. "I've remembered so much, Lars love, especially that I have always been in love with you, in spite of the way I treated you!"

"It's almost worth nearly dying to hear you say that, Killashandra Ree." He sounded stronger now, almost exultant!

"I'll remember that, love. I'll remember that, too."

The moment she disengaged the channel, Killashandra Ree left the office to meet Lars Dahl at Shankill Moon Base. Exit, triumphant, stage center.

ABOUT THE AUTHOR

Anne McCaffrey was born in Cambridge, Massachusetts. She graduated cum laude from Radcliffe College, majoring in Slavonic Languages and Literatures. Before her success as a writer, she was involved in theater. She directed the American premiere of Carl Orff's *Ludus de Nato Infante Mirificus,* in which she also played a witch. Her first novel, *Restoree,* was written as a protest against the absurd and unrealistic portrayals of women in science fiction novels in the '50s and early '60s. Ms. McCaffrey is best known, however, for her handling of broader themes and the worlds of her imagination, particularly in her tales of the Talents and the sixteen novels about the Dragonriders of Pern. She is the winner of the Hugo Award, the Nebula Award, and the Margaret Edwards Lifetime Achievement Award.

Ms. McCaffrey lives in a house of her own design, Dragonhold-Underhill, in County Wicklow, Ireland. Visit the author online at www.annemccaffrey.org